Strike at Richmond

A Modern Novel

Steven P. Locklin

grey gecko press

Published by Grey Gecko Press (www.greygeckopress.com).
Printed in the USA, the United Kingdom, and Australia.

Library of Congress Cataloging-in-Publication Data
Locklin, Steven P.
Strike at richmond / Steven P. Locklin
ISBN 978-1-9457605-8-7

First Edition

For William and Thomas

"Blood cannot restore blood, and government should not act for revenge."
                    — Abraham Lincoln, May 17, 1864

CHAPTER ONE

Nov. 19, 1863

DESPITE THE DAY'S COOLNESS, sweat saturated his clothes. He gulped in air as he ran along the tree-lined street. He didn't know what street he was on; he could only tell his general location in Gettysburg by the prominent college building and by the Lutheran seminary to the southwest. He remembered the cupola of the seminary well; he had been standing in it with John Buford the first day of the battle back in July. It seemed like a long time ago, yet it was only four and a half months... with Jackson Prescott and Parker Stallard... and all that gold still missing.

It was stupid to be thinking of that as he ran down the street, pushing himself to the utmost, his legs screaming with fatigue and a blister from inside his left boot shooting pain with every step. But he had to keep going. He couldn't slow down, couldn't give in to the pain and fatigue. The Confederate spy in front of him, barely fifty feet away, kept up a torrid pace, looking back every few seconds to see his pursuer. Twice the Reb had yelled out in panic as he ran, but there was no one to pay heed to his exclamation. The streets were empty on this Thursday afternoon.

"They're all at the ceremony," Colonel Andrew Brison said to himself under his heaving breath. He unbuttoned his over-coat, slowing down and losing precious seconds and distance, but he thought he would gain it back without the cumbersome garment. He cast it aside onto the front porch of a small house set close to the street and increased his pace.

The Reb cut across the street and down another, Brison closing the distance. A milk cart drawn by a single horse approached; the Reb cut behind it, and Brison lost sight of him for a moment. When he got past the cart himself, the street was empty. He looked to the left and saw nothing, but a few more steps brought him to an alley, where he glimpsed the Reb turning the corner of a house.

They were now in an area where the buildings were closer together and the street fighting in July had been fierce. Holes pockmarked the buildings from the bullets that had failed to find their targets.

Brison pulled his pistol from his waist and slowed down, for he understood this would be a good place for the Reb to turn and ambush. He reached the alley's end and found there was another way out behind the building on his left. He charged down this new path between the building and a fence with trees overhanging the path. Just as he reached the midpoint between the alley and the upcoming street, a shadow darted from a recessed doorway and crashed into his side, sending him against the fence. Brison cried out in surprise and pain as his head and shoulder hit squarely against the solid wooden fence. He looked up to see eyes wide with fear in the Reb's young face. He was just a boy, barely fifteen or sixteen. His matted-down light-brown hair hung down to his shoulders from underneath a hat. He made a panicked noise and scrambled down the path towards the street with Brison, back on his feet, just yards behind him.

He was just a youth, but he was here to help kill the president of the United States.

The Reb reached the street and disappeared to the right, the way to the town's center. Brison came right after him and rounded the fence corner, and just as the Reb came into view, the boy looked over his shoulder and tripped over his own feet. Brison was on the boy in a second and pinned him down into the dirt, grabbed the boy's arm, and pulled it behind his back.

"Ahhhh... I ain't done nothin.'" The Reb struggled as Brison pressed down on his back. "I ain't done nothin.'"

"Son, I'd be much obliged if you would stop movin' like a worm fresh from the ground," Brison said. "You're done running for now." As he finished, he accentuated his point by pulling the boy's arm toward the middle of his back. The boy shrieked, then Brison let his arm drop into a more comfortable position. "You're coming with me now, boy, and you cause any more fuss, I'll break your arm good and proper. You understand?"

"Yeah," the boy snorted into the ground.

Brison picked the boy up and grabbed him by the arm and neck, ignored the look of an old man walking past them, and hurriedly marched with the boy until they came upon a doctor's office in a corner house. Brison knocked on the door but didn't expect an answer. Everyone of prominence was up on the hill at the two cemeteries, Evergreen and the new national one where the battle's Union dead were being moved from their hastily placed graves in the hot days of July. With no answer, Brison kicked the door in and threw the boy onto a chair.

He needed privacy for what he was about to do.

"I don't know nothin', mister, I told you." The boy clung to the chair like a solitary boat in the ocean.

Brison had pulled his Colt from his waist and pointed it at the boy as he looked around the room. He found a length of rope in a side storage closet and quickly tied the boy up in the chair. All the time, the boy protested, insisting he had done nothing to deserve this treatment. When Brison was finished, he grabbed another chair, turned it around, placed it in front of the boy, and sat down. He began in a calm, reasonable voice.

"You and I both know I don't have much time. I know what happened at the meeting in Harrisburg. I know you were the messenger between the Knights of the Golden Circle in the capital and the agents here. I followed you here and saw you deliver the message to a man who rode off not twenty minutes ago from that building at the college." Brison paused to see the effect his words had on the boy and was pleased to see the youth's eyes widen. "I also know that you or someone you know stole my horse and my goods back at the college there, which is why I had to chase you down by foot.

"What I don't know and what you are going to tell me is what your message was and what your group is planning. How are you planning to attack the president?"

The boy's eyes suddenly narrowed, and a smile crept onto his face that now carried the distinct righteousness that an advantage of knowledge creates. He wiped blood from the corner of his mouth with his shoulder.

"You won't git nothin' from me," he said menacingly. "And you'll be too late for it to do you any good anyhow. I know who you are. You're a Yank colonel even though you don't wear no uniform. You got to take me in to your right fine and mighty general or some such. You can't do nothin' to me here."

Brison tilted his head to the side, paused, then threw a fist into the Reb's gut, hurling air and spit from the mouth. The boy moaned and struggled to gain his breath, sounding like he was about to spill his stomach onto the floor.

"You see, son, that's where you're in error." Brison got in close to the Reb's face. "I'm not bound by military regulations concerning treatment of prisoners. And you're a spy, so I am well within my power to hang you right here at the Diamond if I wanted. Or easier still, just put a bullet in your head right now. I'm under orders from President Lincoln himself. You understand what that means?"

"You're... you're bluffin'," the boy said with a smile, "and your orders won't mean nothin' in a few minutes anyhow."

Brison went for the jaw this time and connected solidly, sending the boy and chair back over onto the floor. When he reached the boy's face this time, he had his knife pulled from his boot. He flashed the wide, well-sharpened blade in front of the boy's eyes. Blood came from a hole where a tooth had been just seconds before, and the boy whimpered through mixture of spit and blood.

"Tell me what I want to know, or I'll take this knife and slowly gut you like a pig. And I do mean slow." Brison did his best to sound crazy. He had to convince the boy he wasn't bluffing, because he knew what the Reb had said was true... he had only minutes. "How are they going to do it? How are they going to kill Lincoln?"

"I'm bleeding... I'm bleeding," the Reb said.

Brison took the knife and placed the point against the boy's side and pushed it slowly through the shirt and into the flesh.

"Noooooooo!" the boy shrieked. "Nooooooo, I'll tell you. I'll tell you."

Brison pushed a little harder. He had to be careful. He didn't want to sink the blade in too deep too quickly.

"Aghhhhhhhh! Don't do it! Don't cut meeeee!"

Brison grabbed the boy by the shirt collar and pulled him off the floor, chair and all, with his powerful right arm. His left shoulder still bothered him even after all these months. "Tell me how they're going to do it."

The boy had started to cry. "I don't want to die... don't want to die. You'll kill me after I tell you."

"I don't make war on Rebs as long as they aren't doing me any harm or have given me what I want. Tell me and I'll take you to the closest Army authority with the recommendation that you not be hanged until the president can give you a pardon. Of course, if he's dead, that won't happen, and the military will either hang or shoot you at their discretion."

"I don't want to die," the boy sobbed.

Brison was surprised at the speed of his breakdown.

"They're going to shoot him when he comes back into town at the train station after the talking up on the hill. Please don't kill me."

"How many?"

"Oh, God. I'm bleeding."

"You'll live. I said how many?"

"Two. They're going to shoot him at the station."

Brison pulled back from the Reb. There were upwards of fifteen thousand people milling about the town today, many of them soldiers. The railroad platform would be filled with officials, both military and civilian. They couldn't help but get caught. There would be no chance at escaping the station even if they were successful. Brison looked down at the boy and, for a split second, gave him a look that denoted contempt. This boy was good... very good for his age, Brison thought. But shooting Lincoln at the ceremony would be just as impossible to escape for the same reason unless the agents wanted to sacrifice themselves. That didn't seem likely, but then again, this whole idea of assassination was not part of the rules of war. That was why he'd been investigating this small group connected to the Knights of the Golden Circle; they were radical and rash. Yes, an assassination of Lincoln would never be sanctioned by Jeff Davis and Richmond. This was the work of zealots. But would they be so fervent in their desire to sacrifice their freedom?

He looked down at the boy, who had now composed himself and was looking up at Brison with his head down, his eyes locked up in his eyebrows. Yes, the boy was good, but not good enough. Brison pounced on him again, the knife now up underneath the chin.

"Try again, this time the truth," he hissed in anger, and it was genuine because he was growing desperate. "They wouldn't try at the station or the ceremony. Too many people to get into the way. No chance to escape." He pushed the knife into the soft tissue underneath the chin.

The Reb swore at him, hatred invading his face. "Despots need killin'."

"You won't tell me how, then you're no good to me alive anyhow." Brison removed the knife from the chin, brought it down to the boy's side again—the same spot as before—and plunged it in.

No shriek this time, just an exclamation of pain and a look of absolute shock. The realization that he was going to die in this room swept over him.

"No, no, nooooo," he pleaded. "I'll tell you the truth, I'll tell."

"The blade's half in, son," Brison said. "I lean on the handle, and you'll be dead before I wipe the blade clean."

"All right, all right, oh God, it hurts," the boy begged. "Please no more."

"You're delaying. Enough." Brison made a motion to lean in on the knife.

"Sharpshooter... there's a sharpshooter... at the ceremony... right now."

"The ceremony is at the cemeteries on the hill. There's no vantage point, is there?"

"Yes, there is. There's a barn... used as a storage. Oh, God, it hurts..."

"How can he see Lincoln through all the other people on and around the speaker's stand?"

"Got a spotter with a glass."

Brison knew he had to take a chance. He couldn't drag the kid through the streets and make it in time. The ceremony was supposed to have started almost two hours ago. He pulled the Reb up again, and the knife edged a little deeper, evoking a quick intake of breath.

"I have never spoken truer words than I'm sayin' right now to you," Brison said. "Tell me which barn it is and I'll not kill you. If I go and find out it's the wrong barn or you told me another lie about something else, as God is my witness, I will come back here and put this knife clean up under your ribs. What does the barn look like?"

"It... is white with a red thing on the right-hand door that faces south. It's a shape with three points."

"A triangle?"

"Yea, that's what they call it. It's got a lot of holes and such from the battle."

"What road south out of town is it closest to?"

"Oh, God almighty, it hurts. Please take the knife out." The boy's eyes were closed tightly.

"Which road?"

He opened them again, and the contempt returned. "I... don't... know. I don't know the names of the roads around here."

Brison pulled the knife from the boy's side and grabbed a clean-looking tablecloth from nearby and held it over the wound, which wasn't bleeding all that much. He grabbed the boy and dragged him over to a closet just off the front room. It would do. Three minutes later, he was out the door. With urgency, he surveyed the street, which now had some activity, a couple of buggies and a lone rider coming north along the street at a slow canter. The rider was another youth of perhaps twenty or so. He gave Brison a worried look as the stranger came charging up to him.

"Son, I need your help something fierce," Brison said, grabbing the horse's bridle.

"I'm a temporary deputy marshal," the young man said. "Name is Timmons, Al Timmons. You look familiar. I seen you around town recently? I don't forget a face if I've seen it enough."

"My name is Colonel Brison. I'm with the War Department on special assignment with the president." He flashed the non-descript badge he had been given to try to give him some semblance of authority when he wasn't in uniform, which was much of the time in recent months.

"There's a lot of you people around, 'specially right now with President Lincoln and all the other fancy suits in town," Timmons said with a wary smile.

"Look, I don't have time to explain; I need your horse. The president's life is in danger. Do you know the lay of the land south of town up by the cemeteries?"

Timmons seemed to take to the seriousness right away, but the young man was still wary until he suddenly carried a look of recognition. "I remember you. You were with General Buford the first day back in July. I was helping with the horses with his unit, trying to lend a hand when you and General Buford met up with General Reynolds outside the Seminary. I was there."

"I need your horse now, Timmons. I promise you I'll get it back to you today." Brison glanced down the street, desperation controlling his decisions now. If Timmons didn't acquiesce... Brison started to reach for his sidearm.

"I can't give you my horse. It's not mine to lend, sir, but I'll give you a ride to wherever you need to go." Timmons held out his hand to help Brison up. With a murmur of thanks, Brison swung up behind Timmons, who smartly turned the chestnut around and headed south along the street.

As they got closer to the Diamond, the activity increased with street vendors displaying souvenirs left on the battlefield and gathered up in the last four months, selling to the thousands of visitors who had recently mobbed the town. Brison looked to the left and caught a glimpse of the last remnants of the military hospital that he had seen on occasions he had been here since July, looking for the lost gold shipment he knew lay hidden somewhere south of town down among what he called "those blasted boulders." That area carried many other names now.

"Cut over to Baltimore Street, where the crowd is up at the cemeteries," Brison said.

"What's the fuss about, Colonel?" Timmons asked.

"Assassination, Mr. Timmons. Assassination."

The traffic was becoming more of a problem. There were buggies, buckboard wagons, and even a pair of Concords mixed in with vendors, children running about, and coffins... many score of coffins. On the side streets, they were stacked four high after delivery. The locals awarded the contract for moving the dead from their battlefield graves to the national cemetery, and it was still underway even as the ceremony today dedicated the grounds for that purpose. In his visits, Brison had wondered at the changes this small town had undergone since the day he rode in the back of a drummer's wagon with a damaged shoulder in late June.

They cut to the east and approached the Diamond, the center of town. The pair received more than a couple of raised voices at the speed they were moving as Timmons negotiated the moving obstacles. Brison thought he had lucked out immensely—Timmons was an accomplished horseman. When they reached the Diamond, he was forced to slow down to almost a stop. It was packed with people who had not decided to fight the crowd up to the ceremony and were waiting for the procession to return.

Brison was still uneasy.

"Do you know the land up near where the reviewing stand is?" he asked.

"Pretty well," Timmons responded. "I've been all over since the battle, gettin' my share of pickins' from the field. What do you mean assassination?"

"I believe someone is going to try and murder the president."

"How?"

"If I can trust a Reb spy in pain and under the threat of death, a sharpshooter. He said the shot would come from a barn south of the reviewing stand."

"I'm not an expert, sir, but I don't know of a barn—"

"He said it was white with a red triangle on it," Brison interrupted.

"I can't say I know of such a barn up there."

They continued to weave their way through the traffic on Baltimore Street, heading down a hill before they headed up the rise toward the cemeteries. By chance, Brison turned and looked over his shoulder and saw a two-story brick house situated on the corner of a side alley, boarded up on the first floor with an unbroken window on the second floor that faced south. It was open.

"Colonel, if you'll allow me, sir. I wouldn't know about such things, but I've heard the soldiers tellin' stories. Wouldn't a sharpshooter want to take a shot from higher ground? You know, from above?"

"You can aim at a target from below if you have a proper view with no obstructions." Brison turned back again at the window, and this time, he saw a figure briefly near the opening.

"But with all those people up ahead and up there on the hill, how could they have the grit to shoot him up there?" Timmons continued. "You only git one shot before everybody would be runnin' around like greased lightning—"

"Pull the horse up and cut in behind the building on the left!" Brison barked.

"You don't have to be ornery," Timmons said, turning the animal. When they were blocked from the street, Brison jumped from the horse and moved to the building's edge.

As he peeked around the corner, Brison thought out loud, "They would have to fire from a higher position, and they would only get one shot. They would want to make it count." He couldn't see the window clearly because of an overhang from a building farther up the street. "The sharpshooter would want to have a clear shot for a goodly time... and the president would be riding a horse or sitting in an open carriage... and the Reb would be able to see the procession coming back from the cemeteries all the way up this street."

"You've got me all goin' every which way. I'm thinkin' it was a mistake givin' you a ride. You're talkin' like a crazy loon."

"I'm taking an awful chance," Brison said to himself, then grabbed Timmons by the coat collar. "Listen to me well and there will be a monetary reward. I want you to ride on up to the ceremony and track down Ward Lamon. He'll be near the president on the speaker's stand. He's a big man. Tell him you have a message from me, Colonel Brison. He knows me, as does the president. Tell them there will be an attempt on the president's life now or in the next few minutes and to take care. You understand?"

"Yes, Ward Lamon, big man, president in danger, and you're Colonel Brison." Timmons half-smiled. "You sure you ain't crazy?"

"Ask my wife, and she would agree with your sentiment," Brison said as he headed down the side of the building. Timmons spun the horse around and made his way onto Baltimore Street and up the hill to the cemeteries.

There was no real reason to think this was the right decision, but Brison had a feeling in his gut, and it had served him well in the past. All he could go on was figuring the Reb boy had told him only a partial truth when he pressed on that knife. The boy had been instructed properly on how not to give up everything, just enough to ward off destruction. That window would be a good place to fire at an oncoming target down the street, but there were infinite possibilities. He approached the house and almost ran into a woman herding along a pair of boys with a hand on the back of each of their necks, their chances of avoiding a switch dimming by the moment. As he got to the house, he paused, feeling vindicated by what he saw. The windows on the bottom floor were boarded over, but the back door was not, and there were three horses, saddled and tied up. One of them was his. He crossed to the door, looking up at the window at the far corner as he did so. At the door, he pulled his Colt, slowly lifted on the latch, and pushed the door open.

As expected, the kitchen was not in working order. Crates of items covered the stove and tables. Brison listened for any sound from inside the house but couldn't hear over the crowd in the street. A single doorway led to the rest of the house, so he took it. Next up was the dining room off the hallway, which led to the first floor's main sitting room. The floors were without rugs, so he was careful as he stepped, knowing that at some point, the floor could announce his presence if those upstairs were at all suspicious.

The street noise increased, and he heard someone yell that the procession was on its way back into town. Then came the voices from upstairs and a sound of shuffling movement. He started up the stairs as quickly as he dared, which meant carefully shifting his weight onto the next step, praying the wood would not give him away or that the increasing noise from the street would drown out a creak. Eyes shifting between the landing and the top of the stairs, Brison made his way up to the second floor. The room facing down the street was at the hall's opposite end from the stairs. He heard the voices more clearly now.

"You need the rifle closer to the window?" a voice asked.

"No, this is perfect," a second voice said. "I can see all the way down the street, and no one can see us. The crowd won't be able to tell where the shot came from at first, so it'll create confusion. They'll be runnin' around like chickens from a fox."

"I'm powerful scared, I don't mind tellin' ya," the first voice said.

"Just be ready to git to the horses," the second voice said.

Brison moved slowly down the hall. He caught a glimpse of a figure moving into his field of vision. It disappeared and then came back. It was the sharpshooter adjusting his stand. The doorway was directly at the hall's end, and a second door to the right was open as well. Brison was just half a dozen steps from the sharpshooter's room. He could now see the shooter and his position about six feet from the window, set up on some crates with the rifle resting in a wooden V-bracket.

It was a Whitworth.

Brison had fired one before right here outside of Gettysburg. The Rebels' best sharpshooters used the English-made Whitworth; it gave one hell of a kick, but it was deadly for over half a mile. This man had to be regular Reb army. No untrained Northern sympathizer would have planned this out so well. The organizers might be members of the Knights of the Golden Circle, but this shooter was borrowed from the Army of Northern Virginia.

Brison was now just at the entrance to the side room, planning to take out the first man, then get the drop on the sharpshooter.

From the side room flew a shadow into his peripheral vision. He tried to turn, but he collapsed in agony as a shoulder plowed into his side and forced the pistol from his hand, driving him across the hall and into the far-side wall. Brison's head slammed into the wall, and he was briefly stunned as he slid to the floor. The first man brought up his arm. A knife flashed into view, upraised, ready to strike down into his chest.

"Damn Yankee," is all he said, his arm reaching its apex. Down it came, headed for the just below the breastbone, but to the Reb's astonishment, his arm met a viselike two-handed grip. The Reb cried out in surprise and frustration and tried to pull his arm free to strike again, but he couldn't break free. He swore under his breath as they struggled, and then Brison gained leverage and got one leg under himself, put his weight on the leg, and threw the other up into the Reb's body. The knee caught the Reb just below the stomach, and he groaned enough for Brison to know the hit had done damage. He glanced over at the door, but the shooter had not appeared, which told Brison the man was concentrating on his target.

He probably only had seconds before the president was in the Reb's sights. What had happened to Timmons?

Brison could tell he was stronger than this one, even with his shoulder still weakened from the Stallard affair. He twisted the knife hand while throwing his body against the Reb, whose face registered true astonishment at what was happening.

"Corporal ... help me," he said.

No reply came from the room. Brison continued until the knife slipped from the Reb's hand into his. Before the Reb could respond, Brison plunged the knife into his chest all the way to the hilt and stepped back as the Reb slipped to his knees, then to the floor with a gurgling sound mixed with a sigh. Brison spun on his heels and brought his own knife up from his boot. Seeing no threat, he moved to grab his pistol on the floor, but he never got there. As he reached the door, he saw the sharpshooter in position pulling back the hammer in final preparation. Brison took two steps and hurled himself at the shooter. The Reb never moved his trigger finger inside the guard as Brison plowed into him, spilling the two of them onto the floor. The Whitworth clattered off its perch onto the floor without firing.

The sharpshooter spun up into a crouched position and produced a knife of his own as Brison climbed into position to strike again, lamenting that he hadn't struck with his own knife first. The Reb swore under his breath, shifting the knife in his right hand. Brison knew that the assassin would strike quickly if he was to have any chance at setting up his shot. From a low crouch, the Reb lunged at Brison, the knife slashing for his middle and nipping through his shirt. Brison countered by throwing his hips back and to the right as the Reb went past. Unlike the dead man in the hallway, this Reb was stronger and stocky with bull arms and legs. Much shorter than Brison, his strength was in his compactness.

They faced each other two strides apart.

"You've already missed your shot, Reb," Brison said.

A smile appeared on the Reb's surprisingly clean-shaven face with wire-rimmed spectacles. All the easier to escape suspicion in Gettysburg. Not too fancy, not an unkept cracker, just a fellow who wouldn't bring attention to himself. "Abe won't be leavin' until dinner time, I'd expect."

He came at Brison again, slashing with his right hand and grabbing for Brison's right arm with his left, missing entirely and suffering as the Union colonel himself grabbed the Reb's arm and turned the knife away. Brison shoved hard against the smaller man but was met with solid resistance, so he lowered his shoulder and, not fearing the knife, threw them both against the wall. The Reb swore and spit in Brison's face, pushing against the bigger man, then throwing his knee up near Brison's groin. Brison disengaged and staggered back only to be hit again as the Reb came off the wall low and drove into Brison, sending the colonel against the shooting stand and over the crates onto the floor and on top of the Whitworth. His knife spun from his hand against the far wall. The Reb kicked a crate to the side and took two strides as he prepared to jump and drive down with his knife. Brison rolled to his right and grabbed the Whitworth. Miraculously, his right hand found the trigger. The Reb growled as he leaped. With no time to aim accurately or steady himself, Brison pulled the trigger.

The Whitworth exploded, the bullet hitting the Reb directly in the middle of the chest.

For a moment, Brison lay on the floor with the dead sharpshooter covering his lower legs. Then he shoved the man off, slid along the floor to the wall, and rested, his heart beating through his chest and his arms shaking from the exertion. He wondered why there were no shouts about the rifle shot, but then, as his head cleared, he heard a band playing in the street. No one had heard the report. He gradually became aware that his right hand was hurting, and he looked down at two of his fingers misshapen and bent at angles he had never seen before.

"Bloody Whitworth does have a hell of a kick," he said, mustering up his best English accent.

Chapter Two

HE RAN HIS FINGERS along the delicate carving on the desk's edge exactly as he would run them along a woman's body, slowly savoring the sensation of the wood's firm surface. Arthur Collins might have an old-fashioned name and, as a historian at American University, an old-fashioned occupation, but he was not an old-fashioned man. He was skilled in the manner of lovemaking. He smiled to himself as he thought about it. He relished encounters with newly graduated former students who had fallen under his classroom presence. In his mid-forties, he still commanded a room with his deep voice and dark beard, salted with white, and he had a wife who looked the other way as long as he was discreet and attentive to her as well.

He was active on social media, blogging on topics beyond what he covered in his lectures. He used the internet extensively for early research on subjects. He belonged to an online fantasy football league. He purchased the latest cellphone immediately upon its release and always had to eat at the newest trendy restaurant in Georgetown the week it opened. Arthur Collins was a modern, forward-thinking man in all aspects except for his love of history and antiques. He exhaled with wonder as he continued with his hands along the desk's edge, a permanent smile carved into his face, his eyes aflame with delight.

"Yet another conquest I should be jealous of, darling," the voice said from the study doors. Stephanie Collins leaned against the doorframe, smiling with her arms folded against her chest. "So, you finally got that desk you've wanted all these years."

"Yes, old man McWharter finally agreed to part with this," Collins said. "Fifteen years I've been asking him to sell it to me. Fifteen years."

"Really, Arthur. You'd think it was made of gold." Stephanie shook her head. "Just what is the significance of this desk again?"

Collins looked over at her with his head tilted down, giving her the same glance he reserved for a student with an ill-conceived question. "This desk was built in 1869 and was a gift from President Ulysses S. Grant to former Secretary of War Edwin Stanton and was delivered upon Stanton's confirmation by the Senate to the U.S. Supreme Court. Except Stanton didn't get to use it much, because he died just four days after his confirmation."

"You wrote an abbreviated biography of him, didn't you?" Stephanie asked.

Collins nodded. "Always been fascinated by Stanton and this desk ever since I saw it at McWharter's house Christmas party that year."

"It *is* a beautiful desk."

"And it only changed hands twice in the last 150 years. McWharter's family has had it since the late 1800s." Collins sat down behind the desk and pulled on some of the drawers.

His wife turned from the doorway and disappeared with her voice trailing behind her. "I don't want to know what you spent on it."

After polishing the desk for half an hour, Collins set about moving his work materials into their new home. He was deciding what would go where when he dropped a folder onto the floor, its contents spilling in a broad mess under the desk. Annoyed and swearing to himself, Collins slid underneath the desk to retrieve the papers when something caught his eye. It looked like the simple head of a nail that had worked its way from its home and now protruded from a corner brace where the drawer housing met the flat top of the desk. Unless you were underneath the desk and specifically looking for it, a person could easily have missed it. There was a metallic ring not unlike a washer around the metal pin.

"What the hell is this?" Collins asked. He felt the pin and gently pushed it. He was met with resistance, so he applied more force, and with a sharp sound, something gave way inside the desk. He immediately knew what he had found, a secret latch that opened a hiding place. He quickly crawled out from under and pulled the top drawer to find that the back end of the drawer had partially opened. Because of age and the lack of use, the false back was hard to move beyond halfway, but after a few moments of manipulation, he gained access. He reached in as far as he could with his arm and found a soft leather pouch.

He giddily unfolded the pouch's ties and gently withdrew the folder papers inside. Within seconds, he ascertained that he was looking at a legal document dated August 5, 1859, signed and notarized in New York City. He sat down in his chair and flicked on his lamp as the sunlight faded. He sat quietly without a call to his wife for thirty minutes, reading the document all the way through. When he was finished, he thought about the significance of what he just read, then looked over it a second time. He repeated the names of the principals and grabbed his laptop and accessed the internet. It only took him a few quick searches to get the information he needed.

He literally shook with trepidation.

May 12

Adrian Torrez stood with his back to the room, looking out his White House window with his hands behind his back, when his executive assistant opened the door, slipped in, and held the door closed behind her.

"Your three o'clock is here," she said.

"Arthur? Great, let him in. Tell Senator Golden's office he can get twenty minutes with the president if he agrees to support our position on the immigration reform add-on. If not, there is no sense in their meeting this week, next week, or next year."

"You want me to say exactly that?" she asked. "Shouldn't that come from you or your deputy?"

Torrez gave a wolfish smile. "Put your best foot forward, Susan. The senator is in for a dogfight next year, one of the few really contested seats, and he's going to need the president's coat tails and he knows it. I just want him to sweat a little. I'll call his office at the end of the day after he's had time to stew a bit. Bring Arthur in. Thanks."

Torrez was curious about what Collins wanted to see him about. They saw each other on occasion even though they traveled in different circles, having been friends for more than twenty years, going back to when they were students at Yale. Torrez smiled at the memories of their exploits; their off-campus keg parties were still the stuff of legend. Collins had gravitated to a life of academia, while Torrez could never have had that kind of life. He liked his life among the power brokers inside the beltway. When his boss was done with his two terms, another elected president always needed expert staffing or perhaps a company or two in need of a board member, perhaps even a chairman. After all, having the title of White House Chief of Staff on your resume was unique.

"How are you, Adrian?" Collins stood next to one of the chairs in front of Torrez's desk.

"Arty." Torrez swung around the desk, grabbed his friend's hand, and hugged him briefly. "How are you doing? And how is Steph?"

"We're doing great. I appreciate your seeing me here on short notice."

"Anything for you. Of course, it always helps when you talk in mysterious phrases and tell me you've got something. I think you used the words, 'pretty incendiary to show me.' That tends to pique my interest."

"I don't think I'll disappoint you." Collins settled into his chair as Torrez traveled around behind his desk. "I'm going to give this to you, but once you're done with it, I hope you would return it to me as a historical find that I can have and turn over to the university for its archives."

Torrez gave a puzzled look. "Well, I don't normally agree to something before I've seen what I'm talking about. What the hell do you have there, Arty?"

Collins withdrew the leather pouch from his briefcase and held it out. "You look it over and tell me what you think we have here. I believe you can make more use of it than I ever could."

Torrez opened the papers and began to read. After ten minutes, he whistled softly and looked up at Collins. He reached over to his phone and punched a key.

"Yes, sir," his secretary's voice said from the speaker.

"Susan, cancel my appointments for the next ninety minutes," Torrez said.

He continued reading for another ten minutes. All the while, Collins kept quiet, biding his time by checking email on his cellphone. After he was done with that, Collins just sat looking around the office until, finally, he couldn't contain himself anymore.

"Well, what do you think?" he asked.

"Have you shown or talked to anyone else about this?" Torrez said without looking up.

"Adrian, I'm not an idiot. You and I both know if that holds water, it's worth perhaps billions if used properly."

"If used properly. I assume you checked to see if we're talking about the same company?"

"It's right on the company's website, the whole history, right there," Collins said. "Except for, of course, what you have in your hand."

"And the minority owner?"

"Yes, his great, great grandfather. You know the senator has his own website as well, and he is very proud of his heritage."

The implications swirled in Torrez's head. The possibilities were almost unlimited, beyond comprehension. But his ordered mind immediately knew his first task.

"Arty, we have a unique opportunity." Torrez smiled just as he had before with his secretary. "Let me take care of this. I'll see you get compensated—seven, perhaps eight figures. If I'm able to use this correctly, I'll handle the risk and you won't have to worry about anything."

"I appreciate that, Adrian. I thought you would be in a position to best use this."

"I am indeed."

June I

THE BAT FELT GOOD in his hands. It had been a while since he took some hacks in a cage. Jason Sparks, his six-foot-two-inch frame balanced evenly on his two feet in the left-handed hitter's box, moved the bat through the hitting zone, waiting for the machine to deliver the eighty-mile-per-hour pitch. He could see the arm pick up the ball... more weight on the back foot... the ball appeared at the top of the machine... the bat moved slightly now near his left shoulder... a timing mechanism... the ball came at him, right down the middle... push off the left leg, drive toward the pitcher, whip the bat through the zone, snap the wrists at the right moment.

Whack!

The ball screamed on a line north of the batting machine and headed up higher now to drive against the netting a hundred and twenty feet away before dropping harmlessly to the ground. Another ball came, not exactly in the same place, but he still managed to put a good swing to it and got a similar result. He started to work up a sweat as ball after ball came in at him until, finally, he finished up with his five tokens and yielded the cage to another hitter, this one less than half his age.

"Nice hitting, pops," the kid said as he passed. "You must have been really good when you were young."

Sparks turned back as the kid closed the door and settled in.

"Pops?" Sparks said under his breath. "Who the hell says 'pops' anymore."

Just as he approached his bag, he could hear his cellphone ring from inside. When he saw the display screen, he saw it was the director's private phone. A Sunday morning call from Raymond Connelly probably wasn't a good thing. He answered, and Connelly responded without a greeting.

"Sparks, meet me at the location I'm texting to your phone immediately," he said.

"What's the problem, sir?" Sparks kept it formal with this director, unlike his predecessor. He had gone from friend to someone he barely knew in a matter of weeks. That was all it had taken for Connelly's congressional approval to go through, he was so well connected and respected in the intelligence and political communities. It had been a slam dunk for the president.

"The president's chief of staff is dead," Connelly said. "And it wasn't an accident. This is going to be a joint Secret Service/FBI investigation, Jason, and I want you on scene with me as soon as possible."

Sparks stopped loading his duffle bag and stood dumbfounded next to the bench. "What the hell happened, sir?"

"Just get to the scene now. I'll meet you there. And Jason..."

"Sir?"

"Not a word to anyone."

Connelly hadn't called Sparks by his first name more than two or three times in the last four months, and here he had done it twice in thirty seconds. Connelly was more than a little anxious. Sparks could understand why. Adrian Torrez. Damn, this was going to get messy. He already had a feeling in his gut, and he didn't have any information. Sparks looked over at the kid rifling balls all over the batting cage. Had it ever been that easy?

Sparks grabbed his bag and hurried through the batting cage office and out to his black Chevy. He loaded the address into his smart phone's navigation app and saw that the drive was only going to be thirty-five minutes. Maybe he could make it in twenty-five.

CHAPTER THREE

Nov. 19, 1863

IT WAS GLOOMY OUTSIDE, and as Brison was about to find out, President Lincoln's mood was not any better. Brison had spent the afternoon with a rather indignant captain who took charge of the bodies of the two assassins in the house on Baltimore Street and the gut-sore young man back in the locked office closet. With help from Ward Hill Lamon, the captain was sworn to secrecy on the goings on, and the young surviving Reb was under armed guard and headed for the Old Capitol Prison, where he had an appointment with Brison at a later time. But for now, Brison needed to talk to Lincoln, and he was meeting resistance in the form of Lamon, of all people.

"Colonel, I know the president usually accepts you at all times." Lamon blocked the door to the car with his imposing bulk, his longish hair and goatee intensifying his presence. They both swayed with the train's movement, having left the Gettysburg area half an hour before. "This isn't a usual circumstance. He is feeling poorly, I'm afraid, and he's been grum all afternoon. He's lying down, and I don't want him bothered."

"I'll not take but a few minutes of his time, Lamon." Brison tried to keep an even tone. "He'll want to see me. There *was* an attempt on his life this afternoon."

Lamon's face screwed up like it was in a vice. "And I've agreed to keep it quiet because that's what Mr. Lincoln desires. But he is to remain undisturbed... for now."

"Sam Hill, man." Brison was tired, and his formerly dislocated fingers hurt like the devil, but he maintained his composure. "Please, just ask the president if he will see me."

Lamon shook his head and was about to poke his finger into Brison's chest when the door opened and Lincoln eased his frame through the opening.

"Gentlemen, if the purpose of your words together is to determine whether I'm to be disturbed or not, I'd put forth the notion my presence would render your conversation a penniless exercise," Lincoln said. He offered a small smile. "Mr. Lamon, I'll see the colonel straight away. Please have someone bring me a wet towel."

Lamon mumbled something in response, and in a moment, Lincoln and Brison were alone in the car. The president lay back down on the small couch in the compartment and closed his eyes.

"You will excuse me, Colonel," he said. "I'm afraid I have some sort of malady. I have been feeling poorly all day, and along with this, my words at the ceremony today didn't take well."

"I'm sorry to hear that, sir, but I needed to speak with urgency with you," Brison said. "The lead we were following out of Philadelphia led me to Harrisburg and then, unbelievably, down here again where I have such recent history. Sir, there was a well-formed attempt on your life this afternoon. Three men, two set up as sharpshooters in a building in Gettysburg."

Lincoln opened his eyes.

"I was able to put an end to it," Brison said.

"I see not without some damage."

"Not important. What is important is that this group connected to the Knights of the Golden Circle seems better organized and willing to go beyond reasonable conduct of war. Assassination... a foul business."

"If you would, the report."

Brison spent the next ten minutes giving Lincoln the details, including the last-second fight in the second-floor room. Just as he finished, Lamon returned with a wet towel, and Lincoln placed it over his forehead.

"I will include everything in my report," Brison said. "Extra measures should be taken, as all this business marks the beginning, in my opinion, of a new effort."

"I agree," Lamon said. "If I may say again, sir, you take your safety as being solid as a rock when it is not."

Lincoln exhaled and shifted uncomfortably on the couch, placing the towel back on his forehead after it had slipped down with his movement. "I am grateful to both of you for your efforts, but for this moment, we shall not discuss it. I would prefer to rest as we continue to Washington. However, I do need to speak with the colonel alone for a few minutes."

Lamon excused himself, looking to Brison like he was not at all happy with his president or the colonel. Lincoln immediately sat up and motioned for Brison to bring a chair close. In the low light of the lamps, Lincoln's face carried a pallid appearance. It seemed the president was weakening with every encounter they had, which left Brison melancholy, for with the war swinging in the Union's favor, the coming year was still going to be another bloody affair.

"What happened to your hand, son?" Lincoln asked.

"A couple of misshapen fingers, sir. Nothing time won't take care of."

"Still, I *am* grateful. Don't let my words here detract from that thought, but we must move on to other issues."

"Sir, I need to talk to the young Reb we have under guard," Brison said. "He might have information."

"Let General Sharpe's people meet that problem for now." Lincoln looked Brison directly in the face. "I have yet another matter where I need your discreet inquiry talents. Do you feel you are up to the task? I doubt there will be skullduggery with this assignment." He offered a small smile.

"I am at your service, sir."

"Have you ever heard of Augustus Raven?"

"Can't say as I have."

"He is the owner of Raven Ironworks in New York, on the Hudson River a ways up from the city. I have met him on one occasion, I believe. He is one of the larger cannon and munitions manufacturers for us. Has been since before the war. A tough bear of a man, not unlike your description of that William

Smythe you wrestled with back in the summer. Raven's supplies have been of the highest quality. His efforts there I have no quibble with, but I've received disturbing words about him and his business that I would like you to investigate."

"What is it?"

"Complaints, rumors, whisper talk that he is more devious than he appears. Competitors of his have sent word they are having difficulties with accidents, suspicious activity, and outright intentional damage. No one has the gumption to come right out and let everyone at the ball know what's on their mind, but that might be because they're afraid of the man. He's like a coyote hangin' around the back forty."

Lincoln stopped for a moment and rubbed his eyes. To Brison, it was obvious the man was suffering from some illness. Lincoln leaned forward and continued. He seemed anxious to be done with the conversation. "The other manufacturers have not sent any official complaints through procurement or the quartermasters. A friend of mine, Samuel Bixby of New York City, fielded these complaints with the knowledge he has my ear. His and their concerns seem worthy of investigation, but we must do so with discretion. Raven's contributions to the war effort must not be curtailed in any manner. They are too valuable, particularly in that we are closer to our calling than ever before."

"And if I find this Raven fellow is behind accidents and such with his competitors?" Brison asked.

"We will decide on the course we must steer at that time." Lincoln got up wearily from the couch and moved to a corner table, picking up a sheet of paper among others loosely thrown about the top. "Go and see Bixby. He is familiar with the men involved in this intrigue. Let me know what the goings on are with Raven." He motioned to the bandaged hand of his visitor. "Be mindful of that hand, Colonel. Give it time to heal as best you can. I broke a finger or two in my youthful days when I was rafting down the Mississippi."

"Thank you, sir. I will. Surely you don't think we should let Raven have his way by unfairly harming his competitors."

"I have a sense there might be more to this whole affair than even Bixby knows, but that might be just my ol' Illinois lawyer's distrust makin' an appearance. Whatever the case may be... we shall see."

Brison moved to get up from his chair. "How did the speech go today at the ceremony?"

"I told Lamon after I finished that it didn't scour." Lincoln handed over the sheet of paper he had picked up. "It wasn't enthusiastically received, I'm afraid. Would you like to read it?"

"Yes, sir."

Brison took the paper and immediately realized Lincoln meant for him to read it presently, not at his leisure. He was surprised by its brevity. It took only a few minutes to read the remarks. Lincoln had sat down on the couch and was about to place the towel on his face again when Brison finished reading.

"Sir..."

"Yes, Colonel."

"These... are very good words."

CHAPTER FOUR

SUNDAY TRAFFIC WAS LIGHT, so he made it to the site in thirty minutes. It was on a wooded stretch of secondary road in rural Virginia west of Arlington. A single ambulance without lights on sat by the side of the road. Sparks pulled behind it and got out of his car, then walked on the sheltered side of the ambulance and found five vehicles parked in a row in front: two state trooper vehicles and three black SUVs with tinted windows, blatantly announcing their government agency ownership. What caught Sparks's attention immediately was the dark blue BMW located just inside the tree line on a not-often-used path that was large enough for a car. Several suits milled around the car along with two people in jumpsuits with crime scene investigation lettering.

As Sparks walked up the path, the familiar figure of Connelly came down to meet him. Connelly wore a suit and appeared to have been at church that morning. He was a man of average stature with auburn hair a bit longer than a buzz cut and was clean shaven around a slightly misshapen nose, no doubt broken more than once. Connelly was in his late fifties, but they had been hard years.

"This is going to be a hell of problem, Jason." Connelly stopped Sparks, holding a hand up. "I've already talked with Director Pearson. We're pairing you up with an agent from his investigative team. The two of you are going to work point on this investigation together. I want to know now if that is going to be a problem."

"Don't think I can work and play well with others?" Sparks mused.

"Griffin left behind a lot of shit after Gettysburg... the House hearings, the public thrashing by the press. You and I both bent the hell out of the truth under oath. The whole damn affair almost unraveled and still could. One of the few things I thought worthwhile he left behind was the position he carved out for you. You've done some good work; now I need your best. We're never going to be as close as you and Griffin were, but I need you to give me that same effort. Are we clear?"

"Sure, I'll give you what you need."

Connelly seemed relieved. "Good. Let's go."

The pair walked up the remaining hundred feet to the tree line. The BMW seemed undamaged, and as they reached the left side, one of the techs handed Connelly a clipboard.

"Single shot, nine millimeter or something in that neighborhood, left temple," the tech said. "Initial dusting found some prints, but obviously, we'll need to get the car into the lab for a full workup. I tried to get a field match on a couple already, but they were Torrez's. No signs of anyone else being in the car, at least on our initial pass. No sign of a struggle or distress on his part. His White House identification and wallet are on his person. It looks like someone just popped him with his window down as he sat in the driver's seat."

"Okay, Chris," Connelly said. "How long before you'll be ready to move the body?"

"Twenty minutes or so."

"What was the time of death?" Sparks said.

"I'm guessing about midnight, roughly ten hours ago. Liver probe says it's about then."

"Thanks, Chris," Connelly said. "Finish up." Then to Sparks, "Secret Service is here."

Four individuals walked up the grassy slope to the tree line, led by a woman wearing a dark skirt and matching sports jacket with a white blouse. She was tall, maybe five foot eight, with an athletic build. Her light brown hair was tied up, and she wore dark glasses, so Sparks couldn't tell the color of her eyes. She walked right up to Connelly and Sparks, flashing her Secret Service identification at Connelly without giving Sparks a second glance.

"Director Connelly, I'm Special Agent Bethany Taylor," she said. "I'm with investigative support, and I'm here to lend any assistance with the investigation. Director Pearson informed me the two of you had arranged for me to run point with one of your people."

"That would be me. Jason Sparks." He held out his hand, which she took with a firm handshake. "I thought Secret Service protection didn't extend to the Chief of Staff."

"It doesn't, but the president can issue an executive order for protection for any individual or order an investigation into any criminal act against an individual, especially someone on the White House staff. He was notified of Torrez's death the minute it came into our office, ninety..." She looked at her watch. "... six minutes ago. Sparks, you're well known after all that Gettysburg business and the lost gold. I enjoyed reading all about it in the Post for two weeks. Must have been an uncomfortable situation for the two of you." A small smile appeared beneath the dark glasses.

"You're going to have fun," Connelly said to Sparks. Then he spoke to both of them. "I'll leave the two of you to handle this from now on. This is a joint investigation, but the FBI has ultimate jurisdiction. I recognize, as does your director, Special Agent Taylor, that Torrez was a high-level member of the administration, so the president's first call after he was informed of the murder was a conference call between Pearson and myself. We agreed that, for national security reasons, the manner of Torrez's death will remain classified for now. He died in a car accident. The president's press secretary will handle outgoing information for now, and all questions to us will be, until we know more, directed to the White House. Are we clear?"

"Yes," they both said in unison.

"From all indications, this was a professional job, so if that is the case, why would someone with connections to hire a professional hit want the president's chief of staff dead?"

"We'll work on it as quickly and thoroughly as we can, Director," Sparks said.

Connelly spun on his heels and headed down the slope, telling them over his shoulder to keep him informed.

Sparks looked over at Taylor and then down at his own appearance, jeans and a Miami Hurricanes baseball T-shirt. "Sorry for the outfit. He called me while I was in the batting cage."

Taylor didn't respond, hands on her hips.

"Just trying to get a few swings in before breakfast. Had to come straight here when I got the call. Feel free to step into the conversation."

Taylor removed her sunglasses, revealing eyes of aquamarine, a sharp contrast to her hair. "I have you at a disadvantage, Special Agent Sparks. I had time to pull a profile on you. I wanted to see who I would be working with. Your record is impressive, and you get high marks in many different areas except when it comes to working with others. Seems you have a problem with delegating tasks, micro-managing yourself right into working alone."

"You're subtle. Just come right out and say what you're thinking." Sparks started walking back up to the car.

Taylor followed. "I'm wondering if we're going to have a problem."

"Not unless you judge me based on some politically-slanted profile jacket. If you make a conclusion based on that alone without seeing me in action, then yeah, we're going to have a problem. So what am I going to find when I do a little research on you?"

"I'm normally assigned to the Emergency Response Team," she said. "I've been with the Service for three years after leaving the military. I rate expert in numerous weapons. I train in mixed martial arts twice a week. I received special forces training but washed out near the end of training because I broke my ankle. Decided not to go through it all again. I love cats, and I don't understand anyone who doesn't. I got to my position because I'm great at what I do, and I don't take bullshit from anyone, particularly traditional, macho, boy's-club crap."

"Like I said," Sparks said as he smiled back at her, "you're subtle."

"We'll be cool if you just treat me like you would anyone else you're paired up with on an assignment."

"Be careful what you ask for," he said under his breath.

AFTER FINISHING AT THE site, Sparks and Taylor left in his car, heading back into the city. They stopped for fifteen minutes so Sparks could change into a suit, because their next stop was the White House. While he was alone in his bedroom, he called in a favor from a friend of his at the Hoover building and asked for them to give him a rundown on Taylor. As he worked on his tie in the mirror, he smiled. *Got to get on even footing, after all.*

Soon, they were on their way into Washington in unusually light traffic and arrived at the White House just after noon. Taylor had called ahead, and Torrez's entire staff had been called in, as well as any staffer that had frequent contact with Torrez. Taylor learned that the president wanted to talk to them as well. Sparks had been to the White House on two occasions, but never to the Oval Office, and he had never met President Douglas. As they were led through the staff offices, Sparks noticed the absence of banter among the staffers who had arrived, and he gave a glance to Taylor, who also gave him a face that showed she understood they were under scrutiny.

"It's going to be next to impossible to keep the circumstances of Torrez's death a secret for long," Taylor whispered as they approached the president's office. They were led in by Stephen James, Torrez's deputy chief of staff. He was a short, thin man in his mid-thirties, already balding with square-ish glasses and the distinctive gaze of someone who was already overwhelmed beyond his capacity to cope.

"Mr. President, this is Special Agent Jason Sparks from the FBI and Special Agent Bethany Taylor with the Secret Service," James said. He turned to an assistant and asked that the meeting just be the four of them.

If having charisma was a necessity to run for president, then John Douglas was overqualified. He would carry a commanding presence even as a high school janitor. A former football player, Douglas stood a shade under six foot four, weighed in at a trim 220 pounds, and worked out five days a week for an hour before he began his day. Sparks knew this because he had read the latest People magazine while waiting for a haircut. At only forty-five years old, he was the youngest president since Kennedy, and the Camelot comparisons had dominated the election cycle.

As he circled from behind the Resolute desk, he was jacketless, yet dressed for church. His rich tan went well with his black hair with a hint of gray at his temples. Sparks thought to himself that whether someone agreed or disagreed with his politics, Douglas was the kind of leader Americans always wanted, a guy who looked the part but could back it up with intellect. He had three degrees: a bachelor's in economics and international relations and a law degree from Stanford. After serving in both houses of Congress, he had been elected with 58 percent of the vote, which constituted a landslide compared to recent elections.

"Agents Taylor, Sparks." He shook both of their hands. "I appreciate your coming in directly from the site to brief me directly."

"We would also like to ask some questions as well, Mr. President," Taylor said.

"Of course. Would the two of you like coffee? God knows I need it right now." He gestured to James, and the deputy chief of staff slipped out to make the request. "What did you find out there?"

"What were you told, sir?" Sparks said.

"The only information I was given this morning is that he was found in his car by a country road in Virginia and it appeared not to be an accident. I can't imagine why Adrian would be in Virginia. His home is in Maryland."

"He was murdered," Sparks said. "Shot once in the head from close range. No shell casing left at the scene, nothing apparently taken from the car. There were boot prints leading away from the car over a wooded ridge for about a quarter mile, where they led to a paved nature trail parking lot. The killer probably had a car parked there. We're checking to see if anyone using the trails saw someone or a car there this morning."

"It was probably stolen," Taylor said, "and it was parked on pavement, so no tire tracks."

"You're telling me this was a professional, not some random robbery gone bad?" Douglas said.

"It wasn't sloppy and was well thought out," Sparks said. "If it was a professional hit, then, Mr. President, our first questions, given his position within the government, are how does this relate to that position and what is the motive behind this act?"

"I've been friends with Adrian since we were working on our undergraduate degrees at Yale. He was one of the main players in my campaign and was the natural choice for Chief of Staff when I was elected. His work on the transition team made my administration's transfer one of the smoothest remembered around these parts."

The staffer arrived with the coffee and distributed it.

When the four of them were alone again, the president continued. "Making political enemies in this town is unavoidable. Every decision or policy you make leaves yourself open to a fresh attack or, at the least someone or group who will file the transgression for retribution down the road." Douglas smiled. "You need a scorecard to keep everything straight." He took a sip of coffee. "But murder. My first thought would be that it is not connected to politics."

"Everything in this city is connected to politics," Sparks said.

"In a way, yes, but the violent removal of my chief of staff..."

"Sir, what has been Torrez's manner recently?" Taylor asked. "Did he seem preoccupied, worried about something?"

"The nature of our relationship, because of the nature of my job, has changed since my election," Douglas said. "We don't have time for bullshitting about the old days or worrying about getting a new set of brakes on the car. Our interaction was restricted to business. If something was really bothering him, it would have to be life-altering in its scope. I haven't seen such behavior. Perhaps his co-workers who aren't so well insulated..."

"We'll be talking to the staff after our meeting here," Sparks said.

"How about people who would hold a grudge from the time before your run for national office?" Taylor asked.

"No one comes immediately to mind," Douglas said. "Adrian was near the top of his class. He was a member in numerous clubs and charities through our fraternity. There were people who didn't like him necessarily, but you could say that about anyone."

"What about women?" Sparks asked.

"He played the field, but..." Douglas held up his index finger. "... he was always up front and honest with the women he dated. He wasn't one to get tied down, even after college and law school. But the women always knew he wasn't going to be exclusive, and he didn't demand it of them. Adrian was no hypocrite."

Taylor looked over at Sparks. He noticed a slight rise in her eyebrows, taking it in as a look of skepticism. She turned back to the president.

"Would he date married women?" she asked.

"Well, you would think a type-A personality like Adrian's would go after married women because they enjoy going after the unattainable, but he never did when we talked about such things. I can't speak to whom he was dating recently. Again, there are members of his staff that might know more."

"What about his finances?" Sparks asked.

Douglas responded while taking a drink of his coffee with an upturned palm. "Someone has his financials, I'm sure. Everyone in the White House is an open book; Taylor's boss sees to that. Kind of comes with the territory. No, Adrian was solid with his money as far as I could tell. He was going to make a hell of a lot of money in the private sector once our time here was over."

James, who had been sitting idly by, moved into the center of the room. "Sir, we need to go over your afternoon schedule and the press conference on Adrian."

Douglas nodded. "Both of you will please keep my office informed as you make progress."

"Mr. President, you realize the manner of his death will get out pretty quick," Sparks said. "We can't say it was an accident, then fight off the press when it's leaked that it was a murder."

"I haven't spoken with my press secretary yet—she's up next—but I imagine we will say the details of his death are being investigated, then come back that it was a carjacking, something in that manner."

Sparks's thoughts flashed back to the previous year and the shooting death of the FBI's deputy director.

"Our directors made it clear we get to stay out of the limelight on this one," Sparks said. "At least until we have answers. We'll leave it up to your administration and the people in our respective bureaus with a higher pay grade than ours to deal with the press."

They shook hands again, and James led them out of the office and directly to a conference room, where he furnished them with a staff list and an organizational chart. He had marked the staffers who were already in the office, waiting to see if they needed to be interviewed. The two agents dug in and interviewed a dozen staffers over the next two and a half hours and mined little important information except that Torrez didn't socialize with anyone on his own staff other than for an occasional drink on a Friday night. It was clear they would need to interview his latest female acquaintances to see if something unusual showed up. They were preparing to leave when a staffer knocked on the meeting room's door frame and asked for a moment of their time.

"Am I to understand you are heading up the investigation into Adrian's death?" she asked.

"Yes, we are," Taylor said. "And you are?"

"Rachel Evans. I have something he asked me to give to you... or give to the people heading up the investigation if he were to disappear mysteriously. I know it sounds weird, and God knows I felt incredibly uncomfortable when he gave me the envelope."

"He literally told you if he were to disappear?" Sparks asked.

"That's what he said. He seemed antsy about it." Evans stepped in. She was dressed in jeans and a Southern Cal sweatshirt, her dirty blonde hair loosely covering her shoulders. "I only went on two dates with him, but about ten days ago, he gave me this envelope and told me to keep it in a locked drawer and tell no one I had it."

"Did you sleep with him?" Taylor asked.

Evans was taken aback, then recovered. "I understand your need for information about his personal life, but really?"

"Why would he entrust you with something important to him when you had been on only two dates," Taylor said, "unless you had been intimate with him?"

Evans gave a bemused smile. Sparks thought she would have given a different reaction had he asked the question.

"Yes, we slept together, but that was a few months ago," Evans said. "I recognized right away what type of man he was, and anything long term was out of the question. He was exciting and very nice but not the marrying kind."

"Then why would he entrust this envelope to you?" Sparks took it from Evans.

"Honestly, I don't know. We got along fine, but we didn't have much contact recently. He just suddenly showed up at my desk..."

"Ten days ago," Taylor said.

"And he said nothing other than to keep it locked in your desk," Sparks said.

"I remember distinctly," Evans said. "He asked me if he could trust me with something for a short time, and he said not to be alarmed but that he wanted some papers protected, kept in a non-official place. I half-jokingly asked him if it was something illegal, and he said no but that I should give it to the lead investigator if he disappears under unusual circumstances. I honestly thought he was joking. He kind of had that dry sense of humor. Then he said he would be back to pick up the envelope in a couple of weeks."

"You never looked inside the envelope, even after you were called in today?" Sparks asked.

"I'm a good girl," Evans said, smiling at Sparks, "and I'm smart enough to know when to let curiosity go unfulfilled. And it was sealed."

"You did say he seemed uncomfortable about it when he gave it to you," Taylor said.

"I didn't think it at the time, but when I heard about his death this morning, I started thinking about our conversation when he dropped it off... and the more I thought about it, the more I remember him being off, not like we had been on our dates. Not distant, mean, or anything, just... different."

"You have a card?" Sparks asked.

"I figured you would need it." Evans had been holding it since she walked in. She gave Sparks a big smile as they exchanged cards. "Call me if you need anything."

"I will," Sparks said. "Thank you, Ms. Evans."

The second Evans left the room, Taylor gave a small laugh. "Really?"

Sparks smiled at her, then abruptly went to the door and called out for Evans to come back. When he spoke, it was in a low voice that only Taylor could hear. "This is vital, Ms. Evans. Did you tell *anyone* that you were holding a package for Torrez? *Anyone?*"

Evans held her hand to her chest and looked uncertain after Sparks's change in tone.

"No, not a soul."

"Okay," Sparks said. "Please don't tell anyone about the envelope. It never happened, you understand? It's for your own protection."

She left, and Sparks closed the door.

"You think she's telling the truth about not looking in the envelope?" Sparks asked.

"I was wondering if you really had your head in the game, the way she was filling out that USC sweatshirt," Taylor mused. "I don't know. Let's see what we have here."

Inside the envelope was a business letter dated ten days before on Torrez's personal stationery rather than on White House letterhead, which Sparks found interesting. With it was a sheet of paper with an itemized list. They sat down next to each other and read the cover letter in silence.

To the lead investigator,

I trust Ms. Evans has given you this envelope per my instructions I gave her upon her taking possession. I can assume my disappearance or death has caused quite a stir. The purpose of this letter is to give you a start on gaining my freedom or catching my killer. Ten days ago, I met with an old friend of mine, a history professor at American University named Arthur Collins. He brought me a rather amazing set of documents from a century and a half ago that carry astounding importance.

Since you are reading this, then it is clear I have made an error and now find myself in dire circumstances, most likely at the hands of Sterling Raven. He will, of course, deny involvement in my disappearance and you will have no proof unless you have the documents in question. I have given them back to Collins for safekeeping and he will be able to turn them over to you. Once you see the documents you will understand their importance to Raven.

Adrian Torrez

"Sterling Raven is the owner of Raven Industries," Sparks said. "His company is right up there in defense contracts with Lockheed Martin, Boeing, and General Dynamics."

"If Torrez was worried about his safety, why the hell doesn't he just spell out what he knew in this letter?" Taylor asked.

"I don't know. But I do know a little about Raven from what I've read in magazine profiles. Raven Industries is worth many billions, and he owns well over controlling interest. There are rumors of his influence in Washington beyond the lobbyists on the hill. He's not a man to be trifled with."

"With this letter, Torrez has implicated Raven in his own murder."

"It's an accusation with no factual evidence," Sparks said.

"This Arthur Collins must have it, and he could be in danger as well." Taylor was already at the door. "I'll get his address."

Sparks looked over the letter again once Taylor was gone. He got to the part where Torrez wrote, "... he brought me a rather amazing document from a hundred and fifty years ago..."

Sparks gazed at the portrait of one of the presidents from the nineteenth century, he couldn't remember which one. All he could mutter to himself was, "Not again."

CHAPTER FIVE

Nov. 23, 1863

BRISON WAS TOLD THAT Samuel Bixby's home would be a handsome building off the newly expanded Central Park, facing directly west onto the grounds. Brison's trip had been uneventful, a train through Philadelphia, then on to just outside New York, where he boarded a ferry across to the island of Manhattan.

He disliked large cities. The crush of human contact along the streets multiplied until all forms of misery were on display. Orphans ran around like separated sheep being chased by the owner's dog. They ran in small packs of three or four, grabbing for whatever wares they could from vendors' carts, sometimes even brazenly snatching a man's pocket watch right out of his hand. Street people lay in corners, attempting to be out of sight from the policemen. Small groups of young men appeared ready to pounce on any unsuspecting person. The city seemed to be one large, clogged mess of humanity, like a conflagration of river logs at a mill. Give him the openness of New England, with its mixture of meadows and forests, small towns placed neatly with the landscape... not this overtaking of the land.

Brison rode on a new chestnut gelding he purchased in New Jersey before taking the ferry. Such was the life of an official on government business. Money made arrangements all the easier. He moved from the backstreets onto the main thoroughfares and finally onto Fifth Avenue, where he was told it would run along the east side of the park. Lincoln's personal secretary,

John Nicolay, had wired Bixby of Brison's intentions, and it was agreed that Brison was to arrive unannounced. He was not to see the financier at the man's offices on this Monday afternoon, a decision that gave Brison cause to wonder if Bixby was concerned about whose eyes would see them together.

As he moved north along the avenue, the scenery improved with fine buildings, smartly turned-out carriages with horses of fine grooming, and people strolling along the walkways despite the chill of the late November afternoon. With his preferred dress of jeans, a simple shirt with a heavy overcoat, a broad-brimmed hat, high boots, his Colt tucked snugly inside his coat, and his Spencer displayed prominently in its leather holster on his saddle, he grew more aware of his uniqueness when compared to his city companions. Still, he wasn't as conspicuous as if he had worn his colonel's uniform.

After a time, he arrived at the southern end of the vast parkland, now under construction with massive teams of horses and wagons moving men, materials, and dirt. No doubt they were rushing to complete some level of work before the snows of winter settled in. Another fifteen minutes of riding brought him to the designated address. The upper-scale red-brick building faced the park and rose four stories. It was well maintained with fresh paint and brass gas lights on either side of the tandem front doors. A stable was located just down a side street, and after procuring a spot for his horse, Brison knocked on the door as late afternoon hurled itself toward dusk.

A male servant opened the door and immediately seemed aware of who Brison was and ushered him into a library off the main foyer that was impressive in both its size and the number of volumes it contained. Instead of sitting down, Brison lightly ran his fingers along the bindings of a row when Bixby came into the room.

"My one great vice, I'm afraid. You are Colonel Brison." Bixby was slightly older than Brison, by the colonel's estimation. He was of average height with a broad belly and brown hair with a healthy mustache and sideburns that came together. He wore spectacles and immediately took them off to clean them after shaking Brison's hand. He carried a broad smile, but his teeth were poorly maintained, despite his station. "Books are man's soul bared for self-examination, Colonel. Not a day that goes by where I don't thumb my way through for some choice words. Are you a man of letters?"

"I studied at the Vermont College. Business and bookkeeping." Brison settled into a chair that Bixby offered. "My family has a pair of dairy farms, and I also learned woodworking as a young man, for profit and to make our family's furnishings."

"Ah, I like a man who uses his hands and not just his brain, and vice versa," Bixby said with a laugh. "Can I offer you a whiskey? I don't ever partake until the end of the business day, but seeing that it is candle lighting anyway, will you join me?"

"I would appreciate it, sir."

With drink in hand and a few minutes of idle chat about his trip, Brison moved to the reason for his visit.

"Mr. Bixby, the president informed me lightly about the issues with some of the arms manufacturers in New York, northeastern Pennsylvania, and Massachusetts and said you were the one who brought the suspicions upon Augustus Raven."

"It is a nasty business, Colonel. Our mayor here, George Opdyke, is a staunch Union man and we're drawing many troops from the immigrant population, but Boss Tweed and his Tammany Hall Democrats are a tough nut to crack, I dare say. They dominate city and state politics. That's why I have been one of the first members of the Union League for those of us who recognize the moral issue at hand supersedes our financial interests with the South."

"The riots in July showed the city wrestles with her loyalty," Brison said. "I saw a building burned out on the avenue here. Was that from the riots?"

"If you're talking about near Forty-Fourth Street there, that was the Colored Orphan Asylum, and yes, that was from the riots. The Irish's desire lies in not having the Negro as competition for their jobs." Bixby put his drink down and pulled his spectacles off to clean them for a second time. "People will always do what they figure on the ledger is the best result for themselves. You can't blame the poor souls, but the killing of innocents back in July..." He shook his head. "Inexcusable."

"What do the problems here in the city have to do with Augustus Raven?" Brison asked.

"It's all related, Colonel, that it is. Raven will show you he is a strong Union man with one face, but put him under strong scrutiny, and he will reveal another face. He is as strong a conservative Democrat as is possible. His money will be behind Lincoln's opponent next year for sure."

Brison knew he had to be careful, but he felt compelled to raise the point anyway. "If I may beg your pardon, sir, you are known as leaning more towards the Radical Republican theology than the moderate course of the president. I must take an impartial view of all of those involved in doings I investigate. It would be a motive to bring discredit to bear on Raven."

"Ha!" Bixby thumped his chair with his hand and put his spectacles back on his smiling face. "I do so like a man who speaks his mind. I distrust a man who couches his questions like he's walking in the woods with bear traps all around. No, I don't see the world the same as Augustus Raven, but I have many friends in my life who disagree with my views, particularly about the Negro. But my concerns with Raven are not political but financial. Colonel, what does Raven and his competitors produce?"

"Weapons of war."

"And if one doesn't fuss over the death of men, what would be in the best interest of Augustus Raven?"

"To extend the war as long as possible without crippling the Union," Brison said.

"You are astute, sir." Bixby took a drink of his whiskey, set the glass down, and walked over to the window of his library. "Raven is a wealthy manufacturer already, Colonel, and the war makes him more so each day this bloodletting goes on, for that is what this is, a bloodletting..." He turned to face Brison again. "... to purge us of our sins against God. But Raven cares not about the morality, only about the financial gain, and he has an eye to the future."

"Beyond defeat of the South?"

"I haven't had a direct conversation with him about this, but from words I have had with him in recent years, yes. He looks to the future. We all know after the war is over, everyone's eyes will turn towards the west and expanding this country undivided to the Pacific. And while we are doing that, Raven believes we will be supplanting Britain and France as the world's dominant power... and we will need the weapons to establish that dominance. But I apologize as I digress from my point. Your issue here is not Raven's militaristic goals in twenty or thirty years."

"No, the damage to his competitors."

"Right." Bixby returned to a chair next to where Brison was sitting, handing him a fistful of newspaper clippings he had retrieved from his desk. "I took these myself from newspapers during the past six months. There have been accidents causing delays at five other manufacturers in direct competition with Raven."

"But Raven's contracts with the government are solid and immensely profitable," Brison said. "And from what I determined in speaking with the quartermaster general himself before I left Washington, Raven could not take on significantly more contracts than he already does with his existing factories."

"Montgomery Meigs," Bixby said, his eyebrows raised. "You have done some sneaking about before coming to see me. Are you sure Meigs was forthright with you about Raven? Those two have a close relationship."

"I was unaware."

Bixby displayed his crooked teeth. "Meigs and Raven go back a time, but for now, that's unimportant. Indeed, Raven lacks the resources to expand his contracts immediately... unless he obtains them through acquisition."

"The competitors default on their delivery dates and lose the contracts, and Raven moves in to obtain the working factories and obtains new contracts."

Bixby responded with a tip of his head.

"Who should be my first visit?" Brison asked.

"Carl Trichard is the owner of the Tri-North Foundry in Springfield, Massachusetts. You should talk to him first. He had two incidents last year, including an explosion that killed five workers. He swore to me it wasn't an error by one of his people."

"I'm familiar with Tri-North. After I meet with him, I'm going to pay a visit on Raven. Can you give me any insight into the man beyond what you've already said?"

"You will need to take care." Bixby took off his spectacles and began to clean them again. "He is smart and ruthless. And he feels he's entitled to everything he has and much that he doesn't. He is a vindictive soul and cares little about the people around him, except his closest advisors and assistants, but I would gather his concern for them is only as a benefactor with absolute loyalty as his expected return. I say take care with him because I have heard rumors of poor-performing employees disappearing, but that may be just humbug scattered about by outsiders, I don't know. I do know that in business dealings, he can be as destructive as one of his own cannons." Bixby put his glasses back on and stared directly into Brison's face. "I would appreciate if you kept my name out of any conversation you have with anyone connected to this business from now on."

"I understand, sir."

"I sincerely hope you do, my man. I sincerely hope you do."

BRISON HAD TOLD BIXBY he was headed to Springfield first, but as he spent the night in a New York hotel, he changed his mind about with whom his next conversation would be. Raven's main foundry and his home were located outside the town of Newburgh, about sixty miles north of the city on the Hudson River, so the next morning, he put down extra funds to secure a place for his horse and himself on a train for the two-hour ride up the east side of the river. At the small village of Beacon, he exited the train and took a ferry that crossed from Fishkill Landing to Newburgh. By half past noon, he was riding through the town, getting directions to the Raven Foundry, which was located south of town on the west side of the Hudson. Brison had seen it at the tail end of his train ride and was impressed by its size. It dominated the landscape, and Brison imagined it must command a good amount of the available labor force.

He made his way down the road as it carried along a ridge above the river. It was frigid for late November, and an early blue sky in New York City had yielded to gray with a spitting of sleet. This was nothing compared to the cold and snow he had faced months ago in Minnesota, but Brison found himself fighting a desire to turn around and find lodging and send along a courier with a request for a formal meeting the next day.

The factory was a mile and a half from town. The activity on the road increased as he approached. Dozens of rooming houses were cut into a hill to his right in rows of five. Brison estimated their capacity to be in the mid-hundreds. Next to houses was a large barn that appeared to have been converted into a meeting hall with a dry goods store attached that was the subject of a great deal of activity.

The factory itself had four expansive red-brick buildings with immense smokestacks that were, even now, belching black smoke in a perfectly vertical mirror to themselves. Another building stood half again larger than its brick neighbors, only this one was made of wood and carried no stacks. There was an assortment of administration buildings, stables, an open black-smith's station, and what appeared to be a kitchen with a line of men waiting to go in. The combined fragrances of baking bread and meat caused Brison's stomach to rumble with longing. This is all he could see at the entrance to the foundry, as he was stopped by a guard at a gatehouse that sat where the road split from the foundry's entrance and continued along the river.

At first address, the guard was unimpressed with Brison's badge and desire to see Augustus Raven, but after a stern word, he agreed to send a message up to the main offices. Short-ly, a woman approached from the administration building and walked directly to Brison with a fire in her eyes that matched her red hair. She had a hint of freckles on her cheeks and wore her hair up off her shoulders that were bare except for a light shawl, despite the cold. Her dress was a deep blue with a hint of satin on the frills, but the material itself appeared to be linen. She wore an apron over the front, though at first glance, she didn't seem to be the type of woman who would be found work-ing long hours in the kitchen. She did not wear a crinoline to broaden the dress—her manner was too practical for that—and it wasn't necessary, for her figure filled out the material in a way that had Brison steadying himself and remembering his vows to his Louise Elizabeth. His wife was also a fiery red daughter of Erin, and this woman could have passed for her sister.

"You be Brison?" Her eyes flared a brilliant green.

Brison tipped his hat. "I'm Colonel Brison, ma'am. I'm attached to the Bureau of Military Information, but I report directly to the president. It's on his orders that I'm here."

She crossed her arms and said, "Mr. Raven is a very busy man, and you are unannounced."

"I would have sent word requesting an appointment, but I thought a chance meeting might be possible. And you are?"

"Cathleen Byrne. I be Mr. Raven's personal assistant on all matters outside of the foundry."

"I'm pleased, Miss Byrne. I can set up a time for tomorrow if Mr. Raven would prefer, though he will want to hear what I have to say, I'm sure."

Byrne stood for a moment, looking Brison up and down. "You don't wear a uniform, Colonel?"

"Mr. Lincoln prefers that I keep a quiet way about me." Brison smiled. "Do you think Mr. Raven could see me for a few minutes?"

"He is overseeing the fixin' of a problem in one of the buildings, but I gather he would want to at least see what you want. Come along then."

Byrne led Brison up the small hill to the large office building with the name "Raven" in large semi-circle letters. Underneath was the image of a black bird, its talons extended as if capturing prey. The imagery's significance wasn't lost on Brison. He reminded himself of what Bixby had intimated.

He was led into a comfortable sitting room with thick rugs and drapes and windows that faced out onto the compound. A fully stocked stove stood in the corner, and a full basket of wood sat nearby. Brison took a direct route to warm himself. Byrne offered tea or coffee, and when Brison found out Raven preferred tea in the afternoon, he requested the same. One wall was a bookcase with many histories and some Shakespeare mixed in with a few military textbooks. There was a single book on a table beside a deep, high-backed chair, and a copy of *Scientific American* was with it. The book was *Great Expectations* by the British author Charles Dickens. He had heard of it, but he hadn't read it himself. It had come out just a couple of years ago. Brison noticed there was a bookmark two-thirds through the volume.

There had been much ado about it in the newspapers a while back.

Byrne returned with tea after a few minutes and told Brison that Raven would be joining him within the hour and to enjoy a cigar and "a bit of reading," as she put it. Brison asked if she would give him a brief tour of the foundry, but Byrne deferred and left him alone. Brison took a cigar from a table box and settled into the chair nearest the stove and drank his tea while reading the first pages of this Dickens book he had heard so much about.

Augustus Raven swept into the room thirty minutes later, spouting orders to the male assistant trailing behind him. He stopped long enough to finish his thought, then dismissed the young man and stood with his hands on his hips and looking at Brison, who had risen from his chair. Raven was a smallish man with small features except for heavy, light brown eyebrows, beard, and mustache. His eyes were a striking bright blue, and he was said to have the ability to go long periods of time without blinking. Bixby had said it was a most unnerving trait for those whom he met. His suit looked fitted by a New York City tailor, and the material's quality was evident even from across the room. He held a book in his left hand.

"You are Colonel..."

"Brison." He stepped forward to shake hands, looking down at the much shorter man. "Colonel Andrew Brison. I'm an agent with the Bureau of Military Information on special assignment for the president."

"It's about damn time the president and the quartermaster got around to us." Raven walked up to Brison and shook his hand while staring intently into the taller man's face. "I appreciate you coming all the same. I was worried Washington was looking upon its armament producers as a codfish aristocracy that could take care of itself."

"I can assure you the president is very concerned about the recent delays in materials because of the disruptions." Brison glanced at the book. "Important book? You haven't set it down since your arrival."

"Shakespeare, Colonel. I carry one of his missives around with me much of the time. I do admire the language."

"What play is that?"

"Richard the Third. Can I offer you a something stronger than Cathleen's sometimes-disappointing tea?"

"No, thank you. I'm content with the cigar, and the tea is fine. I know you're a busy man, and I'm here to gather as many facts as I can to see what the Bureau or even a small detachment from the Army could do to keep production up. The tipping point of the war may have been reached this year, and in the coming year, we need to take it to the Rebels. The president wants to be assured there won't be a problem with the supplying of the troops. And as your factory is one of the few that has been incident free..."

"I'm afraid I can't claim that on my ledger anymore, Colonel," Raven said, taking a drink of whiskey he had poured himself. "I was just about to telegraph the quarter-master. Half of my cannon production was halted not yester-day, and I'll be hard pressed to meet my quota for the month. Some devil of a southerner in disguise is who's behind it, I'd say. They damaged three quarters of the lathes—stripped the gears, I say—and now I've got to make do attempting to funnel our work through the surviving machines. Repairs will take me a few weeks, but I'm confident this will be no more than a small setback, Colonel."

"I'm concerned your factory has fallen victim as well. I came here first because the quartermaster said your oper-ations should be the model the others should follow. Now you tell me you have suffered the same fate."

Raven upturned his hands.

"Do you believe it was agents from within or some sort of skullduggery from outside?" Brison asked. "I need to de-termine how the acts were accomplished."

"I would gather it's from agents within my workforce. I'll route out the scoundrel before the week is out. I don't need some government bureaucrat gumming everything up." Raven's voice carried an edge to it.

"I hardly believe helping you find the person or persons behind these problems is 'gumming everything up,'" Brison said. "You have people who can do the interviewing?"

"Of course."

"Then go about doing so. If you would have your charming assistant give me a list of your employees who work in the actual foundry, I will travel over to Springfield and see Carl Trichard at Tri-North. He's had steady problems."

"He'll whine about something, I'm sure." Raven returned to a soft manner, but those eyes kept staring right through Brison.

"I'm sure once I gather the information I need, I'll be returning." Brison stood up. "I won't take any more of your time today, but I will set up an appointment with Miss Byrne for my return. Thank you for the cigar. I always say keep a good cigar in your pocket." Brison shook Raven's hand, showing no intimidation from the industrialist. On his way out, he stopped at Byrne's desk and made an appointment to return in two weeks and made his way to his horse. The gray afternoon was still spitting freezing rain as he made his way back into town and found a small hotel to spend the night.

BRISON SENT OFF A telegram to Washington saying he had met with Raven, and he apprised the president that he was now preparing to travel to Springfield. After that, he had dinner of venison and boiled potatoes prepared by the wife of the hotel owner. Then he put on his overcoat and went outside onto the porch for a cigar. He had been sitting on the front steps for a few minutes when the lone figure of a woman appeared, walking down the roadway on the same side as the hotel. Brison watched her with casual interest until she passed in front of the establishment next to the hotel and the light from inside lit up the red hair cascading down her shoulders. When she passed in front of the hotel, she gave him a quick glance.

"Not a very pleasant night for a stroll, Miss Byrne," Brison said.

She stopped short and peered at Brison until he lifted his hat and she could see his face in the window light. "Land sakes, Colonel Brison. I didn't see it was you sittin' there. I avoid the kind that stays at this here place. I was going to give you the Jesse for speaking to me."

"I'm sorry if I startled you. As I said, it's a miserable night to be walking, and by yourself. I know this is a small town, but you never know when you might run into a highwayman or worse."

"I was just on my way to my boarding house down the street. I most often take a ride from one of the guards to the edge of town and I walk home. I thank you for your concern, Colonel, but I can take care of myself." She pulled a small pistol from out of her pouch purse and showed it to him.

"Ah, a Philadelphia Deringer; a good choice for a lady." Brison smiled. "I had no doubt you can take care of yourself, Miss Byrne. Still, may I walk you the rest of the way to your boarding house?"

For the first time since he met her, she smiled at him, and he realized just how dangerous she could be to his vows. Even in the dim light of the night, her beauty was brilliant. Brison had never strayed from his marriage to Louise Elizabeth, and even now knew he wouldn't here, but he found himself saying the word "discipline" over and over in his head as he lifted himself off the steps and began to walk down the road with Byrne.

"Did you enjoy your discussion with Mr. Raven?" she asked. "I always enjoy seeing people's reactions to having met him for the first time."

"I wouldn't be a fair gauge for you, as I was given an introduction to him from an acquaintance beforehand."

She gave a small laugh. "He is a most interesting man, and I find working for him to be most unusual. I don't think I will ever sour on this position."

"It is unusual for him to have a female personal assistant," Brison said. "Do you find yourself having to fight the battle for seriousness every day? I imagine many men would dismiss your station."

She gave him a side glance and then took his arm. "As I said before, Colonel, I can take care of myself. Woe is the businessman who doesn't take me seriously when dealing with Mr. Raven. He has never been anything but a gentleman to me. He thinks of me as a younger sister, and he requires of me the same tasks as he would give to any other assistant, and he expects me to complete those tasks all the same... and, sir, you never answered my question."

It was Brison's turn to smile as he looked into her eyes. "He tries to be an intimidating man, but I'm steadfast. Not many men can have that effect on this person."

"What about women?"

"Now *that* is entirely different."

"Are you married, Colonel?"

"To an Irish lass like yourself, in fact. Your likeness is quite similar. I'm of the mind that you two could be sisters."

"And does she intimidate the Union colonel?" Byrne stopped and turned her back to the street, so Brison turned his back to the dark alley between a pair of businesses to face her.

"She does on occasion, particularly when the children and I are caught doing something we're forbidden to do. She gives us the Jesse on an order of a preacher in his best Sunday manner. The children and I often have to skedaddle in an awful hurry."

"Ske... dad... dle?"

"The troops are fond of the word," Brison said. "It's used when they talk about an orderly retreat... or not."

Byrne gave him another one of those smiles, and Brison began to feel guilty about his thoughts when he heard the sound of a foot on rocks. Byrne's eyes grew wide. She made a quick intake of breath, and Brison heard a sound coming from above and behind him just before his world became dark.

CHAPTER SIX

ARTHUR COLLINS'S HOME WAS in a wooded neighborhood outside the I-495 Beltway in Maryland, not more than eight miles from where Adrian Torrez lived. On their drive out to the house, Sparks and Taylor had discussed, with no resolution, why Torrez had left the letter with the young assistant but failed to leave any clue as to what motivation Sterling Raven would have to kidnap or murder the president's chief of staff. Torrez expected that his status would have precluded violence against him by Raven, an expectation that had cost him his life—that is, if Torrez's letter was connected to his murder.

Sparks turned onto a long drive that carried them away from the main street up a hill to a beautiful colonial with gray paint and black shutters. The house sat on a three- or four-acre lot with a healthy tree canopy. A separate three-car garage faced the drive as they pulled up in front of the house, all three spaces filled with a Mercedes sedan, a Ford SUV, and a Chevy Suburban.

"How democratic of Collins," Sparks said to himself as they exited their car.

There was no activity outside the house, but Sparks still got a sense that something was wrong. It was a beautiful May afternoon, yet none of the windows were open, and, more disconcerting, the curtains were closed on all the downstairs windows. He scanned the property carefully once they got to the steps leading to the front door.

"Curtains drawn, windows shut, yet the garage doors are all open," Taylor said.

"I noticed."

They rang the doorbell and waited, but after a minute, no response came from inside. Taylor peered into one of the right-side windows that accented the front door, using her hand to shade the light from around her eyes. Sparks did the same on the left side but could see nothing other than a short hall with a table and flowers. Taylor gasped and swore.

"We should have had the locals perform a drive by," she said, pulling her gun from her underneath her jacket. "There's someone strapped to a chair in there, and he's not moving."

Sparks pulled his own gun and gently turned the handle of the door, meeting no resistance. They slipped inside with Sparks going left and Taylor right through the first floor, clearing one room at a time. On her way, she felt for a pulse on the man slumped in the chair in the middle of the living room and, finding none, continued to clear her side of the house. Once they met, they went upstairs and cleared the second floor, which left the basement.

"Is that Collins, you think?" Sparks asked as they got to the basement door.

"Don't know, but he's dead... and he was tortured," Taylor whispered.

They slowly made their way down to the basement, furnished with a large couch and a couple of deep chairs with a full bar lining the far wall. Sparks would have been impressed with extra-large, high-definition television and sound system, but both he and Taylor were more concerned with the figure of a woman lying on the couch. Bound and gagged, she was unconscious.

"Someone gave her a sedative, just enough to keep her out for a couple of hours." The paramedic sat back on his legs next to the couch. "She's already starting to come out of it."

Taylor sat on the couch next to the woman, whom she knew from the purse identification upstairs was Stephanie Collins. The restraints had been removed, and Collins was stirring, bringing her hands up to her face.

"If she seems okay for you to leave her alone for a minute, would you go up and ask Special Agent Sparks to come down?"

The paramedic nodded and left up the stairs.

"Mrs. Collins... Stephanie, can you here my voice?" Taylor asked.

"Yes... I feel groggy. What's going on?" Her eyes opened and fluttered, and then she forced them open to focus on Taylor. "Who are you?"

"I'm Special Agent Taylor with the Secret Service."

"Secret Service?" Collins looked around the room and realized where she was, and suddenly, her memory came back, and she grabbed Taylor with a vice-like grip. "Men, in my house. Arthur... where is Arthur? They wanted Arthur."

Sparks came down the stairs and joined the two women, kneeling next to Collins.

"You're safe, Mrs. Collins," Taylor said. "The house is secure, but I'm afraid your husband has died."

Sparks put his hand on Collins's shoulder as tears welled up in her eyes and she cried out and started to sob. "We're sorry for your loss, Stephanie. I'm Special Agent Sparks with the FBI. We're going to give you a few minutes, but we need to hear what happened to you before the men drugged you." Sparks pulled Taylor away from Collins, and the two of them went halfway up the stairs so she couldn't hear them.

"Our team is already starting to process the scene. From what I can see, Collins was briefly tortured, beaten, and selective knife wounds were administered," Sparks said. "My guess is it didn't last long before he gave them what they wanted, then he got two shots to the chest. They didn't bother to collect their brass. Looks like a nine-millimeter."

"So whatever information Collins had from Torrez is probably in the hands of Raven or whomever was willing to kill two people to obtain it." Taylor looked down at Stephanie Collins, now turned and sitting upright on the couch but still sobbing quietly into her hands. "It's unlike professionals to leave someone behind that reveals anything of importance. Strange."

While Sparks went back upstairs to coordinate with the FBI agent now placed in charge of the crime scene and to hold back the local police homicide detectives from trying to wedge their way into the investigation, Taylor went back to Stephanie Collins and put her arm around the woman in comfort as the now-widow tried to compose herself. After a time and repeated attempts at convincing Taylor to let her see her husband's body, Collins calmed down enough to answer Taylor's questions about the attack.

"It was this morning, early," Collins said. "Arthur had gone to the store to pick up some bagels and coffee. He didn't have a class today, and we were going to go into the city and have an early dinner." She broke down for a minute, then gathered herself again. "I was in the laundry room. I only caught a glimpse of someone before he grabbed me from behind. I screamed, but he put something over my mouth, a rag or something. He was big—over six-feet tall—and very strong. Then a second man grabbed my legs, and the first man covered my eyes. I tried to struggle, but they were too strong."

"So you never got a look at a face?" Taylor asked.

"No."

"Did they say anything to you or to each other?"

"One of them whispered in my ear that they only wanted my husband and if I was quiet, they wouldn't harm me. That's all they said. They tied me up, and then I felt a needle in my neck. That's all I remember."

Taylor got up from the couch as Sparks came down the stairs.

"She can't give us anything to go on about what happened here," Taylor said.

"All right, then let's see if she can help us in another way," Sparks replied, then turned to Collins. "If we are going to catch these men, we have some more questions we need to ask you. Are you up to it, Mrs. Collins?"

Collins took a deep breath, exhaled, and looked straight into Sparks's eyes. "I think so."

"Good. We believe these men were after something that was in your husband's possession, something valuable. Did you notice anything different about your husband over the past few weeks? Was he uneasy, preoccupied?"

"I can do you one better than that," Collins said. "He told me he was working with his old friend, Adrian Torrez, the president's chief of staff, on a project or investment, I don't know, but on something that could bring in a lot of money. But he was worried about it."

"Did he give you any specifics?" Taylor asked.

"No. But he was checking outside the house frequently, and we haven't been going out in the evenings at all. I was really starting to get worried about it. He had me cancel a couple of dates with other couples, and we were supposed to go to Jamaica on a little mini-vacation and he postponed it. I asked him about all this, and he was sympathetic, but he just told me it was better if he kept it to himself."

"Did he show you anything involved in this project?" Sparks asked.

"No. He keeps important papers in a safe in his office."

"A safe?" Sparks had been in the office and found it ransacked. The two men had thoroughly gone through the space, ripping books off the shelves, pulling a couple of paintings down, forcing their way into an antique desk, and emptying the drawers. No safe had been visible. "Where is it?"

"It's a floor safe next to the door, underneath a hinged floorboard covered by a rug." Collins made a move to stand, but Sparks stopped her and nodded to Taylor, who understood his meaning and went upstairs to make sure the forensic guys had had time to remove the body from the living room.

"And at no time did he show you any papers or whatever this thing that he was involved with Torrez?" Sparks said.

"The other agent already asked that not a minute ago," Collins said, her voice edging at Sparks.

"I'm sorry, Mrs. Collins. I just want to make sure you aren't overlooking something that could be important. Even a small moment in passing could be vital."

"He never told me the details. As I said, the only thing the man said to me was that they wanted my husband and not me. I kept asking them what they wanted. I told them to take whatever they wanted but not to harm us. Do you think his business with Adrian had something to do with this?"

"We don't know for sure, but there is a strong possibility," Sparks said, noting Taylor's return down the stairs.

"They've cleared the living room," Taylor said to Sparks. Then she turned to Collins. "Please show us the safe, but please don't touch anything as we go upstairs."

They led Collins up the stairs onto the main floor. She paused to look in the living room and saw the empty chair where her husband had died. Sparks heard an intake of breath and a moan. He took her arm and gently pulled her away from the room. When they reached the office, Collins took the lead, closing the door halfway.

"They pulled back the rug to look underneath," she said. "The rug is in the wrong position."

Sparks pulled back the rug and saw a simple hardwood floor. "It's well hidden."

"Arthur was especially proud that you couldn't see the opening. The hinge is hidden inside the baseboard, here..." Collins used the toe of her right foot and pressed against the baseboard. There was an audible "click," and an eighteen-inch section of floorboard next to the wall popped up. Sparks pulled up the section and found a recessed safe with a combination lock staring up at him from six inches below.

"You don't happen to know the combination?" Taylor asked.

"It's the day we first met," Collins said. "January 19th, 1983. One... nineteen... and thirty-eight. The dial doesn't go up as high as 83, so he reversed the last number."

Sparks called a team member over to dust the dial for prints and, after a minute, was told there were no discernable prints available. With gloves on anyway, he spun the dial to open the safe on the first try.

"Do we have your permission?" Sparks asked Collins.

"We have nothing to hide."

Inside were the usual items you would expect in a safe: passports, a Rolex watch, birth certificates, and other assorted papers. Sparks took the contents over to the beautiful desk that dominated the office and sorted through the items as Collins and Taylor looked on. He went further into the pile with nothing of obvious importance catching his eye. It appeared to be a dead end, and Sparks was beginning to get frustrated. He was about two-thirds of the way through the files when Collins pointed at a folder at the very bottom sitting at an angle away from the other files.

"I've never seen that before," she said.

It was a yellowish envelope, sealed with tape but with no writing visible on it until Sparks flipped it over. Marked in the top right-hand corner was a name printed with a Sharpie: Torrez. Without a word or hesitation, Sparks grabbed a letter opener from the desktop and cut open the envelope. Inside was a single white sheet of paper with a block set of random letters—about fifteen lines of fifteen letters—and some additional printed letters and numbers at the bottom. A grouping of nine listings read:

    P A-16-4-7
    T A-4-1-32
    P A-7-3-22
    T A-3-2-17
    P A-8-6-10
    T A-1-2-8
    P A-9-2-43
    T A-3-3-5
    P A-21-4-33

A small arrow at the bottom of the page pointed to a sentence. Sparks turned it over and read the sentence out loud.

"Take not the first letter but the last," he read. Then, without looking up from the paper, he asked, "What did you husband do for a living, Mrs. Collins?"

"He was a professor of history at American University."

"What was his expertise?"

"The 1800s."

"The Civil War era?" Sparks closed his eyes with a pained expression.

"Yes, he was researching a book on the former Secretary of War, Edwin Stanton."

"What's the problem, Sparks?" Taylor asked.

"Anything else he really concentrated on?" Sparks continued.

"Well, his first book was on Civil War-era spies and the codes they used," Collins said.

"Why am I not surprised?" Sparks said. "Damn, I really don't want to go down this road again."

"What is it?" Taylor asked. "Some kind of code?"

"I'm afraid so, and it's addressed to Torrez. This might be what these men were looking for, or it's a clue to find what they were looking for. Mrs. Collins, I'd like to take this envelope and this paper with us. I'll need to have it analyzed."

"Of course," Collins said.

"You think Collins left a coded message for Torrez, something he would know how to decipher?" Taylor asked.

"My guess would be yes," Sparks said, still staring at the paper. "The universe has an extremely bizarre sense of humor."

Chapter Seven

BRISON REGAINED CONSCIOUSNESS WITH the feeling that his shoulders were going to be pulled from their sockets. He moaned out loud in pain as he tried to focus on his surroundings. It was barely light, and he was staring at a row of bricks five feet in front of him with his arms tied together above his head. As he became fully aware, he realized he was hanging from his tied hands, suspended over a black hole, his feet dangling below him without support. He twisted around as best he could to see what was around him.

He was hanging in a well.

From the pain in his upper body and the light filtering in from above, Brison estimated he had been hanging for a good amount of time. He tried to pull himself up and swing his legs to the walls, finding success in the latter, but he was too weak to pull himself up while walking up the wall. When he reached the point where he needed to pull in the slack on the rope, he found his hands were tied so that it was impossible to grab the rope with both hands. After ten minutes of trying different methods of getting pressure off his upper body, Brison gave up and called out to see if any of his captors were above him. In looking up, he also realized the well he was hanging in was situated inside a building, not outside. No one responded to his cries, so he hung there, drifting in and out of consciousness with no knowledge of how much time had passed.

Then, from above, he heard a door swing open and multiple pairs of feet shuffle toward the well's entrance.

"Aye, he's awake all right," a high-pitched voice said. "Brison, how you doin' in there? You comfortable? Been good to get off your feet, I'll wager." He laughed at his own joke and pulled on the rope back and forth to swing its burden with enough play that Brison's legs gently tapped the bricks. "We got some questions for you, and you had better answer straight up, lest I cut this here rope and send you down to the bottom. It's got water, but it ain't no good and no one will hear you callin' out, as this barn is off by itself and no one comes around much. You understand?"

"Raven put me here?" Brison croaked through his dry throat as best he could.

"I'm what you might call—" The voice turned away and spoke to another. "What's the name? Wait, I got it. An independent contractor." Back to Brison, the man grabbed the rope again and shook it, causing Brison to dance against the bricks. "You haven't earned the right to know who put you in this predicament. You just do as I say and maybe I'll pull you up out of the hole. Then again, maybe I won't, but I certainly won't if you don't give me what I want."

Brison looked up into the face of his tormentor. He was just a kid about the same age as the Reb he had captured back in Gettysburg, grinning with a missing-tooth smile, hat pushed back on his head revealing a mud-streaked face framed by dark brown hair.

"You sure look like a Rebel sympathizer," Brison said. "This is what I'd expect from your kind."

The kid yanked on the rope again, this time forcing Brison's entire body to slam into the bricks with such force that new pain shot through his upper body. "I ain't no dirty, stinkin' Reb, you asshole. I wouldn't be caught dead with the likes of them."

A new voice came from above, this one deep with a rough texture. "Enough! Get on with the questions."

The kid murmured a reply and leaned over the edge of the well as if their conversation was private.

"The boss man knows he has to keep me in line," he said with his voice lowered. "I appreciate it. I've got to learn to stay on that line, straight at the task at hand. You can appreciate that, can't you, Colonel Brison? Anyway, what was your reason for coming up from Washington?"

The question came abruptly, and for a moment, Brison was confused. "I told Raven why I was here."

"Who said I worked for Augustus Raven?" the kid said.

"I came up here to help keep Raven from having the same problems with production that some of the other foundries have had, that's all," Brison said.

"My boss believes there's more to it than that, and we want to know what you know."

"There've been problems at various factories up here, and the president was concerned. I was sent to investigate, as Raven was one of the few factories that hadn't had major problems. The president wanted to see if whatever Raven is doing here, security-wise, could be given to the other manufacturers. That's it. Now bring me up and cut me loose."

"What did Sam Bixby tell you in New York?"

"Bixby?" *Had they been following him all the way from Washington?* "He told the president that some of the armaments manufacturers were upset about their problems, and Bixby suggested I start with Raven, as he hadn't had any problems and his factory was close to the city, so I went here first. Who do you work for?"

"Again, I ask the questions. What was in the telegram you sent yesterday?"

"What did you do with Miss Byrne?"

"I don't like repeating my words, Colonel. I'm asking the questions. The lovely Miss Byrne is fit and fiddle, she is. We sent her along her way, so there's no use you fussin' about her. What was in the telegram?"

Brison was slammed into the wall again, this time on his bad shoulder, forcing out an involuntary cry of pain. They must be working for Raven. Nothing else makes sense, does it? Byrne had led him near the dark alley and, by her movement, had maneuvered him to turn his back to the darkness. "All I put in the telegram was that I had gotten nothing of importance from Raven and was heading to Springfield. That's all."

Again, the kid swung the rope and Brison crashed against the bricks. This time, his head tapped hard against the wall, and he nearly lost consciousness. It was beginning to get harder to breathe.

"I don't have anything to tell you!" Brison shouted as best he could, struggling to gulp in the stagnant air.

The kid disappeared from the top edge, and Brison could hear the murmur of their voices. At the end of the conversation, the deep voice drifted down with strange clarity. "He won't tell us anything useful. Wait a couple more hours, try one last time, then shoot him and drop him down like the others."

Brison tilted his head back, overwhelmed by despair for the first time since he sat in the field south of Gettysburg with the body of a certain lieutenant from Massachusetts. He tried to focus on his surroundings, begin to figure out how he could gain any kind of advantage. When he opened his eyes, he was looking directly into the grinning face of his tormentor.

"I'm supposed to let you marinate a bit and then we'll ask you the questions again," the kid said.

BRISON DRIFTED IN AND out of consciousness, so he didn't know how long he hung there. His shoulders and arms became numb and sweat soaked his clothes despite the cold. During one of his more lucid moments, he realized that he had pissed through his pants and down his legs, but the embarrassment didn't register because he knew his life would be over soon if something didn't change. The next time he was awake, he thought of Louise Elizabeth and the children, and sorrow swept through him like a wave of nausea. And then, after yet another time of unconsciousness, he shook his head to force alertness back, and he seethed with anger at those who put him here and at himself for giving up so easily.

He tried again to lift himself by grabbing a foothold on the well's walls, but his arms were so weakened, he was no longer able to lift himself more than a few inches. As he tried yet again for the last of a countless number of times, he heard the door open, and the kid's face appeared above him at the rim.

"Well, Colonel, you best repent and begin your prayin', cause your time is up," the kid said. "I'll be quick about it."

When Brison spoke, the words croaked from his throat. "Pull me out of here and I'll tell you everything you need. Just don't drop me down into the well. Please."

"I can't do that, Colonel. Boss man would come down hard on me if I didn't do what he says."

"Well then... go to the devil."

"How'd you ever get to be a colonel?" the kid said. "Not too smart. No, not too smart." Then a pistol appeared at the rim, pointed down at Brison's chest. "When you get to hell, tell 'em I said hey." He laughed as he pulled back the hammer.

The laughter was cut short by a sudden thump, and Brison cried out as the falling pistol hit a glancing blow on the side of his head and dropped down into the darkness. As he tried to clear his head again, he looked up to see a figure turning the handle on the yoke that held the rope above, and he felt himself lifting up out of the dark and toward the rim. He saw that the figure was hooded and was having difficulty turning the handle when he suddenly stopped. He was above the rim, and his hands were pulling him out of the well and swinging him down to the outside. The relief when his arms came down in front of him was palpable. He sighed as the burdened disappeared. After a moment, his eyes finally beginning to focus clearly, he looked into the face of the hooded figure and saw those Irish green eyes wide with concern.

They belonged to Cathleen Byrne.

Brison sat, dumbfounded, staring into her face until he managed a thin smile.

"In my work, I'm usually not the one in need of saving, Miss Byrne," he said, "but since you're my rescuer, a note of thanks is in order. Though one needs to remember I wouldn't have been here at all had it not been for you."

"I had no part in these doings, Colonel." Her voice was soft, without the edge it had during their previous meeting. Her brow was still furrowed with concern. His words had not lessened her fear. "I only saw them at the last moment before they hit you. They grabbed me and said they had no quarrel with me and I could go, but I was to speak to no one about this. The older man put his hands to my throat." She reached up with her own hand to pull down her dress collar. Her neck was blemished with bruising where one might place their hands to strangle someone.

"I'm sorry you were attacked as well."

"I've had worse done by me own brothers, I have." She produced a knife and began to slice through the rope binding his hands. "We best be leaving. I don't know when others might return. I have a horse a little ways away from here. We must hurry."

"Where are we?"

"A storage barn about three miles south of town. It doesn't look like the property has been used much in many a year."

When Brison's hands were free, he struggled to his feet and fell against the well. The time hanging had worn him down. Byrne handed him a canteen, and he took a long drink, the cold water spreading through his insides. After a moment, he felt better. He was still wobbly on his feet, but his head was clear. He knew they had to move.

"Did you bring a weapon?" he asked, checking on the unconscious boy.

"Just my Deringer."

She grabbed his hand and led him to the barn door, where they peeked outside. The boy's horse stood alone, tethered to a collapsed wagon. Brison untied the horse and slapped it on the rump to spur it off into the distance. Byrne pointed over a ridge above the barn, and they set off as quickly as he could as he began to gain strength. Within ten minutes, they reached her horse and headed off, with Byrne directing Brison toward the town.

"You're going straight into town?" Byrne asked. "What if they're after you?"

"I'll be discreet about my goings on. I have other questions. Did Raven order my abduction? And... how the hell did you find me?"

"I don't know about Augustus." Byrne gripped tighter around Brison's waist as they moved the horse across a small ravine. "Nothing came from me, I can tell you honestly. But I don't know about him. The two men who attacked us were not men I had seen before at the factory, and I know most every face there. This morning, I saw the boy back there in town. I took my horse and followed him. He was lacking in his mindfulness, for he never turned around once on his way. I know this area pretty well, so when he turned up off the main road, I circled around and watched him from the ridge above, and he headed straight to the old barn."

"Why didn't you go to the sheriff?"

"Because if Augustus was involved, that's the last place you would want to find help," Byrne said. "And yes, I considered it possible that he sent those men. It makes sense. You were in his office just yesterday."

"And you felt confident enough to just dance in and knock him on the head from behind?" Brison said.

"I grew up with four brothers—two older and two younger, Colonel. I can take care of myself if you don't mind."

Brison smiled and shook his head.

They reached the town by way of a side road not often traveled during the cold months. Brison figured that was why they didn't meet anyone even though it was near midday when they arrived. They swung around to the side of town where Brison's boarding house was and made their way in through the back. Brison was relieved to find his belongings, including the Spencer, safely tucked away in the closet in his room.

Byrne, hands on hips the entire time he gathered his things, spoke not a word, but she furrowed her brow as she watched.

When he was ready to leave, he finally looked at her.

"Are you sure no one saw you follow that boy to the barn?" he asked. "Because you'll be in serious trouble for what you've done, and somehow, I believe even if he has taken a cotton to you, it won't stop him from doing away with you. I'm sorry to be blunt, Miss Byrne, but it is what it is."

"You're just a-goin' to ride off now, are you?"

"I need to inquire about the problems at another of the factories up here, look into it for myself. Maybe I can connect the nasty goings-on up there to Raven. Incidentally, you have heard nothing about the problems at the other foundries?"

"Well aware of it, I am." Byrne had removed her head covering, and her red hair perfectly cascaded over her shoulders. She was directly in Brison's face. "I'm Mr. Raven's assistant, but I have never seen nor heard anything that would cause me to be suspicious. As I told you, he has never been anything but a gentleman with me. I deal mostly with staff and dealings with suppliers."

"I'm guarded that you'll be found out."

She reached up and lightly touched the side of his cheek, a far-too-intimate gesture. Brison felt the blood fill his face.

"As I said, I can take care of myself. No one saw me, of that I'm certain." The sides of her mouth turned up a bit, not quite a smile. "I will not go seeking information on Mr. Raven for the likes of you or any other man, nor will I tell him of your suspicions. I saw a man in trouble, and I did what had to be done."

"For that, I'm eternally grateful." Brison cleared his throat, despite it not being necessary, and motioned for the door. "You should go ahead to your horse alone and go about your business, lest there be prying eyes."

"I will be seeing you again, Colonel?"

"As sure as a New England winter, Miss Byrne."

CHAPTER EIGHT

Present Day
June 1

SPARKS AND TAYLOR LEFT Collins's wife with an agent and stressed the need for her to be in protective custody until the situation was resolved. The forensic crew was working the house as Sparks and Taylor drove back downtown to the Hoover Building. Reports of Torrez's death had hit the news; it was the lead story on every broadcast and getting straight through coverage on all the 24-hour news channels. The story was that he had been killed in a car accident, but the details were still not known. Most of the channels were already spinning the story forward to who would be taking charge of John Douglas's White House staff and what the political implications were for the administration's ability to deal with Congress.

Once they were inside the building, they went straight to a lab where Sparks's favorite tech, Tom Becker, was waiting for them, his feet propped up on his desk while a Golf Digest magazine hid his face. It didn't move even though Sparks and Taylor made considerable noise walking in.

"Not going to do you any good, Beck," Sparks needled. "I'm still not giving you any strokes next time."

"Won't need 'em. I've got a good idea here to help me with my game, Special Agent Sparks. Going to strengthen my grip a little bit and work on my backswing not being so upright. A little time on the range, and I'll be taking your lunch money." Becker dropped the magazine to just below eye level and caught a look at Taylor, and his eyebrows arched up and his feet dropped down.

"Hello," Taylor said.

"Jason, you could have at least let me know you were bringing company home when you called me," Becker said.

"Agent Bethany Taylor, this is my full-time lab guru and part-time hacking dog on the golf course, Tom Becker," Sparks said. "Sorry I didn't clue you in, Tom, but I've got something I need you to look at."

Taylor shook hands with Becker, who looked clearly uncomfortable in his jeans, golf shirt, and ball cap as he glanced at Taylor's business suit. "What's up?" he asked.

"You heard about Adrian Torrez, I assume?" Sparks said.

Becker pointed over at the television on the wall. It was on a cable news channel, but the sound had been muted. "I was watching America's finest journalists turn it into a national story that will affect the politics in Washington for the rest of Douglas's term. I could only take twenty minutes."

"We're only dealing with the cause, not the politics," Taylor said, then motioned for Sparks to turn over the coded message.

"Torrez wasn't the only person to meet an unnatural end today." Sparks pulled the envelope from a small briefcase with a latex-gloved hand. "Torrez was in contact with a college historian named Arthur Collins who was tortured and executed this morning, after Torrez's death last night. In Collins's safe was this envelope, and inside was a single piece of paper. I wanted you to have a look at it." Sparks slipped the sheet onto Becker's desk and turned it around so it was upright for the lab tech. "It had Torrez's name on the outside and this inside. It looks like a code of some kind."

Becker read the brief contents while slipping his gloves on. "Whatever happened to simply having an encrypted file on a laptop? Jason, you just bring out the old school in people, don't you?"

Taylor gave a small chuckle. "This happened to you before?"

"Oh, Jason is the king of finding people with written codes," Becker said.

"That whole Gettysburg gold thing," Sparks said to Taylor.

"Ahhhh."

"This looks like an Ottendorf cypher," Becker said.

"Ottendorf?" Taylor asked.

"You remember National Treasure, the movie?" Becker began copying the letters and number down from the paper onto his notepad.

"Sure, loved it," Taylor said. "Not so much the sequel."

"Remember the scene when they are looking at the back of the Declaration of Independence? They found an Ottendorf cypher. It was a Revolutionary War cypher."

"Collins's wife told us he had published a book on Civil War codes and spies," Sparks said.

"Well, this cypher predates the 1800s," Becker said. "I don't know what the letters at the beginning are, but the grouping of numbers could be pages, lines, and words."

"But there are two separate letters as well," Taylor said.

"Could be the publication to look for." Becker was now using a magnifying glass to search both sides of the paper. "We'll need to see this man's house and talk to his wife again. If this was for Torrez, then it would be something they had in common, something the two of them would instantly understand so Torrez would have a starting point." Becker read aloud the hand-written sentence on the back. "Take not the first letter, but the last."

"What do you think that means?" Sparks said.

"Just what it says," Becker replied. "If this is an Ottendorf cypher, then the last number would be the line of the text, and Collins was telling Torrez to take the last letter in the line. That's how you would form the word. But it's useless unless you know what publication, what book, magazine, or newspaper should be used."

"Something they both had in common," Taylor said to herself. She was thumbing through a notebook. "They both attended Yale, were in the same class. They didn't often socialize together in recent years, according to Collins's wife. Give me a minute." She stepped out of the room to make a phone call.

Sparks took the opportunity to get some coffee from the machine down the hall, then returned and looked over Collins's letter again, this time with the plastic covering Becker had placed it in.

    P A-16-4-7
    T A-4-1-32
    P A-7-3-22
    T A-3-2-17
    P A-8-6-10
    T A-1-2-8
    P A-9-2-43
    T A-3-3-5
    P A-21-4-33

"It alternates between P and T at the beginning of each line," Sparks said, "but the second letter each time is the same... A."

"Then three sets of numbers nine times," Becker added. "The first letters could be the publication and Torrez is supposed to use two different ones."

"What do you think would be the best chance, publication-wise, to start with?" Sparks asked.

"Maybe a book they both had read and liked... a reference book they both used, or a favorite author. Too many variables. You're not going to crack this unless you have more information about the two men."

The lab door opened, and Taylor walked in with her cellphone against her ear.

"I'm waiting for Mrs. Collins to come back to the phone," she said. "I asked her about her husband and Torrez. Their time at Yale together creates many possibilities, but I figured it would have to be something they had in common more recently, wouldn't it, if Torrez was supposed to recognize it."

"You would think so, but it could be a publication they both were involved with back in college that was important to them," Becker said.

Taylor held up her hand and listened for a full two minutes without uttering a word. When she spoke, it was with a conciliatory tone. "Mrs. Collins, would you give those to the agent in charge before you leave for the safe house so that he can deliver them to us here at the Hoover Building? Yes, ma'am, I think they are important, especially since they were in the safe. What was the date of publication? All right, yes, I'll make sure they're returned to you. Thank you again."

Sparks and Becker both had upturned eyebrows as Taylor ended the call and joined them at the desk with the letter.

"They weren't as close friends now as they had been in college," she began. "As she said at the house, they had been working more closely on something the last few weeks, right about the time Collins had become more secretive. But they had gone to dinner a few times over the years since Torrez had become more powerful in D.C. and Collins had settled into his teaching at American. I asked her if there was anything they did together, and she said they went fishing a couple of times with some other guys in Vermont, and then, almost in passing, she said they had both been proud of a time when they both had dueling letters to the editor published in both the New York Times and Washington Post on the same Sunday a number of years ago. They had a barbecue to celebrate, and they had teamed it up with a reunion for the Yale gang that were living on the eastern seaboard. Mrs. Collins said her husband kept copies of the two newspapers as mementos." She paused with a wry glare.

"And?" Sparks said.

"We were right there with them staring us in the face," Taylor said. "They were in the safe with the envelope."

"Ahhhh, that could be it," Becker said. "Jason... the first letter in each sequence. Post... Times... Post... Times."

"The second letter could be the section, the same for both editions," Taylor said.

"Then the page number, and the second number in all cases is six or less, which means it could be the column, and the last number could be the line... or the word," Becker said.

"I'll call the team and make sure those newspapers come straight to us right now," Sparks said, scrunching up his face as he took another drink of his coffee. "Maybe we can order out for some decent coffee while we wait."

IT TOOK NINETY MINUTES for the newspapers to arrive with the agent from Collins's house, and Sparks spent the time going over his notes from the White House interviews. Taylor spent the time extracting Torrez's financial records he had to file each year with her office and went over them with Sparks. Nothing was remarkable about Torrez's finances—more than one IRA, some investments with a popular brokerage house, some real estate probably tied to family assets from his parents... nothing offshore, and no large sums appearing in recent months. No large debts other than his car loan and a small mortgage on his townhouse, certainly nothing to raise red flags. He took one or two vacations a year—usually with a lady friend—to the Caribbean or Hawaii, but other than that, he didn't spend lavishly.

When the agent arrived, Sparks signed for the envelope and pulled out the two newspapers, dated August of 2002. They laid the two papers out side-by-side with the cipher sheet between them.

"Okay, the Post, A section, page sixteen, column four, line 7," Becker said. "Take not the first letter but the last."

"That would be an n," Sparks said.

"The second sequence is the Times, A section, page four, first column, line thirty-two," Becker said.

"That would be the letter a," Taylor said.

It only took them five more minutes to go through the remaining seven sequences. Becker read out the nine letters in order: "n – a – m – a – g – o – n – i – c... Namagonic. Sounds Native American."

"Search for it," Sparks said.

"Well, lookie here," Becker said. "Up pops Seymour Lake in the Northeast Kingdom of Vermont. It's up there in the corner near the Canadian border and New Hampshire. The lake was also known by natives as Namagonic, or 'salmon trout spearing place.'"

"Mrs. Collins just said they went on fishing trips up to Vermont," Taylor said.

"You wanna bet on where they went on those trips?" Becker said.

"I'll call Mrs. Collins back." Taylor punched into her phone. In just a few minutes, she was off again. "Arthur Collins owned a place on this Lake Seymour. Mrs. Collins never went up there, and he owned it before they were married. He went up there twice a year for fishing with friends. At least that's what she said."

"What do you mean?" Sparks asked.

"I don't know, just the tone of her voice," Taylor said. "It could be the stress she's under right now, but there was kind of an edge to it, like this place was a point of contention with her."

"When was the last time he went up there?" Becker asked.

"Ten days ago," Taylor said. "She offered up the address and the keys to the place."

"Road trip!" Becker said.

"Sorry, you need to process this letter and the rest of the Collins house evidence," Sparks said. "We need to know who we're dealing with."

"I get cabin fever never getting out of the lab," Becker said with a smile.

"Next week, we'll hit the golf course and you can debut your new swing," Sparks said.

"I've been known to play a few rounds in the summer," Taylor said. "Or are your get-togethers exclusively male?"

"A professional who uses a gun on the job, and she plays golf." Becker laughed. "Be still my heart."

"You really don't need to encourage him," Sparks said. He gently tugged at her arm and headed for the door.

WITH A FEW HOURS of light left, Sparks arranged for a charter, and they boarded the plane at 3:00 p.m. for the ninety-minute flight to Burlington, the largest city in Vermont. The weather was fair and the flight smooth, and they landed just before 5 p.m. They took possession of a company car made available to them at the airport and were on their way to the lake a few miles south of the Canadian border in what locals called the Northeast Kingdom. The late-afternoon sun filtered through the trees as they made their way along the secondary roads. The invigorating air coming in from the open windows was a welcome relief from the muggier day they came from just hours ago.

"I asked that a state trooper join us on site," Sparks said over the rushing air.

"We don't need a federal warrant. We have written permission from Mrs. Collins." Taylor held back her swirling hair.

"I know. Still like to have a local rep around. Makes them less like we're tramping in over their territory. Plus, I gave them the address, and they'll know exactly which cabin belongs to Collins. Save us time tracking it down. We'll probably only have an hour or so of light before it gets dark."

They passed through a handful of small towns, the quintessential postcard tour of the state's summertime charm—mountains and open fields green with grass or crops. Sparks counted six dairy farms before they were even halfway across the state, crossing from Burlington on Lake Champlain in the west to the eastern border with New Hampshire. Sparks noticed that Taylor had been quiet since the drive began, looking over her shoulder at the light traffic behind them on the twisting roads. Sparks could see that her anxiety was increasing. Finally, as they approached the small city of Newport, Taylor pulled out her Sig Sauer P229 and checked its readiness.

"This is a standard issue Bureau vehicle, right?" she asked.

"Yes."

"Additional weapons in the trunk, right?"

"Yes." Sparks looked back and forth between her and the road ahead. "You want to tell me what's going through your mind? We haven't been partners even a day yet, so I can't read it."

"I don't know, just got a weird feeling. Something doesn't feel right. You don't feel it?"

"Feel what?"

"I get this way when an investigation goes too smooth and too fast. I've been checking behind us, and we aren't being tailed—too hard to do that on these secondary roads in the country."

"What's bothering you?"

"We're assuming because the safe wasn't compromised at Collins' home that whomever tortured him wasn't successful," Taylor said.

"He gave them the location of whatever that he and Torrez were involved with directly, so the need to get into the safe wasn't necessary," Sparks nodded.

"They may have already been to this fishing camp ahead of us, or they might be waiting for us."

"We'll be careful. And if we can't get a thorough search done by dark, we'll get some state troopers to babysit the place overnight if need be." Sparks slowed the car down as they reached Newport and were caught up in traffic. "Your hunch could very well be correct."

It took them twenty minutes to get through the city, and Sparks lamented not taking a more remote route around as the lake lay to the east. They came to a set of gas stations just off Interstate 91 near a small town called Derby. They met up with the state trooper Sparks had requested, and after a brief meeting, the trooper—an Officer LeClair—took the lead to drive them the last twelve miles to a town called Morgan next to the lake. The evening was cooling down, and the sky was turning overcast. It was approaching a quarter past seven when they reached an intersection of two roads converging and a simple country store. LeClair was quickly out of his car and held up a hand sign to Sparks and Taylor to hold on while he went inside the store. He was back out in under two minutes.

"Just double-checking which place we're talking about here," he said at Sparks's driver-side window. "This store doubles as a post office, and the woman at the counter knows every place on the lake." He handed Sparks a map of the lake, which presented itself as an upside-down L with the long stretch running north to south. "The Collins place is on the west side, just south of Wolf's Ledge, which is right at the inside elbow."

"Wolf's Ledge?" Taylor asked.

"An old tale you might hear from the old-time locals. It's a grouping of rocks visible from the water about eighty to a hundred feet high. Collins doesn't have any close neighbors. He owns a place and a good bit of land on either side. Likes his privacy, I guess. Rare nowadays, with the buildup around

Seymour during the last forty years. We take this road south right from this intersection."

LeClair led the way as they descended from the ridge where the intersection was down to a small valley where the western shore of the lake met them in just a few minutes. They turned off the road where a small wooden sign that said "Collins" marked the entrance between a pair of healthy birch trees with their pristine white bark.

Sparks remembered his time as a Boy Scout and how birch bark on the ground was a coveted find because of its ability to help even the greenest of scouts get a fire started. They eased down the dirt road and approached the tree line. Sparks noticed that Taylor was surveying the land on either side of the road and behind them as well.

"Sparks," she said.

"I don't like it either. Can't see a damn thing in the woods."

The woods were shrouded with what little overcast light was filtering down from above. They were inside the tree line only a couple of hundred feet when they came upon a clearing where a neat, well-kept cottage greeted them in the gloom. There was no sign of activity, and a first glance showed no signs of break-in damage. The building itself was about sixty feet by forty feet and was raised up on a foundation of cinder blocks that allowed access to the underside of the cottage. A separate barn was located off to the right, which appeared to be an addition that was built a considerable number of years after the cottage.

The three of them met at the simple front porch.

"The camp's been opened for the summer," LeClair said. "Shutters are off. Wind chimes are hanging up here." He pointed to a set of chimes hanging silently in the stillness. "Fresh firewood is stacked up here. Someone's been here since before the spring."

"Collins's wife said he was up here for some spring fishing just last week," Sparks said. "LeClair, we need to clue you in on something. The people who killed Collins are obviously dangerous, and we believe they are linked to yet another murder. And it's distinctly possible they know about this location. You're not just babysitting us here. You need to stay sharp."

LeClair's reaction seemed a bit too casual to Sparks, but the agent didn't emphasize his point further, as Taylor was already at the door with the set of keys Collins's wife had provided them.

Later, Sparks wished he had taken the time.

CHAPTER NINE

Nov. 27, 1863

CARL TRICHARD WAS A plain-dressed man who carried with him none of the presence Brison had found with Raven. They sat in Trichard's office in Springfield, just ten miles from Brison's farm, and the yearning to see his family came strong to the Union colonel. He had thought about riding to see them before attending to his president's business, but duty took precedent.

Trichard had welcomed Brison with enthusiasm into the drab workplace. Trichard's foundry was half the size of Raven's, but the smoke constantly belching from the stacks revealed a lively business. Trichard wore a dark gray suit with a black tie and suspenders. His jacket was folded over a nearby chair, but he didn't feel the November chill, because the office stove radiated with the glow of a well-stocked belly. The owner had dark hair with a full beard and a mustache, thick and unkempt, framing a face accented by a tiny nose and brown eyes. He had offered Brison a spot of whiskey upon the colonel's arrival, but after a polite refusal, he offered up a mug of toxic coffee that he accepted with gratitude. After a few words about his ride into Springfield, Brison wasn't surprised with Trichard's first question.

"So what did you think of Raven? You didn't let that horse's ass sell you a bag of shit?" Trichard didn't smile with his coarse words.

"I knew what I was in for, sir. I had been forewarned by Samuel Bixby."

"Ah, good old Sam. He's a right proper businessman, I'd say. He'll drive you a hard bargain up to a point but always is fair and deals with everyone as the Good Book would hope. So you knew what to expect with Raven?"

"Just why do you and your other competitors up here in New England believe Raven is behind the damage being done to your businesses?"

"Because we all have had our problems with transportation mishaps, suppliers losing orders, important employees being hired away, incomplete materials being delivered without explanation—meaning they left the supplier intact but show up at our businesses short by a considerable amount. Then, in the last six months, we've had accidents at all of our factories. Nothing catastrophic, mind you, but enough to slow down orders by weeks." Trichard offered Brison a cigar, and they both lit up their smokes. The owner continued. "Our gracious Union quartermaster has shifted more of his orders to Raven."

"Meigs."

"Can't say as I blame him," Trichard continued. "I would do the same if I were in his position. But really, Colonel, the six or seven of us up here are having similar problems, and Raven over in New York hasn't had a lick of trouble. Smells of rotten fish, I say."

"He told me he had an intentional act in his factory that set his schedule back not the day before I arrived."

"And you believe him?"

"Not necessarily." Brison thought it best not to mention having spent ten hours hanging in a well. "The point is, I was sent here at the president's request to ascertain if these acts against you gentlemen are coordinated and who is behind them. Have you any suspicions on any of your own workers? He would need someone on the inside to facilitate the disruptions."

"I have a few names my foremen are watching, but we haven't been able to catch anyone in the act, not even whispered rumors," Trichard said.

"I'd like to talk with those men, one at a time."

"I'll arrange it. Do you want to speak to them this afternoon?"

"No, tomorrow in the afternoon. And don't announce anything in advance. I want to pull them from the line."

"As you wish, Colonel," Trichard said.

HE NEEDED A GOOD night's sleep and his body still ached from the attack in Newburgh, but Brison could not resist the draw of his home, Louise Elizabeth, and the children. In the weeks after the Stallard affair, he felt this same yearning he was certain every man in the war felt about their families. In September, after delivering the news of Jackson Prescott's death to Abigail Stinson on the Massachusetts coast, he came home for a two-week furlough and found his absence had been hard on his family and returning to duty was difficult. Louise Elizabeth asked him about resigning his commission and returning home to again join her father's furniture making business in Springfield, but he fought off her inquiries with words of duty and responsibility. It was a challenge at the time, and Brison knew now as he approached his home in the dusk of this late November afternoon, the challenge awaited him again.

It was near the dinner hour. The inside of the house carried a glow, and smoke spilled forth from the kitchen chimney. Jennie, his seven-year-old, was the first to see him through the dining room window as he tied his horse outside. She always seemed to be the one to see him first, as she was the one who knew everything that went on at the house and surrounding land.

"Father!" her muffled scream erupted, followed by the voices of his two other children, ten-year-old Mary and four-year-old Patrick.

The side door where he stood burst open, and they charged out of the house, Jennie leading the way and jumping into his arms. She wrapped herself around his neck, sending shooting pain through his bad shoulder. Brison felt little of the pain through the joy. Mary hugged him around the waist, and Patrick grabbed a spot on his leg. Their weight and screams of delight overwhelmed him, and he staggered for a moment.

"Father, we missed you so much," Mary said. "Mother didn't tell us you were coming home."

"This is a surprise for all of you, but I can only stay tonight before I have business in Springfield, and then I have more work for the army."

He kissed each of the children in turn; first Jennie with her reddish pigtails still fiery even in the subdued light; then Patrick, named after Patrick Henry, the first signer of the Declaration of Independence of whom Brison's own grandfather was an acquaintance; and after the other two had run back into the house, Mary, his oldest, who was beginning to look like her mother, except her hair more auburn than red. She had those same gray eyes that held one's attention from the moment you looked in her face.

He would never admit it to anyone, but Mary was his favorite, if only by small margin. She held the same love of working with her hands and already seemed especially gifted with creating things. After a long hug, Mary turned and skipped inside, just moving past the figure standing backlit in the doorway.

"Andrew, you could have sent me a wire that you were coming around." Louise Elizabeth grinned, arms crossed in front of herself.

"I don't think the president would care that I was using the wire services for arranging an evening with a bonnie lass." He reached for her and kissed her before putting his arms around her. "Besides, I didn't know myself until a day or so ago."

She held him tightly even after he tried to pull away. "How is your shoulder?"

"Feelin' a bit like barking at me right now, but I'll be fit as a fiddle after a meal and a good night's sleep in my own bed."

"Did I hear you say you are only here for the night?" she asked.

"Yes, my love, I'm afraid so."

She gave him a withering look. She was three inches short of a full foot shorter than him, but she still could be intimidating about certain things... and his absence from home due to the war was one of those. "Well, come inside. We're having lamb stew with fresh bread I just baked today."

"Perhaps we could have a little music tonight after dinner." He glanced over at the piano in the parlor.

"Mozart or Brahms?" she asked over her shoulder.

"Whatever you would prefer," he said, knowing well that she would always play Mozart over any other composer.

"We shall see, Mr. Brison."

SHE WAS NAKED UNDER the covers, draped against his body, her hair smelling of perfume. He was barely awake now after a comforting meal and some music from the piano while he sat on the couch with three children and the cat. Then came the evening prayers and goodnights for the children while he put his horse in the barn for the night. Finally, when they were alone, came the physical pleasure they both had missed in the weeks he had been gone. Content and exhausted from the last week, he was drifting off when her whisper brought him back.

"We need you here, Andrew. Have you not done enough for Mr. Lincoln? I am afraid every time I see you the luck that brings you back to me will be gone."

"Dearest, the president needs my services, and I daresay there are many men fighting who are more in danger than I shall ever be."

"I know."

"And there are people up here in the North who are doing harm to our country, Louise Elizabeth, and the president says I'm useful in helping bring those people to justice. How could I turn my back on Mr. Lincoln and on the other officers and men who have already died?"

She brought herself tighter against him, her softness melting his resolve. "We've said this all before."

"I believe we were in the same situation." He kissed her perfumed hair.

"Yes, I believe we were. You are a cad, sir, using your charms on me then casting me to the side as you charge off to war." She lightly smacked his chest at her joke.

"You know it is hard being away from my family—from you, my love. Our country is facing a difficult time, and I believe this war will determine what our country will be for generations to come. And I believe Mr. Lincoln is our best hope to lead us proper-like out of this war when it is over. I have his trust, darling, and I can't fail him again."

"Andrew, we had words on this before," she said. "You said Mr. Lincoln himself didn't blame you for that gold going missing, and you helped keep it from the Rebels. Why not let go of your guilt? There is no reason to still have it."

"It is hard."

"What are you tasked with this time?"

"You know well I can't tell you of my task until all is over and done." Brison brought his hand to her face and kissed her for a long moment. "Yet you always ask me. Are you a Rebel spy? You know there are many lurking about in Washington and other places. Perhaps I should have you investigated."

"You have found me out," she mocked. "Perhaps we could come to some arrangement to secure your silence." She reached her free hand down to caress him and felt his growing excitement. "I am encouraged by your reaction."

"You are wicked, Louise Elizabeth." Brison kissed her again. "I was almost asleep a moment ago, and now look at us. I must ride out early in the morning."

Her smile was brilliant, even in the candle-lit room, and she pulled on him so his body moved on top of hers.

WITH A BRAVE FACE to the children, Brison helped make breakfast and enjoyed the meal with them before saddling his horse and heading back to Springfield. He arrived close to the noon hour and was accepted in by Trichard, who insisted they have a meal before Brison began his unannounced interviews. Trichard had a list of eight employees he said could be involved in direct action against the factory, two of them being supervisors. He was straightforward with them, explaining that he was from Washington on a fact-finding mission to investigate the deliberate acts that had plagued them over the recent months. He asked direct questions and took notes in front of the men. When the afternoon was done, he went right back to the notes from one particular meeting with a supervisor in charge of in-house transfer of cannons and munitions within the factory. He went through their conversation.

"Mr. Browning... first name?"

"What is it with more questioning about all this?" Browning said, failing to hide his contempt. "We all did our talking about all this weeks ago."

"I'm here to ask the questions again. First name?"

"John."

"You are the second shift manager on the floor?"

"Yes."

"Back on the dates when the last two incidents occurred, do you remember any behavior you would deem unusual?"

"From my men?"

Brison resisted an impulse to raise the antagonism. "Yes."

"No."

"Any of your men strike you as being disloyal to Mr. Trichard or to the Union? It could be anything, a word spoken in a conversation."

"Look, you... Colonel, as I've said all along when asked about these goings on, I haven't seen nothing, no how. If I would have seen something, I'd have spoke my mind." The supervisor appeared relaxed, but Brison could see his leg bouncing in steady rhythm, and he fumbled with a button on his overcoat. He was a smallish man with narrow black eyes and no facial hair, his forehead extending back to a sparse ridge of hair far back on his vertically proportioned head. When he spoke, he averted his eyes from Brison on each opportunity. "These here problems didn't happen on my watch."

"I'm aware of this, Browning. They all happened in the early morning hours before the morning shift workers arrived. We're checking the night watchman as well. But some of the damage, Mr. Trichard says, were acts some of your men or yourself would have the knowledge to do."

"That don't prove nothin'. There are many who work with the machinery. Like I told them all before, if I knew something important, I would have spoke up."

Brison had talked with Browning for another five minutes, but nothing useful resulted. Compared to the others, Browning's attitude was the most suspicious, but Brison debated on whether it was too obvious. He asked Trichard about Browning, and the owner was aware of the supervisor's gruffness but said the man was his best supervisor, his people usually excelling in turning out their quota. But the man was difficult to handle, and Trichard had had to discipline the man six months before for taking a drink on the job. Brison asked about the man's habits after work and found out most of the workers went to a couple of taverns on the south side of Springfield. A little coin and a choice question to Browning's immediate boss gave Brison the name of Browning's establishment of choice: the Patriot Bridge, located next to the bridge of the same name that crossed the Connecticut River.

Brison waited outside in the shrouded gloom of the November dusk and watched men come and go for about an hour when he saw Browning, walking alone with his head down, come up the street and turn directly into the tavern. Brison wasted no time crossing the street and moving down the alley to the tavern's side and found the back entrance to the kitchen and storage area. Getting a frown from a worker wearing a stained apron with arms covered in grime, Brison slipped in the back door. He made his way into the short hall leading into the main tavern, stopped short, and peered around the corner to survey the crowd. He spotted Browning immediately; the supervisor was hunched over in the opposite corner with his back to Brison's position, involved in an earnest conversation with a second man. This man was carrying the talk and punctuated his point with a jabbing finger at Browning. Brison knew this kind of man, one who assumed control of a group whether he was new or not, tough, demanding, and ruthless. Even from across the tavern, Brison could tell this was a man with whom one didn't trifle.

Given the tavern's design, there was no chance Brison could maneuver his way over to have any chance at listening in on their conversation, but he thought at least he had someone else to investigate as a possible lead. He had just decided to maintain his place out of sight when Browning's companion rose with an empty glass and walked toward the long bar that ran on the wall to the right of Brison's position and gave the colonel a chance to see his face clearly. It matched the demeanor, clean shaven but with dark eyes and hard-angled features except for the nose, which looked like it had been broken multiple times. He was a good-sized man, like Brison, with the upper body of a blacksmith. He approached with a scowl and dropped the glass on the bar and dug into his pants for payment.

"I need a whiskey, and I want a clean glass," he barked well above the general noise from various patrons.

Brison tried to become part of the wall around the corner. It was the same low voice from the well, the man who handled the young kid who was about to put a bullet in Brison's head when Byrne intervened. This was the man who'd ordered Brison's death with as little concern as stepping on an insect. The colonel slid along the wall and retreated to the kitchen, keeping his eyes fixed back up the hall until he bumped into the same worker who had seen him when he walked in not three minutes before.

"Aye, what the Sam Hill you think yous doin' in my kitchen, you dumb-ass donkey?" The worker shoved Brison. "Get out."

Brison muttered an apology, tipped his cap, and backed out the door. He turned up his collar, walked across the road, and found shelter in the porch of a business a door down from the tavern. He felt for his Colt as he thought about the implications of that man meeting with Browning. The kid at the well never admitted being in the employ of Raven, and Byrne said she had never seen the kid or the men who had laid Brison out before. That meant nothing as far as proof, for they could have been hired separately by Raven or they could be a party unattached to Raven. But there was good reason to believe that man was involved in the damage at the foundries. Why else would the nervous Browning be meeting with him on the same day Brison had interviewed the employees? It also meant Raven, or whoever knew Brison, was still alive and had come to Springfield. And if they knew Brison was alive and here, then it wasn't beyond reason that they would know about his family. If Raven was behind this, he would know. He would make it vital to know everyone he was dealing with in every aspect of his business.

A shiver swept down Brison's back, and it wasn't from the night.

CHAPTER TEN

Present Day
June 2

LEAVING LECLAIR OUTSIDE TO search the grounds, a jacketless Sparks entered the cottage with Taylor, and after clearing the rooms, they returned to the living room. The cottage was simple, furnished with comfortable furniture, including a leather recliner situated next to a seven-foot stone fireplace, apparently built using material found on-site. The living room ceiling peaked at twenty feet, and pine-log beams were used to reinforce the roof. The lake side wall consisted of glass windows, offering a partially tree-obscured view of the water a hundred feet away. The other walls were adorned with photos of family and various Vermont scenes. Sparks found himself envious of Collins for having such a getaway location for fishing and relaxing away summer afternoons. Then he remembered Collins was lying in a morgue.

"So what do you think?" Taylor said. "Another safe up here?"

"I doubt it. We're going to have to do this the hard way, since Mrs. Collins had never been up here. One of the bedrooms was converted into a study. I'll start there, and you start on the kitchen and out here in the living room."

The study was unremarkable, just a desk, a chair, and a single bookcase, the kind you buy at an office supply store and put together yourself. No computer, but Collins could have brought a laptop with him. Sparks guessed that this study wasn't used all that much. He gave the room a professional going-over, especially given how Collins had hidden the safe in his home, but found nothing that resembled a document Torrez would have left with Collins. Sparks went through the books, moved and examined all the furniture, and felt along the floorboards. After twenty minutes, he moved on to the other rooms.

The bedroom seemed out of place for a fishing cottage. It had a king-sized bed with puffy pillows. The end table was filled with condoms, lube, and some sex toys, and on the floor in the corner was a sex swing. Sparks looked up to see a hook situated above his head.

"I don't think there was a hell of a lot of fishing going on at this place." Taylor stood in the doorway with a smirk on her face.

"I think you're right."

"The kitchen has no cutting boards, no frying plate to cook a catch, just some basics for quick, easy meals."

Sparks picked up a wedged-shaped hard foam pillow similar to ones he'd seen advertised in the back of men's magazines for helping out in certain sexual positions. "Collins doesn't fit the stereotype of a college history professor."

"I found a television with a DVD player in the living room," Taylor said. "There are some action movies and quite a lot of porn... couples' stuff."

"Couples' stuff?" Sparks grinned.

Taylor rolled her eyes and gave a fake annoyed voice. "That's what they said on the boxes."

"Okay, so Collins used this as a getaway for playtime with coeds. Mrs. Collins, I have a feeling, was aware of this place's use, but I really don't think it matters to us. Where would Collins hide a document?"

"The barn maybe?"

"Possibly."

They walked out into the living room. Dusk was approaching, and as Sparks had feared, the overcast skies meant they had little time before dark and would probably have to return in the morning for a complete go-over. The rooms were not brightly lit. Sparks stood, leaning against the couch and looking around the room, while Taylor went to the front door to call out to

LeClair. Before she got to the door, Sparks called her back into the living room.

"What is it?" she asked.

Sparks nodded toward the wall where a dozen or so framed photos of Vermont scenes were displayed. The largest was placed just off center in the middle. It was an aerial photo of Seymour Lake taken during the winter with fresh snow covering the area around the lake, a blue upside-down L-shaped sapphire shrouded by pristine white. The frame had a nameplate on the bottom edge, but it didn't say "Seymour Lake." It said "Namagonic."

"Nameplate," he said.

"Shit, I didn't check behind the larger photos," Taylor said. She took down the frame and flipped it over. The frame had a backing plate, but just by holding the photo frame, she could tell it was overly heavy and something was placed between the photo and the back. "There's something here."

She pulled a large envelope from behind the photo and quickly opened it. Inside were legal papers held together with a large paperclip. They were obviously old, and in the upper right-hand corner was the date Aug. 5, 1859. On top of the papers was a more recent folded paper with modern type from a laser printer. Side-by-side, they looked over the paper together, reading the first page. It was a legal brief discussing what significance the accompanying document carried. The synopsis said the document from 1859 was a binding contract, witnessed and recorded in New York City between one Augustus Raven and a Justice Mallory, combining their two companies into one with Raven retaining 51 percent ownership and Mallory 49 percent.

Taylor placed the document on the table and was about to take a photo when they heard a cry followed by the staccato bite of automatic weapons fire. The glass of the picture windows shattered, and Sparks felt the bullets heat the air around him as he instinctively threw himself into Taylor and onto the floor. The firing continued in a sweep, starting where they had been around the perimeter of the living room, carving destruction along the walls and into the furniture nearby, shattering and splintering everything in a sustained burst of fire. Sparks rolled off Taylor and felt wetness on his arm; she had been hit. He made a quick inventory of her and saw a wound on her upper arm near the edge.

"You hit any place else?" he asked.

"I don't think so. I'm okay, just took a small chunk of my arm, no bone. But it's bleeding already pretty bad. I'll hold it until we can get a tourniquet on it. Inventory... I've got my Sig, two spare clips, and a knife." Taylor held the gun in her right hand while her left applied pressure to her upper right arm.

"We've got to assume they took out the deputy." Sparks had pulled out his Glock from his back holster. A fresh burst of fire tore into the wall where they had been standing and stayed focused on their position. "Move!"

They crawled to the hallway leading to the bedrooms and away from the concentrated fire until they were sitting in the hallway with their backs to the opposite walls from each other. Taylor's left hand was covered in blood, and she was biting her lip in pain, but she looked at him with calm, focused eyes.

"They'll come in the front and from a window in the back bedroom, opposite sides," she said through a grimace. "Pinch us in between."

More bullets slammed into the walls at the hall's entrance for five seconds and then stopped. Three seconds later, a metallic object struck the floor and hissed to life, followed immediately by a second and third, creating a cloud that began to fill the living room.

"Gas," Sparks said under his breath. He crouched and brought Taylor up into a similar position. Together, they moved down the hall a few more feet, and Taylor turned her arm to separate it from Sparks.

"Quickly, get me something for a tourniquet," Taylor said. "I can't fight with my hand over this hole in my arm."

Without a word of acknowledgement, Sparks slipped into the bedroom and brought out a shirt from the closet, ripped off the long sleeve, and, after removing her jacket, tied the shirt sleeve above the wound. He was relieved to see it was just a shallow entrance wound through the outer arm, very nearly a graze. He handed her the remaining shirt. "Keep the pressure on when you can," he said. "It should start to bleed less. Stay in this doorway here. It's the bathroom and doesn't have a large enough window for them to breach. I'll cover the bedrooms. You cover them coming through the main house."

Taylor nodded in response, the tear gas edging into the hall, but not enough to cause incapacitation. Sparks slid down the hall so he could see the windows in both of the back bedrooms, and immediately, he saw two figures forcing open two of the windows in the main bedroom. He turned back to Taylor and caught her glance. He motioned out to the living room, and she shook her head.

Back to the bedrooms, the second bedroom looked quiet, the windows intact. He moved along the wall until he was at the master bedroom door. He counted in his head to three and swung around the door frame. In an instant, he assessed what he saw. The first man was looking right at him, his weapon trained on him, with the second man sliding the second part of his body through the window. Sparks fired, hitting the first intruder square in the chest. At the same time, a short burst flew past his left shoulder and through the open door.

Sparks moved his aim a fraction to the right and caught the second man as he turned. Two rounds later, the second man was crumpled on the floor. Sparks dropped low and peered back up the hall, finding Taylor looking right back at him. He held up two fingers, made a downward motion, then pointed once more at the living room. Again, Taylor shook her head and returned to her observation.

Sparks ran to the master bedroom window, peered out at the surrounding forest, and snatched his head back inside as glass splintered from shots fired from across the clearing that served as the cottage's parking lot. He glanced outside and fired off two rounds at two more figures edging toward the building. As he pulled back in, he heard a shout from the hallway followed by three rapid shots from the Sig. There was automatic response fire, and Sparks turned the corner of the bedroom in time to see the hallway splinter debris onto the floor. Taylor swung into view and fired off three more rounds before yet another gas canister fell to the hallway floor. Sparks surveyed the two bedrooms again, found no movement, and returned his attention to Taylor, who now was coughing and moving crouched on her feet to Sparks' position.

"There are four, I think," she said. "Can't count accurately with the smoke... could be double counting. Think I caught one."

"Okay, we're retreating to the master bedroom," Sparks said. "Two windows face the parking lot at the front of the building, but there's a side window that goes directly into the woods."

Another gas canister was pitched into the hallway, closer to their position.

"They're driving us to this end of the house," Taylor said, then swore. "The papers. They're still on the table in there."

"Master bedroom." Sparks gave her a shove, took a deep breath, and moved back down the hallway. He tried to keep his eyes shielded from the smoke, but he didn't have much success. Tears already filled his eyes from the irritation. He reached the corner on the side obscured from the living room and peered around the corner. His attempt was met with bullets ripping into the wood paneling just above his head, wood fragments hitting his face before he snatched his head back behind the corner. Through the smoke, he had still been able to see all he needed to see. The papers on the far table were already gone. He moved back to the master bedroom, coughing the last yards as he miscalculated and took a breath before he was clear of the smoke.

"They've already got the papers," he said, moving to the window.

Taylor responded with an expletive, maintaining her post at the hallway's entrance. Outside, Sparks saw movement along the far tree line.

"They're withdrawing now," Sparks said. "They've got what they came for." He looked over at Taylor. Her bleeding was under control. She kept her attention on the hall. Back to the window, Sparks saw no movement, but then he heard a powerful motorboat engine start and immediately accelerate. "And they came by the water."

They climbed out of the bedroom window and split up, each clearing two sides of the cottage and nearby grounds. It was Taylor who found LeClair's body in the woods on the north side, a single gunshot wound to the center of his chest. She called Sparks over, and they ran down to a set of ledges that extended from the shoreline thirty feet into the lake. The powerboat, already half a mile away, was heading directly away from the Collins's place, no doubt to where a vehicle waited for them. If they were smart—and Sparks was sure they were—it was probably two or three vehicles of differing types.

"We've got a dead trooper. You're shot up a bit. We've lost the biggest lead towards finding out about what the hell is going on here." Sparks didn't try to hide his frustration. The entire assault on the cottage had lasted less than fifteen minutes. Whoever was behind this whole operation was extremely well funded and trained. "This went bad real fast."

"It wasn't all bad, Jason," Taylor said. "We saw the brief for a few seconds, and we might be able to go on what we saw."

"What'd you get from it?"

"Contract, 1859, between two men named Justice Mallory and Augustus Raven. Raven was to own 51 percent of some company and Mallory 49 percent."

"Guess we have some more historical research before us," Sparks said. "By the way..."

"Yea?"

"You get any more of those uneasy feelings again, make sure you slap me on the side of the head to pay attention."

THE ASSAULT TEAM LEFT the boat on a small sandy section located on a cottage-less tract of land. Inside the tree line were three vehicles: a painter's van from a business in Newport, a family van, and a nondescript sedan with a luggage rack on top. Wordlessly, the group of eight men put their equipment in the painter's van and went to their assigned vehicles. One man with sandy blonde hair pulled a Boston Red Sox cap out of a soft-sided bag and prepared to climb into the driver's side of the sedan. He called out to the other two drivers as they prepared to do the same.

"Washington location... 48 hours... no excuses," he said. His thick Massachusetts accent matched the ballcap.

The three vehicles climbed through the woods up to the main road on the east side of the lake. At the top, two turned right and one turned left. They all sped off into the gloom of early evening.

IT WAS ALMOST THREE in the morning when Sparks and Taylor checked into a motel outside of Newport after they spent the entire night going over the crime scene. An hour and a half of that time was consumed dealing with an angry and grieving group of troopers at the scene. Sparks took a back seat as Taylor worked to explain the situation and went methodically with the investigators from the state over just what happened and why it wasn't their fault that a trooper had been lost.

There were three other bodies at the location: the two in the master bedroom and the one near the living room back door that Taylor had, indeed, taken down through the smoke. They carried no ID and no cards. Each had about $200 in cash. A print reader allowed them to send in the three sets of prints down to Washington, but none of the three were in the system. They also didn't appear in either Vermont or Canadian databases. Despite their exhaustion, they scoured the cottage again with the help of the troopers in case there was anything else of importance they had missed before the firefight.

Then came the quiet ride back to Newport and a visit to the emergency room for an eight-stitch job on Taylor's arm. Then they checked into the motel, and Sparks bid Taylor a goodnight with the stipulation that they would go over what they knew in the morning when they were rested and had a couple of hours to drive back to Burlington. Even with his fatigue, Sparks decided to shower. Despite having not eaten in over twelve hours, he dropped into bed without so much as a candy bar and was asleep within minutes.

CHAPTER ELEVEN

Nov. 29, 1863

BRISON RODE THROUGH THE dark, pushing his horse with a cruel drive, cursing himself, and fearing for his family. He dreaded what he might find at the house he had just left a few hours ago. The war was coming to his home, threatening the one place he always found joy. It was a pestilence just as deadly as scarlet fever or the pox, and, like the others, one he might not be able to fight off. He also thought of another farmhouse in Ohio where another family was butchered a few months ago for no reason other than to inflict emotional pain on someone. This time, the action would be directed at him. He should have moved his family into town to stay with his father-in-law and had them put under protection. It wouldn't have been difficult. Brison filled with rage at the thought that something could have happened to his family. The possibility of harm to his own family, however inconceivable before this Raven business began, was now very real.

Brison swung his horse to a stop just below the ridge less than a quarter of a mile from his home and swept off the animal while simultaneously pulling his Spencer from its leather holster. He started on a dead run, cutting through the woods he knew so well, having hunted in them for rabbits and deer. His breathing was labored, and his body barked at him for all the suffering he had come to in that well back in New York, but he paid it no heed. He clipped a branch and lost his balance, falling down a slope and jamming his bad shoulder yet again. The pain seared through and around to his back. But he was back on his feet in an instant, and within a couple of minutes, he came over a rise and saw the lights of his home. The downstairs lamps were lit, but the upstairs was dark. With haste, he scanned the area around his home as far as he could see with what moonlight was available to supplement the house lamps. Nothing seemed out of the ordinary.

He made his way down the final slope and approached the barn from the back. A quick look inside and a survey of the interior revealed nothing sinister, so he half ran, half trotted to the side of the house. He tried to quiet his breathing and gave himself a moment so he could listen for any noise coming from inside, but he was greeted with just the slight movement of the bare trees nearby. Now he was up on his front porch, and here he saw, for the first time, evidence that something was amiss. The two front porch chairs were overturned and discarded to the side. With the Spencer now in one hand, he slowly lifted the latch and pushed the door inward. Light greeted him, and he eased his head around the door and into the gap.

An explosion of sound startled him, and he fell against the door frame. The bullet just missed him and split the wood in the wall next to him. He heard a pained scream, and he looked to see Louise Elizabeth sprawled on the floor, favoring her shoulder and crawling away from the light. She was crying.

"Elizabeth, it's me," Brison said as he rushed to her side.

She sobbed as she grabbed him so tightly, he was pulled down, losing his balance on his knees.

"Andrew, oh, my savior, Andrew," she said. "I thought you were them come back."

"Mother!" It was Mary, peaking down from the stairs with the other two children right behind her.

"It's all right, children," Brison said. "I'm home. Your mother thought I was a thief breaking into the house. Go on to bed. There's nothing to be afraid of. We're sorry the rifle woke you all. Everything is right as rain."

The two younger children disappeared up the stairs, but Mary stood her ground, seeing that her mother was crying.

Brison separated from Louise Elizabeth and moved to the stairs where Mary was up against the slats below the railing.

"Mary, mind me. All is well. Your mother and I are fine. The gun went off by accident, and neither of us are harmed. Go on now, to bed with you."

"But Father, Mother is crying." Mary already had her mother's natural skepticism; Brison took note for future reference.

"She just was scared by my come a-callin' in the middle of the night is all." Brison put his hand on Mary's cheek, then gave a short tug on her ear like he always did when putting the children to bed. "I need you to make sure your sister and brother are back in bed."

Mary looked around her father's shoulder, then back into his face. She wasn't convinced, but she finally yielded to her father's wishes. "Good night, Father."

When he turned back to his wife, Brison found her sitting in a kitchen chair, her arms tightly wedged between the folds of her dress between her knees. She was trying to steady herself, taking deep breaths, before she looked up at him with watery eyes.

"I could have killed you... could have killed you," she said.

"But you didn't."

"They were here..."

"Who?"

"... left not twenty minutes ago."

"Who was here?"

"Three men. The children were asleep. I went out to move the horses into the barn because I forgot to get Mary to do it. They covered my mouth and told me to hush up or they would harm the children."

"Did they harm you?"

"No, other than handling me roughly. They just forced me back into here and sat me down in this very chair."

"Were they highway men... robbers?"

"No, Andrew. They knew who we were, knew who you are and that you work for the president. They were only here for five minutes, and only one of them did any talking."

"What did they want?"

"He said I was to relay a message to you." She took his hands in hers. "He said you were to drop whatever business you were doing and tell them back in Washington that there was nothing left up here to do. He said you should head back to Washington or they would come back to harm us, and then he shook me by the shoulders and made me repeat what he said. And then he left that." She nodded over toward the table. It sat in plain view, as out of place in her kitchen as a plow or a cannon's ramrod, sitting in the table's exact center. "He said you would understand his meaning."

It was a bullet.

Dec. 6, 1863

BRISON PULLED HIS HORSE into an alley as the carriage he was following got caught in a tangle of traffic in front of the Willard Hotel. Whenever he was in Washington, Brison never ceased to wonder about the amount of activity he found in the city no matter the time of day... or night, as in this case. Here, it was near enough the midnight hour, and five carriages jockeyed for position in front of the hotel. The one that interested Brison was the one farthest from the entrance, for it contained Augustus Raven, having just arrived in the city from New York by train, then visited a private home just ten miles north in Maryland before coming into the city.

Brison had been following Raven since a week ago at his family's home. He was dusted up with anger, all the way back to Raven's factory grounds where he intended to confront the bastard directly along with as many militia men as he could procure along the way. He had moved his family in the night to his father-in-law's home in Springfield and spent a good hour explaining to him why he needed the two soldiers Brison was going to have stationed at the house for the duration of this business.

The next day, armed with a wire message from Washington giving him authorization, he got the protection he desired despite the skeptical prostrations from an otherwise bored captain. A hard ride had gotten him into Newburgh in the middle of the night, but it had not kept him from slipping into the boarding house and waking up a stunned Byrnes, who was dismayed by not only the story about his family but also his appearance. He had learned from her that Raven was traveling to Washington in a day for an important meeting and had seemed preoccupied since Brison's visit. He slept on a couch in her room—he protested, but she insisted, despite the appearance of impropriety. He did need sleep, after all. When he awoke the next morning, she was gone.

Brison's stomach grumbled. He had missed dinner, and looking at the Willard reminded him of the wonderful meals he had had there. Though he was never privileged to stay at the Pennsylvania Avenue hotel just a stone's throw from the president's mansion, he had eaten meals there as a guest of others. His favorite dish was the roasted goose with cranberry sauce and ribbon cake for dessert, and he'd pay twice the normal coinage for a helping of that right now.

As Raven's carriage moved closer to the entrance, Brison tied up his horse at a rail on the same side of the broad street as the hotel. He glanced down the thoroughfare and could make out the Capitol building from what light welled up from the city. Hat lowered, Brison slipped into the Willard's main lobby and looked for a corner from where he could observe Raven's arrival.

"Andrew Brison... Colonel?" The voice came from an open office door and belonged to the hotel's business manager, one of the Willard brothers—Joseph. "Come in, come in." He waved at Brison to join him in the office. He wore a major's uniform, but his jacket lay on the side of his desk. He had a thick mop of hair and heavy sideburns on his squarish face. The Willards were from Vermont, so when Brison was introduced some months back, he and Joseph had struck up a casual friendship.

"Joseph, what are you doing up at this ungodly hour?" Brison asked. "You can't possibly be finding numbers work at midnight, can you? And are you not in the Army? What the blazes are you doing here?" He said all this with a smile, but he stayed at the entrance to the office and refrained from entering.

"I've had myself transferred to Washington," Willard said, standing at his desk, "and my superior officers are letting me visit the hotel on occasion."

Brison thought of asking on Willard's wife, but he had heard whispers of Willard's involvement with a woman—not his wife—who was in the Old Capitol Prison for spying. He thought it best not to draw the conversation there. Besides, just then, Raven walked into the lobby and headed straight for the front desk.

"Joseph, I would love a talk despite the late hour, but I need your help," Brison said, showing his credentials. "I'm working for the president on some private business, and I need access to any room in the hotel."

Willard's face scrunched up in a frown. "I don't know, Andrew. I can't very well have your roaming into any room at this late hour no matter what business you are conducting for the president. This hotel is the finest one in Washington and—"

"Would you rather have me arrest Augustus Raven in the lobby of your hotel right now? Or better yet, maybe tomorrow during the day, right in the middle of a well-populated lobby?" Brison hated this tactic, but he was desperate. "Look, I might not need to do anything more than wander through the halls upstairs. Please, Joseph, I'm asking for a favor."

"Augustus Raven is arriving now?" Willard brushed by Brison and swiftly moved across the lobby. From Brison's vantage point, he saw his acquaintance walk right up to Raven and greet the industrialist. Brison couldn't hear what was said, but Willard gave instructions to his people behind the desk, and after shaking hands with Raven, he made his way back to the office. He found Brison standing just inside the still-open door. "He'll be staying in Room 436. What is your business with Raven?"

"That's between me, President Lincoln, and Raven," Brison said, "but this much I can say. Augustus Raven will eventually have much to answer for if I am to have anything to say about it."

Willard stood for a moment making his decision, went to his desk, and retrieved a key from a drawer. "This key will get you into any room, but so help me God, Andrew, if you bother any of our guests unnecessarily..."

"I'll be on my best behavior. You said he's staying in 436?"

"Yes, but he's not going there straight away. He asked me the room number of another guest, and I felt he was going to go there straight away."

"Who was the other guest?"

Again, Willard hesitated, but as before, his decision fell on Brison's side of the ledger.

"He's on the top floor—the fifth—in the corner room on the northeast side. It's Edwin Stanton, the war secretary. He's renting a room for a time this week."

BRISON PRESSED HIMSELF AGAINST the wall around the corner from the hallway. He had made his way upstairs a few minutes after Raven and two other men left the lobby and now stood around the corner from Stanton's room at the end of the hall. The two guards stood outside the door, talking in low whispers, smoking cigars next to an open window. Brison stood for a few minutes, trying to think of a way to slip into the room next to Stanton's. Willard had said it was empty, a rare occurrence for this hotel. He was fifteen feet or so from the door, and his being observed would be certain. He didn't recognize either of the guards and was sure he hadn't seen them at the Raven foundry, but he couldn't be sure if either or both had been the ones who sacked him next to the alley in Newburgh.

Then came an increase in noise from outside the hotel... raised voices, near enough shouting, made louder because of the open window forty feet away. Brison peered around the corner and found that both guards had their heads and shoulders outside the window, obviously watching whatever altercation was taking place on the street below. Given the hour, it was certain to draw the attention of guests, staff, and soon someone of legal authority. Brison took his chance and moved quickly along the carpeted hall to the door, used Willard's key, and opened the door. The door handle made a noise as he turned it, but by the time one of the two guards turned from the window, all he would likely see of Brison was a brief glimpse of a coat and trousers and the door closing.

"Timing is the luck of the fortunate," Brison said under his breath as he locked the door behind himself and turned up the lamp next to the door.

The room was finely furnished with a four-post bed, a handsome sitting chair, and a chest of drawers with an oval mirror. The curtains were drawn, and the light from the gas lamp danced against the silk-like material. Willard had told Brison that this room was connected to Stanton's room, as these two were often rented as a suite. Brison swiftly moved himself next to the door between the rooms and put his ear to the seam between the door and the frame. He could hear voices immediately, speaking in normal tones, but he was not able to decipher any words. The door would have to be opened to overhear the conversation.

Brison went back to the lamp, turned it down, and re-turned. He slowly, patiently eased the pass key into the lock. He waited for a particularly loud exchange as the voices became raised in argument and turned the key, then the knob. Once it was free from the latch, Brison let the knob turn in his hand as he moved the door only enough to allow him to hear the men now locked in a heated exchange.

"What you are asking about is foolhardy, Augustus, and you know it. I can't let you send in agents of your own down to Richmond, for God's sake. If they failed and were discovered, it would be disastrous."

The voice was Stanton's. Brison had met the man on a couple of occasions and knew his voice well.

"The bastard has been a thorn in my side, and I'll not have him benefit off my work these past three years." Raven matched Stanton's intensity. "I want my partnership with him eliminated from my ledger, and I'll remind you again about how much you and Lincoln benefit from my good will and my money besides the cannon, ammunition, and firearms my factory produces for the war effort."

"Augustus, let us calm ourselves a bit," Stanton said. "We are attempting to reach the same end, are we not? I am sympathetic to your plight, my good man, but it would be political suicide if the matter isn't handled in a most delicate manner."

"I don't need your permission, Edwin. I could just send my agents to Richmond. I could have done so without this meeting, but given our relationship, I thought my chances of success would be better with federal help, and I believed you would be open to rendering assistance. It appears I was wrong. Is my method distasteful to you?"

"God no, man. Justice Mallory is a traitor to the Union, working there directly with Jeff Davis. If I had my way, when this war is over, all in that illegal government in Richmond would hang together as surely as we whipped the Rebels at Gettysburg. I have the stomach for what you wish to propose, but I'm a member of the president's cabinet, damn you, so I must be cautious. When I accepted the president's request that I take over as the Secretary of War, I thought he was a buffoon, and he's not, not by a jugful. I've observed him, on many occasions, move his pieces like he was playing chess, maneuvering souls into doing his bidding."

"I think you overestimate him," Raven slipped in.

"No, you and many others are tasking the opposite."

After a few moments of silence, Brison heard the brief clink of glass. He guessed a brandy was being poured into someone's glass. He smelled the cigar smoke through the small opening he was listening through. Finally, Stanton spoke.

"Perhaps there might be a way for your demand to be satisfied," he said. "We could have a military action cover your agents, give them protection for as long as possible under the umbrella of an actual foray into Virginia."

"Is something like that being planned?" Raven asked.

"Preliminary... I don't desire for you to take this as an affirmation of your demand, but let me look into it a bit. There is a colonel... Kilpatrick. He's proposing an action that might fit our needs."

A key was being slipped into the door to Brison's room. He didn't take time to close the door he was listening at, but he made a quick move to the window and slipped behind the curtain and slid up the glass. He didn't wait to see who was entering the room, climbing out the window and stepping onto the frame. There was no ledge, nowhere to go but up, so he reached up and tried to grab onto a ledge... his hands falling about six inches too short.

The only way to reach the roof line would be to jump, but if he failed, it would take a miracle for him not to fall all the way down to the street. Taking no time to think or weigh the options, Brison bent his legs, then thrust himself up and barely curled his fingers over the edge of a ledge. He pulled himself up until he stepped on the top of the window frame, got a solid foothold, and reached up again, this time to the roof's edge. After a moment of adjusting, he swung himself up and over onto the roof.

He took a moment to exhale and collect himself before taking a careful look to see if anyone was investigating the open window. He saw no one. The roof was relatively flat with a slight tilt so rainwater could escape through numerous gutters. Several large, tarped, box-shaped bundles were arranged in rows. No doubt the Willards used the roof as storage. Brison moved swiftly south toward the Pennsylvania Avenue side, looking for a hatch and a ladder down to the floor he just left. He spotted it a hundred feet away and approached it without hesitation, all the while going over what he had heard in the conversation between Stanton and Raven.

It was disconcerting that Stanton was involved with Raven, particularly with what Brison had learned about the New York industrialist in the past ten days. Raven wanted Stanton's help with something to do with a man named Justice Mallory, and it had to be done in Richmond of all places. Mallory was in Richmond, and Raven wanted something done. It sounded almost like Raven was planning to kill Mallory. And Stanton objected until he began to present an idea and it involved a man named...

The hatch cover wasn't closed. It was open, propped up by a wooden dowel. Open in the middle of the night.

A boot sounded heavy on the wood, and Brison turned in time to see the glint of a knife coming at him from above, its thick blade dull in the lamp light that filtered up from the street. Brison threw his hand up and grabbed the arm of his attacker and jammed his hip into the man's side at the same time. They staggered together and lost their balance, falling against one of the tarps, locked in a struggle over the knife that Brison was keeping barely above his chest. The man was near enough his size and solid, and strengthwise, he was Brison's equal, pushing against the colonel's upper body and jamming him against the tarp, not allowing any movement to the side. Brison had his Colt in his belt and his own knife in his boot, but they were as useless as a pair of fine leather shoes during mud season unless he could put some distance between the two of them. All he needed was a second, but his strength was going into keeping the knife from plunging into his chest.

They both let out cries of pain as the effort continued. The attacker used his left arm to shove against Brison's throat. At the same time, he pulled his knife arm free and tried to reroute it down and from below into Brison's stomach. The knife came forward and flew into where the attacker thought would be the soft flesh under the ribcage, but instead, it struck the side of the tarp as Brison twisted his torso to the side.

Brison brought up his right knee and hit the man's side, eliciting a pained grunt. It gave him a free split second to go for the Colt in his waistband, but as he drew it, the attacker slammed his knife arm into Brison's gun hand, and the Colt spun off into the darkness.

Brison grabbed for the knife arm and threw his weight, shouldering the attacker off balance, but the man's strength kept him on his feet. Despite Brison's try at limiting the man's knife arm, it swung around again. Brison braced himself while turning to the side again. He felt the pain as the knife cut through his side, low, just above the waist on the fleshy side. Again, Brison threw his weight against the man and finally separated the two of them.

"I can't believe I have to kill you myself." The voice was the same deep tone Brison had heard at the well and in the saloon. "My fault for putting my faith in a stupid boy. Now hold still, Colonel."

The man lunged at Brison but was sidestepped. He swore as he spun around. This time, he faced a figure in a fighting stance, bent over slightly with knees flexed, ready to take on the attacker. Only now, there was a knife in the colonel's hand.

"Well, it seems the odds have evened up a might," the man said.

Brison didn't respond but kept shifting his weight as the two of them moved in a semi-circle away from the tarps. Brison felt wetness underneath his clothes, but he could tell the wound was not deep and probably would just leave a scar. Louise Elizabeth would give him a tongue lashing from now on every time she saw it. It was a strange thought to have in the middle of a knife fight.

They continued to circle, looking for an opening, but Brison was doing more than that. He was looking for where he thought the Colt had landed. The man gave up a little ground, and then Brison caught sight of the Colt out of the corner of his eye, lying just five feet to his left and slightly behind him. He quick-stepped, and in one lunge, he got to the pistol. He swung it around while holding his knife arm out in defense, but he needn't have done so, because when he turned, the attacker was at the hatch and already halfway through the opening.

Brison cried out in frustration, but the latch slammed shut when he was still five steps away. He reached the covering, lifted it, threw it off the hole in the roof completely, and peered down into the building. The ladder traveled just fifteen to twenty feet, and the attacker was already at the bottom, sprinting away from the base. Brison thought about firing a shot, but he decided against it. He needed this man alive if possible. Replacing the knife in his boot, he slid with expediency down the ladder, catching a splinter in his left hand as he went down, all the while watching the attacker run down the carpeted hallway and disappear around the corner at the stairs. He still felt the blood underneath his shirt; the wetness was spreading.

He reached the stairs and started down, taking the steps sometimes two at a time and nearly pitching forward onto his face early on until he realized he needed to pull back a bit or end up unconscious on a landing. The attacker was a full flight ahead of him and pulling away. He was a better runner, so Brison resorted to the cliché shout of a pursuer.

"Someone stop that man!" he yelled.

A couple down below looked up to see the man sprinting at them from above. To his credit, the gentleman in a fine overcoat pushed his lady to the side none too gently, but the attacker had all the momentum and threw a shoulder, which launched the poor fellow into the wall, and he crumpled to the floor. Five seconds later Brison, reached the couple.

"I'm sorry, ma'am." Brison tipped his hat and continued.

He was on the second floor landing when the man reached the lobby, where a good number of people were milling about.

"Willard!" Brison yelled again. "Joseph, someone. Stop that man!"

Two officers—both lieutenants—near the front desk stepped in front of the man, but he slashed at them with the knife and shouldered his way past them and out through the front entrance. Brison was down to the lobby in a few seconds and charged through, despite one of the lieutenants reaching out to try and stop him. He reached the outside to find one of the bellmen flat on his back, much the worse for wear.

"The bastard ran right over me, the son of a bitch," the bellman said.

It didn't take Brison much time to locate the man. He was across Pennsylvania Avenue and running to the east right past where Brison had been when he observed Raven's carriage arrive at the hotel. Dodging a military wagon loaded with supplies delayed Brison another five seconds. He sprinted through the soft earth and reached the other side just as the attacker met up with another man who was holding two horses, and in a moment, they were both mounted.

Colt withdrawn, Brison yelled, "Halt!" and aimed at the two figures. Maybe he would get lucky and only wound the attacker. One of them was quicker and fired off a shot at Brison as he ducked behind a tree, and by the time he recovered to return a shot, they were already charging down the street in the direction of the Capitol building. Brison assumed they would make a turn soon and head toward Swampoodle, and there would be no point going after them if that was where they were headed. Brison was alone, and it was the middle of the night. The chance of his having a difficult time was high. The shanty town was among the rougher places Brison had ever been in, and that was during the day. If this attacker had accomplices, then Swampoodle would be just the place for him to have hired them.

Suddenly, Brison felt very tired, and the Colt was heavy in his hand. His arm dropped to his side, and he turned to re-cross the street where he knew a bewildered and possibly angry Joseph Willard would be waiting for him.

Chapter Twelve

Present Day
June 4

BRIGHTON MALLORY'S OFFICE WAS in the Russell Senate Office Building, one of three such buildings that housed offices for Senate members. Built in 1909 and situated at Constitution Avenue and First Avenue Northeast, it was perhaps the premiere example of Beaux Arts architecture in the United States. It was also the oldest of the Senate buildings and had been designed by the firm of Carrere & Hastings, who had been heavily influenced by designs like the Louvre. Mallory was a Republican from Arizona and the chairman of the Senate Committee on Appropriations; his office suite was impressive in its elegance of design and austere feel.

It was well furnished, but there wasn't a hint of opulence that Sparks could see. The carpeting was lush, and the desk/chair combination was a sturdy dark wood with hand-carved designs. The walls held photos and illustrations of places and people that Mallory no doubt considered important—an illustration map of Arizona; photos of the Grand Canyon; a rugged evergreen forest that Sparks assumed was somewhere in the northern part of the state; the stadium where the Arizona Cardinals played; a shot of what looked like retired vintage airplanes with a nameplate on the frame marking it "Pima Air Museum," which Sparks knew was on the southeast portion of Tucson; a sailing photo taken on a large body of water; and finally, a sunset shot in the desert somewhere.

Sparks and Taylor had been waiting for fifteen minutes.

SPARKS AND TAYLOR HAD flown back into Washington the day before and agreed that their first effort would be researching the two names they remembered from the papers they had glimpsed for just seconds before the attack in Vermont, Augustus Raven and Justice Mallory. With the help of a search engine, it took them only minutes to find information on Raven. That was because his great-great-grandson had plastered much of Augustus Raven's life history on a company website that belonged to Sterling Raven—Raven Technology Industries—the very man named in Torrez's letter.

Sterling Raven was very proud of his family's heritage and this massive company's origins back in the pre-Civil War days when Augustus had grown the iron manufacturing business into a weapons manufacturer because he saw the coming war as an opportunity. Of course, the website's language was couched in patriotic phrases declaring Augustus's fervent support of the anti-slavery cause. Sparks and Taylor knew immediately they had their link to the present and to the murders of Torrez, Collins, and now the trooper in Vermont. Someone thought the business papers dated in 1859 were important enough to kill for, and Torrez had pointed a finger directly at Sterling Raven.

The other name from the 1859 document, Justice Mallory, was harder to come by. They found no apparent references to the name, at least on the internet and from the time of the Civil War, for the first two hours of searching. Then, while Sparks was having his fourth Diet Coke and a granola bar, Taylor and Becker found a reference to Justice Mallory in an online document about Jefferson Davis's Confederate administration in Richmond. It was mentioned in a history textbook written in the early 1900s with sections available online. The website demanded a paid account, so Becker opened one, and a couple of minutes later, they found the section that mentioned Mallory by name.

When Davis was forming his original cabinet in 1861, he chose Christopher Memminger as his Secretary of Treasury. Memminger had been a South Carolina delegate to the provisional congress that formed the Confederate States of America and was the chairman of the committee charged with writing the Confederate Constitution. With the outbreak of the war, Memminger was faced with a daunting challenge because of the Confederacy's severe constraints. He turned to a friend who had spent time in the North before the war but was a South Carolinian by birth and was considered an excellent businessman.

Justice Mallory held a large Charleston-based business but was known before the war for his investment in businesses in New York and Pennsylvania. While he never held an official position in Richmond, Mallory was known as a close advisor to Memminger and then, as the war progressed, to Davis himself. In February of 1864, Mallory died in a carriage accident after leaving Davis's Richmond home late one night.

Memminger tried different tactics to shore up the Confederate economy...

That was the only reference they came across, but it gave Becker an idea.

"I know you two didn't get a real good look at those documents before the cabin was turned into Swiss cheese, but wouldn't it be plausible that if there was one direct descendent from those two in that company that they may be others, particularly from the Mallory side of the equation?" he asked.

"And maybe someone Torrez knew," Taylor said. "Someone in Washington."

"Torrez, through his office, dealt with people from the private sector as well as inside the Beltway," Sparks said. "It's kind of a jump to assume it's someone in government."

"Yes, but it's a start," Taylor said.

Sparks made a call to Torrez's assistant at the White House and requested a log of every visitor Torrez had received in his office or meetings he had had outside for the past six months. At the same time, Becker started work with a staffer on procuring telephone records for Torrez's work and cell phones for the same period. With everything connected to their investigation given top priority in the Bureau, by early that night, they had the list of people Torrez had been in contact with. Eighty percent of them were political in nature. They had been poring over the list for only a few minutes when Sparks caught himself taking a quick breath.

"Whoa, now there's a name that jumps right out at you." He flipped the list so Taylor and Becker could see it.

"Brighton Mallory?" Becker said.

"Senator Brighton Mallory... from Arizona," Taylor said. "I have heard the name before. He's on an important committee, I remember now. I've heard his name before. I'm surprised it didn't pop right into my head when we started."

"Senator Brighton Mallory, Republican from Arizona," Sparks read aloud from a congressional reference book the FBI compiled with each new session. "Chairman of the Senate Committee on Appropriations. Fifty-eight years old, married with six children. Considered one of the power brokers in the Republican Party and has so far stayed out of the limelight but is considered a strong possible challenger for the party's nomination in the next presidential election. Considered a middle-of-the-road conservative. Family is wealthy, and he owns a large complex of residential buildings in the foothills of the Catalina Mountains outside of the Tucson."

"I'm looking up his own website," Taylor said as she started tapping away at the keys.

"It says here he began his political career as a state representative in Arizona for two terms while he was running his family's commercial real estate business," Sparks said. "Then he ran for a House seat in the mid-nineties and served just one term before running and winning a Senate seat. At the same time, his family—he has a brother that helps run the business—had gradually bought up a lot of desert land outside of Tucson, and with the growth in retirees flocking there in the last twenty-five years, they made huge profits. The family has diversified its interests over the years, and Senator Mallory is worth about thirty-five million. His brother is worth considerably more and has spent much more time running the businesses, all still privately owned."

"This is interesting," Taylor murmured.

"What's up?" Becker leaned over her shoulder with a smile.

"There's nothing on Mallory's official congressional website, but look what I've found here," Taylor said.

"The Mallory family tree going back from Brighton and his brother, James," Becker said. "How'd you get this?"

"This is one of those family tree websites, you know, the ones that help you research," Taylor said. "I have an account myself, but I can't release the Mallory information even though someone from their family has been doing research. I need a password to get into their account."

"Let me take over." Becker slipped over to his desktop and pounded away at the keys while Taylor went back to Sparks, who was making a call on his cellphone.

"Tank? It's Jason Sparks. I'm good. Listen, I need to pick your brain for a couple of minutes. Can you spare them?"

"Who's that?" Taylor whispered.

Sparks waved her off and continued. "Can you give me a quick rundown on Brighton Mallory? Yeah, the chairman of the Senate Appropriations Committee." Sparks listened for a good two minutes before responding. "I appreciate the lowdown, Tank. One last question. You used the word 'ruthless' just now, so he's got political enemies like everyone else, sure, but would you consider him capable of unethical behavior?" Sparks nodded as he listened and then thanked the person on the other end and ended the call.

"Who's Tank?" Taylor asked.

"Friend of mine who used to work at the Post," Sparks said. "He knows everyone in Washington who's been here for any length of time. Frickin' walking encyclopedia on the movers and shakers in town."

"Why Tank?"

"Used to be a fullback," Sparks said. "He didn't say a lot more than what was in our dossier, but he said Mallory is an incredibly adaptive political animal. That's how he's maneuvered himself into his position without a lot of exposure. He also said he's as ruthless as a hired killer. Tank's exact words. But there hasn't been a single whisper about any connection to anything shady. He's just badass, politically."

"You asked if Mallory could be unethical?"

"He said it wouldn't surprise him in the least. In fact, it would be more of a surprise if he wasn't."

"I'm into the family tree website," Becker said.

"You hacked it?" Taylor said. "Crap, Tom, that's illegal."

"Shhhhhh." Becker smiled.

"All we want is a quick in and out," Sparks said. "See if Mallory can trace his family all the way back to Justice Mallory, late of the Confederate States of America."

"Someone in his family created an account recently, and they were piecing together a tree that, let's see, does go back to the early 1800s," Becker said, now flanked on either side by Taylor and Sparks. "And lookie here, his direct line ancestor was, in fact, one Justice Mallory."

"So we have a modern-day weapons manufacturer and a United States senator, both linked by family to a document dated from the Civil War," Sparks said.

"I'm getting déjà vu all over again," Becker said.

"And someone has shown they are willing to kill—and kill prominent people—to gain possession of that document," Sparks said.

"So who do we go see first?" Taylor said.

"Let's start with the senator."

BRIGHTON MALLORY, TWO YEARS short of 60, was an inch or two over six feet and, by Sparks's estimate, probably weighed about 220 pounds. His brown hair was turning gray and hung over his ears, which seemed unusually small for a man of his size. He wore dark wire-rimmed glasses that framed his strong face well. After shaking hands with both Taylor and Sparks, he spoke briefly with his assistant about appointments later in the day and then had the office cleared before taking off his suit jacket and sitting behind his desk.

"I haven't received an urgent call from any agent with either the FBI or Secret Service during my years here that I can recall," Mallory said, rolling up his shirt sleeves. "Normally, something this last minute is difficult to accommodate, but the very fact you want to talk with me personally piqued my interest. Just what is this about?"

"Your family history, Senator," Taylor said.

"And murder and attempted murder... and a business document that is a hundred and fifty years old," Sparks said. He paused as Mallory gave him a raised-eyebrows look that seemed rehearsed. He continued, "Senator, a professor at American University was killed yesterday morning—tortured for information beforehand—about a document from the Civil War era. Special Agent Taylor and myself were about to recover the document when we were ambushed at a cabin in Vermont by a professional extraction team. We were lucky to escape; however, a state trooper was killed. We had a thirty-second look at the documents before we were attacked. Your great-great grandfather Justice Mallory was mentioned in a partnership with a man named Augustus Raven."

"My great-great grandfather?" Mallory asked.

"Yes," Sparks said. "You were aware of him?"

"Well, yes. My father did a lot of research into the family, but I was never very interested in it myself. Justice was a friend of Jefferson Davis, the Confederate president, and was a businessman in Richmond and elsewhere. I think Davis wanted Justice for a position in the cabinet but was turned down, if I recall. You don't read about Justice in the history books much. He was kind of a behind-the-scenes character. I do remember he died during the war in a carriage accident." Mallory paused and glanced at both Sparks and Taylor, then his eyes narrowed. "What on Earth does a document from back then have to do with murder and me?"

"That's what we are trying to ascertain, Senator," Taylor said. "We know that two men have died because of it in the last thirty-six hours. Has anyone been in contact with you or your office about this document at all in the last six weeks or so?"

"No, but what was this document about? You said a partnership. A business partnership? I can't imagine what that would have to do with me other than my family ties."

"It must have value beyond just historical significance," Sparks said, "for this kind of effort to take possession."

"This is all so bizarre. I'm beginning to become worried that my name might be dragged into something that could damage me politically through no fault of my own." Mallory got up and moved over to the window with his back to them. He put his hands on his hips when he turned around and faced them. "Of course, I will help you both anyway I can. I have nothing to hide, but you have not been truthful with me, and I don't particularly like you both coming into my office and asking questions when you yourselves have been practicing some crafty obfuscation."

"Senator?" Sparks said.

"Murders over a document... a college professor and a state trooper. Perhaps the purview of the FBI because of the interstate aspects, but why is the Secret Service involved here? Is there some financial ramification coming from this or danger to the president? You aren't part of the intelligence community per se, Special Agent Taylor. Why are you here?"

They had expected this question and had agreed that if they needed to, in order to explain Taylor's involvement, they would reveal the circumstances surrounding Torrez's death, though they would leave out the letter implicating Sterling Raven.

"I'm here because this murder of a college professor is tied to the death of the president's chief of staff," Taylor said, staring straight into Mallory's face to read his reaction.

Mallory's mouth dropped open halfway, and his eyes widened. "Torrez didn't die in an accident? It was deliberate?"

"Yes, sir, and we have information connecting the two murders. Anything that ties to the White House staff and could affect the president's safety is of our concern. So, Senator, back to part of the question you didn't answer. Do you have any idea why this document would be so valuable?"

"There has never been a mention of a document in anything I've learned about Justice Mallory. And as I said before, I'm worried about my name being dragged into something of which I have no prior knowledge." Mallory sat back down in his chair. "Your respective departments are playing it pretty close to the vest, aren't you? How long do you think you can keep it quiet that Torrez's death was not an accident?"

"If the mainstream press gets a whiff or some random blogger starts a fire on the internet, it will be announced that it was a botched robbery," Sparks said.

"After your history with being loose with the truth, Agent Sparks, I'd think Ray Connelly would be more sensitive to how manipulated information can come back and bite him in the ass." Mallory revealed a perfect set of teeth. "Frankly, I'm surprised you still have a job."

"Senator," Taylor interjected.

"That's okay, Bethany. It's a valid opinion." Sparks gave Mallory a shrug. "Director Connelly wanted us on this because we're good. The decision about withholding the manner of Torrez's death is between him, Secret Service Director Pearson—"

"And the president," Mallory said.

"Torrez was his chief of staff," Taylor said.

Mallory drew in a breath and gave a soft whistle. "The president has a reelection campaign coming up; he'd better be careful. Anyway, I don't know why my family was linked to this document, but I would appreciate a heads up when you two come up with a concrete answer. Can I count on you letting me know discretely in advance?"

"We can give you a heads up, Senator," Taylor said.

Five minutes later, after Mallory had explained that he was headed back to Tucson for a fundraiser and for a long weekend at his family's estate, Sparks and Taylor walked out the front doors of the Russell building onto the broad sidewalk and headed to the garage.

"What was your impression?" Sparks asked.

"I don't know. His reaction to the news on Torrez seemed genuine enough, but he was pretty aggressive with that shot at you."

"Just a little emotional sleight of hand. He knows more than he's telling us, though I agree he didn't know about Torrez's death. But there is more to his involvement than what he told us. And you know why?"

"He didn't once ask about what else we saw in the document and who his great, great grandpappy was dealing with back during the Civil War," Taylor said.

"You'd think if his political rep was so important, he'd at least want to know the other names in the document."

"Maybe he already knows."

"We should put a detail on him in Tucson," Sparks said. "Whether he likes it or not."

"What do you want to do now?"

"Well, we've talked to one side of the equation. It's time to talk to the other. Somehow, I believe it's going to be a little more adversarial."

"I haven't been to northeastern Pennsylvania recently," Taylor said with a smile. "We asked for a profile of Sterling Raven. It should be completed by now. We can swing by the Bureau before calling it a day. Or we can just get it emailed to us."

"Instead of flying a charter up there, I'd like to drive," Sparks said. "I want to make a short detour. I need to see someone."

Taylor gave Sparks a questioning look. "So mysterious. A lady friend?"

"As a matter of fact, yes."

"The infamous Jason Sparks has a girlfriend?" Taylor teased. "How come my dossier on you didn't have that little fact?"

"You're the first person outside of the two of us that knows, so please, a little discretion, Special Agent."

She pulled an imaginary zipper across her lips. "Why don't you drive up and I'll fly up later in the day and meet you up there tomorrow evening?"

"All right, but no running into Raven's office on your own."

"Yes, sir." She gave him a mock salute.

Sparks shook his head and said to himself, "And you wonder why I like working alone."

Chapter Thirteen

BRISON, WRAPPED IN HIS overcoat and wearing his favorite wide-brimmed hat, leaned against a pillar on a side porch of the Executive Mansion. He was smoking a cigar in the dark by himself, the glow illuminating his face every time he took a puff. It was late, and he had been waiting for two hours, but he needed to speak to President Lincoln. He had tried every day since the incident at the Willard, but the president had been recovering from an illness and had not been seeing visitors. It had not been Brison's imagination that evening on the train from Gettysburg—Lincoln had been ill. But today, the president's secretary, John Nicolay, had sent for Brison after having held the colonel at bay before Lincoln was feeling up to seeing visitors. He would save Brison for the day's final meeting.

Just as he was finishing the cigar, Brison saw Nicolay at the side door motioning him to follow.

"It has been a long day for the president," Nicolay said without further explanation. He silently led Brison through the shadow-dominated halls as the lamps were turned down for the night. They climbed to the second floor and came upon the same office Brison had visited on previous occasions. Nicolay knocked gently on the door frame, turned on his heels, and faded into the gloom, leaving Brison to enter the office on his own.

"Ah, Colonel, how good to see you." Lincoln was coatless, but he carried a shawl over his shoulders that slipped off as he walked over to shake Brison's hand. "I do apologize for your having to wait in the dark. I wasn't expecting my visitors to take up the hours, but as I recall, my brief residency here should have prepared me." He grinned and shook Brison's hand and held out his own toward one of two chairs next to the fireplace. "I just stoked the fire so we can have the warmth to ease our conversation."

"Thank you, sir."

"After what John told me you relayed to him in your effort to see me in recent days, I expect harsh treatment from you." Lincoln settled into his rocker and put his reading glasses to the side, resting them atop a book that Brison figured was his regular evening reading. "Please do not read the delay as a signal of indifference. I have great concern for your family."

"I was only trying to impress upon Mr. Nicolay the severity of what I have encountered during my investigation," Brison said. "I'm relieved that you are over your illness, sir, and I understand the delay."

"So, I read your notes you left with John, but do go over the events since I saw you last on the way back from Gettysburg."

Brison spent the next thirty minutes detailing his visit to the Raven's factory, the assault and his being held in the well, the escape and his visit to Springfield, the warning left with his family, and his following Raven back down to Washington. He finished it up with the altercation on the roof of the Willard, for the moment leaving out his eavesdropping on the conversation between Stanton and Raven.

"It seems each time I give you a task, your life becomes like an alley cat fight," Lincoln said with a bemused look, which Brison found hard to fathom coming from the dark recesses of the president's eyes, made more so by the shadows moving from the fireplace.

"Sir?"

"Long periods of posturing followed by a vicious mauling." Lincoln readjusted his shawl. "The business against your family is quite disturbing, Colonel. Are you sure you have left them in safe hands? We can move them temporarily under the watch of the closest brigade."

"As I said, I have left them with my father-in-law. He is a wealthy man with many friends in the local militia. My family will have a safe guard about them. I am more concerned about another matter. I am compelled to reveal these details to you now."

Lincoln nodded slightly. "Continue, Colonel."

"The conspirator within your administration who we failed to learn the identity of from Parker Stallard back in July, I'm afraid I may have learned his name. I just told you that when I followed Raven to the Willard four days ago, I was attacked by someone who I believe was working as an agent for Raven, who probably was the man who threatened my family and had me in that well in New York. What I didn't say was that before that scrap, I was listening in at a door on a conversation between Raven and... Edwin Stanton."

"You saw and heard the two in conversation?"

"Didn't see, but I know the secretary's voice. We've met on two occasions here in this building. Raven also called him by his first name. I made a few discreet inquiries and learned that Raven and Secretary Stanton are friends going back to when Stanton worked as a lawyer in Pittsburgh, before he moved to work in Washington. And the meeting took place in a room at the Willard that was rented by the secretary."

"Their friendship doesn't preclude a conspiracy on the problems up north in the foundries. Please tell me what you overheard."

"I did hear them discuss that Raven was upset about someone named Justice Mallory," Brison said. "Said he was working with Jeff Davis in Richmond, and his words carried the meaning that Raven wanted a permanent resolution to his problem. And by permanent, I mean Mallory's death. Stanton was trying to calm Raven down and discourage any action being taken, and he cited political objections, sir, not moral ones."

"Raven was advocating the murder of this individual?" Lincoln asked.

"That was my conclusion, sir. Then, after a moment, Secretary Stanton suggested an alternative action involving the movement of troops to Richmond, allowing for an opportunity for Raven to do what he desires."

Lincoln sat forward in his rocker, the fire's light now leaving half of his face shadowed and half in the light. The effect gave him a harsh glare, and Brison was taken aback as the president spoke. "Colonel, I have trusted you as I have trusted almost no man in all my days. I desire to understand this clearly. You are telling me that my secretary of war suggested a federal troop movement to Richmond that could provide cover fire, so to speak, for Raven's agents to kill a close advisor to Davis?"

"That is what I cyphered from it, sir, but I was interrupted before I could hear the rest of the conversation. There was a mention of a name, someone named Kilpatrick."

Lincoln began rocking in his chair and seemed not to hear Brison's second sentence.

"Sir, do you know of anyone named Kilpatrick?" Brison asked. "I don't know of any officer by that name, though I have been away on your business for so long that there will be many names new to me."

"I haven't been approached with any such action against Richmond, though I have often asked it of my commanding officers. I wouldn't be opposed to our forces taking a stroll down the streets of the city. But again, such a plan hasn't been brought before this office."

"And such an officer, Kilpatrick, you know nothing of?" Brison asked.

"No. But during the dormant winter months of war, many plans hatched are hatched while hands are idle." Lincoln rose stiffly and poked at the fire and dropped a smallish log into the flames. He was silent for a full two minutes, to Brison's estimate, and returned to his rocker. "Colonel, I want you to turn your attention to Raven and this matter, and leave the problems up in the foundries alone for now. Perhaps you stirring up the hornet's nest up there might have Mr. Raven quietly curtail his activities. I'm not convinced Edwin Stanton is guilty of anything more than calming down an old friend who brought him an outlandish plan, but I can't fully discredit your account either. And from what you've said, you have no evidence tying them to any Southern sympathizers in the North, like those

Knights of the Golden Circle. The secretary has done fine work in sharpening our war effort, and I can't afford to lose him. And a scandal of this magnitude—I daresay you must realize this as well—would end this president's opportunity for another term. So... we will wait a bit, like a good hunter, and see if patience can give us what we need. While we do so, Colonel, I'm ordering you to move your family to a place of safety for a short time until this matter is resolved."

"Sir, I really don't believe it's necessary, especially if we refrain from pursuing our investigation in Raven's people in New York and Massachusetts. We have a small farm to maintain. My wife needs to be there to oversee the men we've hired while I am away. And she is with my father-in-law, as I said, and he will take care of them, I'm sure."

"I only worry for their safety, Colonel," Lincoln said. "If you believe them to be safe. Perhaps a visit up there for a few weeks would be a benefit, a furlough through Christmas."

Brison's heart leapt at the opportunity Lincoln was suggesting, but then he thought of all the men who would suffer in winter camps, and guilt got the better of him. "Sir, I spent a good amount of time recovering from my shoulder wound, and we need to investigate Raven and this Mallory. And should we not look into the relationship between Raven and your Secretary of War?"

"A man turning down a furlough? I must be more tired than I thought and ready for sleep." Lincoln smiled. "I would suggest to you that when your president gives you an opportunity for a furlough, you accept. Remember, if you're correct about what you heard, any action would require a parry at Richmond. Rest assured, Colonel, if a matter like that comes to my attention, I will call you back to Washington with haste. Go home and be with your family."

"I still believe I should remain in Washington and make inquiries here, but I could travel back up to Springfield. With your permission, I would like to make a side trip back to Newburgh, where Raven's foundry and factory are located. I might be able to glean valuable information from Raven's assistant. She is the one who saved my life at the well."

"I encourage you to move forward," Lincoln Said. "Just let the boys at the telegraph hall know where you are so if something is brought to me, I can notify you. I will also make discreet inquiries through Nicolay as to this Kilpatrick fellow."

"Move with caution, sir. These people have tried to kill me twice, and if Raven is behind it, as I believe he is, then ruthlessness seems to be the order of the day. There is something going on here besides some fouled-up machines at some of our arms factories."

Lincoln stood up and reached out to shake Brison's hand. "I agree, but we will wait and see what comes our way, Colonel. Now, go see your family and enjoy the holiday. I will have your furlough entered in officially through John tomorrow. Take the necessary funds from the paymaster."

"Thank you, sir. I shall return regardless of the circumstances after the new year."

"We are about to begin another year at war." Lincoln finished shaking Brison's hand and took a deep breath followed by a distinct sigh. "I pray it will be the last turning of the calendar that finds us in such a state."

"I as well, Mr. President."

Dec. 15, 1863

CATHLEEN BYRNE SHUFFLED INTO the boarding house off the main street in Newburgh, a light dusting of snow on her shoulders and hat. She took a moment to loosen her overcoat and shake the wetness from her hat, her auburn-red hair tied up in back, her face flush from the unusually cold early evening. She moved over to the stove, situated at the junction of a small dining room and the front desk area of the house, and warmed herself from her walk. Rubbing her cheeks to get the blood going, she smiled at the desk clerk, Tommy Malone. He was a tall, awkward boy of fourteen who worked in the early evenings during the week for his mother and father, who owned the boarding house. His face lit up with a beaming smile whenever Byrne paid attention to him, and she had taken notice of his attentiveness. She was flattered by his lovesick manner, but she tried to walk the line of politeness without giving him reason to think she was leading him on. She was, after all, twelve years his senior.

"Tommy boy, how are you this evening?" she said.

"Right as rain, Miss Byrne. I sure wish you would let us send a carriage out to bring you from the main road on nights like this, I surely do." His smile extended from one side of his face to the other. "You being our best tenant and all. You deserve it."

"Oh, a little walk never hurt no one, even on a cold night such as this. Is your mother in the kitchen?"

"Yes, ma'am."

"Would you please ask her if I could get a plate? I know she's done serving, but I was kept late at the factory, and I'm famished beyond knowing." Byrne gave him a smile, and his delight radiated back at her.

"I'm sure we can get you something." He stood up from his stool and moved from behind the desk. "We had a delicious chicken stew with brown bread tonight. I can set you up a table if you'd like, ma'am."

"I don't want to be bother, Tommy. Just... could you bring it up to me in my room? I'm tired and just want to eat and rest."

"I'll bring it up straight away," he said. "I'd expect you want tea as well?"

"Oh, you know me well, indeed. Tea would be especially welcome on a night like this."

Still grinning, Malone bounded off down the hall toward the kitchen that made up the back half of the first floor of the boarding house. Byrne made her way up the stairs to the third floor and down the hall to her corner room. There was presently only one other tenant on the third floor, and he was in the room next to the stairs, which was the way she preferred, liking to keep to herself. On more than one occasion, Raven had offered to give her quarters on the factory property, which would have been more convenient but likely would have put even more demands on her time. No, she liked her privacy away from her work.

She opened the door and placed her things on the adjacent table and lit the lamp that resided there. Closing the door, she took off her overcoat, went to a mirror, and worked to let her hair down. As she finished rearranging her hair, the lamp in the far corner suddenly brought light into the room. Byrne swung around in shock to find Brison sitting in the chair, hand on the lamp, his rifle upright and leaning against his right leg.

"Lands sakes, you scared me! I almost screamed by bloody head off." Byrne put her hands on her hips, glaring across the room.

"I'm sorry for the intrusion." Brison moved his rifle to the side so he could stand, hat in hand in front of him. "I needed to talk to you again, and it's best if I'm not seen. I came in through the window from the back roof over the barn that's connected here to the house. We need to discuss matters with Raven."

"I told you, Colonel. I helped you before, but I won't be searching for tidbits you can use to drum up charges. I'll not be a spy against Mr. Raven."

"I know. I don't want to put you in a poor position, but I need your help... your country needs your help. And this doesn't have to do with the goings on up here. There is another matter."

Byrne held up her hand and put her finger to her lips. Seconds later, there was a knock on the door. A muffled voice came through the door. "Miss Byrne, I have your dinner, and I also brought you a warming pan for you."

Brison moved swiftly and lightly to the corner out of view, and Byrne opened the door.

"Thank you so much, Tommy boy." Byrne took the tray with her dinner.

"I can put the warmer in your bed." Malone's voice exuded eagerness.

"No, thank you. I can take it myself." She took the long-handled bed warmer from the cart Malone had parked in front of the door. "I do appreciate your helpfulness. Tell your mother I'm thankful and that I'll have the coming month's rent to her the day after tomorrow. Will you do that for me?"

"Yes, ma'am, Miss Byrne. I'll be back with some hot water for you."

"Thank you, Tommy boy."

With the door closed, Byrne listened with her ear to it as Malone moved away down the hall. After a few moments, she resumed with Brison but with a more playful tone. "What new matter concerning Mr. Raven is worrying that handsome face of yours?"

"I should let you eat first. I can hold my questions." Brison lifted off the linen covering the stew and bread, taking a deep breath from the aromas. "Oh, this does smell good."

"Are you hungry? I can have them bring up some more, but I don't think we should give Mrs. Malone a reason to call for my leaving. I'm not allowed to have men visitors."

"No, I ate a couple of hours ago—a big meal—on the road before I got to Newburgh. I'll just sit here in the corner until Tommy boy returns with the hot water. No use him hearing our conversation."

Byrne nodded in return and set about preparing a place to eat her dinner. About ten minutes later, the boy returned with the hot water and received another smile plus a bit of coin for his troubles. She sent him along and listened again for him to head down the hall and return to his desk on the first floor. When she was satisfied he was gone for the evening, Byrne went about finishing her meal and told Brison to continue.

"To begin, I've been instructed by the president to suspend my investigation into Mr. Raven's possible involvement with intentional damage to competitors' factories."

"The president... you mean President Lincoln?" Byrne stopped eating. "The president?"

"Yes. I told you I worked on special assignment for Mr. Lincoln."

"I remember. I just hadn't thought on it, I dare say."

"There is another investigation I've begun, and it, again, involves Raven," Brison said. "Are you familiar with someone named Justice Mallory?"

Byrne stopped mid-chew and took a healthy drink of her tea. She settled herself before responding. "I've seen the name, and it's strange you would come here in the night with that name on your lips."

"Why?"

"Mr. Raven never mentions that name, but I've seen it on documents pertaining to the company... at least... older papers with the company. But I can't recollect the particulars. I got the impression that he was an old business partner of Mr. Raven's. But he has never come to the offices as long as I've been employed there, and I started a good year before the war began. I would certainly remember if he had been on Mr. Raven's appointment calendar."

"But it's definite that you have seen Mallory's name?"

"With certainty. What skullduggery does this have to do with?"

"I'm prevented from revealing the facts. Cathleen, have you ever heard of the name Kilpatrick?"

"No, not with Mr. Raven."

Brison sat and pondered a moment, watching as Byrne finished her meal. "Back to Mallory, you said there had been no mention of him by Raven. Was there any mention of him by anyone else in the company?"

Byrne finished her tea and went over to the basin and proceeded to wash her hands again, but this time, she also wiped her face, all the while seemingly lost in thought. When she was finished, she returned and sat on the edge of the bed next to Brison.

"I did hear one of the foremen grumbling about Raven, then speaking words not too kind about Raven but praising Mallory. I remember now because the name was repeated by another worker. There was some mention that Raven hated Mallory."

"That confirms what I already have heard myself," Brison said.

"That's all I can recall."

"Do you think I could get a look at those records? The ones where Mallory is mentioned?"

"Wouldn't be difficult with Mr. Raven in Washington, but he does have men watching the goings-on around here."

"I would still like to try. I need to understand Raven's motive for what I believe he might be trying to do."

"And that is?" Byrne asked with anticipation.

"Illegal. That's all I can say."

Byrne understood, but then she put her hand out and touched Brison's arm. "Colonel... Andrew, there's something I need to tell you. I'm scared, and you need to be careful."

"I also endeavor to be careful."

"You don't understand. The boy from the well—the one I hit on the noggin to prevent him from doing away with you—they found his body in the river just downstream from the shack. He had been shot in the head. I've been looking behind my back ever since that day they brought the body into town. I fear you're in danger if you're discovered here. Raven is a powerful man, and there must be people who work for him that are of the worse sort."

Brison held her hand and squeezed it for reassurance. "I have had another run in with them in Washington, and I came through it intact. But I dare say I'm worried about you. After my escape, was there any difference in Raven's manner?"

"He did seem in bad temper afterwards but not directed to me," Byrne said.

"You need to continue your duties as you have before, but I need to ask you to bring me the documents that pertain to this Justice Mallory. Would you be willing to do that for me?"

Byrne hesitated, but after a moment, she nodded her head. She licked her lips and held her mouth open slightly, looked into his eyes with a hopeful expression, and squeezed his hand in return. When she spoke, the vulnerability in her voice struck him, for it was the first time he had heard it from her.

"I don't know what you think of me, Colonel... Andrew, but rarely have I had a man in my bedroom and certainly never here. I find myself wishing the circumstances were different—"

"I am a married man."

"—and if you weren't such a gentleman, I dare say I don't know what would become of us tonight."

Brison felt the blood rush to his face, and he looked to the side. He wasn't a man tied strong to his faith, not like his Louise Elizabeth, and his vows didn't carry the barb of sin for violation, but he regarded himself as an honorable man, and he was proud of it. His vow to his wife was, at the very least, a promise, and he always kept those close to his heart. He looked back at her and offered a weak smile.

"I have embarrassed you," she whispered.

"A little, but not because I don't think you are a beautiful woman. I've never been so sorely tempted, but I would dishonor my Louise Elizabeth, and that is something I dare not do. She has been the brightest light in my life and has brought me children any man would be proud to call his own. But Cathleen, if ever a man would become weak, it would be with you. You are extraordinary."

"Shhhhhhhh." She put her finger to his lips and released his hand. "I release you from your dilemma, Colonel, for the moment has passed." She smiled again. "She must be an exceptional woman."

"Yes."

"Despite your comfortability with honorable intentions," Byrne said as she righted herself, "I will retrieve what documents I can procure. Though I honestly don't know what I'll be looking for."

"Anything that would explain their prior relationship and perhaps why Raven has such a dislike for this man Mallory. Can you obtain them quickly?"

"I can look into them tomorrow," she said. "How will I get them to you?"

"I'll return tomorrow night—late, after the other boarders have retired."

Brison moved to the window after picking up his rifle and slid the frame up, the cold air bursting in. He paused for a moment, then went swiftly to Byrne and gently kissed the cheek of her astonished face, disappeared through the black hole, and slid the window down.

Chapter Fourteen

Present Day
June 4

SPARKS DETECTED THE AROMA coming through the open window, and it made his stomach grumble, as he hadn't eaten since noon. It was approaching 8:00 p.m. as he knocked on her apartment door. She was making spaghetti sauce. He had taken off his tie and left it and his suit coat in the car with his overnight bag, so he stood there, sleeves rolled up and a couple of days' beard growth when Brenda Munson opened the door. That long raven hair alone would have taken most men in, but Munson's most striking feature was her brilliant hazel eyes, a perfect contrast to her hair. They were what had surprised Sparks when she removed her dark glasses the first time they were together on the Gettysburg battlefield. Those eyes, always searching for knowledge, revealed a singularly intelligent woman who could hold her own in any conversation.

She pulled on his arm and brought the two of them together, putting her own arms around the back of his neck. She kissed him with the enthusiasm he always enjoyed and then gave him a forceful hug, pressing her body against his with familiarity. He felt himself getting that craving she had proven so adapt at drawing from him.

"I can't tell you how happy I was to get your call." Munson withdrew and led him into the kitchen where a small pot of marinara sauce was gently bubbling on the stove. "I thought you'd enjoy some spaghetti. I even have meatballs."

"Oh, that smells so good. I haven't eaten in forever. I hope I'm not causing any trouble, just coming in with a couple of hours' notice. I was swinging up from Washington, and I've got to go northeastern Pennsylvania tomorrow on a case, but it's been a couple of weeks, and I said we could only make this work if we went out of our way to see each other every week."

"No, Jason, this is great. You know I want to see you every chance I can." She laughed and grabbed playfully for his belt buckle and pulled him close. "Like I said, it's been two weeks and we had a pretty intense vacation last month. I got used to certain things with certain frequency." She kissed him again.

"I do love it when you decide to take charge," Sparks said.

"Well, you have to deal with all those alpha males at the Bureau all the time. I figured you like a change of pace now and again."

"That I do."

They had met on the Gettysburg gold case. She had been called to testify during the investigation that followed. After that was resolved, he called her, and they met for dinner a few times before their relationship turned serious. It was Sparks's first serious relationship with a woman since his wife had died twelve years before, and he was beginning to think about how their life together could go if it continued. For the first time, he was allowing himself to consider and make the possibilities real, and he was comfortable with it.

"That was just awful about Adrian Torrez." Munson motioned for Sparks to stir the sauce while she took the pasta, broke it in half, and dropped it into the boiling water. "A carjacking gone wrong, that's just terrible. Are you guys investigating?"

So there must have been a leak coming from somewhere if the Bureau and the White House were now saying it was a carjacking, just as Connelly had said they would do. Sparks pulled out his phone and saw that there was, indeed, a missed call from Connelly with a voice message waiting. Sparks had silenced his phone because he'd wanted to relax and think as he drove to Gettysburg.

"I hadn't heard about the announcement, but yes, we are investigating," Sparks said.

"Are you on it?"

"You know I can't talk about an ongoing investigation."

"Oh, come on. You're telling me that agents don't talk to their wives or husbands about cases they're on?" Munson set the timer for the pasta. "Pillow talk and all."

Sparks smiled. "I suppose, but you and I aren't married, my dear, and so that privilege stays reserved. Besides, you know the Bureau has me on a short lease. If I get in trouble for any reason—"

"I was there, Jason, remember? When Connelly stepped into the job, right before the closed-door hearings began into the Bureau and Griffin's death. He shielded you pretty well, so to me, as an observer, I got the idea he probably considered you an asset he wanted to keep and any leash you were going to be on would be short lived." She leaned against the counter and crossed her arms in front of her chest, giving him a mischievous look.

"You ever think of being an analyst for the FBI?" Sparks chuckled and held out his hand. She accepted and put her arms around him. "Yes, Connelly wanted to keep me as an asset and took heat from more than one congressman, but it won't last forever if I don't keep a low profile. Anyway, I still can't talk about the case."

"Fair enough. Can you set the table? I have to finish making the salad, and you're in charge of opening the wine after you do the table."

"Yes, ma'am. During dinner, I want to talk to you about something."

"Sounds intriguing." Munson grinned.

"I can't talk about the case, but I want your help on it just the same."

SPARKS LISTENED FOR THE rumble of thunder, as he had just seen the flash of lightning through the Brenda's bedroom window. Sleep was coming more difficult than he'd imagined it would after their lovemaking. She was, in many ways, especially in tune with his idiosyncrasies. He enjoyed holding her after sex when they would talk about various things, but when it came time to sleep, like him, she liked to retreat to her side of the queen-sized bed. They both liked having room to stretch out when sleeping, but while she was gone in a matter of minutes, he was unusually left more wired than before.

Something about this case gnawed at Sparks's gut. Two men were dead, one of them a very public figure. Whoever wanted them dead was willing to risk the scrutiny that a murder would bring. Torrez himself had implicated Sterling Raven, but evidence eluded them. Implying Raven was responsible was a long way from proving it. And with the Civil War-era document taken, possibly by Raven's team, then it could very well be destroyed already and the matter ended.

Sparks turned over on his side and watched Munson slowly breathe in and out. For the first time in years, he felt real contentment. There were similarities between Brenda and his first wife, Casey, but there were definite differences that Sparks was pleased to recognize. If Brenda was simply a vague copy of Casey, then he would consider it a warning. Brenda was different in appearance and, in most cases, temperament; it filled Sparks with confidence that he was headed in the right direction with her. He stretched his legs out and pounded the pillow into a comfortable shape and closed his eyes.

There was nothing to be gained anymore tonight.

June 5

TAYLOR ANSWERED THE DOOR to her Wilkes-Barre hotel room already dressed for their visit on Raven. Her eyebrows arched, and she smiled briefly at Sparks as he entered her room.

"You looked rested," she said. "A successful stopover in... wherever you were?"

"Yes, it was great, except I had to get up before six to get up here in time to look over the dossier on Raven. You texted me the meeting is set for 2 p.m."

"Yeah, and his secretary kept asking what our request was all about. I told her it was a matter of national security. Since Raven's company is one of the largest defense contractors, she probably has heard that before."

"Most likely from the Defense Department or Homeland Security, but not necessarily from the FBI," Sparks said. "Hopefully it piqued his interest."

"Well, Connelly called just a half hour ago." Taylor sat on the edge of the nearest of the two double beds. "Raven called his office directly and asked about why we were requesting this meeting. Connelly spoke with him directly and simply told him we were investigating a case and Raven's name came up."

"We'll tell him everything except that Torrez implicated him," Sparks said. "Either Raven is behind this mess or Mallory is."

"I was thinking, perhaps, just maybe, Torrez and Collins were playing both sides," Taylor said.

"I considered that. We'll see how our meeting with Raven goes."

Taylor got up and headed for the door as Sparks opened the dossier and settled into the room's only comfortable chair. "I'm going to get some lunch in the restaurant next door. Do you want me to bring something back?"

"No, I grabbed food on the road."

"Enjoy the reading."

It didn't take more than a minute for Sparks to be surprised by Sterling Raven. The company had been based in Newburgh, New York during the Civil War, but then the offices were moved to just south of Scranton, Pennsylvania about twenty years after the war. Through the years, the company's divisions produced many different types of weapons, evolving as technology changed. Except for a stretch in the late 1800s, the company was well run, and while there was some divestiture in non-military products, the bulk of the company's value was always in making weapons of war. The line of Raven men who ran the company was unbroken from the time it was founded just before the war in 1859.

The same year as the document they had seen in Vermont.

In the years following World War II, Raven Industries became Raven Technology Industries and opened production facilities outside Los Angeles and in Silicon Valley outside San Francisco. They also had opened offices in New York and in Washington, D.C. The company was still privately owned, and there had never been any hint at a public offering.

Sterling Raven's personal history was just as impressive. Fifty-five years old, he was an intimidating 6'5" tall and about 240 pounds. The dossier's photo showed him to have sandy blond hair with a weather-worn face, as he spent much of his free time sailing when he was on the west coast visiting the offices in Los Angeles or Fresno. He played football when he was an undergrad at Notre Dame, then got his MBA from the Wharton School of Business at the University of Pennsylvania. He was a good tight end in college and could have played pro ball, but he went straight to graduate school.

He inherited the family business with his younger sister when his father and younger brother were killed in a plane crash when he was thirty-five. He had worked hard in the last ten years to expand the company's political influence in Washington and had procured four significant defense contracts, each worth close to twenty-five billion dollars. Raven was married with a twenty-five-year-old son and two teen daughters. The son, Samuel Raven, had just graduated with his MBA from Pennsylvania, a Wharton man just like his father. It was obvious who was being groomed to run the company.

The dossier included a list of men on Capitol Hill that Raven was known to associate with on at least a professional level, and Brighton Mallory's name was included, which didn't surprise Sparks, considering the amount of federal business RTI did. Whether there was any deeper relationship, the dossier didn't say. It did include a summary list of properties Raven owned—a villa in France near the Alps, a condo outside of Scranton, a house in Malibu, California, one outside of Fresno, a summer estate on Long Island, and a house on the water in Boca Raton, Florida. The wife and children lived in Malibu full time, and Raven spent more time there than any other residence except during the summer, when he took the whole family to the Hamptons.

Raven Technology Industries gave money to both political parties in equal amounts, always to the national committees and not to individual candidates. Sterling Raven seemed to be apolitical, and his company had benefited no matter what party held the executive branch or control in Congress. The Defense Department and the various military branches were universal in their praise of Raven's products and their application in the field.

Aside from competitive sailing, he had financed an America's Cup entry in each competition since he was twenty-five, and twice his crew had been the U.S. representative in the final competition. Raven was an avid golfer and kept in shape by cycling twenty miles a week. He dabbled in electric guitar and was known to be a big Springsteen and U2 fan, attending concerts as often as his schedule would allow. He was not known to see any women outside of his marriage, and his wife, Lisa, was the CEO of the couple's foundation, which funded cancer research and provided scholarships to economically underprivileged students.

Sparks read through the dossier twice to obtain a thorough view of Raven and came away impressed. How could a reader not be? This was a man born into money, yes, but he had expanded his influence beyond what his father had done and invested heavily in future human capital. He also gave back significantly to charitable causes and was successful in almost every endeavor.

Taylor came back into the room with a cup of coffee she offered to Sparks.

"Impressive reading, wouldn't you say?" she asked.

"You aren't kidding. This guy's too good to be true."

"Too good to be involved in murder?"

"Doesn't seem to be his style, but he certainly has a lot to protect if he was threatened." Sparks closed the dossier and put it next to Taylor's briefcase. "We should take the same tact we did with Mallory."

"Agreed."

To say Sterling Raven was an imposing figure was a first-degree understatement. The dossier had said he was about 240 pounds. "Maybe twenty pounds ago," Sparks thought as he shook the industrialist's hand, a vice-like grip the FBI agent returned with equal vigor. He had blue eyes, and his skin was much darker from sun exposure on the water—it was easy to tell because the skin around his eyes was lighter by the sunglasses he apparently wore outside. He carried the air of someone who knew he was the smartest and wealthiest man in any room he graced. He was dressed in a dark blue suit that Sparks figured was a good month's salary for him, impeccably tailored to his immense frame.

"Agent Sparks, it's good to meet you." Raven motioned Sparks and Taylor, whom he had already greeted, into the two elegant chairs placed perfectly in front of his desk. "Either of you like coffee to get through the afternoon?"

They both politely declined, and Raven settled into his chair, closing his laptop minimizing the screen on his desktop machine, which was open to a multi-graphed business screen continuously updating information from the stock exchange. He folded his hands in front of himself on the desk and said, "Let's get to it."

Taylor and Sparks spent the next ten minutes explaining what had happened since the discovery of Torrez's body, including everything except a mention of Brighton Mallory's connection to Justice Mallory and the 1859 document. Raven listened intently, remaining motionless. When Sparks finished, he paused, and Raven leaned back in his chair, nodding his head almost imperceptibly.

"That's an intriguing story, to be sure," Raven said. "You are sure Augustus Raven's name was mentioned in this document?"

"We only had a look at it for a minute, but both of us saw it plainly," Taylor said.

"If this document—your agreement—is between my great, great, great grandfather and this..."

"Justice Mallory," Taylor said.

"Justice Mallory, I can't imagine it having much importance now, but I can tell you that I will fight any challenge to my family and this company with a furor you can't imagine. This company is my family's legacy, its identity." Raven stood up and walked over to the wall opposite the office's windows. It was adorned with dark paneling, and hanging prominently, taking up two-thirds of the surface, were framed plaques that appeared to be certificates. "These honors here have been bestowed upon this company by every branch of the military, by veteran's groups, senators and representatives, foreign governments, all a testament to the men and women who work for me and our partnership with Washington to provide the tools necessary to keep our country safe from outside threats."

"And you haven't been contacted by anyone in connection with these documents?" Sparks asked.

"I'd contact the FBI directly. You must know I'm personally acquainted with Director Connelly. I'd be on the phone with him the minute a threat was posted against this company. With our national security importance, it would be my obligation. I'd welcome the protection the FBI or any of the other agencies could provide us. We're all linked together."

"So you can't imagine what this old document could be?" Taylor asked. "There's been no mention of it in your family's history. You have to admit, your family prides itself on its history and this company. You must have records from every major transaction ever made by Raven Industries since its inception."

"We do, and you're welcome to them." Raven was back at his desk. "I'm afraid the nineteenth-century records aren't stored digitally yet. It's taken us years just to get the last century done. It's a work in progress, but I know the record keeping was pretty exact, so if you give a year, it probably would be a workable amount of paper to go through.

"But I can't fathom what would be so valuable as to cost the lives of two men. Should I be concerned about the safety of myself and my family?"

"We have no indication there is a threat," Sparks said, "but we have little to go on. It would be prudent for you to take precautions until we're further along with the investigation."

"I have impeccable security that travels with my family and myself. I bet they would rival your Secret Service details that cover the president." Raven managed a smile at Taylor. "I'll take precautions, but I don't believe I'll need outside assistance."

"Nevertheless, I think it would be wise to give us your itinerary for the next month," Sparks said. "Your safety needs may change as our investigation progresses."

Raven nodded in agreement. "I'll have my assistant provide my business and personal plans. And I'll have him make arrangements to get you access to our records from any timeframe you want."

"BOTH MALLORY AND RAVEN know more than they are letting on," Sparks said as he climbed into the driver's side of their car. "You notice how, while dismissing the document's importance by saying he couldn't see how it could initiate the violent actions we've seen, in the next breath he said he would fight any challenge to his family or company?"

"I caught that as well," Taylor said. "Do you suppose Torrez and Collins were blackmailing one or both of them—Raven or Mallory?"

"Possibly. We have Torrez's financials. We'll get a court order for Collins's and see if there were any significant deposits, but I doubt we'll find anything."

"Why?"

"The documents were still in Collins's possession until the attack on us, so if those two were blackmailing, say, Raven, no payment had been made yet. And it could have been a third party we aren't aware of that was responsible for stealing the documents, not Raven or Mallory at all."

"Should we get surveillance in place for Raven and Mallory?" Taylor asked.

"Absolutely, but we're going to have to tread lightly. We're talking about a sitting United States senator and a major military contractor. This could all blow up in our face."

"If the document was taken by the party being black-mailed, then it's over and done with unless we come across something else from Torrez or Collins."

"Tom was going to go over a forensic eval on their recent search activities online, and we can go over their daily activities for the past few months." Sparks shrugged. "Without knowing the nature of the documents and why they were important, we'll be hard pressed to come up with a motive."

"You mean other than simply keeping the document from seeing the light of day," Taylor said.

Sparks turned the car onto the main road, heading back into Scranton. "Raven is the one with the ancestor who began what became a multi-billion-dollar company, and Mallory had the ancestor who disappeared into obscurity during the Civil War. I'll bet present-day Raven is the man with something to lose here."

"I wish we knew what that document was all about, just what Augustus Raven and Brighton Mallory were all about."

"I've got someone working on that angle right now," Sparks said. "Maybe she'll be able to come up with something."

"She?"

"My girlfriend. She's a historian. If anyone can come up with information on those two, it will be her."

"Girlfriend? I'll bet that's the first time you ever used that word about her," Taylor mused.

Sparks thought for a second. "You know, you're right."

June 6

THE MALLORY RESIDENCE AND compound was situated in the mountains north of Tucson, nestled into a notch between two ridges that swept up to the lower part of a much larger peak. In this part of Arizona, loose rocks, scrub brush, small cacti, and larger saguaros dominate the land and make moving any distance a labor of picking and choosing the best route and slowly proceeding.

The compound consisted of a twelve thousand-square-foot adobe-style main house, which faced west with the back porch/pool area backing up against the view of the ridge, and beyond, the Catalina Mountains. The house was fronted on two sides by a five-car garage and a separate servants' quarters. The entire complex had an eight-foot wall and an eight-hundred-foot drive from the complex to the gated entrance. When Mallory visited, two guards were stationed at the front gate and two more roamed the one-hundred-acre grounds.

For the two FBI agents assigned to surveillance, it was impossible to do so without Mallory or his staff knowing they were there. The property was isolated from other residences, and the open territory provided no chance for cover, so Agents Garcia and Harrington resigned themselves to sitting off the access road in plain view. The sun just above the horizon behind them provided a spectacular view of the ridges and mountains to their east, bathing them in a fiery glow. The temperature still hovered around a hundred degrees, but they were content to sit in the air-conditioned car and wait for their relief at 10 p.m. to take over.

Mallory had arrived in Tucson early in the day and had attended a fundraiser sponsored by some University of Arizona boosters. He had arrived at the compound about 5 p.m., and there had been no activity since. As the light faded from the massive mountains above them, Garcia and Harrington broke open the sandwiches they had bought on their way up Oracle Road, past the towns of Oro Valley and Catalina to the access road that took them through the desert from the main road. As they finished their foot-longs and chips, night fully arrived on the high desert.

Harrington had stepped out of the car and was standing behind a three-armed, thirty-foot-tall Saguaro answering the call of nature when he saw the lights coming along the access road. It was a panel van, and it approached slowly, as if the driver was unsure of the road. Harrington picked his way along the eighty feet back to the car.

"Van," he said as Garcia stepped out of the car.

"Kind of late for a delivery," Garcia said.

For the van to reach the front gate, it would have to travel within a few yards of their position. The two agents stood beside the car as the van slid past their position. The baseball-capped driver turned to look directly at them with a grin they could see even in the gloom of dusk.

"What the hell made him so happy?" Garcia asked.

The van continued past them and traveled four hundred feet up the access road and turned into the short drive up to the Mallory gate. The two agents saw the brake lights come on as the van stopped where the guard door was situated. It was dark enough now that the agents' view of the guard door was obscured, but just as the guard appeared in the doorway, a voice came from the desert behind them.

"Hey, shitheads!" the voice yelled.

Garcia and Harrington both turned just in time to take two shots each in the chest from the silenced automatic held by the camouflaged figure standing by the very same saguaro Harrington had used earlier. They fell silently to the ground next to the car as the guard at the gatehouse simultaneously took two shots into his chest before he had even stepped across the threshold. Even as he slumped to the floor, the panel van's door slid open and two figures jumped out and moved directly over the dead guard, moving wordlessly to the back room where the other guard was stationed. They found him just rising from his chair with a perplexed look as they fired more rounds into him before he could even shout a warning from his headset to the two roving guards within the compound.

"They're as unprofessional as we figured," one of the men said to his partner. "Two left on patrol."

One of them pushed the button to open the gate and they pulled the one guard in the threshold inside and out of sight. As they got back in the van, a figure came trotting up to the passenger side door and climbed in. The van proceeded through the gate and made its way up the drive to the main house.

CHAPTER FIFTEEN

Dec. 16, 1863

TRUE TO HER WORD, Byrne brought a parcel of documents and ledgers back to her room the following night. Brison went over them with her for two hours. Mallory had indeed been a minority partner with Raven in the company that carried the latter's name. Signatures from Mallory regularly appeared on some of the documents, items like bills of sale, coal shipment receipts, personnel hiring forms, and purchasing orders for various bulk materials. It showed that Mallory was a significant partner but Raven still had final say in all major transactions.

"There's nothing here that tells us if or why there was a disagreement between Mallory and Raven. There's nothing that shows just how much stake Mallory has in the company." Brison slumped back in the chair, his shoulders rounded in defeat.

"I could go back and see if there are any incorporation papers," Byrne said hopefully. "If they entered into a partnership, there have to be papers somewhere, not only here, but copies with Mallory and copies wherever the business was filed."

"Probably New York, wouldn't you say?"

Byrne nodded.

"Take these back so they aren't missed," Brison said. "And if you would, check on what you can find, but for God's sake, command discretion, Cathleen. If you find something amiss, send me notice. I'll check the telegraph office daily and the post as well. I'll be in Springfield through the new year before I return to Washington. Don't take any risks."

"He may call on me to travel to Washington myself if he decides to have a lengthy stay," Byrne said. "What should I do?"

"Continue on as you would. Go to Washington and do as he asks. Everything should be as always to his eyes. After you look into these documents, I don't want you to do anything else. You have already provided invaluable services. You saved my life, by Lord. I can't repay you in any way in equal measure."

"You do have that effect on people, Colonel Brison," she said with a smile.

He moved to the window again after turning down the light to a low level, picked up his rifle, and slid up the frame. "Be watchful. We will meet again, I'm sure. Let me know if he calls on you."

"I will."

Brison moved through the window, closed it, and made the familiar way over the roof of the attached storage shed. He gently dropped himself down to where he had built up a makeshift stack of crates to get access to the roof. His horse was tied to a tree about two hundred feet in the tree line near a trail that led back to the road further down toward town.

Across the side alley next to the boarding house, a lone figure watched as Brison climbed out of the window and traversed the roof before disappearing. He took a short puff on the last bit of a cigar and dropped it into the mud and slop he was standing in. He left his watching post, made his way onto the main street, and trudged off to find a bottle and a warm bed. His night's work was completed.

Dec. 20, 1863

THE DAY AFTER MEETING Byrne, Brison sent a wire to Washington informing Nicolay to tell the president that he was taking his commander's advice and heading home to Springfield but he found posted news in the office that changed his plans. General John Buford, a friend he had last seen during the battle at Gettysburg in the summer, had died from an illness the previous day in Washington. Brison felt compelled to travel there for the services and did so, making it to the city this morning ahead of the services. He was offered a place as a pallbearer because Buford's staff and wife, Pattie, knew the depth of their friendship, but he instead chose to remain in the background.

Lincoln himself attended the service for the man considered one of the significant heroes of the Gettysburg victory. Brison walked in the procession and helped to attend Buford's horse Grey Eagle, but after that, he slipped away from the service and went over to where Pattie, who was too ill to attend, was staying. He visited with her for almost an hour, much of it alone as he comforted her.

After his time there, he decided on a walk back to the boarding house. He stopped in a small drinking establishment, for he felt the need of a bracer. He was tired from the travel over the past weeks, and he dreaded that another trip was necessary if he was going to see his family, but there was no doubt it was enough inducement.

"Good day, Colonel." A man sat down a table away from Brison and shoved off his own coat. The man was a stranger, but he knew rank insignia because Brison was dressed in his uniform for the funeral. He was a rough-looking sort but clean and well kept, with a sturdy frame and dock worker's hands both in size and appearance. He acknowledged Brison's uniform. "You were attending General Buford's services?"

"Yes."

"Did you know the general?"

Brison funneled up his eyebrows. He didn't feel like an interrogation over a whiskey, particularly on this day. The man's voice carried a distinctive Irish accent, one that came from perhaps having not been raised on this continent. "Yes, I knew him."

"Ah, sad news it was. I hear he was a fine general." The man took a drink and continued, "I read all about his doins' out there in Pennsylvania. I don't know nothin' about military goings-on, but the newspapers said he was a hero, so that's good enough an opinion for me."

"He was a good man."

"You stationed here, Colonel?"

Normally, tavern talk over a whiskey settled well with Brison, but he wasn't in an easy frame of mind. He had already decided this was a one-whiskey stop. "Yes, but I travel some too."

"Name's Flanagan, Colonel. I work construction. Got no work today because an order of materials didn't come in and the foreman sent us all off."

"On a Sunday?"

"Work's gotta be done," Flanagan said. "You posted for the holiday, or you getting to go home?"

Brison was really annoyed now. This Flanagan was going to initiate a long-winded conversation that was going to spread to the war, politics, and the Negro situation or maybe a half dozen other complaints about the capital city. He threw back the remainder of his whiskey and started to pull on his overcoat. "I'm headed home on furlough, and I've got tasks ahead of me before I go tomorrow. Good day to you."

The news of the furlough seemed to brighten Flanagan's face. "You're a lucky man, gittin' to be home with family for the holidays. I wish you a speedy journey, Colonel." He pulled out a pouch of tobacco and took an enormous wad to stuff into his mouth. It was so large that Brison reacted with a smirk even in his dour mood. When Flanagan tried to speak, it was well-muffled by the tobacco. "I love my chewin'."

Brison shook his head as he walked back into the chilly afternoon.

Dec. 30, 1863

Louise Elizabeth filled the small concert hall with music. A melodic flurry of her fingers across the piano's keyboard produced a piece with which Brison was unfamiliar, one she no doubt had been practicing during his long absences over the past eighteen months.

Brison sat alone at the Wednesday night recital put on by the Springfield Methodist Church. The children were with Elizabeth's parents for the night. A two-hour recital was not conducive to keeping children from squirming in their seats. Brison himself found that sitting for a long period of time presented itself with its own difficulty as his shoulder and back would begin to bark if he was motionless for a time. It's not that he didn't appreciate his wife's talent—he often complimented her on her ability and secretly wondered why she had married him in the first place instead of pursuing a career playing in the world's finest concert halls. He truly felt that could have been her life if she had so chosen. He was blessed with her love, and on this night, he sat with contentment amid neighbors and acquaintances listening to her create astounding music.

And yet his mind wandered from the music.

It drifted to Washington and to what lay ahead of him, or at least what he could piece together with the scant information he had to decipher. He had received a parcel by courier from Lincoln that very morning with detailed information about the man Brison had heard mentioned in the Willard that night.

Brigadier General Judson Kilpatrick was certainly an officer of note, graduating from West Point fifteenth out of his class of fifty and went right from class to the battlefront. Within six months, he had advanced four ranks and through the almost three years of the war and had earned a reputation as brave, yet reckless, commander. His record was one of uncommon inconsistency in manner, leading successful cavalry raids through Virginia and Pennsylvania but also having been arrested for selling confiscated horses and tobacco only to have the charges dropped.

He was not afraid to remind everyone of his greatness on the battlefield even to the point of grossly enhancing the reports of his success to superior officers. He was known to keep a mistress in his camp, which Brison didn't find surprising, as it wasn't uncommon, but from Nicolay's report to Lincoln, it appeared Kilpatrick's reputation was one of excess.

Brison always prided himself on not judging a soul until he met them and evaluated their character. He thought he measured up well with that talent, but it would be difficult with this one. Bravery was an admirable trait, but recklessness... that Brison judged harshly.

Along with the report on Kilpatrick was an unsigned note—obviously from Lincoln—that spoke of no approach about a raid into Richmond but pressure was being brought to bear on the administration because of the Union prisoners held in Richmond. Brison had been reading about these prisoners held at Libby Prison. It spoke of extreme conditions, and newspaper editorials were calling for something to be done. Perhaps something might be coming soon. Just as Brison confirmed in his own mind that it was indeed time for him to travel back to Washington, he realized the crowd around him was clapping, as Elizabeth had finished her performance.

"She is such a splendid talent at the piano, Colonel," the dry goods store owner, John Peterson, said over the applause. He was seated next to Brison. "You must be so proud of her."

"Yes, I am," Brison replied, feeling more than a bit guilty for having not listened to the final few minutes of her performance. "The family is very proud."

SHE KISSED HIM WITH a slowness of satiated desire and put her head on his chest.

Brison watched in the near dark as her head rose and fell with his labored breathing. He smiled to himself.

"I find myself longing for a message from the president that my furlough has been extended indefinitely," he whispered as he stroked her hair. "I will miss evenings like this. Music, a meal with good company, and taking you to bed."

Elizabeth took the moment to pull herself closer to him. "Andrew, I love you so, and I have asked you to resign your commission and return home, if not for the concerns for your safety, then to avoid the times when you come home on furlough and scarcely leave me a moment to sleep at night. You have a powerful desire that you unleash upon me every time I haven't seen you in a while."

"Sakes alive, are you complaining, my love?"

He could almost feel her smile in the dark. "No, darling."

"Are you saying I'm too horny when I come back from the war?"

She slapped his stomach. "I'll not have you use that language in the house," she said in a mocking tone. "What would happen if you let slip a foul word or two in front of the children? Then how would you feel?"

"Never you mind worrying about that. I would rather face a cavalry charge from J. E. B. Stewart himself than face your wrath by letting a word slip here or there." He let her chuckle a moment before he kissed her gently on the top of her head. "There is something I need to tell you."

"It's time for you to go back to Washington?"

"I'm afraid it is. And I want you to stay at your father's house with the children until I wire you that it's safe."

"There is so much to do with the livestock and fixin' up the tools and such for the spring, we need to stay here." Elizabeth's voice carried little conviction.

"Your father is helping us with paying the help and they can take care of duties until this business is over with, but until then, I would have less on my mind if my family was safely with your father's extended family of militia men in town. I wouldn't insist unless I felt there was a reason. Please don't get a dander up about this."

She rubbed his stomach with the flat of her hand. "I still feel it's proper that I oversee the men's work at the farm."

"If it makes you feel satisfied with the arrangement, then so be it," Brison said, "but I don't want you working with any of those heavy tools. One slip and I wouldn't be able to hear you play like you did tonight."

"I agree... Colonel Brison."

"Didn't mean for it to come down the road as an order."

She reached up to kiss him, lingering for a moment before she resumed with her head against his chest. "What is all of this business with the president this time? You have been quiet since you've been home. Can you not give me just a little hint?"

"It started out as looking into some foul business with some of the cannon factories up here but has now changed into something else entirely. I have no idea where it will lead, but that's why Washington is now on my compass."

"The children will find it hard again."

"Not any harder than the other children missing their fathers." They remained quiet for a few minutes during which time Brison felt sleep pulling at him, the dull ache in his shoulder subdued for the night. He was drifting off, comforted by the warmth of Elizabeth's body next to his and the covers wrapping them in a cocoon. It could have been a dream, but he thought he heard her tell him something about taking care and reminding him that his first duty would always be to his family and Lincoln asked too much of him. He was so tired, he couldn't remember if he responded.

Jan. 7, 1864

BRISON STAYED FOR THE new year, then traveled by train from Springfield to Baltimore, picked up his horse, and rode from there into Washington and returned to the boarding house he used whenever he was in the city. Since he was not attached to a specific unit—not even the Bureau of Military Information—he rarely wore his uniform unless it suited the situation. He arrived late in the afternoon, took a bath, and changed into his uniform because he was going to need it so he could blend in where he was going. The sun was nearing the western horizon behind the gray covering of a winter sky as he arrived at the BMI office. He was searching for a clerk who worked as one of the assistants to John Babcock, who, together with Colonel George Sharpe, had created the BMI a year ago.

Brison stood in front of an attendant in the outer office and waited for some acknowledgement, becoming irritated when it stretched to over a minute.

"I would like to see Mr. Babcock's assistant, Mr. Pope," Brison said.

"Mr. Babcock and Mr. Pope are both unavailable," the elderly clerk responded without so much as a glance upward. "You can leave a message and/or schedule an appointment for next week."

Brison realized he could get more done with civility than with confrontation, but he was fatigued from the trip and not rightly in the mood for incompetence. Yet he tried again.

"Mr. Pope will want to see me immediately. Please send word along that Colonel Brison is here to speak with him... briefly."

The old man summoned the initiative to raise his head up. "As I said, Mr. Pope is not available..." He looked over the uniformed Brison. "Message or appointment?" He looked down again at his ledger where he was copying information from a messy stack of loose papers.

Brison looked around. Two others were working in the office, but they were at desks in the far corners and were oblivious to Brison and Methuselah here at the front desk. With a sigh, he dropped his riding gloves down onto the ledger the clerk was working on and leaned in on the desk.

"Send a runner to get Mr. Pope or I daresay you won't have a job anymore." Brison's stare grabbed the old man's attention, whose face went from annoyance to fear in moment.

"We don't have a runner now, and I'm not allowed to leave the desk for unannounced visitors. Not my rules, Colonel."

Brison cursed under his breath, reclaimed his gloves, and moved down the hallway to his left as the clerk made a half effort to verbally turn him around. Four doors down, he found a nameplate with Pope's name on it. Brison knocked twice and stepped into the doorway. Robert Pope was standing at his desk talking to another man while looking over what Brison could see from the doorway was a map.

"Robert," Brison said. "Sorry to interrupt, but could I have a quick word?"

"Andrew, uh, Colonel. Good to see you, but I'm paddling in the middle of the stream here, and neither side is close. Can you give me a few minutes and I'll come out to the main office there?" Pope obviously didn't want Brison in his office.

"Better choice, how about me treating you to dinner in an hour or so at Willard's?"

Pope gave a glance at his companion. "Sure, I have no plans. Let's make it eight. I'll meet you in the front lobby. You confident you can get us a table at this late hour?"

"I know the owner, and he owes me a favor." Brison gave a grin. "Eight o'clock it is."

BRISON HAD ALWAYS THOUGHT of Robert Pope as a decent man, loyal to his friends and, from what he had been told, an honest worker who gave a hard day's work for his salary. He was unassuming and didn't draw attention to himself; in fact, he could best be described as average in almost every way—height, weight, amount of facial hair. His voice carried no special nature, and his manner led one to completely forget about him after you had passed him by. He had been married but lost his wife to illness two years ago, had not remarried, and had no children.

As he approached Brison's table at the restaurant in Willard's, he was undoing the buttons on his mud brown overcoat, stuffing gloves into his pockets, and unwrapping his scarf. Yes, he was perfect for maneuvering about this politically dominated city that, during this war, was trans-forming on a weekly basis with all sorts of unique charac-ters throwing themselves about on display. He was invisible, which was why Brison was interested in talking with him, for Pope may have been a bland person in appearance—wholly forgettable—he was, in Brison's estimation, the one person who knew everything about everyone important. That in-cluded both in the worlds of politics and the Army.

Brison rose to shake Pope's hand and offered him the chair at their two-person table in the corner. It was close to the kitchen but away from other tables so they would be able to speak freely.

"I daresay I was surprised to see you, Andrew." Pope settled into his chair.

"Well, I'd like to say I showed up just to catch up, but you know me better. I wanted to cultivate some information, and I was sure you could help me. Then after that, we can catch up on things."

"Always charging ahead, that's our Andrew, but I won't allow you to steer us away before I ask how Louise Elizabeth is. Have you been home to see her and the little ones?"

"I was home on furlough during Christmas time. They're all doing well."

"You're a lucky man, Andrew. She is an exceptional woman. My Mary counted her as her best friend from Massachusetts—really, they were almost like sisters."

"I know, Robert. Mary's death was hard for Elizabeth. We all miss her."

Pope nodded without a word as the waiter brought menus and took their drink orders. Once they were alone again, Pope held up his hands briefly. "So what do you need?"

"You know I'm not attached to the Bureau of Military Information or to Baker's people at Union Intelligence," Brison said.

"But you work for someone important. Your name has come up now and again. They were investigating some businessman up in Philadelphia for suspected ties to Southern sympathizers after a job you worked on. That's how I last heard about you."

"I'm not involved with that for now. I'm working on something else, and I need some background information on Brigadier General Judson Kilpatrick."

"Kilcalvary?"

"What's that?"

"His nickname. Given to him, no doubt, by some of the surviving cavalrymen under his command. They consider him a no-account fool. Too easy with spending the lives under his command. The officers above him put up with him because he brings with him all sorts of newspaper attention paired with measurable results at times. I hear he is fearless, something the men begrudgingly accept, but he still shows such a disregard for his men that one wonders how effective a commander he will be in the long haul. He does have some powerful friends both in the Army and roaming the halls up the avenue."

"I was given a summation on him, and this was mentioned. Anyone in particular?"

"Senator Howard from Michigan... and Howard's got Lincoln's ear."

"Does he?"

"Yes, as I believe you do."

"Is that what you've heard?" Brison asked.

"I've heard you have access."

"Seems secrets are hard to keep around you, Robert."

"I don't need the details, never you mind." Pope paused as the waiter returned, brought their drinks, and took their orders. "Kilpatrick is also ready to blare his own bugle, I hear, with gusto. He'll wake snakes about anything he's attached to if it will get eyes on his person, and there are those in the Army that hate him for it."

"Army's got plenty of those such folks." Brison gave a small laugh.

"That it does. There was also a dust-up a while back between Kilpatrick and a General Custer. It was much ado about a woman staying at the camp, and the talk was she was giving up her charms. She was quite the adventuress."

"Was Kilpatrick reprimanded?"

"No, it was whitewashed, but it was a bit embarrassing to the Army. It died down after a spell. Like I said, he has friends that can render assistance."

"Have you heard anything about him leading a raid into Richmond?" Brison asked.

"No, can't say as I have." Pope sat back and looked about as it appeared he was trying to recall. "There has been a lot of talk about the prison down there in Richmond. Rebs are keeping our boys there in a bad way. I know a lot of talk says we should be sending an army down to free those men. I wouldn't be surprised if we're planning to do just that."

Brison decided to take a longshot. "Have you ever heard of a Justice Mallory?"

Pope tilted his head and took a drink of his bourbon that had just arrived. After a moment, he nodded his head. "There's a Mallory that works in the Reb government. Think he works for Jeff Davis himself. Can't recall the first name."

"It's Justice. Know anything more?"

"Can't say as I do. What's the news on this?"

Brison held up his own drink in a belated toast. "Now, you know this is a one-sided deal here, but back to Kilpatrick. You know where he's stationed right now?"

"No. Somewhere around here, I'd expect. Everyone's biding their time 'til the warm weather arrives, then I'd expect you'll see the ugliness begin again. How much longer do you think the war can continue?"

"Hopefully within the year. Do you know anything about Kilpatrick's personal life, his business dealings?"

Pope's shoulders sagged a touch, and he turned his glass in his hand. "He lost his wife in November the same way I lost my Mary, to the influenza. He has an infant child, I believe. As far as business dealings, I don't know. I could make some discreet inquiries for you."

"I would appreciate it. Have you ever heard of Augustus Raven?"

"Of course. He's the industrialist. Does a lot of production for the war effort."

"Ever heard of them mentioned together?"

"No," Pope said.

"One last question about all this business." Brison leaned forward and looked around to make sure no one was showing interest in them. Satisfied, he continued, "Have you ever heard Stanton's name mentioned with any of these people?"

Pope straightened in his chair away from Brison. "You'll not get rumor from me about him. I've heard of people reassigned to most unpleasant duty when they've come to bad feelings from him. Never met the man and don't want to."

"Land sakes, what are you worried about?" Brison asked.

"I'd just as soon stay away from him. I don't want to come out on the little end of the horn."

Pope's uncomfortable response surprised Brison. "Well, I have met the man, and I admit he comes across like a gruff old bear at times. I don't believe you have anything to worry about from him."

"Well, anyway, I haven't heard any of those others mentioned with him."

Brison decided to change the subject and began to talk about his visit home and the latest news about the children. He knew Pope always wanted to hear about the children and their latest misdoings. The food arrived a few minutes later. Their discussion then flowed from family to Pope's duties at the Bureau while they ate the superb meal. He filed away Pope's reaction to the mention of Stanton as another reason to tread cautiously on this assignment.

CHAPTER SIXTEEN

Present Day
June 7

SPARKS ACCEPTED THE CAR from the attendant at the car rental garage just off the main terminal from Tucson International Airport and climbed into the driver's seat. He started to plug in the address for Mallory's compound into the GPS device on the dashboard as Taylor finished putting their bags in the trunk. It had been five hours since he received the phone call at 4:00 a.m. eastern from Brighton Mallory himself, describing an attack on his house and staff. Local police were on the scene and the family was safe, but Mallory demanded that Sparks and Taylor fly out to Tucson to see what had happened and continue their investigation. He had sounded almost apoplectic on the phone, but then again, Sparks had only been asleep for a few hours after getting back into Washington. He had called Taylor, and they had procured a private Bureau plane for the flight out. Both were rested, as they had been able to sleep on the plane.

They left the airport and drove through the city to the west and north until they reached one of the main north-south streets—Oracle—and took the street out of Tucson and north to the Mallory compound. They had talked briefly about what the attack meant, but having determined sleep was more important, they had suspended their discussion.

"This play could only mean one thing," Taylor said as Sparks maneuvered through traffic. "Someone believes Mallory had the documents in his possession."

"Provided this had anything to do with the documents at all," Sparks replied, "but since I don't believe in coincidences, let's go under that assumption. But then why call in the local police and us? It doesn't make sense."

"Because if he did have the documents, he's responsible for the deaths of Torrez, Collins, and the Vermont trooper," Taylor finished.

"Or..." Sparks held up his right-hand index finger. "... there's a third party involved like we talked about that's playing the two of them against each other."

"But for what purpose?"

"We don't know enough yet. We'll listen to what Mallory has to say."

There were high, thin clouds in the sky over southern Arizona, but it was still already over a hundred degrees as they reached the Mallory compound and were met by a group of police and forensic vehicles. There were also four FBI vehicles from the Phoenix Bureau on scene. As they got out of their car, a bald man wearing a suit and an FBI identification badge clipped to his pocket approached them.

"You Sparks?" he asked.

"Jason Sparks. This is Special Agent Bethany Taylor with the Secret Service."

"Josh Tobin. I'm with Phoenix. Welcome to the high desert. Did you pack plenty of water? It sucks right now, but wait 'till there aren't any clouds and it's early afternoon. Then you'll learn just how wonderful this area is in the summertime."

"Yeah, I get it. It's hot."

"Yeah, all right. Here's what we got so far. Just after dusk last night, a group of well-armed and trained assailants shot down two of ours down by the main road and then also took out the two guards at the gate. There was a single panel van with Arizona plates and no lettering that approached the house. One of the two remaining inside guards approached the van without any knowledge of the attack underway. He also was taken out quickly. We've gotten all this from the surveillance cameras. The fourth guard was able to warn Mallory and his family, and they secured themselves in a safe room the senator had installed when they built the house. There were two resident housekeepers who were not harmed. The assault team, when not finding the Mallorys, went straight to the senator's office and drilled open his safe. The fourth guard was wounded trying to fight them off in a brief exchange of fire. The Mallorys were unable to call out from the safe room because the phones lines for the entire complex were compromised, though the cameras weren't disabled until the van reached the house and they entered."

"How long was the team here?" Sparks asked.

"Fifteen, twenty minutes," Tobin said. "The senator had a cell phone in a pair of pants in his bedroom. After an hour or so, just as the housekeepers were coming out of hiding themselves, he emerged from the safe room and called local police, who, in turn, called us. And Mallory called you. He said you two were already working on this case. Can you read me in?"

"Not right now," Sparks said. "We want to talk to Mallory alone. Then we'll decide how this will be handled jurisdictionally."

They entered the home, which struck Sparks for its beautiful décor set in a southwestern theme, as one would expect. Upon entering, Sparks was greeted by a large living room with a high ceiling. Dark wood beams rose from the south wall all the way to the peak at the north wall. The two deep couches were tanned leather and no doubt left an occupant a challenge upon trying to get up from enveloping comfort.

Almost the entire eastern wall was glass, offering an inspiring view of the mountains that began rising from the desert floor just fifteen hundred feet from the back yard area. There were no shades on the windows; the morning sun would already be obscured by the mountain until near midday. The backyard included a pool and waterfall with a hot tub set off to the side and recessed into the stone patio. The track lighting shone down on the north wall fireplace. Above it hung an expensive-looking painting.

"I could retire here," Taylor said.

"You and me both, except I like to fish in the Keys too much. Though this would be tempting." Sparks raised his eyebrows.

Tobin led them down a hallway and into Mallory's office. The room had one window—also facing the mountains—and deep off-white carpeting with a cherry wood desk and matching wall unit. He had two desktop computers and a laptop he was working on as Sparks and Taylor came in. The room seemed untouched except for the wall safe that had been drilled open with minimal damage to the wall around it.

Under his breath, Tobin said, "Forensics has already finished in here. We told him he could work at his desk if that was all he touched."

As full of bluster as he had been in his Washington office, Mallory was still shaken by the events. Sleep had not been an option.

"Senator." Sparks offered his hand. "I'm glad your family is safe, sir. It must have been a frightening experience."

"Thank you. They are under protective custody at a hotel near here. But my men and yours, this was so unexpected. When you came to my office, I had no idea something like this could happen. What the hell am I involved with here?"

"We're still trying to figure that out, Senator," Taylor said. "This team was extremely well trained, and they knew their way around the grounds. They knew exactly where to cut the land lines. I'll bet they even brought a jammer along to keep anyone here from calling out on a cellphone. They took out our team on the road without a struggle, the same for your men at the gate and one of the two inside. They took nothing except what was in your safe. So, Senator, what was taken from your safe?"

"That's just it. They took nothing."

"Nothing?" Sparks asked as he continued to walk around the room, slipping on a single latex glove and casually picking up items and looking at them.

"I had some personal papers, deeds to some property including this home..." Mallory was reading from a list in his hand. "... copies of a couple of my favorite speeches I've given on the Senate floor, some bond certificates, a couple of old watches that are worth considerable money, passports... All of those items are still there."

Sparks walked over to the safe and put his hands on his hips, his back to Mallory.

"I'm pretty good at reading people, Sparks." Mallory remained subdued. "And you don't believe me."

"I don't know what to believe, Senator. Some frighteningly well-organized people invaded your home and could very well have killed you and your family, and you're back at work this morning like last night was normal. And people like this don't execute an operation like this without being damn sure what they are after is here. They took nothing else. They obviously were focused on a single goal. What were they after, Senator?"

"I don't know." Mallory stood now with his arms out and palms turned towards Sparks. "I'm with you on this. This has to do with these papers you talked to me about in Washington. I'm telling you, I don't know anything else. If I had been contacted, I would tell you. And you can check phones records and emails all you want."

"We will... and we appreciate your cooperation, Senator," Taylor said, "but the body count is rising over these papers. We're up to eight after last night. We can't get a handle on what's going on if you aren't being truthful with us."

"Agent Taylor, I am being truthful. Those papers you both came to me about weren't in that safe, and I don't have a reason for this attack."

Sparks walked toward the office door and said Taylor's name under his breath. They walked out onto the backyard patio and moved to a sheltered portion where there was a gas barbecue and a kitchenette setup. The heat was stifling.

"Why are we out here?" Taylor asked. "It's so damn hot."

"When we get back in, tell the guys to sweep for listening mics but not to say anything if they find any. I just saw one in Mallory's office attached to his desk phone, a high-end version with a long-term battery. Probably voice activated. Again, like everything else in this case so far, either it's related or could be totally unrelated."

"We should continue as if it isn't a coincidence," Taylor said. "I feel like we're looking at a jigsaw puzzle and we've got the edges done, but we can't get a handle on the middle. Torrez and Collins were killed because they were in possession of the documents, we're attacked because we had just come into the possession of the documents, and now Mallory's house was attacked because either someone thought he had the documents or he did have them. If we had only a few minutes more with them in Vermont we would know what this was all about."

"We need to find out as much as we can about the business agreement between the original Raven and Mallory." Sparks pulled his phone from his pocket and scrolled down to Munson's number and hit the call button. On the fourth ring, Munson answered. "Brenda, hi. The little favor I asked you to check into... yeah, it needs to be moved to the top of your to-do list. You think you could ask your boss for a little time off?" Sparks nodded to Taylor as another agent approached them.

"Agent Taylor, we found the van identified from the house video," he said.

"Where?" Taylor asked.

"The parking lot of a doughnut shop on Ina Road down by I-10. It's about a half hour from here depending on traffic."

"Let me know if techs get anything usable, but I doubt they will," she said.

"The plates were stolen from another van four days ago," the agent said and then left them alone.

"I've got someone researching any possible link between Augustus Raven and Justice Mallory." Sparks ended his call. "She knows her way around old documents and archives in a number of states."

"Our next move?" Taylor asked.

"This attack changes the dynamics," Sparks said. "All of the actions up until this point have been directed at others. Now it's been shifted at Mallory, so logically, we should be looking at Raven. He wanted the documents, and he believed Mallory had them."

"After Mallory possibly had Torrez and Collins murdered and then ordered the attack in Vermont," Taylor said. "We need to start looking at both men, their associations, and their employees. It will take some time, but maybe we'll learn something from the Vermont attack or the assault here, some thread to lead us towards either Raven or Mallory."

Sparks motioned for them to head back into the house and the air conditioning. "We've been behind on this from the beginning, and I get the feeling it's not going to change anytime soon."

SAMUEL RAVEN GLANCED DOWN at the ball, then turned his gaze down the range at a distant flag, then back to the ball. He waggled the club as the trigger for his swing. His rhythmic tempo, repeated more times than not, was his strength on the golf course. He wasn't particularly a long driver of the golf ball, but he hit almost seventy percent of his fairways and was a consistent challenge to the other better players at the club.

For this swing, he was trying to hit a slight fade from left to right with his driver, his go-to shot on most of the holes at Raven Country Club, the facility his father had purchased years ago when Samuel was just a boy. He had grown up on this very driving range, hitting bag after bag of new Titleists any afternoon he was able to get away. Now, with graduate school out of the way and with a full year as a vice president under his belt, he was hoping to play more than occasionally. It was always the perfect stress reducer, and he knew he would need that in the coming months.

Not quite as tall as his father, Sterling, Samuel was still well over six feet tall and a solid two hundred pounds with the same sandy blonde hair, dark-tanned skin, and long arms with massive wrists which enabled him to use his smooth swing to launch the golf ball. He started his swing back, shifting his weight to his right side, bringing the club gracefully to the top, then, with just the slightest unhurried hesitation, shifting his weight to the left side and accelerating through the ball and turning his body fully downrange. The ball zipped bullet-like through the air, straight down the range until, near its apex, it began a slight move to the right, a perfect fade.

"Hitting it as well as ever, I see," a smiling Sterling Raven said, hands on his hips, standing thirty feet or so to his son's back.

"Thanks," Samuel said. "That was an intentional fade." Samuel knew full well his father would give him a hard time if the following shot was less than well struck.

"We need to talk in the dining room," Sterling said. "I want to have lunch, and there are some things we need to discuss. And I'm flying to Florida tonight."

"I just started not more than ten minutes ago. Can't we talk after you have lunch?"

"No. I'll buy you lunch. Now." Sterling was already walking away, not waiting for Samuel to move his clubs and ball bags to the cart he had come to the range in. Sterling withheld his anger but muttered an expletive under his breath as he slammed his clubs into the bag.

Half an hour later, they ate in silence while both focused attention on their smart phones, going through emails. It wasn't until lunch was over and the table was cleared that the elder Raven began the conversation.

"We're close to your first anniversary as vice president, military compliance liaison, and you have done well—better than I expected for your first year," Sterling said. "How have you felt your first year has gone? Not exactly like graduate school work, is it?"

"Nothing I haven't been able to handle."

"You did adequately on the X3-A guidance system negotiations with the Navy. I was satisfied with the final numbers."

"Satisfied?" Samuel couldn't hold back his annoyance. "Our final contract came in fifteen percent higher than projections, and I got an extra ten units tacked onto the back end of the deal. That means an extra quarter of a billion dollars over the life of the contract. And you're satisfied?"

"You know I've had high standards for you, and they have served you well. You should be grateful for my guidance, as you wouldn't be the man you are today without it."

"I can't dispute you there." Samuel pocketed his phone and leaned back in the chair. It was time for him to bring up the subject he had been mulling over for the last month. "Father, you raised me to be assertive, so it won't surprise you that I want additional responsibilities with the company. It's time to work me into the decisions that affect the entire company and its long-term direction. You are a long way from retirement, but the process of increasing my involvement should begin immediately." He tried to read his father for a reaction, but Sterling's face could have been made of stone. "You might think I'm being impertinent... impatient, but I believe it will make the company stronger overall, and it will make the transition seamless far down the road when you step aside. It will be a significant part of your legacy, and eventually mine, if the company continues with unabated health under the final years of your watch and during mine."

Sterling looked into his son's eyes briefly, looked at his watch, and then waved over a waiter to their corner of the restaurant. "I'd like a scotch, neat." He motioned for Samuel, but his son waved off anything. He got up and moved to the chair closer to his son. When he spoke, it began as barely above a whisper.

"You *are* being impatient. You're only a little over a year removed from graduation. I could have started you much lower in the company's structure, but because you showed excellence in college and grad school, I felt it warranted a vice presidency. I knew you could handle it, even excel in it. I was having you cut your teeth, so to speak, on the federal contract section. That being said, you are a long way from being privy to all aspects of my dealings. I have a plan for you, a gradual increase in responsibilities."

The waiter returned with the scotch and left.

"It's the word 'gradual' I'm concerned about," Samuel said. "I want to be challenged, father, and I'm beginning to feel stifled."

"Patience is often a vital quality to have in leading a company. I was the same way as you when I was your age, thinking how to speed up my involvement in the company while your grandfather was holding me back... or so I thought. Looking back later, I realized his wisdom. You should trust me."

"What about the Richmond project?"

His father's left eye twitched before both eyes narrowed. "How in the hell did you hear about that?"

"I don't know the details, but in my dealings within the computer system, I came upon a number of folders linked to the master file. What is it?"

"It's none of your concern, Samuel," Sterling said. "Drop it now and leave it to me."

"A new acquisition in play?"

"I said drop it. How is it you know the details of the files in our computer system so intimately?"

"You forget I minored in computer science for my undergraduate. I know my way around our system and don't need assistance from IT."

Sterling took a healthy drink of his scotch. "Richmond is private, and it is vital that it stays that way. I have my reasons."

"We aren't talking illegality here, are we?" Samuel asked.

"You will need plausible deniability, but I wouldn't have this project in play unless I felt it was absolutely necessary. Don't pressure me on this, Samuel."

The son averted his eyes from his father, knowing it was a sign of weakness. He had hoped his father would read him in on Richmond as a sign of a growing trust in his abilities. Now he was disappointed and worried because it would dictate a more aggressive path. And it was all so unnecessary for his father to cling to this secrecy. Samuel knew exactly what was in the Richmond files and what his father was doing. He agreed with his father's assessment and his tactics. He just wished his father would hold faith in his one, true heir.

"As you wish, Father," he said.

CHAPTER SEVENTEEN

Jan. 18, 1864

BREAKFAST AT THE WILLARD Hotel was a grand affair with delicacies to entice the hungry patrons and enough chaos to leave Brison with the opinion that all green Union officers should stand a shift so as to experience a battle firsthand. He knew the comparison was inappropriate, but he had to marvel nonetheless at the carnage laid out before him: waiters scurrying between tables, children under foot and table, patrons in loud discussions with those at their own tables as well as a disturbing number having words with those at nearby tables, or in the case of one man, an argument with someone from across the entire dining room. Brison was standing to the side, surveying the culinary carnage, when Stanley Rose, an assistant to Joseph Willard, walked up to him and leaned in to speak above the noise.

"A fine Monday morning to you, Colonel Brison," he said. "Are you looking to have a good meal to start your week?"

"I was going to try."

"Before you do, I wanted to let you know that when you asked Mr. Willard to let you know if a red-hair lady joined Mr. Raven's party, he passed along the request to me as well."

"Has she arrived?"

"Yesterday afternoon, sir. She was accompanied by two gentlemen under Mr. Raven's employ."

"Did you see her when they checked in? What was her manner?"

"Sir?"

"Was she of good temperament, or did she seem in distress?"

"As a matter, sir," Rose said, "she did seem not to be in the best frame of mind, if I may say so. Is this a personal matter, sir?"

"Government business, Mr. Rose. I would appreciate the utmost in discretion in this matter."

"As you wish, sir." Rose retreated toward the main reception hall, which no doubt carried with it a scene not unlike what Brison was watching here.

Cathleen's appearance was worrisome. It was possible Raven learned of her searching through the records up in New York and brought her down here to keep her under watch, or worse, was going to use her as leverage against anything Brison was planning. It had been unfair to ask her to put herself in this situation; she had already saved his life and put herself in danger, and his reward to her was to ask more of her. Brison's shoulder barked at him, and he tried to move it around to ease the discomfort. It always seemed to do this to him now in cold weather... or when his conscience whispered.

Foregoing a meal, Brison headed back into hall to track down Rose and get Byrne's room number when two men approached him, one from either side. One of them held up his hand to stop Brison.

"Colonel, could we have a word with you?" The one on the left wore a sergeant's uniform. "General Baker would like to have a word with you today at your earliest convenience."

"He says it is of utmost importance," the second man said, dressed in plain clothes. He looked particularly rough in his manner. Brison would not want to face him in a street brawl.

"General Baker? Wants to see me?"

"Yes sir," the sergeant said.

"Today," plain clothes said.

"I'll head right over after I have breakfast." Brison smiled at the two roughnecks. "Would that be satisfactory?"

"You won't mind if one of us stays in the reception hall and heads over with you to Union Intelligence?"

"Not at all," Brison said.

He quickly found Rose and got Byrne's room number, then made his way back into the dining room. If he was going to face Lafayette Baker, he wanted to do so with something on his stomach.

"COLONEL, I HOPE YOU had a satisfactory breakfast at Willard's." Baker shook Brison's hand and quickly went behind his desk. Dressed in his army uniform with a beard as thick as it was dark set against his piercing eyes, he made a formidable presence.

Brison had never met Baker before, despite the general's prominence in the intelligence business that was so much a part of Washington during these war years. He had heard much about the man, including that his work at clamping down on the city's corruption was enthusiastic and tinged with a hand held out for payment. Brison had no direct knowledge of this, only rumors spelled out by people who held hard feelings, so he took it with the measure of skepticism it deserved. Still, Brison was wary. This was a man others, including Lincoln, might trust... but he didn't.

"The meal was fine," Brison said. "It always is at Willard's. Can we get straight on with the business at hand? I'm at a loss to understand while I'm here."

"Don't be elusive with your candor, Colonel. I know that you have worked on certain matters for the president on a, shall I say it, contract basis. I have worked with the president directly myself, but curiously, we have not had the occasion to become acquainted."

"My work for the president is done with the highest level of confidence. I'm bound to keep my work private."

"Oh, I know, I know." Baker folded his hands on his desk. "I had to ferry two men up to Philadelphia to investigate some businessman. It was all out of something you worked on last year. Lincoln never enlightened me with the details. But that's not why I asked you to come by today."

"Is there a problem I need to know about?"

"I don't want to infringe on your confidential relationship with the president." Baker's voice was as smooth and cold as the flat side of a knife. "However, it has come to my attention that you have shown an interest in Augustus Raven's affairs, and I want to know if there are facts I need to be privy to, considering his importance to the war effort."

"Are you investigating Raven?"

"Should I be?"

"If you have concerns about Mr. Raven and whether or not I'm investigating him," Brison said, "I would suggest you discuss the matter with the president. Your reputation proceeds you, General, so if you are looking for some manner of corruption with Raven, I have no direct evidence at this time that he is involved in any graft. If you think there is something there to examine, then I suggest you do so."

Baker began to fiddle with a letter opener, running a finger along the blade as he thought of his response. After a moment, he leaned back in his chair. "I just wanted to be sure we wouldn't be running into each other at inopportune occasions. This is why I've implored the president to centralize our intelligence efforts—all of our efforts. There are too many damned people coming from different angles with no coordination. I certainly don't want to interfere with whatever assignment you have for him. I suppose I was just seeking enlightenment on what the president's business with Raven is and should I be involved. My office carries with it significant resources you could use in whatever your business is."

"I appreciate your concerns, but the president has asked for my services expressly because I'm not attached to any agency. My dealings, shall I say it, stand alone. If I find myself in need of assistance, I can request it... from the president."

Baker threw Brison a look tinged with anger, but it swiftly tempered, and a small smile appeared. "Mr. Raven has helped this office in its pursuits and provides vast armaments of high quality, unlike many of our government's suppliers. I would hate for the war effort to be affected adversely because of some unfounded investigations or by minor charges brought to light in a highly charged political atmosphere."

Brison stood up, collected his hat from the chair next to the one he was sitting in, and deliberately placed it on his head. "General, you needn't be worried, either for yourself or for your friend. And my business for the president will remain business for the president and no one else. With your permission, sir, I believe our matters have been addressed."

"I just wanted to find out your intentions, Colonel." Baker stood and extended his hand over his desk.

Brison shook his hand, spun on his heels, and exited. *So that was how it was going to be.* Raven was calling in favors here in Washington, and it most certainly was going to increase the difficulty of his assignment for the president. And was that just ancillary, or was Baker directly involved in Raven's plans, whatever they may be? Brison knew he needed time to think and perhaps even request another meeting with President Lincoln, but the news he received this morning at Willard's predicated action on another matter, one that could carry with it life-or-death implications.

He needed to get Cathleen Byrne away from Raven with utmost promptness.

Jan. 20, 1864

BAKER WAS RIGHT. BRISON was just one man, and that limited his ability when his assignment entailed keeping watch on someone every hour of the day. That is what would be required if Byrne was in trouble with Raven. For this task, Brison used not only Stanley Rose—who, like his boss Joseph Willard, knew most everything that went on at the hotel—but also a couple of attendants who worked in the kitchen and at the nearby livery stable. They were indispensable because, as with any large enterprise—and Willard's certainly fit—there were aspects of life there that went unnoticed by those in charge.

It was half past three in the morning when a rap on the door to Brison's boardinghouse room awoke him. Upon opening it, he was greeted by the sight of the kitchen worker, Cole, wrapped all up in wool from his head to his feet like he was rolled up in a carpet.

"Colonel, sir, I'm sorry to disturb you, but you told Bobby you wanted to know if a red-headed woman from the Raven party appeared out of her room. He sent me along. You'll need to be as fast as greased lightning. They demanded their carriage prepared earlier tonight but just now made ready to use it."

"They're taking her somewhere?" Brison was already half dressed.

"The woman appeared to be asleep, Colonel. At least that's what Bobby says. He said they told him they wanted out of there off the reel, but he said he would work his damndest to slow them down a bit till yous get there."

"I'm obliged, Cole." Brison tossed the kid a coin, then held out a second. "Give this to Bobby when we get there, and don't hold out on him. You get me?"

"Yes, sir."

The two of them ran along one of the side streets before they ran into Fourteenth Street and they crossed to the west side and made their way to where Brison could see a carriage parked along the street next to the Willard's back alley. When they were about half a block away, Brison recognized his horse tied up to a lamppost ring.

"My horse?" Brison was astonished.

"Yes, sir," Cole said. "We had him all fixed up for you 'cause we figured you's want to follow them."

Brison shook his head in wonder and pulled out another two coins. "One more for the both of you. You'll all be running this town someday."

A smile appeared on the youth's face. "We plan to, Colonel."

Brison saw a figure working on the trace buckle and exhibiting great difficulty.

"Bobby said he'd slow them down a bit," Cole whispered, easing into the shadows along with Brison as a man appeared from the hotel alley and began to speak harshly to the attendant Bobby. The voice grated on the ears, and Brison recognized it immediately as that of the man at the well and on top of the hotel. The man shoved Bobby away from the horse and admonished the young man to get away. He finished tightening up the brace and quickly checked the rest of the rig before climbing into the carriage, which then moved away from the hotel.

Within a few seconds, Bobby came running up to the two of them.

"I held them up as long as I could, Colonel," he said.

"You did excellent work, the two of you." Brison slapped them both on their shoulders as he watched the carriage turn left onto Pennsylvania Avenue and into the shadows of the January night. "Now they didn't hornswoggle you... you're sure, Bobby? The red-headed woman is on that carriage?"

"Yes sir," Bobby said. "It ain't no gum, Colonel. I saw them with the lady. She was asleep and wrapped up in a coat and such, but no bonnet against the night air. That man came at me full chisel when I asked about her. Told me to keep to myself. Thought she was some adventuress."

"No, Bobby. She's in trouble." Brison climbed onto his horse.

"I knew they were scalawags," Cole said.

"Obliged, boys. Get back to your duties." Brison spun the horse, and moved off at a fast trot, and made his turn onto Pennsylvania Avenue, buttoning up his coat as he went.

BRISON'S THOUGHTS TURNED BACK to Springfield, home, and family as he took his horse along the avenue. He saw the carriage making its way down the broad street, casting long shadows against the ground from the streetlamps. He kept his horse a ways back and his head tilted down as if he were just a traveler bundled against the chilly early morning, but his eyes shifted all around him. He moved his hand to the handle of the Spencer, admonishing himself for not checking it before leaving the two boys back at Willard's. He was going to have to trust they took care of it as instructed, though he did feel for his ammunition pouch and found it in its proper place.

With his Colt inside his coat, Brison pushed those concerns out of his mind. Washington was a coarse place, and Brison always felt he had to be on guard from all sorts—those who would steal and would harm to accomplish that goal, especially at night. Baker and his men had done much to soften the edges of vice, corruption, and plain old violence in this odd amalgamation of patriots and traitors, soldiers and citizens, wealthy and poor, and the spiritually devout and the wicked. The Union was still a few years away from a century old, and her capital carried none of the prestige of her sisters in Europe. Perhaps she was a rough diamond, uncut and unpolished, Brison thought, but for now she was only suffering from the ravages of neglect and war.

He trotted past a lantern-lit crew of four men as they struggled to haul a dead horse onto a wagon bed, knowing full well the only reason they were working with any expediency was because this was a main avenue. If this had been a lesser-traveled street, the carcass would sit rotting for days until a crew could get to it. The carriage made a slight turn onto D Street, still heading east and would quickly cross in front of City Hall where Louisiana and Indiana Avenues met. Brison maintained his pace to keep the distance constant, ready to turn off if it appeared they were interested in his presence.

Within a few minutes, the carriage reached the intersection of D Street and North Capitol Street and made a left-hand turn to head north. There were fewer formal buildings out here, the land a mixture of hastily built shacks, drinking establishments, corrals, and buildings erected with more consideration... and money. The city sprawled out to the north during these war years, taking over where boggy, marsh-like land awaited.

As Brison made the turn onto North Capitol, he looked to his right at the unfinished capitol building just three blocks away. He spied the carriage, now moving a quicker pace as it passed a low-quality bawdy house that Brison deduced was such because there were two women talking to a pair of soldiers next to their mounts tied up at the railing. This time of the night and away from their camp... under different circumstances, Brison would have admonished the two officers, but now was not the time. He also knew where they were headed, and it held no surprise for him.

"Swampoodle," Brison said.

It was late at night, and they were taking Byrne there. Washington had trouble with lawlessness, and this Irish shanty town was among the worst. Brison held little doubt as to what awaited Byrne there. He squeezed the reins tighter as his anger rose. Raven was a depraved man if he was casting Byrne out to a brief life as a forced adventuress or if they planned to simply murder her.

He thought about going back to grab those two officers for support, but he worried about losing track of the carriage even if he was able to convince the men to join him at four in the morning. No, he had to save her now, and he was on his own, for she could be dead by daylight.

The carriage turned right and disappeared opposite the printing office, leaving Brison with a choice, either to make the turn at the same place or go a different route. If they had any idea he was following them, he could turn at those shanties and find himself in a dire situation, so he dismounted and quietly led his horse into a small grove of trees off the street and out of sight of anyone. There were no streetlights here, so he could barely see his hand in front of him much less his surroundings. He tied his horse to a tree, hoping it would still be there when he came back.

Even in the night, voices carried through the trees and buildings, and someone was playing a fiddle far enough away that the melody faded in and out. He took the Spencer and ammunition pouch with his Army-issued Colt under his coat and made his way as best he could through the marshy area behind a group of houses that fronted the street the carriage had turned down. Brison prayed they had not continued out of walking distance; he didn't know Swampoodle that well, having only been here during the day on official Army business with other officers and men, but he knew there was a bawdy house or two just down the street from where he was trying to work his way between buildings. The area smelled of dead animals and human excrement, and the stench hung suspended in the cold air. There wasn't a breath of wind tonight.

He stumbled into a row of pots that had been left outside, scattering them in all directions with a clanging that Brison was sure would raise the dead. It did raise the anger of a pair of mutts that barked indignantly, warning him to the leave and letting the neighborhood know there was someone about.

"Idiot," Brison muttered and looked about to see if attention had been raised.

No one seemed to care. He continued between a tar-paper shanty and a structure of some better construction. It actually had a foundation of stone, though it appeared that loose members had been shoved indiscriminately, leaving Brison to wonder how the wood above it survived. He reached the street and looked to the right. The carriage was parked not a block and a half away on the opposite side. There was no activity—they must have taken her inside with haste, despite the hour. What little light there was came from lamps in windows with worn shades, giving the street a hollow, tunnel-like appearance with darkness down the way like one was looking into a well.

Brison walked across the irregular frozen mud and went between another pair of shacks, almost running into a soul, obviously well with drink, relieving himself on the side wall. Brison worked his way through the backyards toward the house where they had Byrne. As he approached, he noticed a small barn—larger than a shed—shoved between a pair of trees that each marked the last post of a pair of collapsing fences. The house had a porch in back and a single door at the top of some stairs. Subdued light came from inside, but no sound, in contrast to the barn, which had stronger light coming from inside, and now... voices.

He moved to the closest side and peered through the slats, as the barn was poorly constructed. Byrne was sitting in a chair in the middle of the floor, wearing only a simple working dress with no coat. She was gagged, and her hands were tied together behind the chair. Her eyes were wide with fear and anger, her attention focused on the two men standing in front of her. Brison could make out both of them; neither of them was the man from the well in New York or the Willard's rooftop.

"Now, you shouldn't fret, deary," the bigger of the two said. "We're to take special care with you. The less fight you give us, the easier it will be for all."

The smaller man giggled and shoved his friend with enthusiasm. Brison took a quick moment to move around the barn, get an idea of the surroundings, and make sure no one else was around. The house remained quiet, no movement against the light in the windows. He heard a slap of skin, and Byrne cried out in pain.

"Damn bitch bit my hand," a voice said. "You're gonna plum wish you hadn't done that, I'll say, you damnable whore."

"Untie me, now," Byrne barked at them. "You're goin' to let me go." Her voice was forceful, but Brison could hear its uncertainty.

"You'll do just what you're told," the larger man said. "You're goin' to give us what we want, and we'll not have to worry about no French pox."

"You'll untie me right along," Byrne said again.

"Oh, and get more than my hand bit," the smaller one said. "I don't reckon so."

"I suggest you two do as the lady says." Brison stood in the doorway, the Spencer leveled at his hip and pointed at the two ruffians.

"Where in the Sam Hill did you come from?" The taller one asked.

"I rode in with General Meade." Brison pointed the rifle at the smaller man. "Untie her or I'll presently put a considerable hole in you."

"We've got no quarrel with you, stranger," the taller one said. "This is just a no-account whore. You want a turn, you can have one." He moved slightly to the side, increasing the distance between himself and his companion.

Brison thought the man was smarter than he appeared. If he was to shoot the smaller man, the tall one would have a chance to rush him before he could work the lever.

Brison glided the barrel toward the taller man. "You a bettin' man? One of you might rush me, but which one will be dead beforehand?"

The smaller man moved behind Byrne and began to untie her as Brison kept the Spencer on the taller man. "I want you to lie down on the floor," Brison said to the big one. "Face down with your hands behind your back. Now, no delay."

Just as the big one got to his knees, Byrne cried out. The small one had produced a knife and held it to Byrne's throat.

"Now you put down that there rifle." He grinned at Brison, as did his companion, who got back up on his feet. "I'll slit her gizzard like a holiday goose, stranger."

"Colonel to you."

"Colonel?" the small one said. "You ain't got no blues on."

Brison brought the rifle up to his shoulder and pointed it straight at the small one's head. "Last chance. Drop the knife."

"Fuck him, Danny boy," the big one snickered. "He won't do nothin'. Just keep the knife on the whore."

Brison issued a small sigh in resignation.

"See?" the big one said.

The Spencer exploded with a sound that deafened those in the barn. Danny's head snapped backward and sprayed red all the way to the far wall and he fell backward. Before Brison could move the rifle to the other man, the taller one was on the colonel with surprising quickness, throwing his body shoulder first and knocking the two of them onto the floor. The force knocked the wind out of Brison, and his bad shoulder sent pain slamming into his brain. There was no time to recover as the man started to pummel Brison about the head with one hand while trying to wrest the Spencer free with the other.

After a moment like this, Brison was able to get his right arm up to ward off the blows and threw his leg up, trying to strike his assailant in the groin. He missed, but he gained a little more leverage. The man threw another right and hit Brison just below the left eye, jarring the colonel back against the floor. Brison felt the barn spin, and he barely kept his wits. The man had given up on getting the Spencer, but as Brison began to get his head clear, the man produced a knife and threw his right arm again, this time aiming for someplace in the middle of Brison's coat. The man found his arm stopped frozen by Brison, whose strength exceeded his attacker and now the man realized the first thrust wasn't going to get home. He pulled back again, trying to clear Brison's defense with his left arm as he prepared to strike when from behind and above a gray blur landed on the back of his head and his eyes rolled up. He collapsed on top of Brison.

Standing over him was Byrne, a ten-pound sandbag lying at her feet.

"I'm much obliged," Brison said as he struggled to his feet, shaking his head and massaging his left cheek.

"Praise be the Lord saw fit to send you to me," Byrne said matter-of-factly.

"Don't be praising just yet. We are a long way from being out of here." Brison turned down the lamp by the door and peered out the small window.

"Danny? Joe? What the blazes happened in there?" A voice called from the porch. "You didn't shoot the bitch, did ya?"

"What are we going to do?" Byrne whispered.

"Tie the big one up," Brison said. "There's some rope hanging on the wall right over there." He opened the door a crack, then yelled in a voice he tried to match to the tall one named Joe. "Gun went off by mistake. Nothin' to fuss about."

"Clayton says not to harm the woman," the voice from the porch said. "There'll be hell to pay if you can't follow simple instructions."

"Yeah," Brison responded, closing the door. He found a wheelbarrow and wedged it into the door. "We've got just a minute or so."

He helped Byrne finish tying the tall one up, then went to the back wall of the barn and kicked at two of the vertical slats. There was already a gap below these two he had seen when approaching the barn, and kicking them out would give him and Bryne a place to crawl through. They pulled the bound man to the gap.

"Stay here for a moment," Brison said. "When I tell you to skedaddle, pull him through and wait for me."

Byrne nodded in response.

Brison found two cans of kerosene by a wall and dumped it out around the floor. Just as he finished, he heard voices closing in on the barn. He looked at Byrne and mouthed the word "now" as he took the lamp in his left hand and cradled the Spencer in his right.

The men outside tried to open the door but met the resistance of the wheelbarrow.

"What in the blazes?" someone exclaimed.

Brison fired off the Spencer and threw down the lamp. The resulting explosion startled him, and the fire leapt across the floor and against the front wall.

"Jesus Christ Almighty!" someone yelled. "Joe? Danny?"

Brison threw himself under the broken slats, grabbed Byrne, and dove into the bushes that marked the yard's back end. Keeping low, they ran north as quickly as they could as far as the bushes could take them, about a hundred feet by Brison's estimation. They paused to see if there was a pursuit. He could hear men yelling, and people from nearby houses were appearing already, trying to see what was causing the stir. Upon seeing the fire, figures began running in multiple directions, so Brison and Byrne joined the commotion, running back to the street and along the same route he had traveled just a few minutes before.

People were yelling "fire," and Brison saw no one paying attention to the two of them. They reached the alley on the street's other side, slowing down because of the darkness. This time, he missed the pans, but Byrne kicked one, and the dogs from before began barking again.

"Mary mother, what is going on out there?" a woman yelled from a half-open window right above their heads.

"Fire, ma'am," Brison responded, and they continued on.

Lamps were being turned up as people awoke to the clamor, so Brison found it easier to make his way back. Within two minutes, they were back at the horse. Brison swung himself up into the saddle and pulled Byrne up right after him. Brison kicked the horse into a quick canter, and they were out onto North Capitol Street, heading directly for the building itself. Byrne, who had been silent through the whole dash from the barn, wrapped her arms around Brison.

"I've got a right bit of thanks I owe you," she said, "for saving me life."

"I'm afraid, Cathleen, your life just became all-overish my dear," Brison said. "Until this Raven matter is done, you are in all sorts of trouble. And I'm afraid I'm to blame."

Chapter Eighteen

Present Day
June 10

THE VAN PARKED AT the doughnut shop in Tucson had proved to be a dead end—no evidence—but the team had found some blood smeared on a hallway corner at the house that was unaccounted for with the family or staff. It was possible that someone on the assault team had injured himself and that might be able to get a match on one of the many DNA databases. Sparks and Taylor had flown back to Washington in the late evening and spent the next day filing the paperwork to get a federal court order to search three of Raven's properties: the main offices in Pennsylvania, the condo outside the offices, and the house in Boca Raton, Florida, where they learned was where Raven was presently staying for the next two weeks. The plan was to execute the warrants all at the same time in three days early in the morning.

While preparations were made through the two regional field offices in Philadelphia and Miami, Sparks and Taylor sat down with Bill Howard, the person Sparks talked to on the phone a few days earlier when they discovered Mallory's possible involvement.

"Tank, good to see you and thanks for coming to us here at the Hoover." Sparks shook Howard's hand and motioned over to Taylor. "This is Agent Bethany Taylor with the Secret Service."

"Thanks for seeing us," Taylor said.

"My pleasure," Howard said. True to his nickname, he was a stocky, strongly built man with the kind of massive shoulders and arms seen on body builders or naturally big men who worked out at the gym every day. The suit he wore was tailor made and cut tight, which accentuated his intimidating presence. Add to that his neatly cut black hair and dark brown eyes, and you had yourself an individual that commanded attention. The only things that detracted from his physicality were the wire-rim glasses he wore. "After I got your call about Brighton Mallory, I did some more digging and came up with some more information on him. I thought you might be calling me again."

"That's Tank," Sparks said with a grin, turning to Taylor. "Bill here was a first-class journalist, political writer with the Post for a number of years until he learned the reality that being in the game could make him a lot more money than writing about it. He's been a much-sought-after political consultant here for the last, what is it now, ten years?"

"Just short of that."

"You want to know deep background on anyone inside the beltway, he can give it to you... for a price. And everyone tells me he's worth whatever exorbitant fees he charges."

Howard smiled, flashing a perfect set of pure white teeth. "And I will be charging the Bureau for my time."

"Damn, let's get going then," Sparks said. "The director will have my ass if I throw too many unusual expenses his way. What did you learn about Mallory you didn't mention on the phone?"

"I'm sure you both keep up with politics here in Washington," Howard began. "Senator Mallory is on the short list for the Republican nomination to run against Douglas next year. In fact, the party insiders say he'll run away with the nomination. He's polling strong in Iowa and New Hampshire, and the party has quietly done some nationwide polling that has him actually ahead of Douglas in a head-to-head. Douglas's people got wind of that Republican poll and just about shit in their pants... sorry." He looked over at Taylor.

"Pleeeeease," Taylor dismissed him.

"Anyway, if Douglas wants a second term, the early money says he'll have to get through Mallory to do it. That is if the senator runs."

"I thought that was a foregone conclusion," Taylor said. "He's expected to announce next month, isn't he?"

"He was," Howard said. "Much of the preliminary work is being done, but I've heard whispers he might wait another four years or might not run at all. I find that rumor to be extremely interesting, because it goes counter to everything I've heard about the man."

"What do you mean?" Sparks asked.

"I told you before he has the reputation of being ruthless as he goes about his work on the Hill. He'll sell out your grandmother and his own grandmother to get a deal done, and anyone who has crossed him has suffered real repercussions."

"Does he have limits to what he would do if enough pressure was applied?" Taylor asked.

"I don't think so."

"Murder?" Sparks said.

Howard threw his head back like cold water had been thrown in his face. "Can you ever predict behavior like that? I don't know. He does exhibit almost sociopath tendencies, it seems to a layman like me. He hasn't cared if people's lives were damaged or even destroyed, but it's still a leap to murder. Would it shock me if I found out he had someone knocked off? I guess not.

"Beside the ruthlessness, he is single minded in his focus—so much so that I can't remember a time when he has changed his mind on a significant decision. He studies all the angles and evaluates, but when he makes a decision, he's all in. That's why this rumor about him not running smells like something is rotting away in the ol' town."

"If he was going to run, made the decision to run, then it would take a monumental obstacle to force him to change his mind," Taylor said.

"Life altering," Howard added.

"Does he have a relationship with Sterling Raven?" Sparks asked.

"The billionaire military hardware guy? Other than on the hill, no. They aren't known to frequent the same circles, which is actually a little unusual. I don't suppose you can tell me what Raven and Mallory have in common with your investigation... and what you're investigating."

"Sorry, I can't read you in, but if the time comes, I'll try and get permission from the director to brief you if we get a signed nondisclosure agreement under penalty of prison," Sparks said.

Howard nodded. "Pretty high-end shit here, huh? Well, all I can tell you for sure is if Mallory comes out and announces that he *isn't* running, something or someone has spooked him in a way no one on Capitol Hill has ever before. And if it scared him, it has to be some pretty high-end shit. Unless it was for extremely high-end monetary reasons."

Sparks looked over at Taylor, who arched her eyebrows in return.

THEY SAT IN THE corner of the Bureau cafeteria, not far from the exit to the roof garden. Sparks was gnawing on a roast beef sandwich, and Taylor was having turkey; both had chosen a fruit cup over fries.

"Mallory isn't thinking twice about running because of family or the attack in Tucson," Taylor said. "The rumor has been around prior to a few days ago. We've got no solid evidence linking it, but you and I both know if what Howard says is true, then whatever was going on with these pre-Civil War documents could very well affected his decision-making process."

"Agreed," Sparks said with his mouth full of sandwich. His cellphone buzzed on the table. He held up his finger to Taylor, telling her to hold on. "Hey, what's up?"

"Any chance you can expense me for the drive up here to Harrisburg?" It was Munson.

"You too?" Sparks joked. "I'm going to be in so much trouble."

"Tell you what," she said. "Next time you visit, I'll have some special requests you'll need to take care of."

"Now that sounds very interesting."

He could hear her chuckle. "I need a new garbage disposal installed, Casanova."

"Oh."

"I'll take your disappointed tone as a compliment. So, I've done some checking, and I found something very interesting. All major business incorporations and agreements are put on file with the state, which, as it is today, was Harrisburg back in the 1850s. Now, everything is stored digitally, even here in ye old Pennsylvania, but not for companies back in the middle of the nineteenth century. I went into the archives and found a logbook that actually lists a business agreement between one Augustus Raven and one Justice Mallory dated August 5, 1859."

Sparks sat up. "Do they have copies of registered agreements?"

"The records are a little sketchy and incomplete in some cases. Here's where it gets interesting. I went looking for the corresponding paperwork that goes with that logbook entry, and it's missing."

Sparks slumped in his chair, his disappointment clearly visible to Taylor across from him. "Well, you did say the records from back then are incomplete?"

"That's not why it's interesting, darling," Munson said. "The company papers were there. Someone recently removed them. I could tell the files around where it should have been were recently disturbed, and the clerk remembers someone asking about that timeframe just a few weeks ago."

"Are you sure?" Sparks.

Before he could ask the next logical question, she interrupted him. "No, there are no surveillance cameras for this part of the building. But you have to show ID and sign in, so I've got a name. But it could be fake."

"Give it to me anyway," he said, writing down the name on a notepad he kept in his inside breast pocket. "I'll check it out. Brenda, thanks a lot. You've been a great help. Head home and read up on the garbage disposal. I'll be by soon."

Sparks ended his call, put his cellphone down, and took a monstrous bite out of his sandwich.

"Well," Taylor implored, "what's the word?"

This time, Sparks waited until he was done chewing before he answered. "Someone's been covering up their tracks. I've got a name, but it probably isn't a real one."

THEY SPENT THE AFTERNOON checking on the name put in the register in Harrisburg. It came back as false. The Florida driver's license number was real enough, but it belonged to an eighty-three-year-old retiree living in Sarasota. When the scanned-in license image was emailed to Sparks and they ran the photo through the database, the face-recognition program produced a hit, but it belonged to a dead ex-convict. The results weren't surprising to either Sparks or Taylor, but it still made for a frustrating day. It didn't get any better when both of them were called up to the director's office as it was closing in on 6:00 p.m.

When they walked into Connelly's office, they were greeted not only by the director, but by Taylor's boss Pearson and Stephen James, the acting chief of staff for President Douglas.

Once everyone had taken their seats at the conference table in the spacious office, Connely said, "Sorry we didn't give you both a heads up on the briefing, but we felt it was time we got together for an update. The networks aren't letting Torrez's death slip away without milking it for every ratings point. So far, the carjacking story is holding up, but we've gotten notice from other people in our investigation that reporters from the Post and the Times, a couple of the largest website news outlets, and some networks are asking questions, sort of firing out salvos to see if anything blows up."

"Neither Agent Taylor nor I have received anything in terms of contact with the media," Sparks said.

"That's because we've insulated you," Connelly said. "You know how reporters work: start chipping away with some of the people with minor jobs and work their way towards the people of interest. If they get a whiff of something irregular, we'll be in a shitload of trouble."

"And we don't need to tell you the stakes when it comes to the president," James said, poking his finger into the table.

"We're aware of all that is at stake here," Taylor said. "Should we be worried about finding something that could embarrass the president?"

"No, not at all," James countered. "Just that our decision to turn it into a carjacking gone bad instead of a murder based on who Torrez was could blow up in our faces."

Connelly held up his hand. "Why don't we first hear what Sparks and Taylor have come up with so far? Give us what you have solid, then we'll talk about conclusions and theories."

Sparks and Taylor spent the next half hour relating the events of the past nine days: the note from Torrez implicating Raven, finding Torrez's friend Collins dead and coming up with the clues to the camp in Vermont, the attack up there after they saw the agreement between Augustus Raven and Justice Mallory and the subsequent loss of the documents, the two interviews with Senator Mallory and Sterling Raven, and finally, the attack on Mallory's compound in Arizona. Sparks then added the last development on the missing documentation in Harrisburg. When he was finished, Connelly, who had been jotting down notes while Sparks spoke, continued writing.

"Forgive me if I'm dense here, but what do you have?" James spit out the words. "A letter from Torrez incriminating Raven and a thirty-second glance at some documents."

"Unfortunately, everything we have is peripheral, I admit," Sparks said. "We don't have anything solid linking Raven or Mallory to the murders, but we know the murders are linked together by those documents from 1859. It's clear those documents are worth a great deal to someone—either Raven, Mallory, or a third party."

"Mallory's estate was attacked in an attempt to retrieve something from him," Taylor said. "We're betting it was the documents, which means someone—either Raven or the third party—believed Mallory had them, which means they believe Mallory was behind the murders of Torrez and Collins." Just then, her cellphone buzzed, and she nodded to Sparks. "It's Becker. Says he has some information on the blood smear found at Mallory's."

"Take it outside," Sparks said. "Maybe they've got something."

Taylor left, closing the door softly behind her.

"Jason, do you suppose Torrez and Collins were blackmailing one or more of these parties with the documents?" Connelly asked.

"I'd bet on it."

"Then why were they killed before the documents were safely in their hands?" Connelly asked.

"That doesn't sound smart," James said.

"They might have known that Collins had the documents and killed Torrez to scare Collins into giving them up. Then, when they were working over Collins to get the location, they crossed that fine line between applying sufficient pain and allowed frustration to get the better of them. Or he gave up the location after being tortured. I think this is the likely scenario, because I'm pretty sure we weren't followed to Vermont. That team we faced at the lake was well-trained and backed off as soon as they had possession of the documents."

"What about identifying the dead operatives in Vermont and linking them with known associates?" Connelly asked.

"Working on it," Sparks said. "The one I took out was a former Navy SEAL who had been dishonorably discharged after being caught running a gambling operation at Little Creek. He worked for an independent security firm for two years but then was recruited away from it by some other firm. But when he left his job, he disappeared off the grid with the exception of an apartment in Northern Virginia and a couple of bank accounts. But there has been no activity on that account in the three years since. I'll bet as we pursue the identity of the other one, it'll be a similar story. These guys work for someone who likes their black ops."

The door opened, and Taylor came back in, but instead of sitting back in her original chair, she stood by it to address everyone in the room.

"They got a hit on the blood we found at the Mallory house," she said. "It was confirmed not to be from anyone connected to the house. We ran the sample through COTIS—"

"Cotis?" James asked.

"The Combined DNA Index System," Taylor said. "We got a hit. It belongs to a Clint Parsons..." She was reading from her phone now. "Former Army Ranger who worked for an independent security firm, Red Storm Security, for eight years after being discharged. He left Red Storm eighteen months ago for another job, but he's dropped off the grid."

"Just like the one we identified in Vermont," Sparks said.

"We've got some shadow groups working here on American soil, gentlemen," Connelly said.

"I made a quick call to Red Storm before I came back in here," Taylor said. "I got the name of Parsons's previous supervisor. They're based in Chevy Chase." She looked at Sparks. "We should pay them a visit."

"Yes," Sparks concurred. "We'll hit Raven's properties in less than seventy-two hours, the main offices in Pennsylvania, his condo, and his residence in Boca Raton, which we know is where he is presently. We'll go in simultaneously and hopefully find the documents."

"You need to link this ex-Ranger Parsons to Raven," Connelly said. "Then you'll have the beginnings of a legitimate case. I want daily updates until the three teams move in, and I want to have real-time eyes on the operation in Boca when you both go in. Raven is embedded with a lot of Washington's political elite, including your boss James, so this has to be done with no fuckups. Is that clear?"

Sparks felt the eyes of the room on him, and he was careful not to look annoyed. He kept his gaze right on Connelly and nodded. "We'll get it right, Director."

THE RED STORM COMPLEX was located just outside of Chevy Chase in an industrial park flanked by apartment complexes nestled between Bethesda and Silver Spring. It consisted of three separate buildings, the largest of which was a four-story glass-and-steel structure that Sparks estimated to be about four hundred feet long by two hundred feet deep. Surrounded by neatly groomed hedges and trees with park benches located in many of the shaded areas, the company's front-porch impression was one of a healthy enterprise. The lobby took the impression to another level as the visitors were greeted by a ceiling that stretched up three floors with a massive stone fountain taking center stage, the water cascading down into a rectangle pool. The walls on three sides were adorned with modernistic paintings, even on the far wall where three elevators were located. The reception desk was not just a desk, but appeared more like a command center with phones, monitors, and workstations for five people.

"Can I help you?" the male receptionist called out from across the lobby. He was dressed impeccably in a four-figure suit.

"What the hell do they pay their people here?" Taylor whispered as she leaned into Sparks.

"My thoughts exactly," Sparks said. "I need to dust off my resume."

"We need to see David Cochran," Taylor said as both she and Sparks held up their identification.

"Do you have an appointment? I don't see anything on Mr. Cochran's schedule this morning." He poked at the keyboard in front of him.

"You don't need to confirm," Sparks said. "We don't have an appointment, but he'll see us. Just tell his secretary the FBI and the Secret Service are here to speak with him. It won't take long, I expect."

The receptionist gave a look over to the lone other person at the station—a security person—then picked up a phone. "There are two agents from the FBI and Secret Service here to speak to Mr. Cochran." He listened for a moment, then nodded. "All right."

"Bad news?" Sparks smiled.

"Mister Cochran's secretary says he is unavailable at the moment and you should make an appointment," he said.

"This will be fun," Taylor said under her breath.

"Tell you what... Matt," Sparks said, reading the nametag. "Call Mr. Cochran's assistant back, please."

Matt picked up the phone and punched the extension in but lost the receiver from his hand as Sparks took it from him.

"Yes, Mr. Cochran's assistant? Margaret? This is Special Agent Jason Sparks with the FBI. I'm here with Special Agent Bethany Taylor. We would appreciate it if you make Mr. Cochran available now, or we'll be back in a couple of hours with fifty men and a search warrant that will effectively shut down your business for the next two weeks. Would you please relay that to Mr. Cochran? Or you can just tell him that we're here to see him and we just need a half hour of his time and a little bit of information. Yes... you do that." Sparks hung up and smiled at Matt the receptionist. "Margaret says she'll be down presently to escort us up."

Taylor looked bemused. "How were you going to pull that off, fifty agents in two hours?"

"You were going to be responsible for half of them," Sparks said.

Cochran's office was neat and austere, a stark contrast from the lobby downstairs except for the desk. It was impressive, intimidating for a piece of furniture; it screamed, "I'm important," when a visitor walked into the room, and it was almost comical to Sparks when he saw Cochran rising from behind it. His chair was elevated above the floor, giving Cochran the ability to look down on his guests. He was a man who, in the era of political correctness, might be called "vertically challenged," and it was clear he was trying to compensate for what his parents didn't give him. He was maybe about 5"5', Sparks guessed.

"Agent Sparks. Agent Taylor." Cochran came down from his throne and shook their hands. "I apologize for my people. They are trained to shield me when they can, but this is, even with our company's mission, the first time I've received a visit from either of your agencies." He returned to his chair. "Either of you interested in coffee?"

Both Sparks and Taylor declined.

"We both know you're busy," Taylor said. "If we could get right to the reason for our visit."

"Of course," Cochran said. "What do you need from Red Storm?"

"We're here, specifically, about a former employee of yours, Clint Parsons," Sparks said.

Cochran reached for his intercom. "Terry, bring me the hard copy file on Clint Parsons. He left here just under two years ago or so." He nodded as he turned his attention to his guests. "I can't tell you I'm surprised Parsons has come to your attention. He left here on his own accord, but his time here was turbulent."

"In what way?" Taylor asked.

"He worked well with his peers, but he battled with myself and other supervisors when they were on jobs in the field. He was... overly aggressive. When he was on a job providing private security for individuals, on two or maybe three occasions, he became physical with subjects either before it was necessary or in excess when it was necessary."

"A hothead?" Sparks asked.

"It was a surprising problem," Cochran said as the door opened and the file was brought in. When the assistant left, he continued. "Ex-rangers are, almost without fault, disciplined and thorough operatives." He glanced through the file for a full minute. "I remember now. He had an honorable discharge and some commendations, but when I interviewed his commanding officer during the vetting process, he said Parsons like to skirt protocols when he felt it was warranted and he was skating on thin ice for the last six months of his service. It was probably a good thing he was leaving the service. Parsons nailed the interview with me as well as the others on my management team. His skills were exceptional, so I decided to take a chance."

"Do you know who he went to work for next?" Sparks asked.

"No, it doesn't say here in his file, and normally, we will put that in a file if it's mentioned in a letter of resignation or if he tells us verbally," Cochran said. "I don't recall him telling me personally what he was going to do... hold on." Cochran called for someone named Walters on his intercom, and within a minute, there was a knock on the door and an executive walked into the office. After Cochran introduced everyone, he continued, "Blake, you remember Clint Parsons."

"Of course," Walters said.

"How close were you to him?" Taylor asked.

"As close as anyone here," Walters said. "He kept to himself most of the time, but we were assigned to the same details half a dozen times, so we would talk."

"When he resigned, did he tell you if he was going to work for another security firm?" Sparks asked.

"I don't remember off hand," Walters said. "What's this all about, if I might ask?"

"It's part of a joint investigation we're conducting," Sparks said. "Was he close to anyone else here at Red Storm?"

"He dated Melissa Cooper in IT for a while, I know that," Walters said, "but she left the company about six months after Clint. They were pretty close."

"We'll need the basics on Cooper as well," Taylor said, "particularly where she went for her next job."

"I want you to know we'll cooperate fully with whatever you need to know as long as it doesn't compromise the security of our clients," Cochran said, excusing Walters from the room. When they were alone again, Cochran's mood shifted. "I want to cooperate, but why are you looking into Parsons?"

"It's a classified investigation," Sparks said. "We couldn't talk about it even if we were so inclined. I can tell you that we're interested in Parsons's activities after he left Red Storm, not for anything he did while he was here. At least so far..."

Cochran sank back in his chair and seemed relieved.

"Mr. Cochran," Taylor said, smiling at the executive. "What were Parsons best skills? Why would someone want to hire him away from you?"

"He was an ex-ranger agent Taylor." Cochran managed a thin smile and clasped his hands together on the desk. "We used him for securing locations and devising defensive strategies to be used in the case of armed incursions. He was on the offensive side of those types of scenarios when he was in the Army, so with some re-training, he was a natural for knowing how to set up defenses. He also kept up his combat skills at a high level."

Sparks' cellphone rang as they walked out of the Red Storm building. When he answered, the Bronx accent of Tom Becker came through.

"We've pulled together a little more information on this Parsons dude," Becker said. "He's been paying taxes like a good boy and he has an address in Silver Spring—a condo—but the company that's been paying him for the past two years is a shell for three other entities. We've only cleared through one of the three, but we hit right away on that one."

Sparks stopped walking, and Taylor was forced to retrace a few steps in response.

"What's the company?" Sparks asked.

"We're playing golf next week, right?" Becker asked. "I want three strokes a side."

"Blackmailer. Give it to me."

"The company paying Parsons for the past two years is an outfit named Corvus, C-O-R-V-U-S," Becker said.

"Say that again," Sparks said.

"Corvus."

"You next to a computer?" Sparks asked.

"Yeah."

"Go online and looked up Corvus."

Sparks waited a moment, hearing Becker's fingers working the keyboard.

"You never told me you were into birds," Becker finally said.

"My grandmother was. She bought a bunch of picture books on North American birds. Was I correct about Corvus?"

"You were indeed," Becker said with a chuckle. "That's why your pay grade is way higher than mine."

Sparks thanked his favorite lab tech and ended the call.

"What's up?" Taylor asked, putting on her dark glasses.

"Becker's crew found out that Parsons has been paid by a shell company for the past two years and that company had three separate entities tied to it, one of which was a company called Corvus," Sparks said.

"Okay?"

"Corvus is the genus that has a number of bird species in it, including... ravens."

A smile crossed Taylor's face, and he nodded. "A link between one of the assailants at the Mallory compound and Sterling Raven?"

"We should be in for a very interesting visit in three days."

Chapter Nineteen

Jan. 28, 1864

THE AFTER-DINNER WHISKEY WAS settling in Brison's stomach, spreading its warmth through his body as he sat in front of a healthy fire in a Newburyport house on the coast of Massachusetts. For the past week, he had secretly traveled with Byrne from Washington, careful not to tell anyone he knew his plans, not even informing Lincoln or Nicolay. He couldn't count on any of his usual contacts for fear that Raven had spies that would seek them out. He couldn't take her into official custody and place her in the army's hands either for the same reason. The best course was to take her somewhere where she could be comfortable and have a reasonable chance at anonymity until this Raven affair was completed.

So he took her to a friend no one knew about.

She sat opposite him drinking her cup of tea, looking at him with her wide, expressive brown eyes, waiting for him to begin the talk he owed her. After all, he had shown up at her doorstep just before dinnertime with Byrne, asking for shelter and a meal, and was welcomed in and fed with nary a question.

"Abby, thank you for taking us in without warning." Brison gave her a smile. "It's more than I should ask of you, but I have no one else to turn to that can help me any more completely."

Abigail Stinson smiled back with familiarity, but Brison could tell the warmth he knew from last spring was being withheld. "Andrew, you know I will do whatever I can to help you."

"I'm sorry your meeting in October with the president didn't result in the desired conclusion," Brison said. "You know the president is doing what's best for the nation."

"He threatened me with arrest if I went public with what happened to Jackson," she said.

Conflict roiled inside of Brison over the death of Jackson Prescott and the loss of the Stallard gold shipment just on the cusp of the Gettysburg battle. Prescott had been forced to become a traitor publicly while working subversively to break up the smuggling attempt, and when he died, the gold's location had died with him. And because of the political climate in Washington and the fall election, Lincoln thought it more prudent to withhold the Prescott story from the newspapers.

"I know, and I'm sorry," Brison said. "After the war, he said... you just need to be patient until the war is won and the heroes' stories can come to light. The way you were speaking to him, threatening to go to the newspapers, it would make his work all the more difficult, Abby, you must understand. Jackson Prescott's story will be told, and he will get his honor back. The president is a fair and just man. He only warned you because of your threat of exposure."

Stinson took another sip of her tea. When she put the cup back onto its saucer, she asked, "Who is this Cathleen Byrne who is taking a bath in my house, and why are you asking me to let her stay with me for a time?"

"She was employed by someone very powerful who I believe has agents in many areas of the government and the Army. This person wants to harm her, and I need to move her out of harm's way while I complete my investigation, because I believe this person has plans much greater than what he has done already. I fear for the union if he is allowed to continue."

"How did you know I would be able to help you?" Stinson asked. "I only came into possession of this house two months ago when my father died."

"I didn't know, Abby, and I'm sorry that you have lost two men you loved so close to each other in time, but I'm desperate."

Stinson nodded slightly but didn't say anything.

"I'll make sure you are compensated," Brison said, then immediately regretted it.

"I don't care about the money," Stinson retorted. "If you say it'll help our country, then of course I'll let her stay with me." She paused, her eyes flaring with anger, but just when Brison thought she was going to give him the devil, the anger subsided. "I've become angry with you these last months around my father's passing and my frustration with Mr. Lincoln's refusal. I feel like everyone has turned their back to me. But I know you, Andrew, that if you could do something now, you would. I owe you my life, and I know you would never do something to harm me."

"I don't blame you for your matter of mind. It's understandable."

"How long do you expect Miss Byrne will need shelter?"

"I honestly can't give you a truthful answer... I don't know."

"If it's important for you, then I'll not ask another question."

Byrne appeared at the door to the sitting room, fully dressed with wet hair, standing and looking hesitant.

"Come in, Miss Byrne," Stinson said. "I have tea. It's still hot and will warm you up after traveling in the cold."

"Thank you. Please call me Cathleen."

"Cathleen, I'm Abigail, Abby to my friends. And since you're going to be staying with me for a spell, I'm sure we'll become good friends."

"I'm staying here?" Byrne asked, looking at Brison.

"We talked about this more than once," Brison said. "Raven has influence in many circles, and I can't protect you without hiding you. No one knows we've come up here, and that will be how I protect you until Raven is brought to justice."

"Just who is Raven, and what has Cathleen done to desire his wrath?" Stinson asked.

Brison told her only what he felt was important for her to know: the reality of the danger Byrne faced from her former employer, including her rescue from the brothel in Swampoodle.

"I found evidence that my employer was guilty of destruction of property belonging to his competitors in the manufacture of arms," Byrne said. "He should stand trial for treason."

"There is something more afoot than simply profiting unfairly from the war," Brison said. "And I need to get back to Washington to find out what he plans."

Brison wrote down a way to get a letter or wire to him that was not through the normal military address but through his boardinghouse proprietor. He made ready to leave even as dusk was closing outside. "I saw a hotel on the way into town. I'll see if they might have a room for tonight, and I'll begin my trip back to Washington tomorrow."

"Surely you can stay here tonight," Stinson said.

"Don't want local tongues to waggle, Abigail," Brison said. "Just tell the gabbers that Cathleen is a dear friend you met in Chicago last year or a distant relative, but for God's sake, Cathleen, keep to yourself as much as possible, and don't use your real name."

Byrne reached for his arm as he opened the door.

"Colonel..." She laid her head against his shoulder as a partial hug, then, aware of Stinson, pulled back. "I know I've thanked you before, but again, thank you for saving my life."

"Remember the well... and the shed in Swampoodle? I was just returning the favor." He smiled at her and then at Stinson, then back at Byrne. "I'll leave it for you to tell Abby that story—not my finest effort. She needs to hear it lest she always think I'm too much of a dashing knight, always saving those in peril."

"Godspeed, Andrew," Stinson said.

Brison winked at her and slipped out into the cold.

Feb. 12, 1864

IT WAS AFTER TEN o'clock at night by the majestic standing clock that stood facing Brison as he sat in a chair he had pulled from a nearby room and tilted back against the executive mansion's hallway wall. He was smoking a cigar and using a spittoon provided by one of the servants. Between puffs, he was digging into a waffle with butter and strawberry jam he had gotten from a cook he had befriended on one of his earlier visits. He had been waiting for two hours, since he received a message from a runner that the president wanted to see him at the end of the day's affairs. Lincoln had just finished dinner when Brison arrived and went into a late meeting while the family retired for the evening. Streamers hung in the main hall a few hundred paces from where Brison sat, the significance of which only came to light while he was acquiring his waffle from the cook.

The lateness of the hour meant the endless stream of people wandering the halls did have an end to it after all. Brison welcomed the quiet. Despite having just bided his time upon his return to Washington from Newburyport, he had not slept well the past few nights. He was anxious for the business with Raven to get along. The war was coming up on three years, and the misery appeared to be a sickness that ate away at one's insides to the point where you just assumed it would be better if the good Lord would just take you away with a shortcut instead of dragging you down the whole route. Still, he was dealt a better hand than the one dealt to the boys already dead in the cold February ground.

"Colonel? The president will see you now." A smartly dressed Negro butler held out his arm gesturing down the hall. His appearance was astonishing, not a smudge on him or a button out of place and his gloves as white as could be, in contrast to the worn, mud-caked carpet they walked down. They went upstairs, and before too long, the butler quietly rapped on the president's office door. There was a muffled response, and he opened it for Brison. With a nod, he let the colonel into the room and closed the door behind him.

Lincoln was seated at his desk working on some papers that held his attention over the mounds surrounding him. He looked up immediately and motioned for Brison to take a chair from the conference table and slide it over to his desk.

"I'll be finished momentarily," Lincoln said.

Brison settled in and took the opportunity to study the man as he did every time they met. As with the previous encounters, Brison was distressed to see a wearier Lincoln. Of course, it was the end of what had proved to be a long day's efforts, but it was more. Lincoln was burdened by the war, and it showed as the months passed by. Just like the last time he met with Lincoln, in the dim light of the single oil lamp and the turned-down gaslights on the wall, the shadows accentuated the valleys of the president's face and hid his sunken eyes.

"I understand that birthday wishes are in order, sir," Brison said.

"Another year in the ledger, Colonel." He took the last of the papers he was working on and set them aside, rose, and walked around to Brison, a smile appearing on his face. "I do hope Halleck and Meade give me what I truly would desire, ending this awful matter before my next birthday." He shook Brison's hand with his left hand on Brison's shoulder. "How are you, Colonel?"

"I'm well, sir, and I think the generals may well have a chance to give us that victory," Brison said.

"How is your family? They remain safe in Springfield?"

"They do indeed, sir. Before we begin with what you brought me here for, I need to inform you of one thing I have done in recent weeks concerning the Raven matter."

"Fitting, for that is why I have asked you here tonight."

Brison then told Lincoln about rescuing Byrne from Raven's men in Swampoodle, taking her up to Massachusetts, and the man he had to shoot down.

"I will accept an inquiry when the time comes, Mr. President," Brison said.

"That won't be necessary. You have the authority to protect those parties vital to the cause. Are you sure Miss Byrne will be safe where she is?"

"Only myself and the person she is staying with know of her whereabouts." Brison paused, then continued. "Sir, the intentional damaging of competitors' foundries aside, Raven is guilty of kidnapping, I suspect murder and attempted murder, and treason if we gather evidence on the foundries—"

Lincoln held up his hand. "You haven't inquired as to why we are meeting tonight, Andrew. Be patient. All of that will play out, I believe. But we have a more interesting matter with Mr. Raven, the one we talked about the last time we spoke."

"The matter of Justice Mallory in Richmond?"

"Yes," Lincoln said. "You see, the clamor of indignation has swept through Washington. The conditions at Libby Prison in Richmond have been made known to all. We need to get those men liberated, and who do I hear in the recent weeks that has a plan to accomplish this but a General Kilpatrick. Word came to me through his political friends, and just today, I met with him to discuss his plan. He was quite enthusiastic, like a rutting buck if I may be so crude. Seems convinced he has the plan to free the men in a quick strike into Richmond with 2,500 men or so. I asked for him to meet with me, effectively flanking any protest from General Meade, who, by my cyphering, holds Kilpatrick with little regard."

"I have heard details of some rather unsavory behavior on his part," Brison said. "He falls short in representing the service, if I may be so bold."

"I have heard the same, but if I eliminated every general in this Army who carries with him the sin of excess, I'd be damn near formulating battle plans myself for the lack of horses available." Lincoln allowed himself a chuckle before turning serious again. "The man has showed himself to be fearless in battle, colonel, and that is a precious commodity I need in my commanding officers."

"Yes, sir. But I've heard he is unashamed to exaggerate his accomplishments. It goes to whether he can be trusted. And if he is now doing the bidding of Augustus Raven and there is some sort of plot afoot underneath the guise of this strike at Richmond, then his motives are clearly suspect, sir."

"Oh, his motives are clearly self-serving, on that I am hoping," Lincoln said. "What we need to do is find out if Raven and my good war secretary are indeed using Kilpatrick and this plan to commit some sort of treachery... and just what it entails."

"I'll need to be added to the detail when they head to Richmond," Brison said. "And I'll need to have a measure of independence."

"I'll send a message to General Meade that I would like you added to the party... discretely. If there is an assassination plot on one of the Confederate government's own, even if it is a personal matter between business associates, I can't put forth a more stringent emphasis to my words on the importance of preventing their success."

"I understand, Mr. President—the election in the fall."

"Not just that political consequence. I'm relating the possibility of outside agencies from across the Atlantic, just like you fought to prevent last year at Gettysburg." Lincoln sat forward. "Governments don't sanction murder of opposing leaders. If this administration were linked to something of that nature, I shudder at the potential returns to such an action."

"I'll see who has their fingers in the pie," Brison said. "And I'll stop them."

"Any means necessary, Colonel."

"Yes, sir. Any means it is."

Feb. 18, 1864

FROM HIS VANTAGE POINT behind a potted plant near the entrance to the Willard's dining room, Brison—dressed not in uniform but in an intentionally nondescript outfit—could see the three people seated at the dinner table not forty feet away. Brison kept his hat low, and he intentionally disguised his face with extra whiskers because Raven's men were sitting in the lobby not too far away and were keeping a close watch on their boss and his companions.

Those at the table had to stop frequently from their discussion, not because of suspicion, but for the well-wishers that approached at regular intervals. Raven was seated with General Judson Kilpatrick and Secretary of War Edwin Stanton, and they were engaged in a discussion that was dominated by Kilpatrick. He gestured with sharp, pointed, deliberate movements. If the conversation Brison had overheard upstairs in Stanton's room was the beginning of their plan for Richmond, this was one of the planning meetings.

Out of the corner of his eye, Brison caught a figure he recognized and immediately made his way across the chaotic lobby and followed the man outside into the cold. They traveled east on Pennsylvania, a moderate wind thankfully at their backs, and Brison quickly overtook the individual until he was beside him.

"Robert, may I have a word with you?" Brison asked.

"I don't know you, sir," a startled Pope said.

"Forgive me. It's me, Andrew Brison."

"Good God, man! You don't look anything like yourself. What skullduggery are you about?"

"Let's keep walking." Brison motioned down the street. "Sorry about surprising you like this, but I just saw you walking through Willard's and I wanted to talk to you."

"Well, if you weren't sharp as a knife, Andrew, I'd find this all looney," Pope said.

"I just need some more scuttlebutt about General Kilpatrick."

"Ah, that makes sense. You've obviously heard about the big excursion the Army is planning with Kilcalvary in charge."

"I haven't been hanging around military circles the last two weeks," Brison said. "What's being spread around? A lot of manure, I'd expect."

"It's about the worst-kept secret of the war. The general has secured support for a plan to take a small, brigade-sized force of men and move against Richmond and rescue the soldiers imprisoned there. All sorts of rumors about when and how. Even the gabbers don't have a clue, but it's assumed it's coming before long. Every soldier coming into the city from Brandy Station is all wrathy about it, so I'd expect the Rebels will have Richmond all neatly sealed up like a barrel of whiskey. Military secrets are the hardest to keep when the commanding officer himself would just as soon put in an advertisement in the Intelligencer and the Evening Star announcing his intentions. It's rivaling the excitement about the grand ball being held for Washington's birthday—it's in four days."

"I was aware."

"I would secure an invitation if you can. Everyone who's important will be there."

"I'll get myself an invitation even if I have to call in some favors," Brison said.

"You going to get yourself on that detail for a visit to Richmond?" Pope asked.

"My friend, I want to say this as gently as possible. My plans aren't for general knowledge, and you shouldn't concern yourself with them."

Brison could see Pope smile in the light of the streetlamp they were walking past.

"I'll take that as a yes, but never you mind," Pope said, clapping his hand onto Brison's shoulder. "My silence on the matter is absolute. Besides, not a soul has ever asked me about you. You're just a stray mutt hanging around town with business to attend to."

"I appreciate the comparison, Robert." Brison pretended to look hurt. "I suppose there are worse things you could have compared me to."

"There are indeed; a few generals come to mind," Pope said with a laugh.

CHAPTER TWENTY

Present Day
June 11

IT WAS LATE AFTERNOON but still scorching with the relentless sun as Sparks and Taylor pulled up behind the surveillance van packed in the shade of a mature oak on the street named for the majority of its brethren that lined both sides of this Silver Spring neighborhood. They walked up to the back of the van, and Sparks rapped twice on the door before it opened and the two of them slipped inside.

"What, no coffee?" a voice asked from the very front of the van. It belonged to Xavier Perez, the audio man, headphones firmly clamped on his head as he listened to the feed from the long-range microphone that was aimed at the house of Melissa Cooper, the woman Clint Parsons had dated when he worked at Red Storm.

An interview of a neighbor earlier in the day confirmed that a man answering to Parson's description had been seen in the last few days at her house, a modest single-floor starter-sized model sitting catty-corner and two houses down.

"No one put in an order when we called earlier," Sparks said. "Your mistake. Any movement?"

"We've had people here since 5:00 a.m., and except for the postman, there hasn't been any activity at the house all day," said Betts, the other individual on the surveillance team. "But we don't have eyes on the back of the house—there's no access from anywhere into the back yard. But the odd thing is, we haven't heard a sound all day either."

"Nothing?" Taylor asked.

"Nada," Perez said.

"You sure anyone's home?" Sparks asked.

"That's her car in the driveway," Betts said. "Neighbor said he saw her arrive home yesterday afternoon, and if the car is here, that usually means she is. Are you planning to take her into custody?"

"We didn't want to," Sparks said. "We didn't want to spook Parsons, and we don't want to take him in ahead of our planned visit to his employer." He felt his cellphone vibrate in his pocket. He looked to see the caller ID and found it was the Silver Spring Police Department. He answered and identified himself, then listened for a few moments. "Go ahead, Lieutenant. Act on the call." He ended the call and looked at Perez. "You're absolutely sure you've heard nothing today?"

"Absolutely, and the first shift guys were specific in that they hadn't heard anything either," Betts interrupted. "What's up?"

"That was the locals," Sparks said. "I had red-flagged Parsons and Cooper with them so they would let me know if they popped up on their radar. They just got a well-being request for Cooper from her employer. Seems she's missed an extremely important meeting today that she was supposed to run and she didn't call in and her manager said that never happens. They called, but she wasn't answering her cellphone. The locals will be here in a couple of minutes."

"I've got a bad feeling," Taylor said.

"We go in with the Silver Spring's finest?" Betts asked.

"Taylor and I will go in with them," Sparks said.

In under a minute, Betts pointed at the screen showing the outside of Cooper's house as the cops pulled up in a single cruiser. Sparks and Taylor got out of the van, hurried across to the opposite side of the street, and flashed their badges as the officers prepared to walk onto the property. Sparks explained the situation and deferred to the senior of the two officers. It would be their call to handle with himself and Taylor there for backup. The two officers went to the front door while Taylor went around the left side of the house and Sparks the right.

Sparks's side was blocked by a backyard fence that cut off access to the right side and back, so he made his way to the front just in time to hear the officers knock for the second time.

"Hello? Silver Spring police officers," one of the officers said. "We've been requested to check on you... Ms. Cooper?"

"Sparks, come around to my side," Taylor's voice barked through his earpiece.

"Can you guys see anything through the windows?" Sparks asked as he made his way across the front and headed for the left side of the house.

"Can't see much of anything through these windows," one responded.

Before Sparks got to the left side, Taylor's voice came through again.

"I've got two bodies on a floor. No movement."

Sparks swore under his breath. "Stay there. We're going in the front." He moved back to the front and let the two officers know what Taylor had seen. The front door was made of heavy wood, but there were sidelights, so one of the cops prepared to break the glass nearest the lock when Sparks stopped his arm and held up one finger to make the officer pause. Sparks turned the knob and was met by no resistance.

Sparks and the policemen cleared the house in about a minute. Sparks was joined by Taylor as he went to examine the bodies. They found no signs of a struggle anywhere in the house or on the bodies. Sparks could tell right away the man was Parsons from the photo he had gotten from Army records, and Taylor showed a driver's license from a purse that showed the woman was definitely Cooper.

"They didn't even try to make this look like a murder-suicide or a break in," Sparks said. "They knew Parsons's training, knew he wouldn't allow for something staged, that he would try to fight them at close range, so they took him out first. Three shots to the chest, one to the head. Looks like just one shot to the chest for her and one head shot."

"The house is immaculate," Taylor said. "At first glance, everything is right where it should be."

"Clean... efficient... cold, without emotion. We can assume they were after Parsons and found him here at Cooper's. They didn't hesitate to eliminate her."

"Professionals."

"Professionals," Sparks said, then yelled out to the officers, "You two see any signs of a break-in?" He received a no from both men, the voices coming from the other rooms. "Professionals, who he possibly knew."

"Could have been his own people with Raven's team?" Taylor half-asked.

"Eliminating a problem," Sparks said. He rose from Parsons's body and called in the officers. "This is officially an FBI crime scene. Our techs will handle everything, and I'll clear it with your superiors. Can you both go out and secure the area around the house while we wait for the teams to arrive?"

"I wouldn't expect you'll find anything," Taylor said. "Parsons might be lying here because he got careless in Tucson." She paused for a second, then tilted her head back. "You know what that means?"

"Yeah. If he was eliminated because he made an error at Mallory's estate, that means Raven has an information source with us."

"He's in the weapons business," Taylor said. "I imagine he has excellent intelligence teams at his disposal besides an apparent special forces-type unit."

"I don't know, Bethany. Every time we run into another body, it makes me think we're into some serious shit here and we've been late to the game all along the way."

"If Raven does have a source with our investigation, then he'll know by now we're planning a raid in less than forty-eight hours. We won't be finding anything of substance, will we?"

"So... we go in twenty-four hours early, without telling anyone outside the team leaders themselves," Sparks said. "Hopefully, the leak is higher up on the food chain, since our team leaders weren't told about the blood swipe we found in Tucson or that it belonged to Parsons. So we go tomorrow morning... and cross our fingers."

AFTER A PRESSURE-FILLED DAY, Samuel Raven was back on the golf course, this time trying to get nine holes in before the sun dropped below the horizon. He was playing alone, as he preferred to do. This wasn't a competitive round, so he tried to sort out many of his problems while he walked between shots. He approached the seventh green, which so happened to be surrounded by trees and was farthest from the clubhouse. Aside from a small, empty restroom building, he was alone with nature in the evening light.

Or so he thought.

He had just finished putting out on the green when a voice knifed through the quiet.

"I'd like to have a word with you, Mr. Raven." The woman was dressed in a black, long-sleeved workout jacket with yoga pants and running shoes, her blonde hair tangled loosely over her shoulders. Her arms were folded across her ample chest, which drew Raven's attention as she uncrossed her arms and put them on her hips.

"Well, you gave me a start," Raven said as he continued to walk toward her, captivated by her beauty. She was wearing makeup, and her blue eyes dazzled even in the failing light. The sun was well below the tree line here. "If you wanted to meet me, all you had to do is come to the party I'm giving next week. Everyone's invited." He smiled as he looked into her eyes, and his anticipation grew as she reached for the zipper on her jacket and slowly lowered it, revealing a USC T-shirt underneath. He subconsciously licked his lips and was already fantasizing about being with her when she pulled out the silenced pistol and directed the business end at the center of his chest.

"I'm here on business, Raven," she said, "and I suggest you clear your mind of any expectations of getting any of what I have to offer."

Raven dropped his putter and put his hands up to his shoulders. His normally controlled manner took a serious hit, his mouth open but words failing to emerge.

The woman issued a small sigh. "I only pulled this out to wake your ass up," she said. "I'm not here to harm you unless you do something stupid. And put your hands down for god's sake."

"Who... who are you?" Raven said.

"You can call me Rachel," she said. "From now on, I'll be your liaison with the party you have been in contact with for the past four months."

"What happened to my previous contact?"

"We rotate contacts occasionally when we're dealing with outside individuals. For the duration of this operation, I will be your contact." From her pocket, she pulled an index card and gave it to him. He could see it was a list of twenty phone numbers. "Those numbers are to burner phones. If you need to contact us, start with the first number. After we have a conversation, cross off the number and move to the next number, as I will be throwing away the corresponding phone after each conversation."

"Look, you people came to me with an offer to help me gain control of Raven Industries," Raven said, picking up his putter. "Aside from basic information you really could have gotten from other sources, you haven't asked anything of me—"

"That's not true. We asked if you were willing to have anything done to secure your control."

"I know, anything. Oh, this isn't about his Richmond plan, is it? He's using his little special ops team to retrieve some document that's important to him and Senator Mallory."

Rachel waved him off. "We're monitoring that situation, of course, but we want you to understand what we mean when we say you're willing to have us do 'anything' concerning your father." Her eyes bore right into him, the gun still pointing at his chest.

"I have no grand affection for the man," Raven said. "He's had his heel on my neck since the day I was born. If you're planning to expose his conspiracy to commit murder with his ops team, then so be it. I can take control and lead the company out of any trouble that would cause."

"And if we decided something more drastic was needed?" Rachel asked.

The realization flooded Raven's consciousness. He could feel the blood rushing to his face.

"You think it would be as all necessary as... that?"

"Probably not, but how would you feel about it?"

Raven's chest began to ache, as if he had gotten sucker punched square in the center. "Surely it can be accomplished without anything happening to him."

"With your go-ahead, we started events in motion that can't be stopped now," Rachel said. "I don't believe it will come to that, but we wanted to make sure you were prepared for anything."

Raven thought for a moment, memories and emotions swirling in his head. Ultimately, he didn't want to see the old man hurt, but the desire to have control over the company was too strong. "I'll handle anything that comes my way."

"Good. Events are moving fast now. You will need to be prepared for things to happen in the next twenty-four hours. Will you have any problems with his officers?"

"No, my father made it clear as soon as I joined the company that he was grooming me to succeed him down the road. The people he has in position are loyal to the family in general, not to him alone. I will have their support and abilities ready and in hand when the transition occurs."

"They had better be."

"Your people promised me larger governmental contracts in the future, a strengthening of the already solid relationship between the military and my company. For my position, all those contracts, what are you going to ask of me in return?"

"As we told you before, when the time comes, we will present our requests to you." With that, the woman Raven now knew as Rachel holstered the gun, zipped up her jacket, and began to step away into the trees. "Enjoy the last two holes. I believe you still have enough light left to finish."

He stood there at the side of the green, the phone number card in one hand and his putter in the other, watching as she melted into the brush and disappeared. He walked to his push-cart and returned the putter to his bag, then looked again in the direction she had left before finally heading over to the eighth tee. His mind was already organizing what he needed to do in the next twenty-four hours.

Chapter Twenty-One

Feb. 19, 1864

CONSTRUCTION SOUNDS RATTLED BRISON'S brain. Hammering coupled with sawing and was filled in with the banter of workers rushing around the outside of the structure that he believed would host the most anticipated non-battle event in months. The ballroom was being erected right here where the Second Corps was camped, and every officer was giddy with excitement over what was coming in just three evenings—the Washington Birthday Ball.

If only the coming excursion to Richmond carried with it the planning and effort Brison was seeing before his eyes. He was dressed in his uniform because from now on, he was going to have to travel within the military circus that was the Union's eastern campaign. Le had bloodied General Meade—and by extension, General Halleck—like tormented youths in the play yard, and rumors were flying that something was going to happen at the top. Pope had passed on a tidbit of information that General Ulysses Grant was in line to replace Halleck, taking over the Union effort.

Brison couldn't confirm that rumor because Lincoln had never mentioned any talk about his generals, but he had heard good talk about Grant. The general had certainly had successes at Shiloh, Vicksburg, and most recently back in Tennessee. Pope had heard other details as well, rumors of heavy drink and long spells of melancholy, yet the same could be said of Lincoln, and Brison remained steadfast in his admiration of that man.

A carriage appeared out of nowhere and almost knocked Brison down but successfully splattered him from the waist down with a spreading of mud. He prepared to issue a swear-filled challenge at the driver until he realized the carriage was occupied by four young ladies, another quartet from the deluge of feminine personages that were arriving with each train from Washington. Whoever oversaw this affair was certainly going to raise the spirits of the officers who would be attending. It was damn near causing chaos at every nearby building, as they had been converted into the ladies' sleeping quarters. Somewhere, a band was practicing, and orders were being shouted in dozens of directions, many having nothing to do with the construction.

Brison was going to stick his head in and see what the decorations looked like, but he settled on continuing with his reason for being here—General Judson Kilpatrick. A quick walk from the horse corral got him to a house where he had been told Kilpatrick was attending a meeting that by now might be concluding. At the steps, he was blocked by a saluting private who could have passed as a bull with his size.

"Colonel, you have business with someone here?" the private asked. "I've been instructed to keep the porch clear, sir. General Kilpatrick is in con... uh, frence."

"Conference?" Brison asked. "He'll want to see me. Can I just smoke a cigar here on the steps while I wait?"

"Well, I don't suppose it would be a problem, no how. Perhaps if the colonel would pony up a cigar for a New York man." He smiled and revealed just a half score of teeth altogether, and those that remained were browned from coffee and tobacco.

Brison thought to admonish the private but decided against it. The man looked tired and probably had been standing in front of the house for the better part of the day. He issued a smile. "Tell you what, son. I've got a pretty good nub here I was going to smoke, but I'll give it to you if you let me sit all the way up on the porch. I'll smoke a new one for myself." He handed the private a half-smoked cigar.

"I'm much obliged, sir." The private's eyes sparked up, and he drew back a grin.

"Just don't smoke it until you're off duty," Brison said, patting the man on the shoulder. "Wouldn't want to be the cause of you finding trouble."

Brison found a group of empty chairs strewn about the porch and parked himself in the one nearest the door. A fair amount of activity was going on inside. Brison put out his cigar halfway as there was a sudden increase in chatter. Hat in hand, Brison forced his way through a trio of officers and made his way over to the door where a group was exiting.

"You have business here, Colonel?" It was a captain, smartly dressed in a full-detailed uniform, his hair slicked back, and his whiskers neatly trimmed like he had just stepped from the barber this minute.

"Colonel Brison," Brison said. "I need to speak with General Kilpatrick. He should be expecting me." The president's John Nicolay had sent a message to Kilpatrick's command informing them of Brison's arrival.

"No one sees the general without my permission." As if to accentuate the point, he put his hand up into the center of Brison's chest. "I received no notification. The general is occupied with important matters, and—"

"I suggest you put your hand down, Captain, before I break your blasted arm," Brison said in a calm manner. He pulled out an envelope that carried Kilpatrick's name. "This is my letter of introduction from President Lincoln."

The captain took the envelope, his face flushed momentarily, but just as fast, a look of contrition showed up as he read the contents. "My apologies, sir. The notification must have passed me by. Come with me." He led Brison over to a long table where the general was pulling his papers together.

Kilpatrick looked up and sized up Brison as the colonel extended his hand.

"General," Brison said. "Colonel Andrew Brison. The president's secretary should have notified you of my arrival, and I have a letter of introduction with me."

"We received no such notification, sir," the captain interjected, glaring at Brison.

"Pay no mind, Lieutenant," Kilpatrick said. "I was aware of the colonel."

The captain handed Brison's paper and gave it over to Kilpatrick, then quickly withdrew from the table. The eyes of an annoyed Brison followed the young officer as he left the room and Kilpatrick read over the introduction letter.

"A hasty retreat," Brison muttered.

"My apology, Colonel," Kilpatrick said, folding the paper. "Captain Starke is young and a bit of a bully over organization, but he's efficient, no doubt. Still, I'll talk to him over his rudeness with superior officers."

"My apologies in advance to you, sir. I know commanding officers don't like to have people dumped on them, especially people they don't know, but I promise to stay out of your way."

"On the contrary, I welcome a man of your talents to my command, Colonel." Kilpatrick offered a seat to Brison and sat down at the head of the table. He was a smallish man with broad, unkempt side whiskers, and he was disheveled. His face was squarish, his mouth a thin line horizontal to the floor with two creases on either side. Brison could tell, contrary to his words, Kilpatrick wasn't happy to have Brison appearing without warning. "The president has informed you of our plans."

"Only that you're making a try to free the prisoners at Libby and on an island in the river, I believe," Brison said. "I obviously don't know any details, though I have to tell you the rumor mill is grinding with full vigor. I heard talk just two days ago at Willards when I was having a meal."

That news brought a smile to Kilpatrick.

"Washington is fraught with tales without substance," he said, "but I can tell you what we're planning will be one of the war's most heralded efforts. We're going to get those men out and rough up the Rebs around Richmond a mite in the process. And if all goes well, we might even have the powder left over to cause a great deal more. It will be just the kind of action to begin the spring campaign on a proper foot and give the army here in the east the snap to put it to Lee."

Kilpatrick tapped at the table.

"What I fail to understand is why the president feels it's necessary to send you, Colonel, along with us," he continued.

"From my talk with him, I believed I had his utmost confidence. Now I find that notion being called into question."

"The president does have great confidence in you, General, and you should see my presence here only as a measure of how vital this mission is to him. I am here as an observer and to lend any assistance I can muster. I do have experience behind enemy lines and with placing myself inside organizations in the north that have designs on Southern victory."

"Damnable Copperheads, right?"

"And the like."

"Are you familiar with Richmond and the surrounding area?"

"Somewhat, sir, but I wouldn't call myself an expert," Brison said. "I'm sure you have people under your command whose knowledge exceeds my own. As I said, the president values your effort, and I have no specific assignment at this time, so he thought I could ride along."

Kilpatrick didn't respond immediately, just silently nodded and again began to tap the table. After what seemed an uncomfortable amount of time to Brison, Kilpatrick tapped one last time harder than the previous and continued.

"Who am I to question or take an affront from our president?" he said. "I have been authorized to take a detail of men, thirty-five hundred strong, and strike at Richmond within a week to ten days. We will split our company with the second group under the command of Colonel Dahlgren, and we will take a two-prong approach to the city and get those boys out of Libby Prison by moving fast and with precision. We'll bloody their nose a bit and move out the peninsula to meet up with General Butler."

"I don't know Colonel Dahlgren."

"Ulric Dahlgren, good lad. He came and sought me out to be added to our endeavor, and I just met with him yesterday. The president met with the lad as well earlier this month."

"Is he related to Admiral John Dahlgren?" Brison asked.

"His son," Kilpatrick said. "The colonel comes well regarded. Just the sort of man who takes what I'm trying to do and gives it the importance it deserves. After the ball Monday, we will be having the next meeting to discuss our plan. I would like for you to attend, so give the lieutenant the information on where you will be staying so we can have a courier let you know as to the time and place."

Brison took this as a dismissal, so he got up from his chair. "I'll let the lieutenant know. Before I leave, I just wanted to give you my condolences on the loss of your wife and child." Brison had just heard of the recent death of Kilpatrick's infant son and the death of the general's wife last year. "I know it must be hard to continue the fight under such circumstances."

He caught a glimmer of softness in Kilpatrick's face. It hung for a moment.

"Thank you, Colonel. It... is... hard, but one must stride forward, because our country needs us." Then the softness was gone, and the hard edge of determination reappeared. "I'll take it to the Rebels and get those men free. Another step towards victory."

Brison nodded, wondering whether Kilpatrick was talking about the war effort or perhaps his own military career.

Feb. 20, 1864

THE NIGHT WAS COLD but still as the two enclosed carriages met going in opposite directions on the deserted road ten miles outside of Washington. The carriage facing the city received a shrouded figure from the other and immediately began heading back. The other carriage began the effort of turning around without its owner. Augustus Raven settled into his seat and faced Edwin Stanton, taking a blanket and putting it over his shoulders to add warmth to the expensive, finely tailored overcoat he was already wearing.

"Why couldn't we meet at Willard's or any other place that has a damn stove?" Raven barked.

"Because I think it's wise we not be seen together as the time for the Richmond plan draws near." Stanton turned up his own coat so his ears were given a bit more protection. "I'd caution you about your activities from now on. Don't want any undue light to fall on what is utmost to you, or at least what you've told me is utmost to you. You have the military effort you wanted. They're planning the attack for a week or so from now. Do you have your men ready?"

"Yes, they're attached to one of the regiments that will be under Colonel Dahlgren," Raven said. "Their identification papers place them with the Bureau of Military Information. I don't know the exact details. Is Dahlgren's group the one that will hit Richmond?"

"I haven't been educated on the details of Kilpatrick's plan, but my understanding is that both groups will meet in Richmond if all goes well. Your men will be able to slip away from the group or stay with them if they meet with success. Either way, they will be on their own."

"They were instructed as such."

"They know where this Mallory will be?" Stanton asked.

"They know where he lives, and we also have a person that knows where he will be if he is not at his home. Once my operatives reach Richmond, they know where to go. There is even a possibility he may be with Davis. He has been spending a great deal of time each week at the president's offices in an advisory role."

"There is much that can go wrong with this. Your men will most likely have to get back to Union lines on their own, and it will be testy for them getting through the pickets. And I can't give them any kind of written documents giving them a pass. Do they understand those conditions?"

"If they succeed with killing Mallory, I don't give a Sam Hill what becomes of them." Raven's eyes were fired in the lantern's light. "Look, all of this, I'm confident about. What I'm concerned about is this trouble I've had with Lincoln's errand dog, this Brison. He snooped around my factory in New York, interviewed my competitors to get information on me, bedded my god damn secretary for god's sake. He was in the Willard when we met the night I arrived and had a brief encounter with my man. Now, the bastard, I think, took my secretary away from my men in Swampoodle, where I had sent her away to be dealt with. I want to have him eliminated."

"Well, then, the news I have for you may cause you a night or two of indigestion." Stanton afforded himself a funneled brow. "I've been informed the president has gotten this Colonel Brison attached to Kilpatrick's command for this troop rescue."

"Damn it, no!" Raven barked, then lowered his voice at Stanton's gesture. "He must have heard or learned our plans. They must know what we are planning to do."

"What *you* are planning to do, Augustus. I only approved a lightning attack on Richmond to free Union prisoners. Anything that happens along with that effort is a side matter, one of the countless ones we have seen during this war."

"You will be implicated as much as I, Edwin."

"I'm not oblivious to the dangers involved with this man Brison," Stanton said. "I've made some inquiries. He's someone who performs special investigations for Lincoln on occasion, sort of an operative outside the normal intelligence community. He was probably asked to investigate all of the problems your competitors were having with their factories."

"I tell you, he must know of our plans," Raven implored.

"If Lincoln has him joining the expedition to Richmond, they could be seeking evidence about a conspiracy." Stanton stared at the lantern, almost like he was trying to draw warmth from the small flame, silent until he felt Raven's frustration and it compelled him to continue. "We need to have Colonel Brison removed from the field. He can't be allowed to disrupt your operatives' plans."

"I'll have my two men from Dahlgren's company handle it while they're on the mission."

"No, you need to have someone else handle it," Stanton chided. "Those two men need to not be involved in anything nefarious before the action begins. You understand, Augustus? I'm sure you have someone suitable."

"I have."

"And it must be done before Kilpatrick leaves for Richmond lest Brison find out about who in the regiment will try for Mallory."

"I'll have someone take care of him as soon as possible," Raven said. "Either he will disappear or it will look like a robbery or such. I understand you wanting me to take the risk with this, Edwin, as I'm the one that asked for this endeavor, but I'll remind you that you are becoming a very rich man out of this war—behind the scenes, naturally—with my help, so my financial well-being is tied directly to yours."

"I don't need the lecture. You should be more concerned on your people completing their assignments successfully. They haven't done so when this Brison is concerned. And I hope your words aren't some sort of vailed threat, Augustus. We have been acquaintances and business associates for many years."

"I just want you to keep it close to your heart that your interests are entangled with mine, permanently." Raven's stare carried a very real tinge of maleficence, and Stanton felt an awkwardness with which he was unaccustomed. Usually, he was the one making those around him uncomfortable.

"Just be certain Brison doesn't leave for Richmond with Kilpatrick's command," Stanton said. He threw his fist into the top of the carriage, and it was brought to an immediate stop. "One more thing you haven't mentioned, and this is entirely on you. The secretary Brison rescued from Swampoodle, I'm sure she can reveal much about your—shall I say it delicately—activities that could be construed as being treasonous. I wouldn't be so quick to kill the good colonel before he gives you the location of the woman. Your people will have to be delicate with how they go about their business."

Raven was halfway out of the carriage when he stopped to reply.

"Oh, they will be."

Chapter Twenty-two

THE ESTATE NEAR BOCA Raton was just off A1A right on the water and next to a nature area on one side so Sterling Raven would have privacy there. The north side was buffered by a few hundred feet of heavy vegetation he had put in when he purchased the fifteen-story condo tower and, contrary to how things are done in south Florida, promptly tore down the tower and replaced it with a less evasive twelve-thousand-square-foot home with so much lush growth, it wasn't visible from the main road.

The estate was Raven's main winter residence, but he still flew in on occasion during the humid summer months and used it as a base to meet with Central American and South American business interests who would fly up to south Florida for presentations from Raven Industries employees. This visit had begun a few days ago when he flew into Boca Raton Airport in his corporate Gulfstream G450 and sequestered himself on the estate. He had planning to do and had been unprepared by the Mallory estate failure outside Tucson. He sat on his back terrace watching the sun creep over the horizon, peeking between thunderstorm clouds hovering between Florida and the Bahamas to the east southeast, pondering his future. His morning coffee, black with two sugars, nestled into his empty stomach as he waited for his cellphone to ring, and, as he expected, it did so promptly at the designated time, 6:40 a.m.

Reinaldo Ramirez was at the front gate.

Raven crossed over to the wall and punched in the code on the keypad to let his number one operative in. Within two minutes, Raven himself opened the front door to let Ramirez in, and they quietly made their way back out onto the terrace. The arms manufacturer had told his house staff to sleep in as he would not need them until 9 a.m. or so. He offered Ramirez coffee, and after a moment, they settled down into the chairs, both facing the sunrise, now obscured even more by the storms over the Florida Straits.

"You have never failed me before, and now you have twice in a row," Raven said, not looking at Ramirez. "I'm quite stunned at the circumstances I find myself in. You killed two federal agents, a number of Mallory's security people, one of your men left DNA behind, and you came away with nothing, the document not in your possession. You had to eliminate your operative and a civilian. Now, a search warrant is going to be issued, and the FBI and Secret Service are going to be swarming over my properties tomorrow. They won't find anything because..." Now he raised his voice to almost a scream. "... I don't have the goddamn papers!"

Ramirez waited to speak. The silence was only intruded upon by the waves sweeping ashore in front of them. Ramirez had been born in Cuba, but his parents had taken him on the perilous gamble across the water to Florida when he was but four years old. Raised in Miami, he served in the Army right after Vietnam, and after he received his honorable discharge, he then cut his teeth during the turbulent cocaine war years in the 80s before turning to a career in privatized security. It was impossible for anyone, even his employer, to intimidate him. After a moment, Raven looked at his operative and made a gesture for a response.

"You've read my report," Ramirez said. "The papers weren't there. As we feared, Mallory apparently is not the individual who is blackmailing you. All that was in his safe was the same photocopy that you received—an enticing tidbit, but useless in a court of law. Whomever has you by the balls is a third party who—again, this is conjecture—is also blackmailing Mallory."

"But who? Mallory's family is the only beneficiary if those papers come to light." Raven's words came through clinched teeth. "And you spent all that effort, eliminated Torrez and Collins, then have someone snatch the papers from you before you can retrieve them. Hell, the fed agents would have reached them before you. You told me you thought those operatives had to have been hired by Mallory."

"I thought so, but my sources say those people were not linked with Mallory. We have a third party here, Mr. Raven, and what we need to be wondering is what Mallory could be black-mailed with over a document that could make him a billionaire. Without it, he continues as a powerful, respected, and feared senator who may be running for president next year."

"There's something we're missing," Raven said.

"You have had no contact with the people who hold the documents?"

"No, not since the contact where they told me to wait until the further instructions would arrive."

"We should consider the Scorched Earth Protocol," Ramirez said quietly.

"Assassinate a sitting United States senator. It would rid me of him, but it wouldn't necessarily eliminate the problem unless you want to visit eliminating his entire family."

"I'm only raising an alternative that, though admittedly drastic, would end the problem with Raven Industries intact."

"As much as it would help me," Raven said, "it wouldn't be a solution, and the investigation would turn into a swarm around me. I need you to find out who has the documents and is blackmailing me."

"They contacted you with burner phones, and they rotate to a new phone after each contact." Ramirez finished his coffee and set down the mug. "I've got contacts trying to determine if anyone has heard of a group trying to exert pressure on you or Mallory. I know it's frustrating, sir. All we can do is continue and let part of my team confirm that Mallory's people aren't behind it while I lead the team in trying to track down the other possibilities."

"I want the Scorched Earth Protocol brought to me," Raven said. "Hard copy. I don't trust even the most secure servers, not when I'm expecting the FBI any day now. I want operational details and all contingencies addressed, *and* I want these all predicated on a method that makes it impossible to tie me to the events. We clear on that?"

"Yes, sir."

"I've got many friends on the Hill and at the Pentagon, but if this blows back at me, they'll fall over each other trying to distance themselves from me." Raven got up from his chair, the signal for Ramirez it was time to leave. "Don't contact me until after the FBI has been through their endeavor here and wherever else they fancy. They'll probably have me under surveillance, so use the secure cellphones and always key the contact with a preliminary call using the code we've established."

"Understood."

Ramirez was headed for the door back into the house when Raven called out to him.

"Reinaldo... find out who's behind this. I can't stress to you how important this is to your future." Raven poured himself another cup of coffee.

Ramirez made a mental note to prepare his own contingency plan should the need arise.

THEY CAME JUST TWO hours after Ramirez left the estate. Four SUVs with tinted windows followed by a black, unmarked panel van with a satellite dish on top pulled up at the gate. Within twenty seconds, they disconnected the gate system and gained access to the grounds. They weren't the first of the team to arrive, however, as others had come onto the grounds from the south and north after a fourth team had cut the power to the section of the security system dealing with the sensors and cameras on the property's north and south perimeters. The vans pulled up at the front door to Raven's house within ninety seconds of turning off A1A, Sparks and Taylor stepping out of the lead vehicle and ringing the doorbell, search warrants in hand.

"Can't say I'm not surprised to see you here on my front porch." Raven had not changed from his meeting earlier with Ramirez, a black shirt, and white linen slacks with a pair of expensive cross-training shoes—the casual billionaire look extended to a cliché.

"We have three federal warrants here, Mr. Raven," Taylor said, handing him the documents as the agents began to swarm past them and spread in different directions. "We are authorized to search and seize any materials that could be considered evidence in our investigation."

"Or you could save us a lot of trouble and just hand over the documents from 1859, the ones with an agreement of some kind between your ancestor Augustus Raven and one Justice Mallory," Sparks said. "The documents seven people have already died over."

Raven didn't respond. His stare chilled the foyer for a moment until he was brushed by one of the agents and looked at the offender with contempt before he regained his composure. "Would the two of you join me on the back terrace? The morning is simply brilliant today."

He led them out the glass doors to the terrace and directed them over to the same table he sat at with Ramirez earlier. This time, there was a thermos pitcher of coffee and mugs waiting for them. Raven motioned for them to sit down.

"We're not here to drink coffee with you, Raven," Sparks said. "We're here to execute a warrant, not discuss the merits of another Florida morning. Now, if it was later in the day and you had some mojitos mixed, I might be tempted to have a drink on the job. But seeing as I don't drink with people I despise, I guess that really isn't an option either."

Sparks was a good-sized man, but Raven's six-foot-five frame loomed over him, and the businessman was trying his best to be intimidating. He ran his fingers through his sandy-blonde hair and sat down at the table. He held out his hands for the two federal agents to join him.

"You needn't be insulting," Raven began, his new tactic having been formulated in his head over the past two hours. "I'm not the murderer you seek. I am the victim, as far as I can surmise, in all of this affair."

"You're the victim?" Taylor asked. "You're... the victim?"

"Yes, I'm being blackmailed by someone who thinks the documents they have in their possession could end my complete control over my company and immediately, if my suspicions are correct, make them worth billions."

Sparks sat down and poured himself a cup of coffee. "Continue."

"I received a Photostat copy of a business agreement drafted in 1859 by my great, great grandfather stipulating that almost half of the interest in his company belonged to Justice Mallory, a business associate who was based in the south. Times being what they were, I can only imagine the two of them recognized the enormous amount of money that could be made with their foundry, which, by the way, already had contracts with the Federal Army well before Fort Sumter. Mallory had put forty-five percent of the money to start the foundry back in the early 1850s, and I guess, with the coming war, they decided there needed to be an agreement written down to protect their descendants.

"I was only sent part of the documents, but I believe they intended the ownership of the business would be passed down to the first-born male child in each succeeding generation or to the second-born male if the first shall die before coming of age or having his own offspring. Whomever has the documents also included the supposed lineage of Justice Mallory, and it filters down directly to Senator Brighton Mallory. My blackmailers believe if the senator learns of these documents, he could sue me for the significant interest of Raven Industries."

"Would that even be legal?" Sparks asked.

"It doesn't matter. Even if the judgment went in my favor, the cost and time litigating this would take up a good portion of the rest of my life. There would be a settlement of some kind—never the full percentage, but a settlement of some kind—and it would come to billions of dollars."

"You just gave us a very powerful motive for murder," Taylor said.

"I suppose it is... except I haven't a clue who the people are that have the document." Raven poured himself his own cup of coffee. "You say people have died because of these documents.

I say you need to look elsewhere. My people were supposed to be looking for whomever was blackmailing me, not committing murder. You will find no proof of my involvement in murder."

"We already have evidence of some of your people involved in the attack on the Mallory compound in Tucson," Sparks said. "We will connect you with that, and that alone will be enough to bring you down, Raven. Two agents were killed in that attack."

"I don't know what you think you have, but you're wrong," Raven fired back. "Just who has been harmed in this affair?"

"The documents were originally found by a historian, Arthur Collins," Taylor said, "and he went with them to his friend and former classmate, Adrian Torrez."

Raven nodded. "This is why the Secret Service is involved with the FBI."

"Don't act like you didn't know they were the ones black-mailing you," Sparks said. "You had them killed in an attempt to get the papers. Then, when we found the papers in Vermont, your team attack us and recovered the papers while killing a state trooper... another reason why you'll be going to federal prison for a long, long time."

"Again, you won't be able to prove I was involved, because I didn't have anything to do with that, because if I did, why would I go about attacking Mallory in Arizona? Revenge?"

"Could be as simple as that," Taylor said.

"I can't afford that luxury. So, you say I attacked you in Vermont, but if I did that, then I would have no reason to attack Mallory's estate. I assume you theorize the parties there were after the documents. And if they were, then it had to be someone other than myself, since I already had them from Vermont. Of course, if I didn't get the documents up there, then a third party has the documents, and I guess you could think I was behind that nasty business in Tucson. But then again, why would I attack him if a third party is blackmailing me?"

Sparks and Taylor glanced at each other.

"Let me make this simple for you both," Raven said, reaching for a folder sitting on the table. "Here is the copy of the docu-ment sent to me a few weeks ago. You'll see the basic language goes along with what I just told you. I'm attempting to be as transparent as possible."

Sparks looked over the document copy from the folder and recognized it immediately from what he had seen for those brief few seconds in Vermont. He handed it over to Taylor.

"You seem to have everything neatly tied up in a confusing knot, but I possess information that will have you reaching for your attorney's number," Sparks said. "We have DNA evidence linking an employee of yours, a man named Parsons, to the Mallory estate at the time of the attack. We know he was employed by you because the shell company owned by you has as one of its subsidiaries a company called Corvus, the genus of large birds that include ravens. Nice name."

"I like it."

"Once we pull in all of the people from your security branch," Sparks said. "We'll find people to turn, but really, all of that is secondary and incidental."

"I don't understand." For the first time, Raven was beginning to allow a worried look to appear.

"You really don't think we would show up here hoping to tear apart your properties here and in Pennsylvania and outside Washington and find all the evidence we would need to convict?" Taylor said.

"Your meeting this morning with... Ramirez, I believe you called him, right out here on the terrace. Our warrant included phone surveillance but also audio recovery from your properties... most importantly, this one."

"What are you saying?" Raven asked.

"We recorded your conversation with Ramirez," Sparks said. "Pretty much sounded like an admission on murder and conspiracy to me, at least from the truck, wouldn't you say, Special Agent Taylor?"

"Sure sounded like it to me," she said.

Raven swore and stood up from his chair, knocking it over despite its significant weight. "You bastard! I want my attorn—"

RAVEN STOPPED MID-SENTENCE. A dull sound like someone punched him in the chest came forth, and his black shirt moved with an unnatural motion. It was followed by a second thump.

This one turned him to the side as his knees gave out. Sparks shouted at Taylor and flung himself to tackle the already-slumping Raven, and Taylor dove to the terrace's stone surface, her gun already out. Sparks rolled and, with catlike agility, pulled Raven behind the edge of a stone grill area that afforded instant cover. Within two seconds, Taylor joined Sparks peering out toward the ocean and the trees to the south.

"Shot came from the trees," Taylor said. "I don't see anyone on the beach or any boats nearby on the water. A boat wouldn't give a sniper a solid base. It has to be from the trees to the south, more near the beach than the road out front." She saw that Sparks had his fingers on Raven's neck. "Is he alive?"

"No."

Taylor swore.

"Tell my men to seal off the area to the south with caution," Sparks said. "I'm going to work my way along the tree line. This guy will already be moving down the beach, but just in case, I'm not going to just charge over there."

He scanned the trees to the south and the exposed beach area where he saw a handful of people walking along the water's edge, where undersized waves lapped at the sand. He shifted himself in preparation to run before turning back to Taylor, pointing at his microphone and earpiece. "I'll inform you as I go. Get the team to swing down A1A to the south."

Without waiting for a response, Sparks started running to the tree line, about two hundred feet. Within a few seconds, he was running along the trees toward the open beach, all the while scanning back and forth into the trees, looking for any movement. It wasn't until he reached the tree line that he saw whom he was after: a single figure dressed in running gear sprinting down the beach at a pace much faster than a distance runner would set during a training run. The person turned around and locked eyes with the FBI agent.

Sparks immediately tore off his suit jacket, loosened and discarded his tie, and charged after the figure who had two-hundred-yard head start on him. He cut across the loose sand, struggling to gain traction until he reached the firmer wet sand near the water and turned more directly south in line with the shooter, who had maintained the lead if not increased it while he was crossing the soft beach.

Sparks then realized the shooter was a woman.

"Taylor, you copy?" Sparks blurted out as he increased his speed.

"Got you. Two teams are headed down A1A."

"Subject is a female wearing a track suit and a black baseball cap. Can't tell the color of her hair because it's either tied up or cut short, but it's a woman, and I'm pretty sure she's the shooter. She locked in on me immediately. She's got a two-hundred-yard head start, and she's bookin'. Tell one of the teams to cut to the beach a half-mile down and we'll try to pinch her in." His breathing was starting to become a little labored.

"Can you tell if she is armed?" Taylor asked.

"She stashed the rifle, but she could and probably has a sidearm hidden," Sparks said. "Tell whoever is cutting her off to use extreme caution."

After three minutes, his shirt was already saturated from the humidity, and he wasn't gaining on the woman. She was obviously a good athlete and was used to running at a high sprint for significant distances. Sparks began to look for the two-man team to come from somewhere to his right as they were coming to the south end of what he knew was Red Reef Park, a heavily treed area on the waterfront that bordered a golf course to the south. But before they appeared, the shooter changed the game.

Three boats were anchored in shallow water just off the beach where a group of a dozen or so people were enjoying the morning sun and warm water. She was already wading out to the group, a gun clearly visible in her hand even from Sparks' distance.

"She's acquiring transportation," he said.

"A car?" He heard Taylor's voice followed by another one of the agents. "What's the make?"

"Not a car, folks. A boat. And she's taking it from some swimmers just south of the park, opposite the golf course." Sparks was now closing the gap and had cut her lead in half. He could clearly see her forcing one of the men away from a speedboat, an approximately twenty footer with double outboard engines in back and an overall sleek design, one of the many speed demons seen running north-south along the shoreline.

Within seconds she was onboard and cutting the anchor line. He could hear the engines' deep-throated voices as they started up. He was down to two hundred feet, and he thought about pulling his own gun and trying for a lucky shot, but the shooter was already hunched down behind the wheel to protect herself. Just as he reached the group, now milling on the water's edge, two of Sparks's colleagues came cutting through the bushes on a path, but they were too far away to be of any help. Sparks charged into the water and made his way toward the two remaining boats in waist-deep water. One of the owners was standing in the water, an astonished look across his face as Sparks came up to him.

"FBI," Sparks said, flashing his identification. "I need to take one of your boats here."

"She held a gun at me and took my friend's boat," the man said. "What the hell is going on?"

"She's a wanted fugitive. I need one of your boats. Which one here is as fast as the one she took?" Sparks watched the shooter accelerating away in her stolen boat, heading south and away from the shoreline to clear herself of the other craft in the area. When the man hesitated, Sparks barked at him. "Which one, damn it! I'll make sure you get it back in one piece."

"Ah, take mine here," he said. "It's almost as fast as Jerry's, and it's got plenty of gas."

Sparks climbed into the boat, which was designed similar to the one the woman took. He pulled up the anchor and fired up the twin inboards, checked for any swimmers that might be around and swung the boat away from shore, and threw the throttle into the full position all in under a minute. He headed away from the shore at a forty-five-degree angle at first, then shallowed it as a way of trying to cut into the lead the shooter had on him. She was a good three quarters of a mile ahead of him, and as they headed south, he could tell he wasn't gaining any distance on her. Suddenly, he realized he could hear Taylor in his ear.

"Sparks, Tomlin said you took after her in a boat. What's your status?"

"She's almost a mile ahead of me, I guess," he said. "I'm not closing the gap much if at all; she's got a fast boat."

"We'll be out of range soon."

"Just head south on A1A and you'll stay in range. She looks like she's going to stick close to the mainland."

Sparks thought she responded with an affirmative, but he hit a larger wave and got jammed against the window frame. The ocean was relatively calm, but a wave occasionally caused the powerboat to jolt and force him to flex his legs to absorb the shock. Whoever this was ahead of him would need to get off the water soon, for she would have to know the longer he was in pursuit, the sooner additional eyes would be on her.

Whatever her plan B was, it would have to include getting back on dry land... and if he didn't close the distance with her, she could disappear into the crowds in minutes.

Chapter Twenty-three

Feb. 22, 1864

BRISON WAS NEVER MUCH of a dancer; it always seemed like a forced movement to him, much to the chagrin of Louise Elizabeth, who loved to dance when she wasn't playing music herself. And he certainly wasn't about to ask one of the belles from Washington and the surrounding area if they wanted to dance, but he had to admit he was impressed by the spectacle before him. He estimated the ballroom was about ninety feet by sixty feet, with a peaked ceiling from which hung numerous flags and large chandeliers full of candles. There was food and drink, and the floor was populated almost continuously by couples moving to the sounds of the orchestra. The war seemed distant to the young officers and ladies, enjoying a night of revelry. Brison marveled how these young people, the country's pride-filled progeny, could separate themselves from the dirty business of massive-scale killing.

Standing off to the side as best he could, near an exit, Brison still was subjected to a constant jostling from the couples coming and going. The scene was sheer, controlled bedlam. Brison smiled and shook his head in wonder and made his way along the wall straight for the table filled with spirits and relieved one haggard corporal of a drink. He continued along until he spotted the man he had really come to the festivities to see, Judson Kilpatrick. The general was holding court off to the side, surrounded by a couple of civilians—most likely members of congress— and a trio of ladies adorned in lavish gowns, their hair long since freed from their hats and carefully curled and hanging in splendor onto their shoulders. Two officers were present as well, a colonel and lieutenant colonel, both of whom gave Brison a wary eye as he approached. As he arrived, he caught the figure of the captain who had given him a hand to the chest at the meeting house a few days ago standing to the side, glaring with a most sour face.

"Ah, Colonel Brison," Kilpatrick said. "Enjoying yourself this evening?"

"Yes, sir," Brison said.

"Colonel Brison is a liaison directly from President Lincoln, sent to join our upcoming expedition as an advisor," Kilpatrick said, hiding the sarcasm well, Brison thought. "Though we aren't able to give details, the colonel's presence demonstrates the importance the president holds for my command and our efforts. Isn't that true, Colonel?"

"Absolutely, General," Brison said with a smile. "The president holds your command in the highest regard and confidence."

The group smiled in response, and Kilpatrick's grin stretched the width of his jaw. "When I presented the president with my proposal, he could barely contain his enthusiasm," he said. "I almost was required to rein him in. His desire was for us to begin that weekend! Can you believe those circumstances? I promised Mr. Lincoln a well-planned, efficiently executed endeavor. Ha, that's clever, if I do say so myself!"

The group laughed at his alliteration, and he continued.

"I don't suppose, Colonel, you can tell the ladies here what your normal duties are for Mr. Lincoln." Kilpatrick smiled with just a hint of wolfish attitude.

"Ladies, my duties are all relatively boring. I'm just the eyes and ears for the president when he needs a voice from inside and outside the capital."

"Oh, I think the ladies would be just happily scandalized if they knew the true nature of your duties, Colonel," Kilpatrick said. "You're a very important man for Mr. Lincoln."

Brison gave Kilpatrick an angry look, then eased up as he addressed the ladies.

"The general likes to task me a bit, I do believe, but he needn't worry. I'm here to render assistance on what I'm sure will not be a one-horse excursion. The general's reputation proceeds him, and I'm sure the president has the utmost confidence in him. If you all would excuse me, I see someone I need to talk to before I lose him in the crowd."

As he left the group, Brison heard Kilpatrick issue a less-than-subtle barb. "Off for some more skullduggery, no doubt." He let it go, as he really had caught a glimpse of someone he wanted to see. He worked his way back to the bar table, and sure enough, he had been correct in his observation. It was Robert Pope.

"Robert! How in the Sam Hill did you get an invite to this oasis out here in the slop of Virginia?" Brison shook Pope's hand.

"Word came down from Baker the BMI should have someone here just to keep a weather eye out," Pope said. "They all expect there are spies hanging from the rafters and hiding behind every buggy."

"Well, they're probably correct. All sorts of critters hangin' around these days. You still hearing a lot about Kilpatrick's raid coming up?"

"It's practically all that's being talked about—so much so, I reckon Jeff Davis knows to get a welcoming party ready for KilCavalry. I suppose your presence should answer my question from a few days ago. You'll be headin' to Richmond soon, I'd expect."

"You never know, Robert," Brison said. "You never know."

"You take care." Pope had to raise his voice as the orchestra started into a particularly loud piece. "This whole thing stinks if you ask me. Military secrets are hard to keep, but this is downright a huckleberry above a persimmon in stupidity. The particulars aren't easily found out, but the Rebs gotta know Kil-Cavalry is coming... and no cavalry charge of a couple thousand men is going do much to Richmond."

"Any chance to free those prisoners at Libby has got to be taken," Brison said.

"I suppose, but I think the saber could cut both ways, Colonel. If he meets with success, Kilpatrick could be promoted and cause great damage down the road."

"You don't have much respect for the man, do you?"

"Can't say as I do, and we've got far too many like him giving the orders." Pope turned to give a thin smile. "I do like this Grant fellow that's coming from the western campaign. We'll see how it goes. But keep your wits about you. I don't want to be writing a letter to Louise Elizabeth about your demise. You hear me?"

"I hear you, John." Brison clapped his hand on his friend's shoulder.

It was near enough 1:00 a.m. when Brison left the ball and picked out his horse from the corral to make the trip back to Brandy Station where he had a tent waiting for him thanks to Kilpatrick's captain. He was not required to be part of the official parade scheduled for the next day, but he'd planned to attend because he hoped to meet up with Colonel Dahlgren, who, from what Kilpatrick had intimated, was going to play a significant role in what was to come. The entire area around the ballroom swarmed with activity, and traffic was heavy along the road back to Brandy Station, even with the lateness of the hour.

Eventually, the traffic thinned out. He was riding his horse at a moderate gallop when he came upon a fork in the road. His return to the encampment was down the left road, but a house was located just a few hundred feet away down the right fork. Lights were on in the house, but what caught Brison's eye was a carriage sitting at an odd angle blocking the road near the house. The team of horses was standing alone with no driver or occupants. He pulled up his own horse and surveyed the situation for a moment, tired and debating whether it was worth his time to investigate when the sound of a woman's scream from up near the house reached him. Now, without hesitation, Brison kicked the horse into a gallop and was at the carriage in seconds. He dismounted with his Spencer in hand.

The house was weathered and small. Brison made a quick evaluation that the land around it hadn't been worked for some time. Light from inside spilled out onto the area in front of the house. The path leading up to the front door was worn down by foot traffic, but other than that, the house looked abandoned.

Brison crouched low and made his way up to the house, scanning what area was visible from the light inside.

He got within twenty feet of the front door when a voice from behind him barked, "Hold it right there, Colonel."

Brison froze as if it were the coldest day in New England. It was the voice of the man from the well and the rooftop of Willard's.

"I've got a pistol aimed at your back, so let's hold that rifle well out to your side with your hand wrapped around it," the voice said. "Good, now keep your other hand well out away from yourself."

"I was wondering when we were going to meet again," Brison said.

"We do seem to meet a fair bit more than one would expect," the voice said. "Carlton, Yates, take his guns. I'm sure he has a Colt in there underneath that coat."

Two men appeared from the shadows. One took the Spencer, and the other roughly unbuttoned Brison's coat and retrieved the pistol. They spun him around, and he finally had a chance to see the face of Raven's man.

"You got a name?" Brison asked. "I figure I've got a right to ask, since you hung me above a well and tried to knife me on top of Willard's."

"Clayton," the man said, taking the Spencer from one of the two others. He ran his hand over it with the care of someone who appreciated a fine weapon. "First time I've held one of these Spencers. Nice rifle."

"I heard a woman in distress," Brison said, looking at the figure of a woman now standing in the doorway.

"We paid the whore to make some noise at the appropriate moment, knowing you wouldn't be able to resist investigating," Clayton said. He was a man of Brison's size with the shoulders of an iron worker and longish hair but clean shaven as if he had just walked out of a barbershop. He nodded, and the two others grabbed each arm and held Brison between them. They held him firmly, but both were just average-sized men, and Brison could tell he held a strength advantage. It was just a matter of whether they would relax enough before Clayton wanted to dispatch him. It was clear Clayton was going to make sure there was no repeat of the first two times they had met.

"Colonel, there'll be no working a Virginia fence here. I need to know straight up where you took the Byrne woman."

"Raven likes everything tied up in a neat box with a ribbon on it, doesn't he?" Brison said.

"Where is the Byrne woman?" Clayton wouldn't bite at diverting from the subject at hand. "It took me a little while to figure out she had to have been the one who got you out of that well, so you returned the favor in Swampoodle. Where did you take her?"

"Go to hell."

Clayton let out a sigh. "This is just a business decision, Colonel. Please don't make me turn it into a personal one. Or don't you remember the warning we left on your kitchen table in Springfield?"

Even though the threat wasn't unexpected, it still made Brison's stomach churn; he involuntarily shuttered. Clayton would or wouldn't get the information from him, but he planned to kill Brison and then Byrne when she came out of hiding and perhaps even Louise Elizabeth and the children. There was no other way out of this. Clayton would have to die to ensure their safety.

"Do you desire your family to be victims of your incompetence?" Clayton asked.

"The Byrne woman is being held at a fort in the north, and there she will stay until called upon to testify for the federal government against your boss, Augustus Raven," Brison said.

"Who I work for is of no matter to you. You have a simple decision: Byrne's life for your family's, a simple enough barter I believe. Clean, easy lines to see. Where is she being hidden?"

"Fort Hamilton. Go. Have at her. You'll just need to get through a few hundred troops and officers who are aware you'll be coming."

"I have spies throughout the Union Army and in a good part of the Confederate Army as well," Clayton said. "My people say no such woman has been brought into camp. Again, and for the last time, where have you got her holed up?" Although unfamiliar with the Spencer, Clayton worked the lever, using his thumb to pull back the hammer, intending to kill Brison with his own rifle.

Clayton's two men unconsciously lessened their grips on Brison and moved a little to either side lest they get hit by an errant shot.

"There's nothing I can do if you don't believe me," Brison said. "I would not risk my family for that woman."

"Maybe not. I asked all polite-like, but you continue to refuse my question. I suppose it will be necessary for me to speak with your Elizabeth... Louise Elizabeth I believe is her name. I'll wager she'll know where you placed Miss Byrne, since it isn't in an Army camp."

"You insist you have accurate information from your spies, but can you really say with certainty that she isn't at Fort Hamilton?" Brison felt the slight distance now between him and the two men, but the one on his left had the Colt in his hand hanging down, pointed uselessly at the mud. Clayton held the Spencer in Brison's direction but not directly at him, just off to the side. He might have enough time. Brison tensed his muscles in preparation for what he planned.

"Aye... before's you all settle your business, you promised me my laudanum and I ain't seen none yet!" the woman in the doorway yelled at Clayton.

Raven's killer turned and snapped at her, "Shut up and get back inside!" He turned his attention from the three of them, now standing ten paces away.

Brison kicked with his right leg at the man standing to his right, hitting him in the knee and sending him tumbling into the muck with a scream at his mangled leg. At the same time, he grabbed the man on his left, wrapping his right arm around the man's throat in the vise that was the crux of his lower and upper arm. He grabbed the man's wrist and squeezed into the tendons as he turned his body behind the man to shield him from Clayton, who had already raised the Spencer and was pointing it at them. There was no negotiation to come, no words of warning. Clayton simply raised the Spencer to his shoulder and fired at the two of them, despite the words of despair from the man who saw what his boss was doing.

The shot stunned the night's stillness, the bullet thudding into the man's body as the breath escaped him with a sound of anguish. Brison felt a burning sensation in the fleshy part of his side as the man became heavier in his arms.

Clayton brought the Spencer down to look at it as he worked the lever, and that was the split second Brison needed. He took the Colt from the limp hand of his human shield and brought the pistol to bear on Clayton. The woman screamed at the violence in front of her and disappeared from the door as Clayton dove three steps to his right and disappeared behind the house and out of the light.

Brison looked over at the other man, but he was scrambling into the darkness toward the road, bad knee and all, more than likely satisfied to wait and deal with whomever remained in the next few minutes. Brison got out of the light in the front yard and slipped quickly against the wall of the house. A dense grouping of trees stood just feet away from his side of the house. He moved in haste, disappearing in their safe darkness and crouching low in their shelter, watching for Clayton to appear.

Brison could hear muffled movement from inside the woman's house, apparently barricading herself inside with whatever furniture presented itself. He continued to look for any movement from Clayton, but after a full minute, he realized the killer wasn't making a head-on assault. Brison opened the action and felt to make sure there were still a full complement of bullets in his pistol. He took one look out front and, seeing no sign of his quarry, crept inside the trees for a look at the back of the house. What light came from the house was more visible out front, leaving the backyard area dark. Brison swore to himself and peered as best he could, hoping for any kind of movement along the back of the house. Maybe Clayton would be careless and come right along the house to check for Brison on this side.

He had waited another minute when he heard a scream from out by the road and the bark of the Spencer, causing him to retrace his steps in the trees until he had a full view of the front yard down to the road where the wagon and horses remained. He didn't have a clear view, but he could see movement between some trees. Then came the sound of another shot followed by hoofs on the ground, charging away from the house back toward the main road.

Caution eluding him, Brison ran down the path to the road, reaching it in time to hear more than see Clayton escaping. What Brison found at the road turned his stomach. The other man was in the mud beside the road on his side with his hands clutched to his belly, whimpering words Brison couldn't understand.

Brison now had a better understanding of Clayton, having crossed paths with him four times now. The killer was cold, ruthless, and totally without humanity. Clayton could have given his accomplice the second horse, but instead, out of shear meanness, he had gut-shot the man and then shot Brison's horse before taking the only other saddled animal for himself. Two other horses were still tied to the carriage, but Clayton must have known it would take Brison time to re-saddle one of those animals, giving him enough time to get away.

Brison went to the man still lying on his side.

"What is Clayton's full name and where is he going?" Brison asked.

"You won't... catch him. That's a rattlesnake, that one. He'd just as soon... cut your throat as look at you. Look... what he did to me. Oh God, it hurts."

"I'll get you in the wagon and I'll get you to a doctor."

"Don't matter," he said. "I'll be gone before that. You... you can do one favor for me."

"What do you need?"

"I don't want to die in the mud. Put me on the buckboard."

Brison helped the man to lie down in the wagon, and he found a blanket to put over him. As he was putting the blanket over the man, his hand grabbed Brison's arm.

"There's one thing you need to know, you being a government man and all," the man said. "Clayton is going to kill a man in Richmond when they go in to take the prisoners out of Libby."

"I know. Some man named Mallory."

The man nodded. "But there's more. They're going to kill Jeff Davis if they get the chance."

"Clayton?"

The man shook his head. "Two others..." His voice was fading. "... with Dahlgren's command."

"That was ordered by whom?" Brison asked.

The man didn't answer.

"Who ordered them to kill Jeff Davis?"

After one last breath, the man's body shuddered. He was still.

Brison leaned against the buckboard and sighed deeply, trying to calm his heart and the fire in his shaking extremities. In the dim light cast from a single lantern hanging from the wagon team, he recognized a familiar shape lying in the mud, cast aside with little regard. It was his Spencer. In his haste to prevent pursuit, Clayton had shot Brison's horse that had the holster for the rifle and so was left trying to handle the remaining horse and a loose rifle. Controlling the animal had won out.

Feb. 23, 1864

THE PROSTITUTE COULDN'T GIVE Brison any information. As Clayton had said, they had just hired her to yell out in panic at the right time as he approached on the road. Brison took her and the two bodies back to the Union command near Brandy Station, where he sent her back to Washington and arranged for the bodies to be buried. He wrote a report out and sent it along by courier for Lincoln, omitting the details about a plot to kill Davis, as he didn't have a code book available and he didn't want to chance that information being seen. Brison didn't want to believe Lincoln would forgo the rules of war and authorize the murder of a head of state, even if it was a government in rebellion.

If he was right about Lincoln not knowing, Brison had a smart guess as to whom the orders came from. If Raven's men knew about the plan to kill Davis at the same time they were planning to piggyback Kilpatrick's efforts with an assassination of their own, then the orders could definitely have come from

Stanton. Brison realized now that his job when he joined up with Kilpatrick's troops would be twofold. He had agents from Raven preparing to break off from the group and kill a man named Mallory, and different—or perhaps the same—agents were charged with eliminating Davis. His task was doubly difficult because they no doubt knew who he was, but he was going in blind. He had no clue of the identities of Raven's men.

Contemplating a fast ride to Washington to see Lincoln, Brison stepped from the house that served as administration building and was met by a young colonel, smartly dressed, walking with a crutch due to a missing lower leg. He had hair tinged with red and a narrow goatee, tall and slender with a competent gate despite his injury. He looked up to see Brison and acknowledged the colonel's rank and continued past him towards the house's entrance. Brison paused at the property's front gate, deciding to smoke the last of a cigar as he pondered his next decision when he heard his name called from the front porch. It was the same colonel whom he had just passed a moment before.

The man held out his hand and said, "Colonel Brison, I just asked for you inside, and they pointed you out. I'm Colonel Dahlgren, sir. Ulric Dahlgren. We have a mutual acquaintance."

"And who would that be, Colonel?"

"President Lincoln. He's a friend of the family, my father in particular. I heard from General Kilpatrick that you would be joining the effort at Richmond, and he said I should seek you out before we leave. You will be assigned to my detachment. The general invoked his prerogative to assign you to me as we will have an important role in the matter at hand. He wanted you to be right there with us."

"I'm sure he explained my role is one of assistance and observation."

"He did indeed." Dahlgren shifted on his crutch. "He also informed me you work personally for the president."

"That's correct."

Dahlgren nodded slightly and offered a smile. "A remarkable man, don't you find him so?"

"I do. It's an honor to work for him."

"Tell me, Colonel, if I may indulge myself, and please, speak freely. What's your opinion of our plans to strike at Richmond? Do you believe we have a reasonable chance for success?"

"The effort must be made, Colonel," Brison said. "From the reports, those men at Libby are under terrible conditions and we must get them freed. And a successful effort will hit at the Rebels' heart. The effect on the mind will be as important as the military gains."

Dahlgren smiled again, his eyes sparkling with mirth. "I may be young, Colonel, but I'm not so green as to not realize you didn't answer my question. How's that for a triple negative?"

It was Brison's turn to give a grin.

"Your reputation proceeds you, Colonel," he said. "I've met your father and have been told of your exploits for the Union. I can say the general opinion is you are one of the Army's best young officers."

"Thank you, sir."

"And it is honorable and fortuitous that you have returned to service despite the injury you sustained."

"Following the example of many men before me. But again, Colonel, you haven't answered my question. It is but a simple one."

"I don't know the details so I'm unable to render an opinion."

"Come now, you know the generalities," Dahlgren said. "I'm sure Kilpatrick spoke of them even though we haven't had the final briefing. May I speak plain? I'm attempting to understand if you have a predisposition on this matter."

Brison was annoyed but hid it to better his station with the young commander. It would be vital in the coming days.

"I think this attempt is filled with risk," Brison said. "And I have hopeful feelings, but as to whether it will be a success, I would give it a one-in-four chance. But... that is still worth the attempt, Colonel. More than enough to try."

Dahlgren nodded and seemed satisfied. "The colonel and myself have much higher expectations."

"As it should be."

"I know you look upon me with the glance of a father down to his impertinent son who has taken on more than he can handle, but don't let my age color your thoughts. I am a more-than-capable commander, and you will be reporting back to Mr. Lincoln that our success was a daring chapter in the Union's ultimate victory."

"In all sincerity, as I said, I am hopeful, Colonel."

"I'll see you at the final briefing then." Dahlgren shook Brison's hand again, gathered himself on his crutch, and moved on.

Though this was their first meeting, Brison had heard of the younger Dahlgren long before that day. He was, indeed, very young—probably the youngest colonel in the whole army—and had nearly died of the wounds that had necessitated the amputation of his lower leg. He had been wounded right after Gettysburg and apparently now was back in charge of a portion of Kilpatrick's command. He was thought of highly competent, intelligent, and willing to lead his men from the front. Because of his father, Rear Admiral John Dahlgren, the colonel was well known in Washington circles, just the type of connection the publicity-seeking Kilpatrick would welcome. The question was, how did Dahlgren and Kilpatrick fit in Raven's plans to kill Mallory and how did they fit into an attempt to decapitate the Confederate government?

A meeting with Lincoln was necessary—and with haste.

Chapter Twenty-four

Present Day
June 12

Even with the throttle opened all the way, Sparks couldn't cut into the shooter's lead. They continued south, paralleling the beaches that were already beginning to fill with people. Plenty of pleasure craft also dotted the waters, enough of them that the shooter and Sparks had to occasionally alter their paths. They had passed a public pier—Sparks didn't know which one—and were continuing south toward Fort Lauderdale as he passed an inlet of some kind. Sparks's legs were taking a pounding since there was sufficient wave action, even with a light-wind morning, to cause the speedboat to shudder with constant jolts.

"Jason, status?" Taylor said into his earpiece.

"The same. She's got it flat-out and heading along the shoreline. I don't think she's going to rendezvous with another boat. My best guess is she's still going to get ashore and disappear in a crowded area. What's your status?"

"Traffic is heavy on A1A. We're bypassing as much traffic as we can with sirens, but the congestion is unreal. We may be ahead of you, but not by much—or maybe not. We've notified Fort Lauderdale Police, and they'll have some officers posted at intersections of main streets leading to the beaches. We've also contacted the Broward County Sheriff's marine patrol in case she heads into the interior waterways."

"She'll bail before that," Sparks replied. "She'd have to go all the way down to where the cruise ships come out of Port Everglades to get access. No, she'll duck in before that. Give her description to the locals and tell them to post as many officers as they can at major beach access points. I'll try to give you all a heads-up when she heads for shore."

"I don't know how fast the locals can get everyone into place," Taylor said. "There's a certain amount of lag time we're talking about."

Sparks was thrown against the side of the window bracing, took a forceful shot to his shoulder, and gave out involuntary swear word. "Just keep on them!"

The skyline of downtown Fort Lauderdale was fast approaching. Sparks had been to the beach area before, but he was far from familiar with the area. He could see a heavy influx of tourists dotting the beaches as far as he could see to the north and south. They were closing in on the city's main beach access and had been traveling flat out for almost half an hour. Suddenly, the killer turned her boat into a steep curve and headed straight in toward the beach. She was going for the shore into an area where the beach was especially crowded with people on the sand and also in the water. A little farther out, two parasailing boats were operating. Sparks couldn't cut down the angle, at least not while maintaining his speed. He was gaining now as she slowed her craft to enter the congestion.

"She's making for the beach," Sparks said. "She's going ashore just short of the first large high rise just north of I think the area around Las Olas. I'm not sure though. Taylor, you hear me?"

There was no response. It was possible that a traffic problem had delayed them keeping up with him.

The killer would be reaching the beach in a minute as Sparks made his turn and tried to cut the angle as best he could. He was maybe two minutes behind her now. He tried to get Taylor on the communications link but still didn't get anything. Sparks caught a break as the woman got out of the boat. A couple of male tourists grabbed her boat and delayed her for a moment as Sparks closed in on their position, but he had to slow to a crawl as there were swimmers in the area. A flurry of movement came from the woman's boat, and she churned her legs through the thigh-deep water, making it quickly toward the sand. Sparks caught her looking back at him to check on the timing between them. Just as she hit the sand, he reached the boat she had left behind. He shut the engine off, jumped into the waist-deep water, and saw the result of the activity. One man was lying face up in the water with an obvious bullet hole in his forehead, and the second was clutching his right chest, up high, with blood coming from his mouth as he held onto the stern of the boat.

"She shot me... shot me," he said, struggling to talk. "We just wanted to flirt with her."

A couple of big, college-aged guys arrived at the boat, wide-eyed at what they saw before them.

"You two need to help this guy to shore and call 911 or get a lifeguard to do it," Sparks said. "He's been shot in the chest, probably hit a lung. He's got blood in the mouth."

"Holy shit!" one of the guys said.

"I'm an FBI agent. Bring in the other guy as well, but he's dead. Tell the first cop you see that Agent Sparks is in pursuit."

"Sparks... got it," the second one said. "Jesus, this guy was shot in the head."

Sparks didn't wait to reply and was already heading as fast as he could toward the shore. The woman was running along the beach in the firm sand, but he knew she would cut up the beach any moment. They were near a congested area of shops and restaurants with a lot of foot traffic. He could lose her in just a few moments if he didn't close the gap. She wore running shoes, and he was stuck in his leather work shoes, now mucked up with sand, so he didn't like his chances. He hit the sand about a football field and a half behind her and chugged up the beach. The woman turned through the softer sand and made for an area where there was a public restroom and disappeared around the corner.

Sparks ignored the stares, a man in a suit completely soaked and running with a holstered firearm obvious to everyone. He pounded through the soft sand and reached the corner she had just turned. He stopped short, pulled his Glock, and peered around the corner. Even before he could focus on the scene in front of him, the concrete near his head spit a chunk of itself into his cheek. He pulled his head back to safety. Two girls in bikinis stood off to the side, mouths wide open and expansive eyes looking at him in wonder.

"Get back over there!" Sparks shouted at them.

"Taylor, talk to me," he said, this time hoping they were back in range. All he got in return was static. What the hell could have delayed them?

He peered again around the corner, this time from a crouched position to present a different target as he appeared. A row of bushes on top of a three-foot wall separated the restroom building from the wide walkway just off the beach, high enough to block any pedestrian view from his position. She had fired from the end of the bushes about a hundred feet from his position. If she was still there, he'd be an easy target once he stepped into the alley.

Sparks swung about and ran around the building's other side, running into another group of people. He had to roughly shove some of them out of the way while being cursed out. He reached the south corner and froze before looking around the corner. She was gone from her firing position of thirty seconds ago. Sparks sprinted to the end of the bushes, where there was an opening for the crowds to access the beach. He scanned the throng swarming along the beach walk and filtering to and from the various businesses and a resort building catty corner from his position three hundred feet away. He was looking for the woman but also if he could see officers stationed in the area.

About twenty seconds into his scan, he caught her walking, not running, along the beach walk just in front of the resort building. He started to sprint through the crowd. She caught sight of him and began to run.

"Sparks, can... me?" Taylor's voice came in sporadic bits.

"I'm chasing her on foot," Sparks said. "We are going past the East Seabreeze Resort."

"Seabreeze is... I got," Taylor said.

The woman disappeared behind the far side of the resort between it and another property with a smaller group of build-ings. As Sparks got to the corner, he glimpsed her rounding another corner, heading in the general direction of a four-story building that was under construction. It seemed empty as he could see no movement on the floors above. Fewer people were here as there were no shops in this area, just the back end of the resort where deliveries were made. He reached the corner, stopped, and gave a quick look in time to see her heading down an alley on the side of the construction site, fenced in and empty.

"Taylor?" he said, running to where the woman had just disappeared.

"I've got you," Taylor said. "There was a massive pileup on A1A blocking both north and south lanes. Where are you?"

"Construction area on the south side of that Seabreeze Resort."

"We'll try and set up a perimeter," she said.

Sparks turned the corner, and the killer was gone. An alley continued long enough for him to see her and a second alley led out, but there was a locked gate at the entrance and another gate in the fence surrounding the construction site. It took him only a moment to know where she went; the padlock holding a chain together had been shot open. He slipped through the gate, scanned both ways, and made his way, gun drawn, along the wall to an opening inside. Just as he moved inside, he heard a noise to his left and above him on a second-floor landing that drew his attention up. Even as he looked up, his mind triggered a warning that he hadn't cleared the area to his right. His life was saved by a simple piece of four-by-four that stood upright as a post and took the full brunt of the bullet from the woman's silenced gun. Swearing at himself for his carelessness, Sparks dove for the shelter of a generator and looked for her position. Just as he was about to call out for Taylor, a squeal in his earpiece sent him grabbing to pull it out.

Someone was jamming their communications.

He saw a brief shadow on the landing above. The makeshift stairs were just thirty feet away, but they might as well have been a mile away, for there was no cover available.

The killer couldn't stay here long. She would have to know Sparks would have backup closing in on their position. She'd have to find transportation out of the area fast.

Another shadow moved against a second-floor wall, and Sparks saw an opening, a second set of makeshift stairs farther down the building. He got to the stairs within twenty seconds and silently made his way up to the second floor. The air carried the odors of dust, paint, and drywall, stronger now that he was on the second floor. He caught a glimpse of the woman. She was making her way along the far wall, picking her way between pallets of materials. She was concentrating on the floor below, moving to try and visually cover as much of the area as she could.

She thought he was still downstairs.

Sparks moved as quickly as he dared to get in position. He was just gaining a perfect place when the woman fired off three shots from her silenced handgun down at the floor below.

"Drop the weapon!" Sparks yelled. "FBI—"

The woman turned on her heel, prepared to fire off a shot at Sparks's position, when instead, she froze in shock. Sparks told her again to drop the gun and prepared to try and drop her with a leg shot when he heard a sound from behind him. Before he could turn, he felt a jabbing pain in his neck just to the left of center in the back. Initially, it felt like a bee sting, but then it began to numb. His eyesight faded, and his motor functions deteriorated within a few seconds. He wobblily dropped to his knees. He tried to turn to see the fresh menace behind him, but the side of his face hit the floor and darkness surrounded him.

The last sound he heard was a familiar voice.

TAYLOR AND THE SUV arrived at the construction site. The three other vehicles separated and sped off in different directions to set up a perimeter. They opted for a tight two-block perimeter and quickly got into positions within four minutes. If they had arrived just a few minutes earlier, they would have seen a Florida Power & Light panel van leaving the construction site and turning south out of the area, weaving its way through the traffic both vehicle and pedestrian.

Taylor and the team found the alley and the open gate and made their way into the structure, clearing the first floor and moving on to the second.

"Sparks?" Taylor called out. Then, seeing the floor, she remarked quietly to her team, "Lots of footprints here, and they're not construction boots."

They moved through the second floor until they reached the landing portion of the floor and found a woman's body lying near the view to the first floor below. Taylor felt for a pulse and found none. They continued to secure the floor. When they were clear, they made it back to the body.

"There's no other way to the upper floors except the elevator," one of the agents said.

"We'll still need to search the building floor by floor," Taylor said. "You two go ahead and make sure the floors above are clear, but be careful. Something fucked up has happened here. Look over here. The construction dust is damp, and this is Sparks's earpiece." She pointed at drag marks moving away from the area and toward the stairs they had just come up. "Someone was dragged away from here." The two agents hesitated for a moment until Taylor motioned them to the elevator. "Go on, but if you find a dangerous situation, either because of the construction or someone's up there, pull back and come back down."

They nodded and left for the elevator. Taylor walked back over to the body and knelt. The woman was dressed in workout apparel and running shoes, still wet from the ocean. The zipper to the jacket was open two-thirds of the way to the waist, revealing a University of Southern California T-shirt underneath. She had taken one shot to the chest and one to the forehead with little bleeding, her vacant eyes half open.

"Well, I didn't expect you to be the big, bad assassin, Ms. Evans," Taylor said. "I just wish you could tell me who shot you. Sparks would never finish someone off with a headshot. And..." She looked around her. "...just who the hell took Jason Sparks from here."

THE HUMIDITY COVERED SPARKS like a soaked blanket, bathing him in sweat and misery. As he became aware of his surroundings, his brain focused on just how loud the frogs were, issuing forth their mating calls in a throaty crescendo. Then he focused on his neck, which felt like someone had hit him with a sledgehammer and then stood on his neck for good measure the entire time he was out. How long had he been out?

As his eyes became able to focus, he realized he was inside a wooden structure of some kind, slightly larger than your standard storage shed. It did have a window; however, it was covered in so much grime, the light was diffused. It was still daylight, so it probably was still the same day. But where was he? The frogs sounded as if they were storming the walls, which meant there were a lot of them, so he must be near a significant body of fresh water.

"Everglades," he said.

With each minute, his faculties were returning, but his neck was going to be problematic for a while. He was lying on the bare floor, no cot or anything, so he raised himself to a standing position with difficulty. He went to the door, which had a simple latch made of wood, much like you would see on a door in the 1800s out in the west. With more than a bit of surprise, he found the door unlocked and stepped out onto the wrap-around porch that seemed totally out of place on a structure so small.

The shed was situated on a dry patch of land that stretched out forty or fifty feet from him. A dock and an airboat sat opposite him with two men lounging about where it was tied up, looking like they were waiting. He noticed a third man to his right, sitting on a barrel just off the porch and cleaning his automatic pistol. He looked up at Sparks with a smile, no doubt enjoying the agent's appearance.

Sparks looked up at the tree canopy, judging the sun to be getting low in the western sky. It was still bright enough that his eyes hurt from the light filtering through the branches. The man on the barrel snickered as Sparks held a hand to his neck.

"Good evening, Sparks," a voice said from behind him and to his left. It brought back a flood of memories and knotted his stomach with a sudden burst of acid.

Sparks turned around slowly and found a figure sitting on another barrel fiddling with a silenced automatic. He was dressed in a Hawaiian shirt, white pants, and boat shoes. He wore a holster over the shirt, and a light sport jacket lay across his lap. He was wearing a dark blue baseball cap with a red B in old English font centered on the front. Sparks exhaled in confirmation of his recognition before he turned around.

"Streeter," is all he said.

Chapter Twenty-Five

LINCOLN POKED AT THE freshly laid logs in the fireplace, arranged them to his liking and moved the horse screen into position. "Mister Nicolay and the others are getting quite used to ferrying you to see me when darkness is about," he said. "I find the practice a bit more... disconcerting. Someday, I would like to clasp your hand by the light of God's graces, Colonel."

Brison sat in front of the president's desk in a chair pulled from a meeting table. The hour was late—past midnight—and the stillness was disturbed only by the hiss and occasional pop of burning wood. He had ridden into the city yesterday and procured a room at a place different from his normal boardinghouse out of caution after the night before.

He was tired. He had acquired a fresh set of clothes after a bath and a shave, so he at least looked more presentable than did the president.

Lincoln was dressed like he was every time Brison had seen him, minus the suit jacket and the familiar stovepipe hat. He fiddled with his suspenders as he moved to sit down at the desk, easing his lanky frame slowly into the chair, a fatigued old bear plopping down next to a tree.

"Your report is disturbing from multiple viewpoints, Andrew," Lincoln said. "I'm concerned for your safety if there are attempts on your life and you've not even made it to Richmond. General Lee's army notwithstanding, you are a valuable man, and I lament the danger you are under. This Clayton fellow seems particularly nefarious."

"If that's his real name, Mr. President. Most likely, it's a false one."

Lincoln shook his head. "So the dying man told you there was going to be an attempt on President Davis's life, not on Justice Mallory?"

"In addition to, sir. I believe Raven's agents will be joining Kilpatrick's raid to Richmond with the express purpose of killing Mallory. I don't know what to believe, but a dying man has no loyalties, especially when his boss just put a bullet into him. He said there would be an attempt at Davis, but he didn't say who was involved, the two men with designs on Mallory or someone else."

"Andrew, be honest with me. Is it possible the attempt at Davis could come from our own troops? Perhaps as part of a plan from General Kilpatrick?"

"The general has the reputation of being brash, reckless with his men, and outlandish with his words. He seems the sort that would welcome such a plan if it was already not a part of his own designs. He has placed me with a young colonel who will be leading a separated contingent for a two-pronged attack into the city, and you know this particular colonel, sir."

"I do? It isn't young Dahlgren, is it?"

"It is, sir. Kilpatrick has him leading the second group, and I am assigned to him. I don't think Kilpatrick trusts me, and his dislike of me is evident. The colonel seemed personable enough. It is admirable, his desire for a battlefield command despite having lost part of his leg. He is so young... and impressionable."

"We could just be crowing at an empty henhouse," Lincoln said. "Raven's people could also have a desire to kill Davis at the behest of someone else."

"Someone who couldn't afford to be connected to the plot if it went astray. Even someone with ties to our government, perhaps... part of our government."

Again, Lincoln didn't respond, carefully running his fingers through his chin whiskers.

"Sir, I don't presume to tell you how to run your government," Brison said. "Land's sake, I can barely run my own house. But I need to hear some particular words, and I need to hear them from you, Mr. President. Is Kilpatrick authorized from this office to assassinate President Davis?"

"Andrew, that's the reason I choose you for the tasks I assign you." Lincoln was suddenly stern. "You aren't afraid to ask the questions that need asking. Too often, we expect someone to have courage without independence, and you cannot have the former without the latter, son. No. The general, or anyone under his command, does not have permission for such an action. It was never raised in my discussion with the general when he came to propose his plan, and there has been no mention of something so reckless in communications with Generals Meade or Pleasonton."

"Could it have come from another source?" Brison asked.

"First you wanted to be certain of myself, now you go for other obvious members of the pride." Lincoln smiled softly.

"You know who I'm asking about."

"Stanton seems involved with Raven, and the industrialist is involved with murder and plots of murder. I'm not trying to whitewash the secretary's shortcomings, and there will be discussion about his ties to Raven, but I would be skeptical about accepting as fact his involvement in a plot against Davis."

"You're cautious, sir," Brison said. "I'm not surprised."

For the third time in their brief talk, Lincoln let silence command the conversation.

"The secretary of war is an ambitious soul," he finally continued. "If he has authorized a direct attack upon Mr. Davis, then he has done so as an act of treason upon this government. I can't make it any plainer than that, Colonel. So... I must put you into great peril once again. You need to learn who in Kilpatrick's camp is charged with assassinating Mr. Davis and stop them. I can't imagine how the course of this conflict could change should we abandon the rules of war. The business is tragic enough as it exists... but a circumstance such as that would send our nation deeper into an abyss from which I fear she would never recover."

"And your orders also pertain to Mallory?" Brison asked.

"Indeed, they do. Can't have assassins working under the guise of our army, Colonel. That wouldn't scour in the least."

"But if Kilpatrick and Dahlgren are not inclined to render assistance to me... I am just one man, sir."

"Do what you can, son. If you must put someone under arrest, the general or the colonel will do so under my order. I will give you a letter you can present to them if the situation presents itself. I cannot express how vital it is that this attempt at freeing the soldiers in the prison there remain this enterprise's sole purpose."

"I understand, sir. Why not issue a command to just that end? Let them know any action further than expressed earlier is not acceptable."

"Ah, this is where political concerns must take precedence. There is an election approaching and a direct order restricting action would pin any failure on this office and this president has enough wolves sniffing about the air."

"I understand, sir."

Lincoln stood, followed by Brison, and walked around to shake the colonel's hand. "Colonel, you have my highest regard, and I will be praying for your safe return. I am hopeful both you and General Kilpatrick meet with success."

Feb. 28, 1864

BRISON, IN UNIFORM, SAT on his mount and fidgeted with his rifle and the other items attached to his saddle. The night was clear and cold, but not bitterly, so he was comfortable in his coat and scarf he had been given by Mrs. Potter back at the boarding-house. He had stopped by only to collect his mail and to let her know he was still around. She hadn't seen him in a while, and she had given him the scarf as a simple token. Louise Elizabeth had nothing to fear, as Mrs. Potter was well into her sixties and looked upon Brison as another son to the three she already had, one of whom she had lost at Chancellorsville last spring.

The last four days had been chaotic, even by Army standards. The north side of the Rapidan teemed with activity as cavalry men from Indiana, New York, Pennsylvania, and Maine appeared with orders to become part of Kilpatrick's endeavor. All was in disarray, with orders being given, countermanded, then issued again. Men and officers were put together without any logical meaning, which gave Brison worry. Traveling in enemy territory with men you weren't familiar with was not a good idea, but Kilpatrick seemed to be oblivious of this fact. The bitter nickname of Kilcavalry carried a ring of truth.

Nearly four thousand men were preparing for this effort, and Kilpatrick was splitting them into two groups with Dahlgren's contingent of five hundred men leaving first. They were given three days of rations, as this was going to be a quick in-and-out operation and they assumed they would be able to raid supplies in and around Richmond. Yesterday, two regiments from the Sixth Corps headed west toward the Madison Courthouse as a demonstration to get Lee's attention, and this afternoon, General George Custer and the Second Michigan Cavalry left, heading for Charlottesville to hopefully destroy various bridges and depots they could find—again, with the same goal in mind.

In the few days leading up to tonight, Brison attempted to keep an eye out for men who seemed out of place, though this was difficult due to the influx of multiple units being thrown together. He kept his distance from Kilpatrick but hung around to observe anyone who might be the two assassins, keeping in mind that the dying man back at the house that night could have been given bad information. It seemed a hopeless task beyond his skills, and as they moved out, he found himself dreading the charge given to him by President Lincoln. He found himself longing for Louise Elizabeth and the children, lamenting how his life had turned in the last three years. After a time as they rode south and east, he had a good talking to himself and cleared his head for what lay ahead. He had a bad feeling about the coming days, and he braced himself for the decisions he would have to make and actions he would have to take.

They crossed the Rapidan easily and ran across a few pickets they easily captured. Brison rode near the front of the column, close to Dahlgren so he could see and hear what decisions were being made. The pace was relentless, varying from a trot to a full-out gallop, so pressing was Dahlgren's desire to carry a swift tempo through Virginia. The conditions were acceptable for the time of year even if the pace was taxing and the half-moon gave them less light than was ideal. The plan, as it was communicated to Brison, was for Kilpatrick's main body to follow Dahlgren's party until they reached somewhere near Mount Pleasant, where they would take separate routes. Dahlgren's command, with Brison, was to swing to the southwest and circle around, cross the James River, and come up from the south of Richmond while Kilpatrick's force attacked from the north. They would storm through the city's defenses and free the prisoners before heading east to the safety of General Butler's command farther out the peninsula.

Through the first hours of February 29, it seemed there was no cause for worry about a force intercepting them before they reached the city. In the darkness of the early morning, they reached the area where the great battle had occurred back in May when Lee had bested Hooker—Chancellorsville. Dahlgren slowed the column, and it became a quiet walk through the remnants of the battlefield, a walk brimming with apprehension and dread as they passed through areas of land torn apart and corrupted by the battle, even now almost ten months later.

Brison rode next to a lieutenant who had introduced himself as Patrick but had remained silent through the following saddle time. They walked along a road, staring at the bones of horses and men clearly visible in the pale moonlight exposed by the elements or left out of the ground entirely. The rib bones of the horses were so numerous, they looked like discarded piano keyboards propped up and apart. In just a few minutes on the battlefield, Brison saw half a dozen sets of human remains, a couple of times with a ghostly hand pointing upward from the ground, imploring those still alive to give them a proper burial. They came upon a skeleton close to the road with the skull clear as day, its jaw split open and eye sockets black with anger at those who passed by.

"Mary, mother of God," the lieutenant groaned when he saw this particular lost soul. "Did they not bury the dead properly here? This is horrible."

"You haven't seen much of the elephant, have you, son?" Brison said.

The young man named Patrick lowered his head to stare at the reins and the saddle horn. "No, sir."

Someone else within earshot snickered, and the lieutenant snapped his head in the direction from which it came.

"Don't pay them no mind, Lieutenant," Brison said. "Not a man here that this isn't causin' a case of the shakes." He had seen worse after Gettysburg, when he spent days trying to locate the body of a certain Confederate and also of a certain lieutenant from a New England regiment to whom this young officer bore a resemblance. It had taken days of looking over rotting corpses being buried as quickly as possible but not in enough haste to avoid the smell of death. It was so bad at times, he would lose what food he had been able to keep down, thus ruining the effort. Away from the worst of it, you might be able to keep down some bread and butter or perhaps a piece of fruit... but you learned, at least in Brison's case, to stay away from meat, even jerky. It turned the stomach, the whole idea of eating meat while there was so much rotting around you. "They try to as best they can, son, but sometimes, mother nature does her best to uncover our sins."

"Still, that was months ago, sir," Patrick said.

"It will take a fair bit more than a few months to cleanse this land... and all of the others like it. You know, Mister Lincoln called battlefields like this hallowed ground. I expect they will always be. So, Lieutenant..."

"What, sir?"

"Maintain your respect lest you wind up like that poor soul back there." Brison pulled his hat a little lower on his face and adjusted his scarf and collar. He felt an uneasiness about his shoulders, as if some malevolent presence was looking over him, fostering the desire to be rid of this place in all haste. The land reeked of death, and Brison found himself almost moving up to tell Dahlgren to move the detail along. Soon, they quickened and were off again at a fast pace toward Spotsylvania Courthouse, where they would turn southwest.

Early in the morning, they reached just outside Frederick's Hall Station and stopped long enough to cut the telegraph wire and tear up the railroad track. Someone in the command mentioned it was the Virginia Central Railroad, and the matter was taken care of dutifully. Brison overheard Dahlgren questioning half a dozen Rebel captives and learned that eighty pieces of artillery were massed just outside the Station, but after further questioning, it was determined the pieces were guarded by a large enough force that the delay would be great even if they were able to capture the guns.

And there now was another concern.

The skies, which had been clear when they set out just a few hours ago, were now darkening with ominous clouds giving every soldier a melancholy outlook, for they knew chances were their ride to Richmond was going to get very wet and very cold. They continued their ride to the south through the day as the weather deteriorated, crossing a few small tributaries and encountering another sobering scene, though it wasn't as unsettling as the night ride through the battlefield at Chancellorsville. The land here, too, had been beaten about by the war—houses and barns burned, churches and other buildings abandoned, and farms empty with neglect even where the houses still stood. Even in winter's grasp, one could tell the land had not been cared for this past year. This was a country worn down. Brison again found himself in a mood that matched his surroundings.

When they were approximately twenty miles from Richmond just past dawn, Dahlgren sent a Captain Mitchell and a contingent of a hundred men down a canal as a scout and raiding party with instructions they would meet up again at the James River later in the day. The decision brought further uneasiness upon Brison, splitting the force up a third time in an area where Lee could have dispatched elements from his main army of Northern Virginia. They were wandering around without knowing their surroundings, something cavalry officers were most likely familiar with, but having never been attached to such a unit, it added to the Vermonter's apprehension.

The one positive occurrence came during yet another strange twist to the goings-on. Dahlgren took the column off on a side road for a good two miles before pulling into a modest plantation that, like most of the area, had seen finer times. There wasn't much in the way of livestock, and the main house and grounds had been ignored. Servants could be seen around the house, but their number appeared inadequate, especially when Brison learned this was the plantation of Confederate Secretary of War James Seddon, whose family was well acquainted with Dahlgren.

The secretary's wife greeted them warmly and entertained them for a time. During this stop, two men—one dressed as a corporal and the other as a sergeant—approached Dahlgren right after he had stepped down from the front porch of the four-pillared house and spoke with him for a good five minutes alone before the colonel's aide had approached. Brison observed them from a short distance away, but he was hidden from view by the horses.

From the manner of the conversation, it seemed a conversation of equals, not one between a commander and two of his soldiers. Brison had been concerned that if Kilpatrick was involved in some conspiracy with Raven's people through Stanton, he would have kept the two agents separate from Brison by putting him with Dahlgren while they stayed with the main group. If these two were the men he sought, it meant they planned on keeping Brison from stopping them through some misfortune or their goal was not the same as Kilpatrick's and Dahlgren's and they were, indeed, just going along as cover for their real intentions.

One of the two men had a mustache and goatee and was of average height with unkempt, longish hair. Brison had seen him in camp before and remembered him because he had one eye that wasn't paired up nicely with the other and he carried a rough personality. The other was taller with a strong physical manner, about the same size as Brison himself. He had the lightest-colored hair Brison had ever seen—almost white—and his skin was as pale as snow. He kept to himself as far as Brison could tell, not speaking with anyone and staying close to the smaller one. They wore uniforms, but they didn't seem to be assigned to any of the other companies on Dahlgren's detail.

Brison had looked through the rest of Dahlgren's group as best he could on a couple of the brief stops, but with the darkness, it was only now in the morning light that he began to see faces. He had spent a night pondering whether he was up for the challenge—why Lincoln continued to have faith in him—and fought off the self-doubt he knew could get him killed. The time last winter and summer with Prescott was a more direct adventure and was therefore easier to handle. This affair carried with it an uncertainty Brison found uncomfortable, disconcerting, and more than a little worrisome. The sky was becoming the gray of unpolished Vermont granite and began throwing a cold spittle at them as if to say, "The worst is coming. boys. Best be prepared."

From the talk among the officers near Brison, they were closing in on the James River and would soon be led across by a freed Negro who apparently knew his way around this area and had agreed to lead the detachment across the river. As they neared the river, already battling fatigue from having been in the saddle half the night and all day, the skies decided it was time to make their way even more miserable.

It began to drench them in a frigid first-day-of-March rain.

Chapter Twenty-six

"I HAVE TO ADMIT, I'm surprised our paths have crossed again," Sparks said, rubbing the back of his neck. "What the hell did you hit me with? You could have broken my neck."

Streeter smiled from behind his dark glasses and motioned for Sparks to sit on the barrel nearest where he was sitting. It was still far enough away that Sparks wouldn't have much of a shot of trying to get a weapon from the hired killer, but he welcomed it anyway. Streeter tossed him a bottle of water from a cooler.

"What, no beer?" Sparks said.

"Same rule applies on both sides of the fence," Streeter said. "No drinking on the clock."

"And we're definitely on the clock."

Streeter nodded without responding.

"For Christ's sake, Streeter, why am I here?"

"Because you showed up with your people at a most inopportune time."

"In time for you to kill Raven." Sparks took a long swig from the water bottle, relishing the coolness spreading through his empty stomach and relieving his dehydration.

"You might have a remarkable ability to find lost shipments of gold, but you've been led around like a dog on a leash during this whole affair," Streeter said.

"Who are you working for?"

"You know I can't reveal that, but I can tell you who I don't work for."

Sparks didn't try to hide his frustration. "If this is some big reveal before you put a bullet in my head, I'd just as soon skip right to the coup de grace."

"I didn't tap you on the head just to drag your sorry ass out to the Everglades so I can get you out of the way. Actually, there are two reasons why you're still alive and why you will still be alive when I leave here with my coworkers."

"Enlighten me," Sparks said.

"The young lady you were chasing so dashingly through the South Florida surf worked for me... at least I thought she did. It seems she had orders that superseded any I had given her. My orders didn't include killing Raven. That action came from somewhere else, and I suspect my superiors of some rather questionable decision making, or she was working for someone else aside myself and my superiors."

"What is it with you and your employers? Seems I remember your previous employer had decided to terminate your services in a permanent manner. What is it with you and job selection? Don't you vet possible employers?"

Streeter pushed up his dark glasses. "When she took out Raven, I had the same thoughts. Sometimes I'm hired through third parties. I don't know, ultimately, who I'm working for."

"Two reasons you said."

"Yes. The first is I have a soft spot for your daughter, and I made a promise to avoid causing her any pain in the future, which kind of precludes my eliminating her father. By the way, how is Jennifer doing?"

"Fine," Sparks said with a glare. "She's going to therapy after what she went through."

Streeter shook his head. "I am sincerely sorry for what I put her through. I wish her only happiness down the road."

"And the second reason."

"I want to point you in the right direction with your investigation."

"Why in the hell would you want to do that?" Sparks asked.

"Because it would benefit my interests, and I think your career needs a little kick start. You're going to get cornered at the

Bureau, the lone agent for special investigations that blow up in his face. I really don't know how you got out of the committee investigations without DOJ charges being brought against you."

"Fuck you."

Streeter laughed and put his hand up. "Sorry... cheap shot. The second reason is truly because I want to point you in the right direction. You looked like you were about to arrest Raven this morning, am I correct?"

"We have evidence his agents attacked Senator Mallory's compound in Tucson. He told us he was being blackmailed over some papers that were damaging to his family's company, and apparently, he thought Mallory had them or was behind the scheme."

"You'll find copies of the papers when your people go through his properties. They aren't the originals, and they aren't complete."

"What is so important about papers that are more than 150 years old?" Sparks asked.

Streeter sat for a moment and looked to debate his next course of action.

"Those papers are a binding agreement between Augustus Raven and Justice Mallory."

"I know that."

"The agreement was that Mallory gave funds to Raven for 45 percent of the company in 1859. They wrote in the agreement that interest would carry over to each succeeding oldest male heir until one of the two owners bought out the other. Mallory died in 1864, but his family was never informed of the agreement, and, in fact, there is evidence in the papers that Raven was responsible for Mallory's death. Raven Industries never went public, so since no contract was ever signed to resolve the ownership, 45 percent of Sterling Raven's company, now worth double digits in the billions—"

"Belongs to Senator Brighton Mallory," Sparks said.

"The lineage checks out."

"So Raven was behind the murder of Adrian Torrez and the history professor, Collins?"

"I have no direct knowledge of that, but it's a safe assumption," Streeter said. "I just know my people weren't involved."

"But your people were involved at the cabin in Vermont. A trooper died up there, Streeter."

"Unfortunate, but in dangerous situations, I can't step in every time I'd like to keep my personal moral code intact. I didn't know you were there until I saw you through the windows."

"So you have the papers, then."

"They've been passed along to my employers."

Sparks took another drink from his water bottle and looked out over the area. The late afternoon light was brilliant coming through the trees, but it was lost on him.

"Did your employers tell you why they wanted to blackmail Raven *and* Mallory?" Sparks asked.

Streeter nodded. "I had the same question when I realized how the two of them were reacting to their situation. It would make sense if Mallory had the papers and was blackmailing Raven for his interest in the company, but I knew he didn't, and now, instead of Raven taking out Mallory, my operative eliminated Raven."

"On orders from your employers."

"Possibly," Streeter said, "which brings into question their motives in the first place."

"Ask your spandex-wearing shooter friend."

"Not possible."

Sparks's eyes grew wide as he assumed the worse for her, and when Streeter didn't dispute his assumption, he said, "Kind of a drastic measure to initiate."

"She and my employers should have read me in. Since they didn't, it causes me to be concerned about my health and the health of these other team members here."

"You need to find another line of work," Sparks said.

"I have considered retirement."

"So a third party was playing Raven and Mallory against each other, but for what purpose?"

"Sparks, I leave that for you to find out. I will be conducting my own investigation into their identity and purpose." Streeter rose from his barrel and put on his jacket, so unusually out of place in the heat of their location. "If you look at the end of the dock, you'll see a small skiff besides the airboat I have. A burner cellphone is hidden in the shack here, and after we've gotten ourselves a reasonable distance away, I'll call you so you can find it. Believe it or not, there is cell service out here. Just tell them you're about two miles north of U.S. 41, just how far west of Miami proper you'll have to figure out yourself. I wouldn't wander too far with the skiff. It will be dark in an hour and a half or so, and you don't want to spend the night out among the wildlife. I hear they have a real serious evasive python problem out here. Twenty footers and such."

"Snakes don't bother me," Sparks said. "Alligators are another subject altogether."

THE HAMBURGER TASTED LIKE a juicy slice of prime rib. Sparks's hunger was so strong, he ate his double cheeseburger in four or five bites. He grabbed the French fries in bunches and did little to continue the conversation they had started on the car ride in from the Everglades to this fast food place along U.S. 41 heading into Miami. It was dark now, a busy evening in the suburbs stretching westward and butting up against the natural wetlands of South Florida's interior. The restaurant was popular. The line to the order counter was six people deep, and Sparks looked at the mass of people with regret.

"I should have ordered two," he said. "The line's too long to wait."

"Two? Jesus, Sparks, you're giving me indigestion just watching you." Taylor's face twisted with mock disgust. "And you've been so concerned with eating, you haven't spoken a word in ten minutes."

"I know it's not the Capital Grille, but all I had for breakfast was a doughnut and coffee, so the last meal I had was twenty-four hours ago, so a little sympathy would be appreciated. Also, I could also be alligator fodder right now so... a little leeway, please."

Taylor held up one hand while taking a sip from her soda with the other. "You need to tell me more about this Streeter character. He wasn't mentioned in your testimony before the closed committee on the hill. I know—I've read the transcript.

Yet, from what you explained, he was instrumental in the situation with your daughter and indirectly connected to the death of a director of the FBI. Now he kidnaps an active agent at the site of a murder of someone who just committed a murder herself. Shit, Sparks, I can't begin to unravel this bullshit."

"I love it when you talk dirty. Any chance I should dump my historian girlfriend and take up with a certain Secret Service agent?"

Taylor gave him a bored look.

"All right, I know this is tangled mess, but unfortunately it's our tangled mess," Sparks said. "Oh, and he killed the assassin."

"Great!"

Sparks then filled Taylor in on Streeter's involvement at the house outside Gettysburg and atop the boulders on the battlefield a year ago and what just transpired out in the Everglades, including all Streeter said about Raven and Mallory and the corporate papers that had brought so much death in such a short amount of time. Taylor listened and sipped her soda, not asking any questions until he was finished and paused.

"You believe what he was telling you?" she asked.

"He could have just put a bullet in my head there at the construction site along with her. It took some effort and improvisation to get me out in the woods and then leave me with a way out while they got safely away. It was important for him to talk to me about who's behind this whole thing."

"Well, let's say he's not trying to misdirect you, that what he was saying was straight up. Collins and Torrez were killed by agents from Raven, who wanted to obtain and destroy the documents after the two of them blackmailed Raven with their existence. They must have been blackmailing Mallory as well because he admitted as much to us, that there was contact. They failed to get the documents, but then this Streeter, hired by someone to get the papers, attacks us at the Vermont cabin and gets possession."

"Then Raven, thinking Mallory must be behind this, uses his own private security force to attack Mallory's compound in Tucson," Sparks said.

"We have the tangible proof of that with the blood from Parsons and his employment with Raven's shell company," Taylor continued. "We heard Raven admit to eliminating Parsons and his girlfriend, so we can follow that lead when we bring in this Ramirez guy. But was there anything at Mallory's place, the actual papers, or did they walk away empty handed?"

"Apparently so," Sparks said. "Then, right when we are about to take Raven into custody, he's taken out right in front of us. Why?"

"Who benefits from Raven's death?"

"Revenge from Mallory for the attack?" Sparks asked. "The sins of his forefathers? Robbing his family of their share of the company."

"A company the Raven family built without them," Taylor said.

"But only because, apparently, there is evidence in the papers that Augustus Raven had Justice Mallory killed." Sparks paused for a moment, and a thought came to him. He analyzed it for a moment and continued, "Do you remember what Tank Howard said about Mallory?"

"When he briefed us?"

"Yes, do you remember?"

"I'd have to go over my notes," Taylor said.

"Come on, remember? He said Mallory was a ruthless S.O.B. who was in line as a favorite going into the primary season as his party's nominee. He's the man the party wants to run, yet Tank heard Mallory was going to announce soon he wasn't going to run this election cycle."

"So he doesn't think he could beat the president." Taylor took another drink.

"Tank said he was single-minded of purpose and he aggressively goes after what he wants... and he wants to be president," Sparks stressed. "Unless the papers represented an obstacle to his running."

"The blackmail on Mallory was not a blackmail in the truest form."

"What if he was promised the papers and the chance at billions if he didn't run this election?" Sparks asked. "He's young enough. He could run in four years when Douglas was coming out of office after his second term."

They looked at each other for minute, neither speaking as they let the possibility simmer.

"The papers were in Torrez's possession for weeks before he was murdered," Taylor said. "Shit, Sparks, I was so concerned about finding you and bring you back out of the Everglades, I forgot to tell you..."

"What?"

"The assassin on the beach was Rachel Evans, the White House assistant who gave us the letter from Torrez in the first place."

For the first time in as long as he could remember, Sparks was genuinely shaken and his mouth hung open. "You don't suppose the decision to blackmail Raven and Mallory could have come from the Oval Office?"

"The president doesn't have hitmen on his staff," Taylor scoffed. "I refuse to believe that's a possibility."

"But he could have people that used the papers as a way to keep Mallory out of the race this time with a promise to give him the papers for a lawsuit against Raven at the proper time."

"Jason, you're moving into serious conspiracy nutcase territory here. Douglas always seemed too smooth to be believable to me, and he plays the political game very well, but we're talking conspiracy to a level that makes Watergate look like jaywalking. You're talking obstruction of justice, blackmail, and murder."

"Streeter said we were being played throughout this whole thing, and I believe him. We've been a step behind all the way. You and I might be under surveillance, and I think we need to take measures to cut off that possibility." Sparks pulled his wrappers together. "Let's get out of here. I need to make a phone call to Becker so we can make plans to isolate our communications when we want to."

SAMUEL RAVEN STOOD WITH his back to the dimly lit room, looking through the window at Washington's majestic nighttime persona. The scotch in his hand had not been touched, for his desire had subsided. He put it on the table next to the window and leaned against the frame, breathing in deeply and slowly exhaling. It had been done. He had committed patricide... just not directly. He had set the events in motion that led to his father's death.

He never really wanted his father to die, but when he looked at it objectively, he understood it was inevitable. His father was restricting him instead of giving him more responsibility, embarrassing him with projects one would give to a competent employee but not to one's legacy, not to the brightest asset in the company.

The woman at the golf course had said that events had been set in motion but by their very nature, they were impossible to absolutely control. Raven now understood what she had meant. And now his future was tied to individuals who would dictate terms. He would remain at the head of his company, and profits would continue to come in. Government contracts were as steady as the rising sun. They always would as long as war needed to be fought somewhere. But there would be decisions whose result would be predetermined, and this raised the bile in his stomach. He wouldn't be in control no matter what he desired.

Had he made a deal with the devil?

He picked up the drink and gulped down the amber liquid.

SPARKS HAD PURCHASED A prepaid phone and dialed Becker's personal cell phone even though it was nearly 10:00 p.m. Becker had answered in a wary voice, surely not recognizing the number, but fell into his usual manner when he realized it was Sparks. The message from the agent was simple: get the equipment together to set up a secure line at his home, and when he did, call back on this new number. Becker paused, but he didn't protest or ask additional questions.

SENATOR BRIGHTON MALLORY SAT in the soft leather chair next to the window of his hotel room. He had fixed himself a drink from the minibar and watched as his entertainment for the evening finished dressing. He was a regular of hers and had grown fond of her in a professional manner, though they both kept their relationship only to the sex and cash transaction. She was his favorite because she was especially talented in one particular area and he appreciated her discretion. She appreciated that he wasn't too freaky and he was always generous with his payments, usually a full fifty percent higher than the going rate. He got up as she approached to say goodnight, his untied robe falling open to reveal his nakedness underneath. She glanced down and smiled, playfully grabbing his manhood and giving it a squeeze.

"I thought we were done for the evening," she said. "Or did I just get all dressed again for no reason?"

"I'm afraid we are done for tonight, my dear." Mallory gave her a kiss on the cheek. "Tempting as you are, my celebration will have to end."

"Celebration?" she asked.

"I received some welcome news today, and I thought a few hours with a beautiful lady was merited, but after my drink, I need to head home and get some sleep."

She smiled in return and brushed back her raven hair and walked to the door, turning as she moved the door's handle. "Call me when you want to celebrate again." She slipped through the door, and it latched behind her, leaving the senator to settle back into his chair. He was satiated physically, and he was satisfied with the news of Raven's death, but the situation was still disconcerting. He had been told that if he followed the instructions given, he would have solid inroads to owning a significant share of a multi-billion-dollar company and he would only have to postpone his run for the presidency by four years. All he had to do was announce he was not running this cycle.

His cell phone rang with a number he didn't recognize. When he answered, he heard a series of odd sounds coming in before a voice spoke.

"Did you enjoy yourself, Senator?" a man's electronically distorted voice asked.

There were having him watched. How else could they have known he was even here? He walked and used back entrances on his visits with his escort and... they must have him under surveillance and had just seen her leave the building. He felt the walls creep in as he put down his drink and sat up, subconsciously closing his robe.

"You have me at a disadvantage," he said.

"We did tell you to keep with your regular routine, and you have done as we instructed. In your position, I certainly would have done the same." The voice chuckled. "We expect your announcement on your withdrawal from consideration for a run at the presidency, and you will suspend your exploratory committee until the next election cycle."

"That is what was agreed upon," Mallory said. "When will I receive the file? The time and manner was never specified."

"No, it wasn't and won't be. You will receive the papers when we deem it appropriate."

"What if I contact the younger Raven and negotiate an agreement to avoid the lengthy and expensive court battle? After all, you got what you wanted ultimately... my staying out of the race against Douglas."

"If you and Samuel Raven can agree on a settlement without a court fight, you are free to do so. We will not intervene. But you will still need to have the original papers in your possession to make them available for authentication."

"I still want to meet with the person in charge of this... endeavor."

"It will be taken under advisement, and I will get back with you on our decision."

"Why was Raven killed?" Mallory was not overconfident with his position, but he found the urge to try and get an answer too overwhelming. "It doesn't matter which Raven was in charge as long as I had the evidence to begin my lawsuit."

"A reckless question, Senator." The voice had an edge to it, even with the electronic distortion. It paused before it continued, "Sterling Raven became reckless. In his efforts to gain possession of the papers, his agents murdered and risked exposure. You, of all people, understand this point, Senator. The loss of life at your Tucson compound could have been much worse."

"Yes... I... just needed confirmation for my curiosity," Mallory said.

"Keep that in check in the future."

"Understood."

"We expect your announcement within the week."

"I was planning on making it tomorrow afternoon."

With that, the call ended. Mallory was left sitting in his soft leather chair, his robe now tightly tied about his waist. The senator reached for a second tiny bottle of vodka and fresh ice, a slight tremor in his hands.

Chapter Twenty-seven

March 1, 1864

Brison had always been pragmatic when it came to the war and the Negro. He was smart enough to understand that there were two distinct ways of life banging heads together in a never-yielding clash of wills. The slavery question really had never been one for Brison. Growing up into adulthood and attending college in Burlington, he had known some freemen and found them to be equal to any other man, just different in appearance. Many of his friends took a narrow view, and he had learned to keep his views to himself around them.

Louise Elizabeth was a staunch abolitionist when they married, but she seemed to become even more so as the winds of war came through Massachusetts, which is why she raised no protest when he enlisted to fight, despite the recent arrival of their third child. Life would be hard for her, with him not being there, but it was softened by her father and other family living in Springfield, and it allowed her to be part of the fight through her husband. With her influence, Brison's views had taken on more of an urgent nature. Slavery was immoral, and the sooner it was eradicated, the better.

That made what was happening before him all the more tragic and disturbing.

They were standing in the frigid, spitting rain as a sergeant and a private worked the noose around a negro's neck, standing up in the saddles of two horses on either side of him underneath a large tree. They had rested in the late night and were on the move again at dawn on the first day of March. They had arrived at the James, expecting that the young man would lead them across at the passable place he'd sworn he was well acquainted with. Instead, they'd been met with swift, high water, and when further observation had found no shallower crossing, Dahlgren had ordered the negro's immediate execution. The man had accepted his fate without protest or pleads for mercy, but now, Brison's gut churned with panic, and he debated speaking to Dahlgren as preparations were made. The moral fight within him finally gave in, and he walked over to where the young colonel stood. A junior officer made a move to step in front of Brison as he neared Dahlgren, but a withered stare from the Vermonter caused the officer to step back.

"Colonel, a word, if I may," Brison asked.

"Brief, Colonel Brison."

Brison lowered his voice so there was a measure of privacy. "Why is this necessary? Has the man committed a crime?"

"The offense will be read momentarily, Colonel."

"But a summary execution?"

"I procured the man's expertise on this area with the stipulation that I would have no mercy for deception. The stakes are too great. He understood this before we undertook this mission, and he knew what the consequences would be."

"He seemed genuinely astonished that he can't find the crossing. Perhaps it is simply an error. You would execute a man for an error?" Brison put his hand on Dahlgren's shoulder, and as the difference in size was considerable, it was like a father cautioning a son.

Dahlgren fired a look at Brison and turned his shoulder away.

"You're standing with the president notwithstanding, colonel," Dahlgren said, "you forget your place. I'm in command, and this is my decision." He turned on his heels and walked away from Brison, but before he was five feet away, he turned his head back over his shoulder. "We have been betrayed."

The procedure went with the hurried tempo of men who were cold, wet, and wanted to get the nasty business over with forthwith. Brison stood shaking, twice over from his anger and from the spitting rain that continued to plague the company. He would try again.

"Colonel, I beg you reconsider. This is a freeman, not a soldier and not a spy. Summary execution is not called for here." Brison had stepped in front of Dahlgren, trying to use his size for intimidation, but again with his voice low as to not outwardly show contempt for the young colonel's orders. "I know you count Mr. Lincoln among your acquaintances, and he is close to your father. I don't believe he would approve of your decision here. Think about what the president would do in this circumstance. At worst, the Negro has intentionally deceived us, but he's not raised a hand or caused direct harm upon anyone under your command. We'll find another way across the James."

"Colonel, I don't know why Mr. Lincoln dropped you in on Kilpatrick's command, but I've come to reckoning that General Kilpatrick dropped you in on me to keep you out of his affairs." Dahlgren eyes were lit with fire. "I will explain it to you one last time. This freeman agreed to my terms before we left Brandy Station, and the terms were that if he deceived us in any way, he would be hanged. I am fulfilling that agreement. If you try to interfere with my command again, I'll have you arrested and we can sort this all out when we get back to Washington."

"I was not trying to interfere with you command, Colonel. I was merely attempting to... counsel you."

Dahlgren shifted his shoulders and adjusted his stance on his wooden leg to bolster his appearance. "I have arrived at my decision, and the order stands."

Another officer stepped up to Dahlgren with another matter, and Brison backed down and resigned himself to the idea that he would not make a difference here. The execution continued with haste, and after the noose was firmly around the man's neck, Dahlgren's assistant read the charges against the accused. The man refused to respond when asked if he had anything to say, and the horse was slapped from underneath him. Mercifully, the man's neck broke clean on the drop and he did not suffer.

Some of the men shuffled their feet and averted their view of the guide, now hanging in the rain, a reminder of their world's ugliness. The company was dismissed, and to further Brison's anger, the guide's body was left there to hang in the rain while they were called to mount up. As he stood next to his horse, he saw the smaller of the two men he was suspicious about speaking with Dahlgren briefly before moving on to his own horse. Brison caught the man glancing his way, but he was sure the man hadn't seen him looking at him as he swung himself up onto his animal. As he settled in, the sergeant in charge of the hanging walked past.

"Sergeant," Brison said.

"Yes, sir, Colonel."

"What was the guide's name?"

"Sir?"

"I asked what was the guide's name."

The sergeant was confused as if the question held no logical purpose. "Martin Robinson, sir." He paused and waited for Brison to respond.

"That's all, Sergeant."

The man continued along, slipping in the mud and swearing under his breath at the damn fool question the officer had asked.

Brison turned his collar up on his jacket and adjusted his Spencer in its holster, and even though he wasn't an overly religious man, he said a small prayer that was as much for Dahlgren as for Martin Robinson.

The company moved along at a slower pace near the James as Dahlgren no doubt wanted to rejoin Mitchell's men before they attacked Richmond together, not from the south as originally planned but from the west, while Kilpatrick launched his attack from the north. As it closed in on mid-afternoon, Mitchell and his men arrived to rejoin Dahlgren's command, and they let the troops rest as they gathered around a campfire to plan what course of action they were to follow. Brison bided his time with a small group of men who were attached to a regiment from New York but had been assigned to Dahlgren's command for no apparent reason. They were a fun lot, all young boys under twenty-four, full of enthusiasm and naiveté yet more subdued than when they started thirty hours or so earlier.

Brison had cut his next-to-last cigar in two to share with one he deemed was the oldest of the group, a corporal with a pitiful attempt at facial hair but strong of stature who seemed to smile an unusual amount of the time. Brison was savoring his last chance smoke when the sounds of battle rumbled in from the northeast of their position.

The officers began gathering the men to move out. Brison kept the two suspicious men under a watch as best he could. If the detail somehow managed to make into Richmond, he would have to be prepared to act against the pair when they broke free from Dahlgren's group—if, indeed, they were the two doing the bidding of Raven and Stanton. It was still possible the agents were with Kilpatrick, in which case Brison had no chance of affecting a deterrent to the plan. But all he could do was handle the situation at hand, and given their circumstances, it was well within the realm of possibility that he might get himself shot by a damned Rebel.

A little after 5:00 p.m., with dusk looming over them, Dahlgren ordered the command east along a road near a village called Westham at a firm pace. It seemed the young colonel was steadfast in his desire to support Kilpatrick's presumed attack from the north of Richmond.

As they got within five miles of the city, the sounds of battle from the north ceased and Dahlgren brought the company to a halt. A dismount was ordered, and Brison and others took advantage of a nearby stream to water the horses. When he returned to the head of the column, Dahlgren was interrogating a picket his advance scouts had captured and brought back to the main body. The Reb was a sorry-looking sort wearing a tattered coat with more holes than material left and one good boot paired with an odd shoe that appeared to be two or three cobbled together to afford minimal protection against the wet and cold. He stood shivering, looking at the muddy expanse at his feet as Dahlgren questioned about what he had heard of the fighting. After holding strong against the questions, the man gave forth a small bit of information when he was offered hot coffee and hardtack.

Kilpatrick's raid had been repulsed.

"We can't go solely on the words of this one mangy Reb," one officer said to Dahlgren, who moved slowly on his crutch to exercise the good leg.

"Aye, I would agree with you, but I think he's telling the truth," Dahlgren said. "Gives him a chance to boast, it does. And the guns have stopped... and you know damn well the Rebs would be kicking up a storm if the general was inside the city or close to it. If he has failed in his efforts from the north, then we've lost our chance to get the boys out of Libby. There will be no chance to affect a success without the two of us attacking at the same time and pushing through. We discussed this."

"We must push forward, Colonel, in case the Reb is lying, see if we can determine if the general has made it into Richmond," another officer said.

Dahlgren nodded to himself as he listened to the officer's words. Brison could tell he had already made his decision. "We'll press forward. We haven't gone this far to simply turn away when there is still a chance they've made it into the city or at least are doing so as we stand here. Gentlemen, let's get the company mounted up and prepare them, for this time, we will come under heavier fire."

The area came alive with movement. Brison readied his mount while maintaining a survey of the area to keep the two men he suspected of being Raven's agents under his eye. As the group prepared to move, a group of slaves who had joined the column over the last twenty-four hours, riding in makeshift wagons, were ordered away as not to slow the company down. As they rode by the group on their way on, Brison saw the terrified despair on their faces in the torchlight. They had latched onto Dahlgren's group in hopes of freedom, and now circumstances were casting them back into slavery's cauldron with severe punishment awaiting.

The group under Dahlgren now numbered five hundred men by Brison's estimate, but now, the blood was up in most of them as they stormed towards the city, swiftly overrunning pickets and even some entrenched soldiers as they moved almost three miles. They reached the city limits, their way eased by the gaslights, but now they were suffering more losses as the Rebs picked them off with more concentrated fire. Brison's horse took a bullet to the shoulder, and he lost control of the animal for a moment. He returned fire at the threat off to his right as he was riding on the right side of Dahlgren's group.

Orders came down the line to dismount and return fire against a fortification that lay less than a hundred yards away. A house partially blocked Brison's view of the position, and in a moment of good fortune he would later relay to President Lincoln in his report, his eye caught two figures riding parallel to their makeshift line, moving south. It was the two soldiers he became suspicious of in the recent hours. In the subdued light of lanterns, torches, and the occasional streetlight, he saw they were not wearing uniforms and appeared to be civilians. Brison checked the wound to his horse's shoulder and found it minor. He pulled his regular coat and hat from his bundle and switched away from his uniform. The risk was great here, for if he was caught by the Rebs from this point forward, he would be summarily shot as a spy. Though he did have an ace in the hole, so to speak, tucked safely in an inside pocket. He swung up on his horse and made at a fast pace away from the unit's position, ignoring the calls at him from the others except for one outburst about deserters.

Within a few minutes, he caught the pair making their way down a dirt road that led down the south side of houses in this western edge of Richmond. They were moving at a fast gallop and paying no attention to anyone or anything to their sides or behind them, which made following them effortless. By their lack of hesitation, Brison reckoned they knew the city well. They knew exactly where they were headed. In his focus on the men ahead of him, he himself failed to be aware of his own circumstances, an oversight that would cost lives and almost change the course of the war.

In a short time, they entered the heart of city and slowed down to mingle with the traffic on the main street. They came upon a red stone building that appeared to be a residence, stopped in front, and disappeared inside. Brison kept to the shadows as best he could, because while he was wearing a civilian's overcoat, his pants were government issue, and so were the union coat and shirt inside his bundle. The night was miserable, which helped his cause, because he had seen only a small group of Rebel soldiers riding north in a big hurry. No one had so much as looked in his direction as he kept his eyes on the red stone.

He didn't stay long, for within five minutes, the pair were back on their mounts and moving off. Brison followed, moving in and out of alleys that availed themselves over the next ten blocks as the pair moved toward their goal. Brison had spent little time in Richmond once before the war, but he had studied a street map provided by Lincoln's assistant Mr. Nicolay and had memorized the significant buildings. He was surprised when the men arrived at a brick house set aside from the street with its own gaslights and a neatness that belied the night's harshness and the circumstances of war.

Just as they arrived, Brison slipped behind a nearby building. The two men dismounted, tied up their mounts, and, for the first time, surveyed the street in both directions. Satisfied that no one was paying attention, they went to the residence's front door. Brison moved with haste, working his way along the street's opposite side before crossing in a casual manner to the same side as the house, his horse tied up in an alley. He ducked into the alley next to the red stone and tried to get a look inside. With a stroke of good fortune, the window in the front room was open enough for him to hear the conversation the two were having with the Redstone's occupant.

"Mrs. Mallory, I don't believe you are acquainted with what awaits you if you don't tell us where your husband is," the short one said. "We have no quarrel with you. We are on urgent business and have important information that must get to your husband."

"Couriers don't come calling in the night dressed like the devil." Mrs. Mallory's voice was sharp. "And I don't like your threatening tone."

"We can't spare the time with this," the tall one said. "We can't, I says."

The short one put his hand as if to hold his companion back. "Please, Mrs. Mallory. My friend here is a most inconsiderate person. He would strike you as surely as a dog likes to hunt rabbits."

Brison couldn't see Mrs. Mallory's reaction to this threat, but he heard a response edged with fear and pain. "I don't know when he will return. Keep your hands to yourself, you no-good Yankee."

The sound of the slap caused Brison to flinch. He heard her crying softly, and he fought the urge to move around and kick in the front door to stop the assault. After a moment, she spoke again. "He is with President Davis, but I don't believe they are at the presidential residence. They are at the home of a mutual acquaintance."

"There now," the short one said. "She can be cooperative and polite. Where does this mutual acquaintance reside, madame?"

"I don't know the address, but it's the brick home on Oak Street with a pair of oaks on either side of the front walk."

"There could be dozens of such homes," the short one said. "You will have to improve your aim, Mrs. Mallory."

A bit more defiance returned to her voice. "It will be the only house on the street with Confederate soldiers guarding it."

A laugh came from the short one. "You have me there, Mrs. Mallory." Then he said to the tall one, "Tie her up and gag her."

Brison made his way back across the street to his horse and was back in the saddle when the two left the Mallory home. He continued to follow them in the mixture of rain and sleet that made this whole enterprise a miserable affair, his outer extremities numb to the point of potentially impeding his ability to fire his rifle if the need were to arise. He didn't have to worry for too long, for they reached their destination within a quarter of an hour. The two slipped into the shadows a full three houses down from what appeared to Brison to be the house where Mallory and Davis were meeting. As Brison took to a side street and moved up against a house, a fear feasted on his gut. What if these two were to assassinate Davis while completing their mission for Raven and eliminating Mallory?

The implications were staggering. The attempt Brison had thwarted just a few weeks ago had been by a radical group based in the North, unlikely a sanctioned effort by Davis's government. Once that boundary was crossed, the conflict would become a dirtier affair than it already was, with war waged in all sorts of dreadful manners. Simply kidnapping Davis would have the same effect, another rallying point for the Rebels and harsh condemnation or perhaps more from other countries. Brison had no choice but to assume he now had two targets to protect.

He hoped that Davis's protection detail was sufficient, and that was filed away in the back of Brison's mind as he worked his way again between houses, leading his horse by the reins.

More activity came down the street. A group of eight cavalry soldiers passed within thirty feet of Brison at a fast trot as he tied his horse to a picket fence next to a house that provided cover from the two men who were now moving in the shadows toward the target house. Two guards stood on the front porch, barely visible from the nearest gaslight a full house away. If Brison saw them, then the two men from Dahlgren's group surely saw them as well.

Leaving his Spencer behind, Brison proceeded with only his revolver and a knife in his right boot, moving swiftly between the third house and the one next to where the two men were moving to the back left corner. The sleet-filled rain was beating down, but Brison ignored it as he followed the two assassins. They split up with the taller one moving around to the side Brison couldn't see while the shorter one moved along the near side. Their plan was obvious. One from each side would take care of the two guards on the front porch as quietly as possible. Brison was surprised there wasn't a third guard walking a post that included circling the house.

With some sort of action happening just outside of the city, one would think the Confederate government would be taking better care of its president. That was an issue Brison pondered for a moment but then concentrated on what he would do next. He could expose the two—that would ensure the mission's failure—but Davis and his government would have significant news to exploit and oh, would the naysayers bring unholy fire down on Lincoln and his administration. *Concentrate, Brison*!

He shivered off the frozen rain and made for the house.

THE SHORTER ONE REACHED the corner first and risked a peek around the corner. The two soldiers stood together at the center of the porch, their attention directed out toward the main street and the miserable conditions coming down on the few souls riding by on horse or carriage. They talked in quiet voices, unbe-

lievably, their rifles resting against the two posts that bracket-
ed the steps up to the porch from the walkway. After a moment
came the sound of a bird whistling a soft, short song and was
followed immediately by the two soldiers turning to face a
threat from each side as the assassins came at them with a
swiftness that defied the cold.

Knives flashed, and both found home at the same moment
even though the soldier up against the shorter assassin was
quicker to react to the threat. The knives were buried deep
into the chests, and hands covered the two unlucky men's
mouths as their knees buckled under the weight of death. In
under a minute, the soldiers were gone, dragged to the side of
the house and dumped into the shadows. Having cleaned their
knives and gathered themselves, the assassins simply walked
in the front door, pistols drawn.

The sitting room at the front entrance was empty, lamps
turned low, but as they stepped into the room, a man dressed
in a businessman's jacket and tie crossed into their view. He
glanced at them and seemed taken aback as he looked at the
two men dressed in work clothes with their hands behind their
backs.

"Who are you? How did the guards let you in?" the man
asked.

"Sorry, sir." The short one's Southern accent was sharp, as
natural as a native. "We have urgent business with Mr. Mallory,
and his wife at their residence directed us here. We must
speak with him directly, as it is a matter of utmost urgency."

"You just don't come barging in here at this late hour.
Where are the guards out front? They should never have
allowed you in the door." The man stepped toward the front
door but was met by a revolver that materialized in his face.
With widened eyes, he made a short burst of sounds that failed
to register as words.

"You would serve yourself well, sir, if you directed us
to Mr. Mallory," the tall one said, the pistol extending out
from his long arm downward at the surprised man. "You'd be
President Davis's secretary, I'd expect?"

"Yes... yes."

"Any servants in the house?"

"There are three darkies in the servants' quarters behind the house, but we dismissed them for the evening." The secretary wetted his lips and re-gripped the papers in his hands.

"You understand what I'll do to you if you're lyin'," the tall one said.

"Yes."

"Let's join Mr. Davis and Mr. Mallory, shall we?" the short one said with his gap-toothed grin.

The three of them moved silently down the hall and slipped into the library, which greeted them with a fireplace filled with a roaring fire and the surrounding wall filled with a built-in bookcase bursting with too many books to be lined up neatly. The room was appointed with dark wood, the chairs were large and leather, the rugs were worn but still cushioning, and the four lamps were turned down considerably for a quiet, subdued feel. The two killers and their escort stood at the entrance to the room, waiting for the occupants to recognize the intrusion. The two of them sat in facing chairs near the fireplace, and they turned their attention to the door in unison. The man on the left immediately stood upon seeing the pistols. He was dressed in a dark suit, but he had removed his tie and opened his shirt. He was thin with a strong nose, an angular face with sharp cheekbones, and chin whiskers. His hair was long and covered his ears. The short killer knew this was Jefferson Davis, the president of the Confederacy.

"Who are you?" Davis asked. "What is the meaning of your appearance?"

The tall one shoved the secretary toward a third chair off to the side. "Sit down."

Both killers ignored Davis and turned their attention to the second man. He, too, had stood, a cigar in hand, the smoke trailing directly up his sleeve as he held it. He was a shade shorter than average in height with dark brown hair that was already retreating from the middle of his head. He had a full mustache and beard with large, penetrating eyes of a light blue. His mouth hung open as if to formulate words that had no chance of revelation.

"Answer me!" Davis demanded. "What is your business here?"

The tall one turned to the president. "President Davis, it is an odd circumstance—and lucky—that we should come upon you this evening. We were not here for you but for you Mr. Mallory." He turned back to Mallory, who had not moved since standing. "We come on behalf of your business partner."

The short one flashed another hideous smile. "His desire is to end your partnership."

CHAPTER TWENTY-EIGHT

IT HAD BEEN TWENTY-FOUR hours since the elder Raven's murder, and Sparks found himself and Taylor back at the estate with barely four hours of sleep. After his 10:00 p.m. call to Becker, he and Taylor had gone back to their hotel rooms in Boca Raton, but once there, Sparks was far from being done for the night. Just half an hour after parting ways with Taylor, he received a call from Becker, who was calling on a scrambled secure line. Sparks had changed rooms from their first night at the hotel, and he had swept the room for listening devices, all the while wondering if he was under the influence of a first-class case of paranoia.

He had had just one request of Becker, to get in touch with Jon Samuel Anderson and let the special operative know that Sparks needed help and to arrange a call within the hour. While waiting, Sparks took a walk out the back of the hotel and around the perimeter, all the while checking for any sign of surveillance. When he found none, he knocked on Taylor's door. She answered in a t-shirt and yoga pants.

"I was already in bed," she snipped without opening the door further.

"Step into the hall for a sec," Sparks said.

Taylor placed her service-issued SIG Sauer P229 on top of the safe next to the door and stepped out, not quite closing the door behind her. "What's going on?"

"Did you sweep the room?"

"I didn't think it necessary; it's a new room."

"Do it anyway. I just checked the perimeter and didn't see anything suspicious."

"Jesus, Jason, don't you think you've gotten freaked out here?" Taylor said.

"I don't know... maybe. Just be careful until we're back with the other agents in the morning." Sparks gave her another good night and went back to his room. Another ten minutes went by before the phone on the nightstand rang.

"Jason, how the hell are you?" Anderson boomed into the receiver, wide awake despite the lateness.

"Sam, I've had a long day, so I'll get right to the point." Sparks briefed his long-time friend who had helped save his daughter's life in Gettysburg last year. Anderson, a special ops expert who freelanced for a number of federal agencies, was Jennifer's godfather. He was also used to receiving late-night calls from his friend, especially when it involved work contracted from outside the agencies' regular activities. When Sparks was finished, Anderson paused for a moment and Sparks waited for him to speak.

"You haven't left anything out?" Anderson asked.

"No, you know pretty much the same as I do."

"You know Sammy doesn't believe in coincidences, Jason," Anderson said. "If someone was playing those two against each other, either they could get the desired result from either Raven or Mallory doing what they wanted or they both were contacted about the papers to confuse the situation. You aren't going to get into trouble briefing me like this? You know the suits up on the Hill were particularly upset with you bringing me in at Gettysburg."

"I have to bring you in, Sam," Sparks said. "I can't trust anyone at the Bureau until we get a handle on who is behind this mess. The only thing we can prove is that Raven's people attacked Mallory's compound outside of Tucson. And Raven is dead."

"By an outside agent that somehow had been vetted and cleared to work at the White House and was tied to your old friend Streeter. A mess is putting all this mildly, Jason. This is a cluster you-know-what. Have you talked to Raven's son? I saw on the news that he takes over as the president of Raven Industries."

"Not yet. We're going to interview him either today or tomorrow."

"You know, it occurs to me that you might be having two separate threads running from the one blackmail," Anderson said. "Getting something from Mallory and Raven's murder might be separate and not retaliatory."

"That thought had occurred. I've just got to see where the leads take us, but I want you on standby. This could go sideways quickly. I'll keep you as up to date as I can."

They agreed on a set time to communicate, and Anderson said he would have a small team ready to go and be anywhere in the country within four hours. Sparks knew he could rely on Anderson, as he considered his friend the most resourceful operative he had ever encountered and loyal beyond normal circumstances.

After those four hours of sleep and a red-eyed drive to the shore, Sparks accepted another coffee from an assistant with the FBI forensics unit who had brought in an impressive order and had somehow gotten everyone's preferences correct. Sparks muttered words about the convenience of smart phones as he sipped his straight black with two sugars. Despite Streeter's tip that a copy of the business agreement between Augustus Raven and Justice Mallory from 1859 was at Sterling Raven's home here on the property where he died, Sparks's fellow agents had not found anything during the day yesterday or this morning. The place had been on lockdown all night with four agents on foot and two more in a command truck that was piped into Raven's own security system.

Sparks was popping a pair of pills for his headache when Taylor appeared in the expansive Florida room and sat on the edge of the white leather couch facing the full-length windows opened out to the ocean. She waited for him to toss back the second pill and chase it with bottled water.

"I really need to get a job that allows me to have a regular sleep schedule," Sparks said, rubbing the back of his neck.

"You would be bored to death," Taylor mused. "Besides, you can sleep when you're dead. We need to have a plan of action, Jason. I think we need to tell Connelly and Pearson what we have and what we suspect. We need backup and the clout of our respective agencies on this, don't you think? I'm not ready to get my head chopped off because we shot too high. I'd like to have a rest of my career if you don't mind."

Sparks didn't answer, but he held up his index finger while he chose his words. "We can't go to them with our suspicions, only with what we have as facts, and some of those we need to keep to ourselves. We don't know what we have here, and we don't know who the third party is here, the one that hired Streeter and then pulled an audible on him out on that terrace." Sparks took another drink of water before going back to his coffee. "We don't know who they are, but we do know they have deep connections within the government."

"All we know is someone was blackmailing Raven and might have been enticing Mallory with a significant portion of the company," Taylor said. "And someone decided to remove Raven from the equation."

"After his people attacked Mallory's estate."

"So Mallory is the prime suspect."

"Too obvious." Sparks walked over as another agent came into the room.

"We've gone through everything except the safe, which we have a warrant for, but the only person who knew the combination is dead," the agent said. "We've interviewed the staff, and none of them remember seeing anything like you two described to us. Oh, Henderson just called in to the truck. They picked up Ramirez at the airport in Miami."

"MIA?"

"No, a smaller airport out in the western part of the county."

"Kendall-Tamiami Executive," Sparks said.

"Yes, that's it. He was trying to leave on a private jet. Flight plan was for Cancun."

"Have him brought to Miramar. We'll interview him before we fly up to Wilkes-Barre or wherever Samuel Raven is now."

The agent left the room, and Sparks finished his coffee in one massive gulp. "I need another coffee if I'm going to get control of this headache."

"Connelly and Pearson aren't going to let us go through this day without a detailed report," Taylor said. "You know that, Jason."

"So we call the bosses and we tell them just the facts as anyone on the team could relate to them. We keep out speculation and circumstantial evidence to ourselves, at least for now."

"I've known Pearson for more than ten years." Taylor stood up and approached Sparks. "His father and mine were frat brothers at Ohio State—not great friends, but they knew each other. Pearson sponsored my application. I've had Thanksgiving dinner at his house, for God's sake. He doesn't strike me as a man who would be mixed up in something like this."

"I used to know someone I thought about the same way, and he almost ended up putting a bullet in my head. And my daughter's."

"Director Griffin was mentally ill."

"My point is we could all be fooled by someone," Sparks said. "I don't know Connelly that well."

"We have no evidence either agency is involved."

"I know. But we have direct evidence that someone who worked in the White House on Torrez's staff was an assassin. A fucking assassin, Bethany! How the hell does that happen? Who vets those people? How does someone like that get clearance to work within steps of the president?"

"You know damn well who vets them." Taylor was face-to-face with Sparks. "Someone dropped the ball big time, I know, but it wasn't me."

"And we're left out on an island, you and me. We don't know who to trust with what we know, and the more we follow up, the more we expose ourselves. The press is smelling blood in the water on this already—Torrez, I mean—and Raven's death is going to hit national at some point as well. It can't help but become that kind of story. The owner of one of the largest private defense contractors is murdered. Jesus, some reporter is going to smell Pulitzer and latch onto this, you watch."

"We can only control what we can," Taylor said. "What's our next step then?"

"We see if Ramirez can get us in the safe. Failing that, we get a team in to open it and you and I will fly up to talk to Raven the younger."

AFTER INTERROGATING RAMIREZ AT the FBI office and learning he didn't know the safe's combination, Sparks and Taylor put the local agents in charge of finishing up his initial statement, which wasn't much because he refused to talk five minutes in, and right after, he said he didn't know how to get into the safe. The pair jumped on a plane and flew back to Washington, but not before learning Raven was in D.C. and wanted to talk to agents in charge of his father's murder. They arrived at Reagan National a little after 4:00 p.m. and just in time to run into gridlock trying to get to the Hoover Building. They were in a company car, alone, when the call came in from Connolly to Sparks's phone.

"I was expecting to be fully briefed this morning, Jason," Connolly said after being informed he was on speaker phone with Taylor present. "The short call last night did little to ready me for the shitstorm that's hitting today. The media's got the story—"

"Taylor and I hadn't seen the televisions as we went through the terminal," Sparks said.

"A major industrialist with the government is gunned down with FBI officers present. Jesus, does shit just follow you around or do you go out of your way to turn over just the right rock?" Connolly's voice crept higher in volume. "I've had to issue a statement that the murder is under investigation and we're going to have a press conference as soon as we've got confirmed facts to give them, but you wouldn't believe what caliber shit cannons are being turned on us. Pearson will be calling you, Taylor, in a short amount of time."

"Yes, Director," Taylor said.

"Since this all started with the murder of the president's chief of staff, when you two get here, we're all going to tramp over to the White House and you're going to brief Pearson and me and then the president on just what the hell just happened yesterday morning and how this all ties in with Torrez and his professor friend and Raven and Mallory."

"Yes, sir." Sparks didn't have a clever response, so he kept quiet.

"Just so I'm in the know a little ahead of the rest," Connolly said, "you two got a theory on what is going on? You suspect Mallory of killing Raven?"

"Honestly, Director, we don't know what to believe," Sparks said. "One thing I can tell you, Raven's killer is coming right back to haunt us."

"Jason," Taylor whispered.

"What do you mean?" Connolly asked.

"Raven's killer, the one I chased down the Florida coast, her prints or DNA are going to come back as a hit on the system, but not one you might expect," Sparks said. "She worked at the White House, Director. She was one of the people Bethany and I interviewed right after Torrez's death."

The director was silent for a good twenty seconds.

"She worked at the White House?" Connolly couldn't help but sound shaken, even with the road noise intruding now that they were moving again.

"Yes," Sparks said.

"When you get here, come straight to my office. Don't bother Agent Taylor. I'll call Director Pearson with the news and tell him we're headed to the White House."

The line cut out, and it was quiet for a moment.

"You shouldn't have told him about Evans," Taylor said.

"He would have known within a short time, as soon as the field report came in from the construction site in Fort Lauderdale. I'm actually surprised he didn't know already."

"We're going to have to be very careful."

THE FOUR OF THEM—SPARKS, Taylor, and their respective directors—met in a small conference room in the West Wing. Coffee was provided, but the tone of the meeting was far from break-room banter. With Pearson's agreement, Connolly demanded a synopsis of their entire efforts since arriving on the scene of Torrez's murder. Sparks then spent a half hour doing just that, with some input from Taylor, detailing all that they had been through in the last twelve days. Sparks knew that everything he was saying had been detailed in his reports back to the office, but he tried to fill in some extra details to give the impression he was emptying the notebook now that he was sitting with them face-to-face. He finally got to his abduction from the construction site.

"When I came to, I was in the middle of the Everglades with an operative I know as Streeter," Sparks said. "The same man that was tied to Richardson during the Gettysburg thing last year."

"I've been read into the details outside the official testimony." Pearson shifted in his seat.

"I haven't." Taylor gave Sparks an annoyed glance.

"That's not important," Sparks said. "Streeter said Evans worked for him but, and he was adamant about this, she had acted on her own when she took out Raven. He's the one that eliminated her at the construction site. He seemed genuinely concerned and perplexed about what was going on here, and he told me he was hired to get the business papers. He confirmed those papers were used to blackmail Sterling Raven, and now, I suppose, Samuel Raven apparently, because Senator Mallory could claim his family owns forty-five percent of a multi-billion-dollar company. Raven told us as much that he was being blackmailed. We thought Mallory might be behind it, especially since we have evidence Raven's people carried out the op at the house outside Tucson, we assume in an effort to get the papers. They left empty handed. Yet Raven seemed to know exactly what was in the papers in the brief time we talked to him before his murder."

"You've moved away from the subject of Streeter," Connolly said. "He's been on our radar since last year, and now he turns up to drag you out into the Everglades. Why did he want to talk to you? And why aren't you dead?"

"He has a soft spot for me because of the relationship he formed with my daughter when he kidnapped her last year. Unless he is pushed, he won't cause me harm in deference to my daughter. He also wanted to see what information I had, though I had the impression he knew more about what was going on than we do. I also got the impression his superiors had directed Raven's murder behind his back through Evans, whom Streeter thought was under his control. And here's the kicker: he doesn't know who his employer is."

Connolly and Pearson looked at each other and gave Sparks a look of disbelief.

"I know it doesn't sound right, but Streeter, in all of my dealings with him, has never directly lied to me. He's omitted plenty, but when he chooses to provide something to me, it's been the truth."

"An assassin with a moral code?" Pearson scoffed.

"He has never lied," Sparks said. "That's all I can say."

"You did the profile on him?" Pearson said.

"Yes, he did," Connolly interjected.

"When you read our reports, it's going to be clear that a third party was involved here to use the papers Torrez and Collins found to blackmail Raven for some reason—could be money or something else—then also turn the papers on Mallory, perhaps incentive for getting behind key legislation on the hill," Sparks said. He decided it was wise not to include his questions about Mallory and his possible bid for the presidency, given they were mere steps from the Oval Office. That could wait until the investigation of Mallory had run its course. At least that was his thinking for the moment.

There was a knock on the door, and an aide's head appeared in the doorframe.

"Director Pearson, you wanted to be made aware if anything broke of importance," he said.

"What is it?" Pearson said.

"Senator Mallory is on television as we speak. The graphics on the screen say he is announcing he is not running for the presidency this cycle." Without a response, he closed the door while Taylor walked over to a television framed in the wall and turned it on. It was set to a cable news channel. Mallory was standing in front of a lectern in the senate building press office. Unlike the people assembled in the White House conference room, Mallory exuded positivity.

"It was with much soul searching that I came to this decision," Mallory said. "My plans are to continue my work in the Senate and help with the legislation that is foremost on the American people's agenda. If, in the future, I feel I can better serve the people by running for the office of president, then I will decide to do so. But for now, and in order to calm all the whispers both quiet and not so quiet here in Washington, I will not, under any circumstances, run in the upcoming election."

As he began to take questions, Taylor muted the sound.

"That's surprising," Pearson said.

"That's an understatement," Sparks interjected. "The political wind had him as the party's strongest candidate to run against Douglas next year, but we had heard there were rumors..."

"We talked with a source, William Howard," Taylor said.

"We all know Tank," Connelly said.

"He had been hearing that Mallory was not going to run until after Douglas's second term," Taylor said.

"This from a man whose M.O. is to never waver from a decision once he's made it, at least as far as political ones are concerned," Sparks said, looking at everyone in the room. "Someone got to him."

"Are you suggesting someone within the administration was responsible for blackmail and murder?" Pearson asked. "That's insane. I admit Douglas's road back to the Oval Office just got easier, but that's a hell of a leap to conspiracy. All you have is conjecture."

"Not really, Director," Sparks said. "Rachel Evans is our link to this building. She killed Raven; of this we have evidence and my testimony. Evans, an assassin, working steps away from the Oval Office. We can't get a stronger link than that, sir."

"If word of this gets out—" Connelly said.

"Everything with this investigation is classified, and it will remain that way for national security," Pearson said. "We'll have closed sessions on it, and maybe we can weather the storm."

"Coming on the heels of Gettysburg, good luck," Sparks said. "We'll all be losing our jobs. I've got private security work I can do. What about the rest of you?"

"You arrogant prick," Pearson hissed. "You always seem to land on your feet, don't you? We have a mutual reason to keep this under wraps and make sure it gets cleaned up."

"No matter who's involved?" Sparks asked.

Pearson narrowed his eyes. "Yes, of course."

Sparks risked a glance at Taylor, keeping his face as neutral as possible. His next stop with Taylor was Samuel Raven... after a song and dance with the President.

CHAPTER TWENTY-NINE

March 1-2, 1864

THE TALL ONE, ZACHERY, tied up the president's secretary and dragged him to an adjoining room as the short one, Wade, held his pistol on the two others. He repositioned his grip on the Colt almost constantly, wetted his lips, and glanced back and forth at what his companion was doing and the two men standing before him. Within a moment, Zachery had closed the door and was back at Wade's side. The four of them stood facing each other in silence, Wade's regripping the revolver the only movement in the room.

"Raven sent the two of you here?" Mallory asked. "For what purpose?"

"Seems, like I said, he desires to end your association." Wade almost giggled.

Davis moved forward. "You both can't expect you will safely make it back to the Union lines without a safeguard from myself."

"We'll do rightly fine," Zachery said. "All we have to do is hook up again with Dahlgren's or Kilpatrick's men. You see, they're just outside of the city, close enough for us to slip back in with them as they make their way."

"My last courier informed us they failed in their attempt to raid us, and I imagine they won't make it back," Davis said.

"We'll make it back, never you mind, Mr. President," Zachery said. He motioned with his head to Wade and directed it at Mallory.

"Mr. Davis, if you would step aside." Wade revealed a crooked, sparse complement of teeth.

"I can pay you both double what you are getting for this." Mallory's voice cracked, and he backed away.

"Can't do that," Zachery said. "It would be detrimental to our reputations, and we want to have steady work ahead."

Wade regripped the pistol again and re-aimed it at Mallory, his eyes flaring with a delight only anticipation of pleasure brings. The smile reached the outermost sides of his face, and that was when he died. The room exploded with sound that caused everyone to flinch as if struck by cold water, even to the point that Davis lost his balance and fell against a table and chair. Wade eased to the floor, the pistol tilting downward as his lifeless hand gave away its control.

Zachery reacted well and spun on his heels, bringing his own pistol up from his belt between the open sides of his coat, turning in the direction of the library's entrance and the cloud of blue smoke. He uttered an expletive, searching for the threat. His finger tightened on the trigger to fire before even seeing the target when he, too, died where he stood. The second explosion blocked out the sound of the .44-caliber bullet pounding into Zachery's chest. A second cloud of blue enveloped the room, and the three remaining occupants were left standing in shocked silence. The elimination of the two killers had taken only seconds.

"Mr. Mallory... Mr. Davis?" Brison said. "Are the two of you unhurt?"

"Yes," Davis answered, overwhelmed by what had just transpired before him.

"Yes." Mallory seemed to regain his equilibrium before Davis. "Who are you?"

"My name is Brison, and I work for the president," Brison said. Mallory looked over at Davis. "No, sir, not Mr. Davis. I'm a special agent for Mr. Lincoln. It is under his orders I'm here tonight. I suspected these two men were assassins sent from a private citizen in the north to murder you, hired by your partner in Raven Ironworks, Augustus Raven. I followed them here through the lines, and I worried they would not only kill you but take the opportunity to murder or take you prisoner, Mr. Davis."

Davis's eyes narrowed. "You're a federal spy?"

"Not entirely, sir," Brison said. "I work for Mr. Lincoln, but my assignments have been exclusively in the north until tonight. I implore you to believe me, sir, this action was done entirely without Mr. Lincoln's approval. He sent me to try and prevent what was about to happen here."

Brison moved to check on the two assassins to make sure they were dead. When he finished, he rose to his feet and faced the two men who were standing together. "I promise you that Raven will face charges for this. And the case would be even stronger if you, Mr. Mallory, returned with me to Washington."

"My place is here, assisting President Davis's government," Mallory said. He held out his hand to Brison. "I thank you, sir, for your assistance. You saved my life."

"Yes, we owe you a debt, Mr. Brison," Davis said.

"Colonel, sir," Brison said. "I hold an Army rank. Mr. Mallory, I can't stress to you in any greater terms that our case against Raven will be stronger if you can testify in person. I urge you to consider that and return with me to Washington. I will guarantee your safety once we are there."

"I want to see him convicted as well, Colonel," Mallory said, "but my beliefs remain with President Davis's government, and here I will stay until this war is over."

Brison nodded. "I will not try to belabor the point." He moved to the window and looked out with his hands on either side of his face to hide the interior light from his sight. "Why haven't the gunshots drawn attention? Do you not have a compliment of men nearby, Mr. Davis?"

"I left only the two guards out front," Davis said. "The Yankees attacking the city drew the rest away. The last report I had was that they had been repulsed."

Brison moved into an adjoining room to check out a window. He was just pulling away from the glass when he flinched from the report of a pistol in the library he just left. He drew his Colt from his waist and took three quick steps to the wall beside the doorway and swung his gun hand and his head around the corner. His eyes immediately locked onto someone doing the same at the other main entrance from the front of the house, aiming a firearm at Davis and pulling the hammer back. Brison fired his Colt on instinct, but his aim was off. The bullet struck the door frame thirty feet away, splintering the wood. The other person's arm pulled back and then swung toward Brison, and in doing so, the figure came partially into the light. It was the man from the well in New York, from the bar, from the rooftop at Willard's, and from the Virginia farmhouse—Raven's hired killer, Clayton.

The wood next to Brison exploded, and a shard cut into the skin next to his eye as he returned another round in the general direction of the killer. Another shot came from the other doorway, but then silence. Brison waited as he watched the adjoining wall for a shadow to appear as it would have to if the killer was approaching, but after half a minute, there was nothing. Then came the opening of the house's front door and running steps on the front porch.

"Mr. Davis?" Brison called out.

"Yes, Colonel." Davis's voice sounded muted. "I'm unhurt, but I'm afraid Mr. Mallory is dead."

Brison stepped into the room and found Davis kneeling over Mallory's body. He was momentarily conflicted on whether to secure the Confederate leader or go after Raven's man.

"Mr. Davis, I reiterate to you, sir, that these events were not the designs of my government," Brison said. "This killer was also an agent of Augustus Raven."

"Go, man!" Davis said. "For God's sake, go! Be that sword of justice for both Mr. Lincoln and myself."

Brison was down the hall and out the front door in a heartbeat, pausing only long enough to check his surroundings once he was on the porch. The rain mixed with sleet had increased. He swept up the street and down before he caught sight of a horse and rider darting down a nearby stretch of open land. He ran back up the street to where he had left his mount, all the while cursing himself under his breath.

You were so concerned with following the other two, you never thought to look behind yourself, you idiot! He must have been hidden in the company and, because he knew of my presence, always kept his distance from me. And with Raven, I should not have underestimated him. Of course he would have an alternative to his first two assassins. If I should have learned one thing from this endeavor, Raven is as organized as he is ruthless.

Brison turned the alley corner and half expected to find the horse gone, run off by Raven's man, but he was relieved to see it as he had left it just minutes ago. The Spencer was still in its place as well. He guided the horse out onto the main street and galloped off. The night was even more miserable than before. A bone-numbing sleet-filled rain pelted Brison as he looked all around him, fearing an alarm had been sounded or that he would run into Confederate troops or city-based militia too soon. It would be a matter of minutes before he would see them—it was inevitable, given the attacks from the two Union forces that had been attempted.

He thought perhaps he caught a glimpse of the rider in the distance. The direction was correct if he was going to try and make it back to Butler's troops on the peninsula to the east. Brison crossed the railroad tracks he knew to be the Central Railroad and caught another glimpse of Clayton along the cut of the tracks to the north and then turning out to an open field to the east. At the same time, he could make out activity along Maddox Hill, which was the prominent feature on the northeast edge of the city and a logical place for defenders in case of another surge from the Federal troops. Brison lost track of the killer, so he cut onto Christian Street, which ran east-west, hoping to see the man once he came down the side of Maddox Hill.

"Halt!" came a cry from Brison's right front.

He brought his horse to a stop. Two militia men were upon him within seconds. Before they could even challenge him, Brison yelled at them.

"I have an urgent message from President Davis that I must deliver!" Brison shouted, knowing the best lie is one couched in truth. "There has been a shooting at the president's residence. He is safe, but I am also pursuing the killer."

"Whoa, mister," one of them said. "We don't knows ya from a raccoon in the garbage. You have orders?"

The second rider pulled a pistol from his holster. The barrel was well cared for as it reflected the light from the nearby streetlamp with great clarity. That was the weapon of someone who knew how to take care of it, and one could assume he was as practiced in using it.

"Damn it, man, I don't have time for you to challenge me." Brison tried to heighten the urgency. "Every second adds to my disadvantage." The sleet took that moment to increase making all three men pull up their collars. "Every second!"

"Do you have papers or orders?" the first man asked.

"I just left a murder scene," Brison said. "The president didn't have time to issue me orders, damn it."

"Let him go, Terrance," the second one said. "I want to get out of this shit."

The first one looked at his companion, who was placing his pistol back in its holster, then looked back at Brison. He pondered for a moment but then threw his head in the direction Brison had been galloping. "Best you watch yourself. There are a bunch of Yankees out there and our boys as well. They're all itching to trade shots in the dark."

"Much obliged," Brison said, pulling on his horse's reins and kicking off to the east. Even as he did so, he was filled with dread because he had just lost time he could never gain back. The killer was on his way back and could either pick his way along until he was back in the Union, join back up with either of the split parts of the Union force, or get back to Butler's army to the east.

The darkness would slow Brison's pursuit, and he had precious little provisions. He thought for a moment the killer might meet an undignified end at the end of a bullet from either side, but he put it out of his mind because he knew he needed the bastard alive. With an apology to Louise Elizabeth, Brison issued a string of swear words for his circumstances, his shoulder barking from the cold. He drove the horse on the road away from Richmond, and when he approached the city's outer pickets, the soldiers, to his surprise, threw up nary a yell. He thought it might be because he was heading out of Richmond that they figured he was just some insane person riding out into the dark and cold and leave him be.

He headed out into the dark, already exhausted with so much more riding to go.

AFTER MIDNIGHT, BRISON STOPPED and moved off the main road in search of shelter and to rest the horse. He found a thicket of dense trees and bushes and threw a small tarp he carried in his saddlebag over him. He used a couple of his matches extracted from a waterproof container he also carried and looked over a crude map of northern Virginia he brought with him.

As best as he could estimate, he was well past Mechanicsville and closing in on Old Church, though he truthfully had no way to tell him how close. The rain had stopped, and the wind freshened enough to speak to him from the trees above. He didn't dare build a fire, partly because he had no dry kindling to even attempt it, and even a modest fire could be seen from a great distance on a dark night. He had dodged Rebel patrols three times since he left Richmond, but he had kept up a good pace despite the difficulties.

He was biting into his second piece of dried beef and debating on whether to sleep for a while when he heard the boom of cannon fire and the crackle of rifles from a distance. It was sporadic in volume but consistent and didn't stop after fifteen minutes. Someone was having a time of it.

Brison got moving again and followed the sound of the gunfire, which seemed to float in air, coming and going depending on how the trees wanted to carry it. For the next few hours, he worked his way north of the main road and along it, trying to keep the sound of gunfire to his right. He figured the Rebs were harassing Kilpatrick's company as they withdrew to the safety of Butler's command to the east.

It was slow going for Brison. His fatigue grew, and he had a fearsome headache to go along with his shoulder. Just as he saw the first light appear from the east, the gunfire increased. Brison planned to swing north of the action and try to get ahead of the Federal group, whomever they were, to form up and get back to

Butler. The first sunlight seeped in through the trees when he heard voices below the ridge he was on. He dismounted, took his Spencer, and moved along a grouping of boulders until he had an unobstructed view of a clearing approximately forty feet below him.

Three Federal soldiers were on their knees facing a group of six Rebel militiamen. One was dismounted and had his pistol trained on the three, backed up by the others. The man on foot and another whom Brison gathered was the group's leader discussed something. The soldiers were haggard and beaten down by what Brison could only imagine was forty-eight hours or more in the saddle with little rest. But it was the discussion between the two Rebels that caught Brison's attention and had him moving his right hand into the trigger area of the Spencer. He moved the hammer into half-cocked position and dropped the lever down and back to chamber his first round.

"Jonesie, we talked about what we'd do if we came across Yanks," the one Brison assumed was the leader said.

"I know we did," the dismounted Reb said. "It's just, I've never killed me no Yank before, and I know yous said it was my duty in all, but it just ain't nothin' I never did before."

"Jesus Christ, I knew you'd be useless," the leader said, turning to look at large man on a mount directly next to him. "Take care of them Yanks, Smithy."

The large one moved his mount a step closer, brought up his pistol, and took aim at the soldier on the left who had begun to cry. Brison's Spencer exploded, and the large man slumped on his horse. Lever down, lever up, and the leader died with a twisted look of surprise. Another working of the lever, and Brison trained the Spencer on the dismounted man and fired again, hitting him high near the neck area and splattering blood on the crying soldier. One more lever action, and he pointed the rifle at the three remaining men who were drawing their pistols and looking up at Brison.

"Drop your weapons, Rebs," he said. "I'll get one of you for sure, and I've got the high ground and plenty of cartridges. The other two will be dead before too long."

"You can't get away, Yank," one of them said. "Our boys are all over these woods. You ain't got a chance in hell."

"Already been there a few times. Seems like the Devil himself is coming right familiar with me. Drop em. I won't ask again."

The three looked at each other and seemed to decide that a one-in-three chance of joining their companions who were already dead wasn't worth it. They dropped their pistols in the slush of wet leaves and muck.

Brison stood up. "You three, up off your feet and get their pistols on them."

Once the three had cover on the Rebs, Brison climbed down from the rocks and retrieved his horse, then joined the others in the clearing. The three were remnants of Kilpatrick's command. They had been separated and found themselves on foot, trying to make their way east as best they could. The Rebs weren't army or even militia, just a group out to help get as many Federals as they could. They were shooting captured men instead of taking them to a Confederate unit and had run down these three just at first light.

"We're all privates, sir," the biggest of the three said. "We're much obliged you came along when you did. Our names are Dugan, Russell, and I'm Cooper."

"Very well, Private. I'm Colonel Brison. I was attached to Dahlgren's command and got separated as well."

"Colonel?" Russell said. "A colonel out here all by yourself, sir? You're wearing a civilian coat and britches, sir."

Brison unbuttoned his overcoat to reveal his uniform and his rank. "Let's just say I was trying to be a bit inconspicuous."

"I bit what, sir?" Cooper asked.

"Never mind," Brison said. "We need to get moving right quick. With light, we can move faster, but we can be seen just as easily. I want these Rebs bound and gagged. We're going to tie them to trees closer to the road. They'll be found soon enough."

"Where should we head, sir?"

"We'll pick our way south and swing around and try to meet up with either Kilpatrick or Dahlgren," Brison said.

They readied the horses they confiscated from the Rebels, tied the spares to a tree, then tied the three to a pair of maples about eighty feet from the road. Brison led the other three off down the road, and while still within sight of the Rebels, he took the men off the road to the south. When they were out of view, he swung them back to the north, across the road, and back into the forest.

"I thought we were heading south to swing around," Dugan asked.

"That's what I wanted them to hear, Private," Brison said with a smile. "We're going to head east on the north side of the river up here, and hopefully we'll run into our boys. You all need to listen to me. I know you don't know me as an officer, but if you stay true to my orders, I'll get you back safely."

"I remember seeing you with General Kilpatrick, sir, before we left," Dugan said. "If you're good enough for them to listen to you, then it would be a stretch for us not to."

They picked their way through the woods, thick with underbrush that made their way difficult. All through the morning and into the early afternoon, they made their way along and twice had to hide to avoid a Rebel patrol, slowing them down further. They continued to work their way east as best they could until they found a ridge with few trees that allowed a better view of the surrounding area.

Brison left the three inside the tree line and rode carefully along the ridge's spine. He saw a group far off to the southwest, and his field glasses allowed him to make out that they were Rebels, grouped to about seventy-five men. They were moving to the southeast and now posed no threat. He moved his view to the east, and after five minutes, a group of Federals appeared at the corner bend about two miles away. What road it was, Brison couldn't tell for sure, but he hoped they would continue to move generally east, meaning they were trying to get to Butler. He returned to his companions, and they set off due east, just north of the Federal company he had seen. Within two hours, they were halted by rear skirmishers from Kilpatrick's men and rejoined the unit as it moved east.

CHAPTER THIRTY

Present Day
June 13

Sparks and Taylor didn't have to fly to Wilkes-Barre to see the new head of Raven Industries. Samuel Raven was in his company's Washington, D.C. offices, so when the agents contacted him, he encouraged them to meet with him there. The Raven offices took the top three floors of a building just over the Potomac in Arlington, not surprisingly a short driving distance from the Pentagon. They had left the White House after a twenty-minute meeting with President Douglas, during which he asked only two questions, both of which were pointed and focused. He listened with full attention. Then the two directors and the two agents were dismissed. Sparks and Taylor called into Raven's offices and learned of their new destination as they exited the White House grounds.

"What tone are we going to take with Raven?" Taylor asked as they rode in the SUV across the river.

"We had his father dead to rights," Sparks said. "He needs to know that. I know he just lost his father, the CEO of his company, but I think we can assume he'll quickly move into position."

"We have nothing that links the son to his father's dealings, including Tucson."

"Yet."

"Can we assume the people who have the papers have contacted him?" Taylor asked.

"I believe that would be a safe assumption. Based on what happens during our interview, we'll need to pull together warrants for his communications with all of the principals."

They arrived at the building, once the home of a major newspaper that had been bought out and cut into little pieces as websites took over as the country's favorite media for news. The two FBI agents were met in the lobby by Raven's assistant and immediately brought up to his office.

After introductions, Samuel Raven held out his hand to a pair of chairs on one side of a coffee table in front of a ceiling-to-floor glass wall that afforded a handsome view of Washington. He sat himself down opposite them without his suit jacket and his tie loosened from his neck.

"What can you tell me about my father's murder?" Raven asked straight off as they settled in. "Any leads at all?"

"The investigation is going full bore," Sparks said, "and we don't normally comment on active investigations, but we can tell you it was a professional contract."

"My father, by the very nature of our family's business, had enemies, but something as brazen as this..."

"There are, of course, many possibilities," Taylor said, "but three come right to the top: one, revenge for past business dealings; two, someone wanted him out of the way because they knew you would bring different priorities to future business; three—"

"You weren't willing to wait for daddy to transfer the company control to his son," Sparks said.

A smile crept to one side of Raven's face, and his eye twitched. "I won't patronize you with a fake display of outrage. I was upset with my father's delaying my move into more significant duties. In fact, we talked about it just last week. We were going to make an announcement in the coming weeks about a new role for me. I loved my father, and no amount of power and control over Raven Industries would have me plotting for his murder."

"We have to look at all avenues," Taylor said.

"I understand, and I could have had my lawyers here to refuse an interview," Raven said. "I have nothing to hide; in fact, I can authorize my staff to give you all emails and phone records for my father and myself and anyone else on my staff. We will cooperate fully."

"How involved were you with your father's dealings?" Sparks asked.

"There were a number of projects my father had running that, as of now, I still don't know the details. And I won't, at least until his will is read. Then I will have access to the company's classified documents. He kept me out of the loop on confidential details. Do you two have me at a disadvantage? Do you two have details?"

"We have evidence your father was involved with a number of felonies." Sparks paused for effect. "Including murder."

Raven's head snapped back. "That's ridiculous."

"The evidence is substantial," Taylor said.

Raven sat for a moment and didn't comment. He stood up and walked to the window, staring out at the Washington Monument in the distance. Without turning back to them, he broke the silence. "My father had a reputation for ruthlessness that was well deserved, but murder?" He turned back to them, straightening his posture. "Raven Industries will cooperate with the FBI as I have stated, but I think it would be prudent for me to have an attorney present to protect not only myself but the company as well."

"Are you certain your father will be bequeathing the company control to you?" Sparks asked.

"Yes," Raven said. "And I have the votes on the board... without question. I think we're done for now." He held up his hand again, this time at the door.

Sparks and Taylor left. As soon as the door closed behind them, Taylor turned to Sparks. "He knew his daddy was into some serious shit."

"The question remains: did he have knowledge beforehand?" Sparks said.

AN HOUR LATER, THEY arrived at Senator Mallory's office unannounced and were met by a staffer whose job it was to say no to every question posed to her.

"The senator is unavailable and will be so for the rest of the day," she said. She was a woman of middle age with a professional suit that reeked of exclusiveness. Her dark-brown hair was in a style that matched her age and was perfectly shaped. She held a thick stack of papers in front of her much like a centurion's shield.

"The senator will want to see us... right now," Sparks said.

The assistant looked at Sparks with an unimpressed expression, then turned to Taylor, who nodded without saying anything. The woman took two steps, picked up a phone, and leaned over her desk, still close enough that she could have blocked the doorway if the need arose. "There are two agents from the FBI that wish to speak to you," she said into the receiver. "Yes, agents Sparks and Taylor... You are supposed to heading out for the meeting with the Desert Caucus... Yes, I understand. Right away." She put the phone down and gave Sparks a withering look. "The senator will see you immediately."

They moved into the senator's office, and the assistant closed the door behind them. Mallory stood at his window, which provided the only light for the room.

"I suppose you're surprised like everyone that I took myself out of the running this morning," Mallory said without turning to face them.

"It was going to be one of our questions, Senator," Taylor said.

"This isn't a formal interview, sir, but we hoped you could answer a few questions," Sparks said.

Mallory turned from the window and motioned for them to sit as he took his own seat at his impressive desk, which looked well used but organized just the same. "Let me see if I can cut down on the number of questions. I really do have a meeting with the Desert Caucus ..." The corners of his mouth raised ever so slightly "... in forty-five minutes.

"Look, I don't like what has happened to me in the last few weeks, and while you may consider me a person of interest in some of this mess, I can tell you unequivocally that not only have I done nothing wrong, I am the injured party in all this."

"At least you're still alive," Sparks said.

"Yes, and look at that," Mallory said. "For God's sake, I'm not stupid enough to strike back at Raven right when the FBI is investigating the attack on my house in Tucson and this whole Mallory-Raven contract business and while I'm deciding about a run for the White House. You must admit it doesn't make any sense for a sane person to attempt. You're going to be sticking your nose into everything I have—emails, text messages, other computer activity. You're going to interview everyone who ever sat next to me at a restaurant or crapped in the stall next to me in a public restroom. I haven't done anything wrong. Someone contacted me, yes, about offering me up the contract that could give me a chance at a huge portion of a multi-billion-dollar defense contractor. I listened. That isn't a crime. Then someone attacks my house, kills your own people and members of my security team, and only by the grace of God, members of my own family. Now someone has killed Sterling Raven, and your wheels are turning about that I had him killed in retaliation. That's crap, plain and simple."

"Have you been in contact with these people who offered you the contract since we last spoke to you?" Taylor asked.

"No."

"Go on," Sparks said.

"I was never pressured or demanded of anything in return for the Mallory-Raven contract. It never got to that point with me. I imagine Raven was positioned to offer a lot more than I in return for the contract. I mean, he could lose a significant portion of his company. As far as my feelings about Sterling, if he was responsible for the attack on my home, I would do everything in my power to bring the hammer down on him, but I wouldn't kill him. I have too much to lose. Besides, whether Sterling or his son is in control doesn't matter if I can legally lay claim to a portion of the company... or a generous buyout." Mallory took a drink of water from a pitcher behind his desk. "I will be definitely running for president in four years."

"In talking with others inside the beltway here," Sparks said. "You are known as a man who ruthlessly goes after what you want, and it was generally considered within your party that this was the time for you to challenge Douglas."

"Why the announcement today, Senator?" Taylor asked.

"Because it will be easier to run against his party's successor than him," Mallory said. "There are a couple of bills I want to help get through before I try for the executive branch, and frankly, I wanted to see how this missing contract business plays out. I don't want it hanging over my head during the campaign. Pretty straightforward, wouldn't you say?"

"It would appear," Taylor said. Her tone sounded unconvinced.

"We're continuing our investigation stemming from the attack in Tucson and the murder of Raven," Sparks said. "Special Agent Taylor and myself will try to keep the investigation secret, but you know leaks are a way of life. Eventually, someone from the Times or Post or somewhere else is going to find out about this whole up affair."

"As I said," Mallory said, "I've done nothing wrong, and whether I'm legally entitled to a part of Raven Industries, well, that won't affect my campaign."

THE TWO AGENTS RETURNED to the Hoover building and set up a workstation in a spare meeting room with all the documentation from the investigation, emailed on secure servers from the field offices in South Florida and Vermont, along with synopses on the physical evidence collected and the lab work completed by Becker and his staff.

Along with three agents assigned to them, Sparks and Taylor pored over the information thation collected in the last two weeks, and Taylor set up a meeting with her director, Pearson, for after dinner at 10:00 p.m. at the Secret Service offices next to the Potomac River across from Reagan National Airport. They spent three hours poring over the reports and the physical evidence, exchanging the documents and taking notes apart from each other so they could compare their conclusions when the time came.

"Let's put what we have together in a summary form," Sparks said when he looked at his watch at 8:30 p.m. "First, let's put what we have as established, confirmed fact."

"Okay, we have eight murders linked to these documents from 1859," Taylor said. "Old college friends Arthur Collins and Adrian Torrez got their hands on them somehow and they both end up dead within twenty-four hours of each other. The documents, we believe, are a business contract between two ancestors of Sterling Raven, the owner of Raven Industries; and Senator Brighton Mallory, who was a strong candidate for president this coming election before withdrawing—"

Sparks cut in, "We find the documents in Vermont but are attacked by a team headed by my old acquaintance, Streeter, and lose those very said documents. Mallory's family compound outside of Tucson is attacked by professionals we can link directly to Sterling Raven, but as far as we can ascertain, they came away with nothing."

"Raven is then taken out by an assassin right in front of us," Taylor said. "And you chase her down only to be taken down, knocked unconscious, and she is eliminated. You are taken out to the Everglades, and Streeter reveals there is, indeed, a third party playing both Mallory and Raven against each other. We don't know his motives, which throws everything he told you into question. The assassin who took out Raven is none other than the White House assistant who gave us the packet from Torrez that led us to Collins."

"Which is the first question we ask Pearson in an hour," Sparks said. "How the hell does that happen? She was a mole directly in the White House, and someone spent a lot of resources making sure she was clean, because we can assume she was checked thoroughly like everyone else on staff."

"There's another thing that has been bothering me," Taylor said.

"What?"

"Why did Streeter leave her body behind?"

"You thought of that too? He knew we would trace her back, and I can't believe his bosses are pleased about that. It's a sloppy mistake."

"Unless he wanted us to find the link to the White House," Taylor said.

"Obviously, he did."

"What the hell is his game?"

"He turned on his employer back during the Gettysburg gold thing when it came to his attention that same employer was going to have him eliminated," Sparks said. "I believe the same scenario is in play here. He said the hit on Raven was not ordered by him and Evans worked for him, so he has sensed an end run around him. I've only had three brief discussions with him in person. He has a moral code, and I feel sorry for those who double cross him and violate that code. He's giving us a chance to muck up the plans of his employers."

"I think that depends on what those plans and goals were," Taylor said.

Sparks nodded. "If their goals were to damage Raven Industries and keep Mallory from running for president this cycle, then they have already accomplished what they wanted."

"What's our next move?"

"You and your people need to see if there is a lead through Rachel Evans, or whoever she was. Someone like that working directly in the White House will be news that will nuke every security agency, with your people being at the epicenter. It's going to be unbelievably ugly unless everything is thrown under a top-secret blanket. I imagine Pearson, Connolly, and the president have been discussing that very point."

"And at some point soon, they're going to shut us down," Taylor said.

"National security... it's a bitch."

PEARSON LISTENED TO THEIR report for twenty minutes, asking questions at just the right moments. When they were finished, he pushed back from his desk and went over to a cabinet where he pulled out a decanter and three glasses. He didn't ask if anyone wanted his whiskey. He just assumed they would need a drink. Both Sparks and Taylor accepted the glasses without hesitation. Pearson downed his entire glass and set it down before settling back down in his chair.

"We've got to investigate Evans thoroughly," Pearson said. "You're right that she is the key if we are going to unravel this thing. Taylor, I want you to spearhead that by starting with tearing down the vetting staff and go through everything they did with her. Director Connolly and I have agreed this is the correct way to go, Sparks, and he wants you to continue with investigating Raven and his son... and Mallory, although the first two should be your priority. The president has stipulated this entire investigation should be classified. The two of you are having your clearance levels raised for this investigation only. The official word to the media once they get ahold of something is that Torrez was killed in a carjacking gone bad and the college professor died in a home invasion, which happens to be a partial truth."

"What about Raven's murder?" Sparks asked. "Next to Torrez, that's the highest-profile murder in this whole mess."

"We'll attribute it to a professional hit with unknown origins," Pearson said. "And we'll hope it eventually fades into the background."

"Someone is eventually going to tie all of this together," Sparks said, the frown on his face apparent.

"We'll deal with that down the road if we have to," Pearson responded. "For now, we button it up as tight as we can and put it all under national security, but..." He paused for effect. "... we've got to find out who is this third party."

"No matter who it turns out to be?" Sparks asked.

Taylor gave her partner a glare. "Jason."

Sparks returned her look. "He knows what I mean."

Pearson registered no emotion except a nod. "Yes, Sparks, I know what you mean, and I want you both to continue unfettered until Connolly and I tell you differently. If this reaches places with political ramifications, then we'll see what happens when we turn it over to the DOJ. A third party has been trying to impart undue influence on a prominent defense contractor and a sitting United States senator. The magnitude of this is obvious. The number of bodies piling up attests to that fact."

"Director, are we already too late on this investigation?" Taylor asked.

"How do you mean?"

"The senator is not running for president this cycle, and Sterling Raven is dead," Taylor said. "Two results linked to these Civil War era papers. Has this third party already attained their goals?"

"The senator not running, yes," Sparks injected. "But Raven's murder isn't logical unless we consider his son. Was Raven murdered because of who he was or because of who his son is? That may be as much of this as anything else."

"So go hard on Samuel Raven, past and present," Pearson said. "Let's get surveillance on him and see. Both of you, I can't reiterate more strongly... be as discreet as possible. These are powerful people that remain in place whether you're here or I'm here or not. They can't stop us from investigating, but they can influence futures if toes are stepped on."

"I've never been one to worry about toe stepping," Sparks said.

"So I've heard," Pearson said, "but after the hearings last year, your name coming up again will be problematic, and I've already discussed this with Connelly. My recommendation is to take you off this solely for that reason. I'm not revealing anything sensitive here, I believe, but he has resisted so far. Ultimately, it's, of course, your bureau and none of my business, but we are working together, so I felt the need to push for that action. Again, nothing to do with your performance."

"I understand," Sparks said.

"Just get this nailed down as fast and thoroughly as you can."

From his pause, it was clear Pearson considered the meeting over, so Sparks and Taylor got up to leave. As they approached the door, Pearson spoke up again.

"Bi-hourly reports, Taylor," he said.

"Yes, sir." Taylor nodded at the director and then glanced at Sparks. It was a look he had become familiar with over the past two weeks. Something was troubling, and it was about her boss. When they reached the corridor, Sparks began to speak, but Taylor squeezed his arm and shook her head, clearly wanting him to keep quiet. Outside, she shook her head again, and a frustrated Sparks shrugged his shoulders. At the car, she dug into a bag she had in the backseat and pulled out a surveillance detector, then pushed Sparks away from the car. She spent the next five minutes going through the car both inside and as much of the undercarriage as she could do. She appeared satisfied after a time and motioned for them to get in and leave. Once they were in the car, Sparks turned the ignition on and turned to look at Taylor.

"What the hell is your problem with Pearson?" he asked.

"Just drive. Give me your phone."

"My phone? Why?"

Without bothering to respond, she took his phone, took the back plate off, and studied it briefly before doing the same to her phone. "Nothing. Well, that's good. And the car is clean as well, but this is the first time we've been in this car in the last two weeks."

"You think someone has us under surveillance?" Sparks asked. "And what did Pearson say that spooked you?"

"You noticed, huh?"

"I recognized the look."

"Two weeks ago, Pearson was fine with you being paired with me on this, and now suddenly he wants to take you off because some members of Congress might think you stepped outside the lines with the Gettysburg gold thing. I haven't known him for that many years, but he has never struck me as someone who gave a real damn about political ramifications. He is very much a find out the facts, fix the problem, and move on."

"Look," Sparks said, "I know I brought up the conspiracy-might-go-into-the-Oval-Office scenario, but you might be starting to see shadows where there aren't any."

"I don't know." Taylor looked away and stared at the scenery.

"We've got the evidence on Raven's involvement in the attack on Mallory's compound. We now need to see what the evidence is on a connection between Samuel Raven and if he was involved in that or in the murder of his father. Forensics is going through all electronic communication Raven has had before and after his father's death, and they're also checking out Mallory's communications throughout this as well. You saw the reports. It looks like Mallory has done nothing except react with indignation at the circumstance thrust upon him. And he dropped out of a race he was expected to be strong in."

"An action that directly benefits the president," Taylor said.

"As we said, Evans is the key," Sparks said. "We've got to see who she is linked up with and who got her into the White House."

"Do you think Connelly is going to take you off the case?"

"He's been really sensitive about P.R. since Gettysburg, and he's antsy as hell that the real details of Griffin's actions will be exposed. He may very well take me off this tomorrow."

"Let's hope we can talk him out of it."

Chapter Thirty-One

March 2, 1864

THE FIRST TASK BRISON set about doing was to search Kilpatrick's remaining men for Raven's killer. Brison reported to the general, informing him that he had gotten separated from Dahlgren's company the night before and came upon the scene with the three privates about to be executed. He remained silent on the entire events at the private residence in Richmond and the murder and attempted murder committed there. With a wave of his hand, Kilpatrick dismissed Brison, allowing him to use the services of a sergeant to search the men as they moved through the Virginia countryside, fearing an attack from a Rebel force and desperately hoping for a chance to join up with the safety of Butler's command in the east.

As discreetly as he could, Brison moved his mount among the soldiers, and after ninety minutes, he determined the killer had not rejoined Kilpatrick's group. It was possible he had turned a different direction and joined up with Dahlgren's company or was working his way alone north to Washington. Brison assumed it would be Washington because that was where Raven would be and the killer would be wanting to make his report to the industrialist... and maybe to the secretary of war. Stanton wasn't far from Brison's mind at any point now. The fact that three men were able to be placed in a federal force driving into Confederate territory had Brison thinking more direct work had to have been done by Stanton's office.

This couldn't have been Raven's operation alone.

Kilpatrick's men continued to move east in a day, bursting with apprehension that lasted through the night as Rebel skirmishers picked at the Federal column, beaten down and ragged after three days and nights of riding. Brison fought the urge to ask for permission from Kilpatrick to ride north immediately on his own, feeling the general wouldn't likely be in the mood to grant the request. The strike into Richmond had been a failure unless Dahlgren had been successful in some small part. Brison spent his time in the saddle cutting himself to the quick about his performance for Mr. Lincoln. He had saved Davis' life, but he had failed to protect Mallory because he had put all his observational efforts in front of him as he followed the two would-be assassins and never thought to worry about his own status. He gnawed on a cigar he had planned on smoking after he had secured Mallory's safety, but it remained unlit, now just something to chew on.

Early the next morning, his spirits and those of the men around him were lifted.

March 3, 1864

ON THE CREST OF a ridge at eight the next morning, Kilpatrick's men caught sight of a fast-moving cavalry group and prepared for a defense until they realized that blue was the color of the day. A round of cheers greeted the first of the group to move through the skirmishers and into Kilpatrick's men. Butler had sent 3,800 men to join up and provide a way back to the safety of the eastern peninsula.

For Brison, as soon as the command was organized and the entire body headed back to the east, he quickly got permission from Kilpatrick to press ahead of the body with an escort to get a boat back and up the Potomac to the capital. He reached a landing on the river, and after a minor difficulty with procuring passage, he got himself on a federal steamer taking a small detachment from Butler's command. The boat ride afforded Brison a chance to sleep as they made their way up the Potomac under the cover of darkness.

March 5, 1864

IN THE SHADOW OF a hearth-bound fire and a single lamp on the desk, Lincoln shook Brison's hand and put his left hand upon the colonel's shoulder. His eyes projected genuine warmth, and the smile was broad enough to show his teeth. The hour was late, and they were alone.

"I praise the Lord you have come back to me safely, Colonel," Lincoln said. "The news from Richmond was not promising. It appears our efforts were not successful."

"No, sir," Brison said. "But there's much to the story that will never see the official record. I'm afraid I must report to you that Raven's efforts were successful. Justice Mallory is dead, killed by the same assailant who has been my adversary during this entire affair. I was not able to save Mallory, sir, but I was able to save Mr. Davis, who appeared to be a target as well."

Lincoln's surprise swarmed his face and his mouth dropped open for a moment before he gained a measure of control. He led Brison to a chair and eased himself back into a facing chair and sat down, a man in the throes of trying to solve a problem, the evidence of which was in the slowness of his movement.

"They attempted to murder Davis?"

"Yes, sir. Fortunately, I was able to stop him, but after I killed the two men Raven sent to kill Mallory, he finished the task himself. I chased him off and pursued him but lost him in the night."

"Andrew." Lincoln had never called him by his first name. "Start over from the beginning and leave out no parcel of detail."

Brison spoke uninterrupted save one question from Lincoln about the hanging of Robinson, the Negro guide, at the river.

When he was finished, he waited for Lincoln to digest the report. The president kept him waiting for a full two minutes.

"Are you absolutely certain Mr. Davis understood this wasn't an effort set forth by this government?" Lincoln asked.

"I didn't have long to convince him of such, but I believe he accepted my word."

"I pray you are correct. The questions that come to mind now... how will Davis and his cabinet react to this assault and what has happened to Colonel Dahlgren and his men? The last word we received was from Kilpatrick and Butler just told of their joining forces east of Richmond. There has been no word on Ulric, and I fear for the boy. This failure to secure the imprisoned troops is sorry full enough, but the loss of young Dahlgren would bring bitterness beyond compare."

"I understand your concern, sir," Brison said. "I only got to know the young man a short time, but he seemed like a fine officer, and the men took to his command well under a difficult trial." He held back his criticism of Dahlgren over the unnecessary tragedy at the riverbank. "Sir, I need assistance going forward with this assignment. We need to have Raven under constant surveillance so we can catch this man who has bested me all along. He is directly responsible for the deaths of numerous people and the attempted assassination of Mr. Davis. But I don't think we can trust everyone within Baker's service, because my presence in Kilpatrick's unit was known to the conspirators. The two I followed who died most likely knew I was there and weren't worried about me because there was someone behind me all the time. I look back at it now, and it is clear my tracking them was too easy. I mistook a lack of concern for incompetence. This man has the evidence we need to bring down Raven, and I believe—"

"Stanton?"

"I have witnessed him myself in suspicious discussions with Raven, and they were able to get three men into Kilpatrick's command."

"That is why you do not trust the Secret Service," Lincoln said. "I tend to agree with your assessment, at least as far as it pertains to this Raven matter."

"You yourself, sir, once cautioned me about the shadow of corruption that covers the government here. Having someone work outside the usual boundaries of the Army and the Secret Service is what you knew you needed. That's why you picked me."

"And others."

"And others. What if you gave me one or two of these others to help with tracking down Mallory's killer?"

"I will consider it." Lincoln suddenly seemed preoccupied, which Brison had never seen before in their talks. "From what you have told me, the two dead men in Richmond directly implicated Raven in Mallory's eventual death. I require you to write out a statement detailing the events in Richmond and what they said. Also the details from the other incidents that incriminate Raven. This is all for me to have if I so choose."

"I understand, sir, but can I watch Raven myself until you decide on the additional men?"

Lincoln nodded. "You can, indeed. Pull that thread as much as you can, and we'll see how the garment holds together."

March 10, 1864

A COUPLE OF HOT baths at the boarding house and substantial meals had Brison feeling well after the Richmond debacle, except for his aching shoulder. And that was exactly how people reacted to Kilpatrick's foray in Virginia. Word had come out of Richmond that Dahlgren's group had been captured in bulk and the colonel himself had been killed and upon his body had been found orders that apparently included an address he gave or was to give to his troops upon reaching Richmond. This address and other papers had been reprinted in the Richmond Examiner and included instructions that Davis and his entire cabinet were "to be killed on the spot" once the captive Union troops had been released.

The enraged Rebels were demanding hangings of the captured Dahlgren troopers while official word from Kilpatrick's command was that these "orders" were fabricated by the Confederates. After seeing Dahlgren's casual disregard of the freeman's life at the river, Brison was of the attitude that the young colonel may not have been of the mind to kill Davis on his own but very well could have been instructed to do so by Kilpatrick. And Kilpatrick could have been prodded to go that extra step by the secretary of war. The papers made no mention of the actual assassination attempt that Brison thwarted.

March 14, 1864

BRISON HAD NOT SEEN the president since his first night back, nor had there been any correspondence instructing him how to proceed. He made some discreet inquiries into the whereabouts of Raven, but the industrialist had not been in his usual places, including the Willard. Brison had sent a letter to Louise Elizabeth that spoke no details other than to tell her he was well and missing her and the children. He asked for her to send a letter in return, hoping he would still be in Washington when it arrived.

In the mid-afternoon, a private from Meade's command arrived at the boardinghouse with a request to meet with the general in the evening. While it was worded like a request, the message mentioned that Lincoln had passed along Brison's name as someone who could help Meade with an investigation. And so Brison found himself riding out to Meade's command as dusk loomed and reached the headquarters a good hour after dark. He was in full uniform, thinking it best to be so for the commanding general of the entire Army of the Potomac.

Upon identifying himself to the general's assistant, he was led into a simply furnished office lit by three oil lamps and a healthy fire that made the room almost uncomfortably warm even though it was still March. Meade stood up from behind his desk and greeted Brison with a handshake and offered a chair.

He was in full uniform despite the lateness of the hour, but the top three buttons were undone like he had been taking it off before a distraction arrived. He was tall, almost equal to Brison, with a slender build and a balding head with a heavy beard and a mustache so thick, one couldn't see his mouth. His eyes were sad, and fatigue was clearly showing.

"I appreciate your coming to see me on short notice, Colonel," Meade said as they sat down. "The president wanted to be kept informed of what, if anything, I could find out about this Dahlgren problem. He informs me you rode with Dahlgren's group but were separated and made it back on your own."

"Yes, sir."

"Was there any statement given to the troops about capturing and executing the Rebel leader and his cabinet?"

"You get to the point with haste, sir." Brison gave a courteous smile. "No, Colonel Dahlgren gave out no such orders, nor did he show me such orders in the brief moments I had with him on the way to Richmond."

"Do you believe the colonel would be capable of issuing such orders on his own, without instructions?"

"I don't believe so, but I didn't know him well," Brison said.

"Do you believe the orders are genuine or a falsehood created by the Rebels?"

"I don't know."

"Give me your best guess, and please be candid, Colonel," Meade said, lowering his voice a degree. "This is off the official record. And... the president alluded to me that you have first-hand knowledge of another event and you already have saved Davis' life, though he didn't give me the details and swore me to secrecy."

"I would say, without examining the orders, that I couldn't give an exact accounting of what happened, but I will say it is entirely possible Dahlgren received orders from a superior to carry out what the Rebels have charged."

"Kilpatrick," Meade said, unbuttoning his tunic one more notch.

"I am aware of his reputation," Brison said.

"He's already placing blame on a dead man," Meade said. "At least in messages within the war department."

"I suggest another name as well, sir. Our secretary of war."

"You have proof of this?"

"Not directly, but I have witnessed myself Stanton's association with a man behind the murder of a Confederate civilian and the attempted murder of Mr. Davis. I do not have direct, documented evidence of conspiracy. I continue to work."

"Did this murder and attempted murder occur just on this strike at Richmond?" Meade asked.

"Off the record, yes."

"Why, then, are the Rebels not exploiting that attempt instead of these Dahlgren orders?"

"It may be Davis hasn't told anyone other than his closest advisors because I informed him, in haste, that President Lincoln was not behind the attempt. And because I saved his life and would have no reason to lie at that moment."

"The damage has already been done," Meade said. "The Rebels are going to stir this up with righteous indignation and make our efforts all that more difficult."

"Are you going to investigate?"

"Already am, but Secretary Stanton will ultimately be the decider of just how this investigation into the papers goes. It's an embarrassment, and no one of sound mind wants to go anywhere near the flame, least of all those who were involved with the raid. I fear also the effect on us is that the Rebs will return in kind, turning this into a dirtier affair than it already is."

"A very real possibility, General."

Meade asked for a more detailed story of Brison's experience in Richmond and listened with keen attentiveness, still fiddling with the buttons on his uniform jacket. When Brison concluded, Meade thought for a moment and asked his final question for the evening.

"Who is the private citizen behind the murderer in Richmond?" he asked.

"He is an industrialist," Brison said. "His name is Augustus Raven."

Meade's head tilted backwards slightly, and he nodded. "I know of this man through my letters with the quartermaster. Never met him myself. I've heard no complaints about his wares, unlike the problems we have had with all of the other shoddy equipment."

Meade stood and held out his hand, signaling the end of the conversation.

"I do hope you the best of luck, Colonel. You have performed a great service for the Union that I'm afraid will never come to light, at least until someone writes their damned memoirs about this whole tragedy."

"I'm not here to be center stage, General," Brison said, giving his hand in return. "I'm here at the behest of my president... and for the Union."

"As we all are, Colonel. As we all are."

March 15, 1864

THE IDES OF MARCH found Brison waking in the mid-morning to a light rain outside and that rigid pain barking at his shoulder like a weathered mutt in the muddy alleyway next door. He had a crick in his neck from sleeping wrong and felt worse overall than he had just a few days ago and worried that he was coming down with a sickness.

And like Caesar all those hundreds of years ago, Brison was going to remember this day as one of reckoning, where he was going to suffer at the wrong end of a knife.

Chapter Thirty-Two

THE NEXT MORNING, AS Sparks drank his second cup of coffee at his townhouse, Connelly called to take him off the case. Sparks spent ten minutes trying to logically make a case for staying on through the investigation's completion, but the FBI director never wavered from the attitude that Sparks's presence as a lead investigator was going to be a political headache when the facts of the case were revealed. And that was assured because the Washington Post had published a story that morning that had sources linking the deaths of the president's chief of staff Torrez and the historian Collins to each other but failed to include the specifics of why they were linked. Connelly was furious about the leak and was so agitated, Sparks told him to take a moment to collect himself and call back, which the director refused.

Unable to convince him to let him stay as an official investigator, Sparks asked if he could stay on as an observer and advisor... strictly off the official record but still available for consultation. Connelly said he would give it consideration, but for now, Taylor was heading the joint investigation, and the FBI's point person to work with her was someone Sparks had never heard of before, a Special Agent Josh Kinder from the west coast. Sparks asked for a couple of weeks off, and Connelly agreed while saying it was going to be his suggestion as well. After ending his phone call, Sparks stood in his kitchen for a time as he sorted through the events of the past couple of weeks and formulated his actions going forward. As he poured himself a third cup of coffee—a rarity for him—his phone rang again and he could see it was Brenda. The thought struck him that he had been remiss in staying in touch with her.

"You're alive!" was her sarcastic response to his answering. "We're going to have to enroll you in another boyfriend refresher course."

"I'm sorry. The case I've been on has been a bit overwhelming... and distracting."

"I have felt totally neglected, Special Agent," Munson said. He could hear the smirk in her voice. "You have to come see me, or would it be better if I came to see you?"

"Well, I just got taken off the case, and I don't think I'd be great company right now. I'm going to take a couple of weeks off, kind of spur of the moment, and let's definitely plan to go away, but I've got something to do first. It might take me a couple of days, but maybe we can fly down to Key West for a long weekend. Could you get away?"

"For a Keys trip? Count me in."

"I'll call you in a day or two, okay?" Sparks asked.

"Is everything all right? You really sound distracted."

"Actually, no. Everything is not all right, but I can't talk about it. You know the drill."

"Best job in the world for a guy who likes to keep his cards close to his vest," Munson said. "Being an FBI agent, pillow talk is verboten. Call me in two days or I'm running away with Paul the maintenance guy. He really looks good shirtless when he's working outside on my park service truck."

"I understand, Brenda. I'm on the clock." Sparks smiled.

Munson laughed, said goodbye, and left him with his third cup of coffee.

Taylor stood in Pearson's office, a manila folder in her left hand, glaring at her boss upon hearing the news that her partner was no longer her partner.

"Director Connelly did this after speaking with you, I hope," she said. "I need Jason Sparks if we're going to get this flushed out."

"Connelly has to deal with the political crap that this could produce just as much as I will," Pearson said. "That's why I need you to focus on Evans and how our vetting process whiffed entirely on her."

"I've got a preliminary report I just printed out when I got here." She handed him the folder. "She came back clean because she was, at least through our normal checks. No affiliations, no missing months or years, no extensive travel overseas, no money issues, no weird posts on social media. All the interviews with family and former employers came back nominal. Director, this person must have been groomed from a young age and led a double life because there are no red flags to see. We're trying to check on patterns of travel within the U.S. She graduated from high school in Oregon, got a political science degree from USC, and worked in President Douglas's office when he was a congressman and a senator and naturally moved into a role with his campaign and the White House when he was elected."

"Someone spent a lot of years and a lot of money to have her as an asset this embedded and this high up," Pearson said.

"And this was important enough to use her on a hit that could have been contracted out to someone outside, thereby not compromising her position inside. They were done needing her there, or they felt she could execute the contract without endangering her cover."

"Keep at it. Interview people at the White House and in her social life outside. Look for regular gaps in her life, like a yearly vacation. It could show up consistent training."

"Yes, sir," Taylor said. "Did Director Connelly tell you when Kinder will be arriving?"

"In a couple of days. He has some details to finish up, and then he'll fly in. He's got your contact info."

"Can I keep Sparks in the loop? I'd like to be able to have him provide insight with anything we come up with."

Pearson thought for a moment, and then he narrowed his eyes. "Connelly didn't expressly say Sparks was off limits, but I'd say keep the contact as light as possible. And he's definitely out of interviews and meetings. Keep it just with you and solely advisory."

"Understood."

HALF AN HOUR LATER, Taylor received a call from Sparks. She was expressing her regret and anger over the decision when Sparks received another call on his cellphone. He put her on hold and came back a moment later.

"You won't believe this," he said.

"What is it?"

"I'm joining you up on this call." There was a pause, and then Sparks continued, "I'm back, and Secret Service Agent Bethany Taylor is on the line as well."

"Okay, this is Dorothy Akers," the voice said. "I'm Senator Mallory's assistant. The senator instructed me to call you both and inform you that someone has hand-delivered paperwork you would be interested in seeing."

"Is it a business contract from the Civil War era?" Taylor asked.

"I believe so. The senator said it was brought to the office this morning and given to one of our clerks with the instructions that it wasn't to be opened by anyone other than the senator. I wasn't in the office this morning or I would have taken it myself."

"Is the senator making himself and the document available to us today?" Sparks asked.

"He's having his lawyers look over the documents as we speak," Akers said. "Then he suggests you agents meet him with Samuel Raven later this afternoon."

"Those documents are the heart of a case," Taylor said. "This isn't a negotiation; he turns over the documents or he will face conspiracy to obstruct justice and other charges."

"The senator fully intends to turn over the documents he just received today once you all meet with the lawyers and a document expert he's bringing in as well. He suggests his estate in Virginia, just north of Richmond, would be a good location."

"I would like to speak with the senator," Taylor said.

"He isn't available at this time. I can relay a message to him that you want to speak with him before the meeting." Akers was trying to sound helpful, but Taylor imagined her standing guard at his door, loyal to the end.

"Tell him he should have just held onto the documents, then called us over to pick them up at his office," Taylor said. "Our patience is extremely thin here, Ms. Akers."

"I'm sure he will cooperate fully at the meeting in Richmond. He is just trying to protect his interests, don't you see? You can't blame him for taking precautions. I'll call back within the hour, and I'll try to have the senator on the line."

"See that you do." Taylor hung up and called Sparks back.

"I wanted to be rough with her," Taylor said to Sparks. "Amazing how the documents show up at Mallory's offices right after he announces he won't run for president."

"This has a weird feeling to it," Sparks said. "If I was Mallory, I'd hold onto the documents and have the lawyers and experts check them out, then call us and Raven, then have the meeting in the Hoover Building. Why at his place in Virginia?"

"Familiarity. Comfort. He probably has security on par with his house in Tucson."

"If I were you, I would take at least four or five with you, that is if you can't get him to come to 935 yourself," Sparks said.

"I can't convince you to get off the bench and join me?"

"I've taken an oath of saneness. My boss wants me on the sidelines for this, I'm on the sidelines. My pension is too damn important."

"I still want your advice," Taylor said.

"Absolutely. Connelly, I think, will approve that."

"I'll text you the results of my call with Connelly within the hour."

AS SOON AS SPARKS was off the line with Taylor, he punched in the saved number for Anderson. Five short minutes later, he was off the phone and in his car. He was going to have to haul it if he and Anderson were going to make it to Mallory's estate in time.

Taylor's phone call to Connelly went as she expected. The FBI director wouldn't budge on having Sparks in on the Richmond meeting. In fact, the very nature of the meeting gave Connelly the impression that Sparks shouldn't be anywhere within a hundred miles of it. Taylor didn't fight and texted Sparks the news instead of calling him. Sparks's response was a simple OK, but then it was followed shortly by the words "good luck."

The Mallory estate ten miles north of greater Richmond was, by most accounts, even more impressive than the desert oasis outside of Tucson, as it was twice the size and commanded a higher profile. The estate sat at the center of 120 acres outside the city with the main house set halfway up a prominent hill that some people would classify as a mountain. The house was designed in a modern style with sharp angles, boxes, and rectangles with glass featuring prominently. A wall set five hundred yards around guarded the main house.

The complex was hidden in trees and expansive landscaping, but inside, the area was open apart from the hill. Taylor could see right away the clearing was done on purpose to create a difficult challenge to approach the complex undetected, and that was just visually, as certainly there were extensive electronic surveillance redundancies built into the property. Mallory didn't take security as an afterthought. Taylor rode shotgun in the first SUV ahead of two other vehicles carrying four men each, leaving the combined FBI and Secret Service detail at twelve, plus overhead support by drones armed with infrared cameras controlled remotely from the Bureau's east coast operational hub. It all seemed a bit much for a simple document turnover, and there weren't expected to be any arrests. Still, Pearson and Connolly felt a need for a show of force prior to taking possession of the documents.

As they approached the complex, they saw two groups of vehicles and a dozen or so security types milling around, giving Taylor the impression the young Raven and the Senator had brought their own details with them. Given the value of the documents and the parties' adversarial nature, it wasn't a surprise to Taylor, but she turned to one of her companions and muttered under her breath, "An awful lot of firepower hanging out together."

They reached the massive parking area to the left side of the complex, and as soon as they exited, Taylor deployed four teams of two to check the perimeter of the structures and develop a threat assessment of the weak areas in the security. As she was finishing up, the remaining four agents with her were greeted by a short, dark-haired man dressed in a tailored suit with an American flag pin on the lapel and a standard inside-the-belt-line accessory, no doubt belonging to a Mallory staffer.

"Agent Taylor?" he said.

"Yes. Are both the senator and Samuel Raven here already?"

"Yes, they are waiting in the main conference hall. If you will please follow me."

Taylor took two of the agents with her and left two at the entrance. The staffer led them down an impressive hallway with modern furniture and accents that fit the house's outside design. A pair of suits stood at the double-door entrance to a conference room. It was four times the size of a normal conference room with a high ceiling and a full glass wall facing west onto part of the open area within the walled property, though trees took up much of the view. Part of the hill north and behind the complex could be partially seen. Mallory stood at one end of the room near a full bar stocked with dozens of liquor bottles, glasses, and beer taps, all wrapped in what looked to be mahogany wood of opulent texture. Raven sat at the table, again adorned in the same mahogany, with three others—two women and a man. They were studying some documents, which Taylor surmised were the ones from 1859.

"Ah, we are all here," Mallory said cheerfully with an edge. "We started without you, as you can see." He introduced Taylor to the three lawyers at the table. Two were Raven's representatives, and one was Mallory's.

With one glance, Taylor recognized the contract as the one she saw briefly in Vermont before the firefight, and she looked first at Mallory and then at Raven, who had an untouched drink in front of him. His face was a mixture of indignation and apprehension.

"Where is Agent Sparks?" Raven asked.

"Not available for this meeting," Taylor said. "Shall we get started? Although I'm at a loss as to why you invited Mr. Raven here. This is supposed to be a simple possession transfer of evidence in a murder investigation."

"Well, I know, but I couldn't help myself," Mallory said, stirring a newly mixed drink.

Taylor stepped closer to the table and took a harder look at the document. It was a contract signed and witnessed in 1859, almost exactly two years before the beginning of the Civil War.

"Ms. Fitzgerald, would you be so kind as to explain what the contract stipulates for Agent Taylor?" Mallory asked.

"This contract was entered into by Augustus Raven and Justice Mallory in 1859," the female lawyer said. "It is a binding deal with the two men sharing interest in what was then known as Raven Ironworks. It allows for Mr. Raven to control the operations with joint ownership between the two men, fifty-five percent by Mr. Raven and forty-five percent by Mr. Mallory. It was duly witnessed and signed by both parties."

"Get to the good part, my dear," Mallory said.

Fitzgerald gave a disapproving glance to Mallory and then one of slight embarrassment to Taylor. "The contract stipulates that if either party becomes deceased, the ownership of said part of the company would be passed down to the first-born male heir. We have researched both parties here, and you can draw a direct line from Justice Mallory to the senator. Of course, the lineage of the Raven family has been an established part of company history."

"I'm going to challenge the validity of property being passed down in perpetuity," Raven said, his first words since Taylor had entered the room. "My family built this company, molded it, reshaped its very nature many times over during the last one hundred and fifty years."

"Because your great, great, great, great whatever grandfather had my ancestor murdered." Mallory's words were sharp-edged knives. "It's all in the papers there, Agent Taylor. Affidavits from two people, including the former president of the Confederacy Jefferson Davis, who witnessed the murder, and a letter from then-Secretary of War Edwin Stanton testifying to the authenticity of the charges, which were never brought against Augustus Raven. Why they weren't brought is a matter of question, but the testimony is clear when you read it: Augustus Raven sent assassins to murder Justice Mallory. And he never compensated the family for its forty-five percent of the company after the war. No member of the Raven family ever compensated the Mallory family and, in fact, hid the betrayal for generations."

"At best, your family deserves what the value of the company was at that time, no more," Raven said.

"Obviously, we are headed to court," Mallory said.

"Well, before that happens, the Secret Service is taking possession of the documents as part of our investigation into multiple murders and conspiracy," Taylor said.

"That is why I brought you here," Mallory said. "I'm simply doing my duty as a citizen."

"Was murdering my father part of this 'duty'?" Raven finally decided to toss back the liquor in his glass.

"I had nothing to do with that," Mallory said, "but after the raid your men perpetrated against my Tucson home and the lives lost there, some would say he had it coming."

"Given the obvious animosity between you two, why the hell did you invite him to this meeting?" Taylor directed her question at Mallory. Not waiting for an answer, she continued, "The joint task force between the FBI and the Secret Service is taking possession of these originals. I assume both parties here have made copies."

"I have to use the facilities," Raven said. He got up from his seat and followed one of Mallory's servants out the double doors and down the hall to the right.

Taylor unconsciously reached for her sidearm and flipped the safety off as discreetly as she could. Something wasn't right.

Sparks and Anderson moved down the hill just north of the Mallory complex. The trees were dense and swayed with the winds of a thunderstorm approaching from the west. Anderson had already checked for cameras, infrared or otherwise, and had found none outside the fence.

The fence was not electrified, but there were sensors in numerous points, so as soon as they cut through or went over Mallory's security detail would be on them. About two hundred feet to the east, there was a gate for a road that cut toward the woods and then east along the tree line before disappearing to the north. Without a word, the two men covered the distance in seconds and squatted at the gate, where Anderson neatly clipped a hole in the fence. They were through and replaced the section so that, from a distance, the cuts were difficult to distinguish from the rest of the fence. They were halfway across the field to the closest building when they heard an engine in the air. Immediately, they could tell it was coming from the northeast, and it was distinctive.

"That's a large drone," Anderson said as they reached a maintenance building set aside from the main grouping. "And I mean a large one."

"Military?" Sparks asked. "It's not stealth."

"Could be commercial, I suppose, but look at the circumstances: a powerful U.S. senator, a defense contractor, the FBI and Secret Service, all together in one location."

"I was thinking a problem with Raven or perhaps the senator," Sparks said. "The third party?"

"Could be." Anderson touched Sparks's shoulder. "It's closing very fast."

Sparks could hear that his partner was correct. "That's not a surveillance drone!" he shouted. "Time for discretion is over!"

They both ran around the corner and headed straight for the main house two football fields away, yelling to anyone whose attention they could get. Two men appeared from a set of doors on the side of the house Sparks and Anderson were approaching, weapons already drawn. Sparks yelled at them to clear the building as he punched his phone for Taylor's number. The two security men hesitated. Anderson yelled there was an explosive drone bearing down on their position at the same time Sparks reached Taylor inside the building.

Taylor had tentatively moved after Raven when he left the conference room and headed for the men's room. She pointed at one of the FBI men, and as she passed him, she whispered, "Gather up the documents and hold them for a minute no matter what the lawyers say." She stepped into the hallway and watched as Raven, followed by his two men, walked right past the bathrooms that had been clearly marked when she walked past them not twenty minutes ago.

"Raven!" she called out. Her phone rang, and the tone told her it was Sparks. She reached for it out of her back pocket as she saw that Raven was ignoring her call and continuing toward the exit. "Mr. Raven, stop!" She answered the call.

"Clear the building!" Sparks yelled. "There's a military drone closing in on the house!"

"What are you talking about?"

"You only have seconds!"

Taylor didn't take even one more. Turning to face the conference room, she yelled for everyone to clear the building. When the reaction was one of incredulousness, she fired a shot into the ceiling and barked out the order again.

Sparks and Anderson were two-thirds of the way to the house, now two hundred feet away when the drone's high-pitched whine filled the air and the small flying bomb came over their left shoulders and flew into the house, hitting just south of the mid-point of the east side. Anderson tackled Sparks, and they both hit the ground. The house exploded in a roar that concussed the two men on the ground, causing them to scream in pain as the blast rolled them along the ground, slamming glass, stone, and wood fragments into their bodies. When they stopped rolling, they instinctively curled up into balls facing away from the blast.

Sparks didn't know how long it was before he ventured to see what had happened to the house, but he guessed later it was about forty-five seconds, because all he could feel was the heat all over his body and the muffled sound as his ears no longer functioned properly. Sparks called to Anderson, who was five feet away and within view without moving his head, but he got no response. He continued to fight, dropping into unconsciousness, trying to take measured breaths and calm himself. He felt little pain, but he knew that was because of the adrenalin, so he concentrated on checking himself for injuries. There were small pieces of material embedded in his skin and clothing, and some bleeding had started. Fortunately, there was no blood around his face, and a check of the back of his head found nothing alarming, so no head injury. But when he felt down to his back right side, the pain knifed through the adrenalin, and he winched. A wave of nausea filled him. A sharp piece of material stuck out of his side, and a move to touch it brought more pain. He couldn't tell how deep it went, so he left it alone.

After these initial moments of recovery, Sparks turned toward the house, or what was left of it. Only a third of the wall facing him still stood, and with the smoke between him and the structure, that was all he could recognize. Flames reached a hundred feet in the air, but for all the destruction and movement, there was still an uncomfortable silence. Sparks stuck his fingers in his ears and wiggled them in a vain attempt to get results. Resigned to having to wait for his hearing to return, he again looked at Anderson, who, thankfully, was moving around himself.

"You all right?" Sparks yelled.

"Checking," Anderson said.

They both struggled into kneeling positions to gather themselves and turned to look at the mansion. Then Sparks felt

Anderson's hand on his shoulder, and he looked into his friend's face, pockmarked with cuts and blood.

"You need to stay down, man," Anderson said. "You've got something sticking out of your side."

"I know. It doesn't hurt too bad."

"Could be an iceberg situation, more of it's beneath the surface than what's showing. Get down."

Anderson called emergency services. Then he turned back to Sparks and found him slumping back onto the ground on his good side.

"Responders are on the way, Jason," Anderson said.

"Bethany was in there, Sam. Go look for her, will you?"

"You're sure you'll be okay?"

"Not much you can do for me. Any bleeding will be internal. Go look for survivors if you're up for it."

"Just scraps and cuts... think I'm ok. I'll be back in a few."

"Sam."

Anderson had already taken a few steps only to stop and turn back.

"Call Brenda."

"I'm on it."

Chapter Thirty-three

March 15, 1864

BRISON FINISHED WRITING A letter to Louise Elizabeth and sealed it in an envelope. He glanced outside to see that the weather had brightened a bit, and he felt he wouldn't need an overcoat against any rain. He walked from his boarding house and encountered heavy traffic even for a busy Tuesday. It was a lengthy walk to the post office building on E Street, but because he woke feeling poorly and with a general soreness, he decided a long walk would be a fine tonic. Between buildings, he caught sight of the unfinished Washington memorial that sat on the vast open area just east of the president's mansion and thought it well represented how events were unfolding in his country. It was a work in progress, but it had stalled, and its future was in doubt.

As he walked, picking his way among the drier places to minimize the amount of mud on his boots, he thought of what his next step should be in bringing Raven before the law. He had his own testimony, which would be strong, but he needed to directly show that the killer in Richmond was working for Raven, and he needed to prove just how well the industrialist knew the president's secretary of war.

On his walk back from the post office building, Brison redirected himself to the Willard and decided to have a meal. He passed through the main doors on Pennsylvania Avenue and went into the dining room, which, as always, was a scene of controlled chaos. He was putting butter on a rather healthy piece of sourdough bread when a hand was placed on his right shoulder. A startled Brison turned to look into the face of his friend, Joseph Willard.

"Andrew, how are you today?" Willard asked.

"A bit peaked, but nothing serious, Joseph," Brison said. "How is business? Though I can see everything here is right as rain. Lands sakes, the money must just be pouring into your coffers."

"I can't complain." Willard turned a chair around that had been set aside as Brison was at a small table near the corner. "You asked me to send word to you if Augustus Raven was back, and here you are, eating in my establishment and saving me the trouble of sending a boy around to your boarding house."

"He's here?" Brison stopped mid-chew and spoke through the bread in his mouth.

"Checked in late last night. The clerk has him in his usual room that he has paid for in advance for the next six months. What's going on with Raven?"

"I just needed to know when he was back in town, Joseph." Brison smiled. "Let's just leave it be."

"Ah, government concerns."

"I'm much obliged."

Willard got up, clapped his hand on Brison's shoulder, and walked away, quickly lost in the movement of humanity between the table and the entrance. Brison hoped he might see Raven in the dining room, but during his meal, he never saw the man, so when he was finished, he crossed the avenue instead of heading for his boardinghouse. It was early afternoon, and Brison made the ten-minute walk to the president's mansion, made his presence known with the guards outside, and walked into the first floor and inquired of John Nicolay, the president's secretary. As Brison waited as inconspicuously as possible for a colonel in uniform, he took a spot in the hall corner watching the heavy influx of people shuffling about the first floor of the residence. Within five minutes, Nicolay, with his dark, swept-back hair, mustache, and goatee, approached Brison with a smile and gave him a firm handshake.

"Colonel, good to see you, sir." Nicolay's thick German accent never gave Brison much trouble, and his manner always seemed to suit him.

"It's good to see you, John," Brison replied. "I need to see him, if possible, immediately."

"I think he's having a bite to eat right now. Mrs. Lincoln was able to remind him to eat today." Nicolay grinned. "Come with me. He always told me to bring you to him whenever you revealed yourself."

They went up the stairs to the second floor and went down the hall, bypassing a line of citizens arguing with a captain and sergeant manning a table meant as a demarcation line between those attempting to get the ear of the president and the man himself. They entered a room, turned the corner to another door that was closed, and with a short knock, Nicolay led Brison into an inner room. Lincoln sat at a small table facing a window, carving slices of an apple. A bowl of nuts and a pitcher of water was placed before him. His face brightened, and he rose to his feet as Brison crossed over to him.

"Ah, John, you have brought me trouble, I'm sure," Lincoln said to Nicolay, grasping Brison's hand and grabbing his shoulder at the same time. "You have a serious look about you, Colonel."

"I do have news, sir."

"Thank you, John," Lincoln said, pausing as Nicolay left the room. "Something must be urgent for you to come see me."

"Yes, sir. Raven is back in the capital. He's staying at the Willard."

"I see."

"You told me to bide my time while this Dahlgren affair was dusting up. I spoke with General Meade, so I believe he'll keep me out of the investigation if Mr. Davis doesn't reveal the murder attempt I stopped. But I believe I need to question Raven in all haste and the secretary of war."

"You're goin' off like a tenderfoot on his first rabbit hunt." Lincoln sat back down, took a piece of apple, and offered it to Brison, who held up his hand. "Edwin is my most effective cabinet member, no matter your suspicions that he could be the man in our house who was helping those Stallard folks last year.

I am trying to balance the scales in my favor without the anyone seein' my finger on the edge, Colonel. If Raven did this terrible thing, then we can arrest him, but I fear his words would bring others to prison with him at a time when we struggle to end this abomination, this war."

"And if Mr. Stanton is the master of dealings of an illegal nature? Do I just ignore the facts I reveal, or do I just not delve any further, sir? I believe you underestimate the Union and its people, sir. We can withstand the truth."

Lincoln took a deep breath and withheld a response.

"At least let me go after Raven's killer," Brison said. "He murdered Mallory and others and would have done so to me if circumstances went against me."

"Provide for me a report on what has happened, what you have proof of, and what you believe you will be able to prove with questioning," Lincoln said. "I will authorize you to pursue an investigation of Raven, but keep details about the secretary out of anything official you put into a record. I cannot impress upon you the importance of this point. Do you understand my order, Colonel?"

"Yes, sir. I will attempt to question Mr. Raven tonight and see if I can start working on tracking down Mallory's killer."

"Go forward with caution, Colonel. I worry about your safety during these matters."

"Well, Mr. President, I always say keep your eyes open and a good cigar in your breast pocket. Everything will come out all right." Brison grinned.

IT WAS NEARLY JUST an hour before midnight when Raven walked through the lobby of the Willard Hotel with two men at his side—his own personal bodyguards—and stopped briefly at the front desk to collect correspondence and then proceeded up the staircase to the rooms above.

Brison had been waiting with a newspaper in the corner of the lobby, listening to a myriad of conversations about the war and how this summer would see an end to the conflict. Despite his love of cigars, he had a headache from the thick smoke hanging in the air as he waited over the past four hours. He followed Raven and his party from a discreet distance and waited at the top of the stairs on the second floor, then continued up to the third floor and so forth until he made his way to the top floor, where he knew Raven occupied a corner double room. The two guards stood by the door in discussion and predictably paid no attention to Brison as he approached.

"Eh, Colonel," the larger of the two men said. "Mister Raven has asked that he not be disturbed until tomorrow morning. He sees no one, even from the Army, without an appointment."

"Gentlemen, you have two choices: one, you let me discuss my business with him and deal with his wrath later, or you can spend the next few nights at the Old Capitol Prison." Brison let his voice carry with increased vigor until the last three words were just short of a shout. Before he could continue while the two guards stammered, the door opened to a coatless but still-dressed Raven.

"It's all right, gentlemen," Raven said. "No need to be skeery, despite the hour. Colonel Brison is more than welcome."

Brison eyed Raven, then the guards, and walked into the room. As he centered himself inside, he heard Raven say something to the guards in a low voice just above a whisper. He couldn't decipher what was said, but he made note of it. Raven closed the door and paused a moment before turning to face Brison.

"Colonel, what is so important that it calls for you to come barking at my door at this late hour? Have you determined who has been behind the destruction at various ironworks up north?"

"No, Raven, I haven't been investigating that at all over the past weeks. I think we both know what I have been working on. I came here to serve notice that I will be calling on you to come in for an official interview. I was there. I saw your agent murder Justice Mallory, and when I find him, I'll have you as well."

"You have nothing, Colonel, because there is nothing."

"The night when you met with Secretary Stanton in this very hotel, I overheard your conversation. I will testify to what was said here, and you will stand trial for solicitation of murder. It will better serve you if you give me the name of your agent before I call you in for an official interview."

"I don't know what you think you heard whatever night that was, but you can't prove anything." Raven reached the door in preparation to open it.

"I noticed you met the knowledge of Mallory's death with no surprise nor suffering at the loss of your business partner," Brison said. "Another point to be taken down for the record."

A flicker of panic hit Raven's eyes, but it was gone in a moment.

"His wife sent me word up from Richmond." Raven's voice offered no weakness. "I only learned it a day ago."

"Convenient. You have the letter as proof?"

"I discarded it after reading it."

"Of course." Brison shifted his shoulders to reposition his coat and walked past Raven toward the door when a voice shocked him into stillness.

"Colonel."

Brison turned to the door that separated the adjoining room and nodded as he recognized the figure framed in the doorway. For the lateness of the hour, he was smartly dressed with his prominent forehead sloping back, his eyeglasses hiding his eyes slightly, and a thick gray-black beard that obscured any tie he was wearing. Edwin Stanton's presence normally would have startled Brison, but he had grown accustomed to surprises since beginning his work for Lincoln.

"Mister Secretary."

"Sit down, Colonel. There is an explanation for all that you fear has happened."

"Sir, I was there. I prevented the agent from killing Mr. Davis and saw him kill Mr. Mallory. The reports have already been given to the president."

Stanton came into the light, his hands in his pockets as if contemplating a dessert choice on a nearly full stomach.

"There is nothing nefarious to prove, Colonel," Stanton said. "The agent was sent down to retrieve the partnership agreement between Mr. Raven and Mr. Mallory, and as far as Raven and I knew, that was the extent of it. And before your next question comes up, the agent was sent during the Kilpatrick raid as a cover for his activities. What happened in Richmond was out of our control and certainly not our intent. The reason he was sent now was because someone else was moving to buy up Mallory's share in the company. Mr. Raven doesn't know who or why, but our agent was supposed to strongarm Mallory to determine if this was a voluntary sale or not. He didn't want to find himself with a new, troublesome partner in the middle of this blasted war. If that agent did kill Mallory, it was under orders from someone else."

"But Mallory's death simplifies things for you, does it not?" Brison said to Raven.

"Actually, no," Raven said. "Justice was not a member of the government down there, just providing expertise for a fee, I believe, as a private citizen. His stake in the company goes to his family, but litigating that during the war is complicated. And when the war is over, who knows how business transactions between citizens here and down there will be decided?"

"Let me guess, Colonel," Stanton said. "The president cited a desire to limit the scope of your investigation now that a real attempt on Davis's life is in play. Look at the how the Rebels are exploiting some pitiful orders that may or may not have been prepared to give to the troops. An overzealous young man's intentions twisted with lies for the benefit of Richmond."

"But an attempt was made on their president," Brison said in a sharp tone.

"Not under orders from this government, Colonel," Stanton said, "no matter what you think you've heard or seen. Have I been helping Raven here with his business dealings with the government? Yes. He is a friend of mine going back to my days working cases in Ohio. You know how the game is played here, Colonel. He has my ear and my helping hand, but his materials have always been superior for the war effort, so I believe the president would accept a certain leeway in this circumstance. I wish we could get more contracts for his arsenal works. But as it pertains to what happened in Richmond, this agent had a different agenda."

"What's his name and where is he?" Brison asked.

Stanton looked over at Raven as if to reassure the industrialist he knew what he was doing.

"His name is Hartwick, Henry Hartwick," Stanton said. "He's a former sergeant in the Army before the war. A very capable individual."

"I know," Brison said. "He's tried to kill me three times."

"As the secretary said, Colonel, he must be working for someone else as well, as we never instructed him to do anything illegal, except perhaps the strongarming on Mallory he was expected to do in Richmond." Raven held up his hands in a mock surrender. "Colonel, we're all on the same side here, fighting to defeat the damn Rebels."

Brison started to say something in return but stopped himself. "Where can I find Hartwick?" he asked.

"I wish we knew," Raven said. "He was supposed to return with Mallory's copy of the partnership agreement. He hasn't shown up, and we are beginning to fear he didn't make it back from Richmond."

"I doubt he was killed," Brison said. "He's too resourceful." Then he turned to Stanton. "Mister Secretary, I believe a meeting between the president and the two of us would be prudent."

"I quite agree. I'll send a courier to your boarding house tomorrow after I set a time with the president."

Brison opened the door and found just one of the guards in the hall, then turned to face Raven and Stanton. "Gentlemen."

THE WEATHER HAD DETERIORATED in the hours Brison had been waiting for Raven to walk through the Willard's lobby. The wind buffeted the three carriages sitting out front as patrons scurried from the partial shelter of the enclosed seats to the front door. One bellman was trying to shelter a woman with an umbrella that became turned inside out and found his efforts wanting.

Brison turned up his collar, pulled down his hat, and turned to walk back to his boarding house. It was considerably colder, and he regretted staying in uniform, as his civilian coat was considerably warmer. The north wind was spitting a rain that bit into what exposed flesh he had, and he knew it was going to be a miserable walk back as he crossed 14th Avenue and headed up the east side of the street, picking his way through the mud. The lamps did little against the dark, with most of the light coming from inside the buildings he was walking past. He came upon a dead horse in the alleyway a city crew hadn't retrieved yet. It added to his melancholy mood.

All I have is my testimony and Raven's admitted association with the man I now know as Hartwick. But association doesn't always lead to conspiracy, and for God's sake, I can't even prove Mallory was killed, not without the testimony of the man at the head of a government in rebellion! And if the president seems to have soured on having public charges brought against Raven, then who am I to give a damn about it? And what is Stanton's role in all this? Could he be the man Stallard was hiding all last winter and spring? There is much about the secretary that needs to be investigated, but will the president let me?

A single rider turned the corner of F Street and 14th Avenue just ahead. Brison just happened to glance up, and it saved his life. Masked in dark shadows with no one else on the street, the rider moved his right hand from behind him and pointed a revolver at Brison, who saw it just a split second before the aim was taken. Out of reflex, he dove for a water barrel just to his right as the rider's gun flared to life and the bullet missed its mark. A second shot came right afterward and hit the barrel. The rider reigned in his mount and prepared to take aim, but Brison partially emerged and had his own Colt in his hand. Another shot from the rider forced Brison to duck, and by the time he came back up, his assailant was galloping down 14th Avenue toward the Willard. Brison took aim and fired off a shot but missed. With the street empty and the hour late, no horses were around to commandeer, so he started running as best he could through the slop, crossing over to the south side as the rider kept on down the street, pulling farther away. Just when Brison was about to give up, he approached the north side of the Willard and saw a stable boy bringing a horse around to a nearby livery. It was the same boy Brison had looking out for Cathleen Byrne all those weeks ago.

"Colonel Brison, sir?" the boy said.

"I need the mount, son. It's official government business." Brison grabbed the reins. "I'll return the horse presently."

The boy stuttered a protest, but Brison was already galloping off after the other rider. He was on the mount for just a few seconds as he crossed Pennsylvania Avenue when the rain intensified into a biting, frigid sheet of misery that Brison ignored, keeping his eyes on the assailant a block ahead. He darted around a carriage, causing the horses pulling it to startle and a series of swear words to come forth from the driver.

They continued down 14th Avenue, headed for the open land where the unfinished monument sat among grazing cattle and slaughterhouse buildings, still unseen through the wind and rain. Brison's hands were becoming unreliable, the cold numbing them of their usefulness. He cursed himself for not having gloves with him. At least he had his Colt inside his coat and his knife concealed at his boot line. He was prepared for when he caught up with this man.

They were, indeed, headed into the darkness of the monument area just north of a marshland. Brison had closed the distance and now was only a hundred feet behind as they crossed a fetid canal than ran along the west side of the open expanse. Lights from the city street lights behind him cut through the dark, and Brison could see the pale ghost looming ahead and to the right of them. Brison grew increasingly worried about losing the assailant in the darkness as his horse stumbled a bit, and it took him a few seconds to gather the animal.

The man cut toward the slaughterhouse and disappeared around a building corner. Brison reined in his mount before rounding that same corner. A pair of lanterns hanging from a nearby doorway provided some illumination, but they were still alone and the shadows reeked of danger. Brison brought his Colt out from under his coat. He eased around the corner and saw the assailant's horse against a far building standing untethered underneath an overhang but with water pouring off the roof onto its backside.

Brison strained to listen for any sound to give away the assailant's position, but the rain and wind made the effort pointless. He scanned the area within his vision but saw nothing. He was about to turn the horse around to back onto the main road when he was stopped short.

"Brison!"

The voice came from behind him at the corner he had just turned.

"I've got a pistol lined up on your back," the voice said, and a familiar one it was. It was Hartwick. "Drop the pistol and dismount."

"You really going to fire that pistol with soldiers around?" Brison said.

"If I must."

Brison had one chance. If he dropped his pistol, he was a dead man. He had to act now. He yanked on the horse's rein, and it reared up, twisting while bringing his front hooves back to the right and toward the sound of Hartwick's voice, giving Brison shelter behind the animal's bulk as he searched for the killer in the gloom. Neither man fired a shot, because there was no target. Hartwick wasn't there, but over the sound of the rain, Brison heard the splash of feet in a puddle. He raced around the corner in time to see Hartwick turn another corner in the direction of the obelisk. Brison kicked the horse in that direction but ran into a group of wagons stored between two buildings, meaning he had no alternative but to leave the horse behind. He knew this was most likely exactly what Hartwick and his accomplice wanted, but Brison was tired of the chase and frustrated by the whole affair to the point where he didn't care. A resolution was coming tonight.

He cut through the wagons, all the while watching for an ambush from the side and keeping a view of Hartwick running ahead of him across the open field toward the monument. At the corner of the last building came the accomplice's attack, but Brison dodged the slashing knife attack and swung his pistoled hand down on top of the man's head, leaving him unconscious in the mud. The rain and wind remained miserable, so it didn't surprise Brison he saw nary a soul except Hartwick running ahead of him toward the monument's base and its stone steps on all four sides. Brison found no cover, so he wondered what Hartwick could be thinking. Then he remembered there was a door to the interior on the east side he had seen the only time he had ridden up to the monument for a closer inspection. But surely it must be locked.

Hartwick reached the base on the south side and disappeared into the shadows of the stone steps on the east side. Brison took a different course and charged up the steps to the southwest corner and made his way along the south side, his gun pointing out ahead of him toward the dark as he ran his left hand along the cold stone. When he reached the southeast corner, he regripped his pistol and peered around the corner. He couldn't see the far corner of the obelisk, but he could make out the single door forty feet away. It was open, and a faint glow came from inside, an open invitation to a deadly confrontation.

Brison had thrown all caution aside. He spared no thought for Louise Elizabeth or the children. He double-checked behind himself, then crossed the distance to the doorway. The hour had come for a reckoning.

Chapter Thirty-four

Present Day
June 14

THE NEXT CONSCIOUS THOUGHT Sparks had was the paramedic kneeling over him and asking his name. As he began to register his surroundings, he saw people running around him with voices shouting, helicopters hovering off with difficulty in the wind and well above the tree line, and two-thirds of the complex, including half the mansion, on fire with the flames reaching high in the air. Sparks identified himself to the paramedic and, just after, saw another emergency vehicle arrive to a group that was already there.

"You've got a piece of metal sticking out of your side, and I can't tell how far deep it goes," the paramedic said. "We've packed the area around it to minimize the bleeding outside. Can't tell about the inside. We're going to medivac you, but there are some folks ahead of you in line."

"I need to talk to the person in charge," Sparks said, trying to shift his position so he could see better.

"Hold on. You got to stay still."

"I need to talk to the person in charge of the scene."

"I don't know who'd that be, but I imagine they're pretty busy right now."

Sparks was going to continue arguing, but then he saw Anderson trotting up.

"Bethany?" Sparks asked.

"She's alive and actually better off than you," Anderson said with a smile, his face and neck area still bleeding from numerous cuts.

"Hey, you need to get looked at," the paramedic said to Anderson.

"I can wait until later," Anderson said.

"Can you bring her over to me? Sparks asked.

"She'll be here presently, Jason," Anderson said. "You need to focus on yourself 'till we get that 7-iron out of your side."

Sparks only nodded and waited. Five minutes later, Taylor came up, kneeled, and put her hand on his shoulder.

"How the hell do you end up worse off than me? I was in the frickin' building." She smiled and pushed his shoulder a little back and forth in a teasing manner. Her left arm was in a sling, and her hand was in a heavy bandage. She saw Sparks eyeing the arm. "Broken bone in the hand, they think, and my shoulder had to be popped back in place. It'll be sore for a while, but I'll be fine. Got some cuts and scrapes. Fortunately, I was in the hallway near the exit. You saved my life, Jason. Thank you."

"What about the principals?" Sparks winced as the paramedic repacked the bandages around the wound and checked elsewhere for broken bones at the same time.

"Mallory is injured, but I don't think seriously," Taylor said. "He apparently reacted well to my warning. Raven was out the door when the missile hit, and he is gone. The drone was his, you think?"

"When you get the team going on this today, first thing is to get a subpoena and check Raven's inventory," Sparks said. "I doubt he would be so stupid as to use a weapon that could be traced back to his company. He has the means, the motive, and maybe the balls to pull something like this off. Shit, what about the documents?"

"I don't know whether they made it out of the conference room," Taylor said. "I told Lane to pull them together and get out of there, but he is unaccounted for, and that business agreement could be buried under that burning rubble over there. Jesus, this is a mess."

Sparks was beginning to feel the effects of the painkillers he had already been given. His mind was fogging up. "Bethany... get Raven in the interrogation room."

"I'll take care of it, Jason," Taylor said.

"I'll call Brenda," Anderson said.

Sparks nodded, put his head back, and turned to look at the fire. The thunderstorm clouds were passing by to the north, but lightning flashed uncomfortably close to the helicopters still hovering nearby.

TAYLOR FORCED ANDERSON TO get medical attention on site after Sparks had been taken away, then interviewed him during the process. She wanted to be able to answer as many questions as possible that were going to come up from Pearson and Connelly. Anderson was non-committal with much other than the specifics on how they got on the property and didn't seem to care that Sparks could be in hot water over turning up at the site, despite being the only reason there were survivors at all.

When the paramedics were done cleaning up Anderson, he called Munson to let her know Sparks was headed to a local hospital but that his wounds didn't appear to be life threatening. He then asked Taylor to follow up as soon as she learned which hospital he would be treated at. Anderson headed off for his car parked off the property to the north, getting a ride from a police officer.

Taylor joined in searching what part of the structure they could as the crews got the fire under control in excellent time. Searching for survivors would take the entire night, and Taylor wanted to make sure she was there for every minute. Her conference call to the two directors consisted mostly of her detailing the events and stressing the lives Sparks saved by showing up where Connelly hadn't wanted him. To the directors' credit, they concentrated on asking pointed questions and gathering details to best deploy resources in the next hours. They both agreed that Taylor would be in charge on site and that aside from the lives of those in the rubble, the recovery of the documents was of paramount importance.

June 15

WHEN SPARKS AWOKE IN intensive care, he found Munson smiling down at him. The lights were too bright. He screwed his eyes shut before putting his hand in from of his face.

"Boy are you going to have a sexy scar added to your collection when you've healed up," Munson said.

"Sam got through to you," Sparks said. "Good. Did the doc give you an appraisal of the damage?"

"Yup."

Sparks shook his quickly clearing head as if to say, "Well."

"You're going to be fine. The piece of metal penetrated only about five centimeters and scratched the stomach, but there wasn't much internal bleeding. They stitched you up great, and you'll be up and about. You were lucky more stuff from the explosion didn't shred the both of you."

"How is Sam?" Sparks asked.

"He was treated at the scene, but you know Sam. He wasn't going anywhere near a hospital unless he was unconscious."

"How long was I out?"

"It's 12:30 in the morning."

"Has anyone been here from the Bureau... Taylor?"

"She's called to check on your progress, but no one has been by."

"I need an update. Is my phone here?"

"You need to rest," Munson said, sitting on the side of the bed. "I told the doc you would want to leave as soon as you woke up."

"Phone please."

Munson sighed but didn't fight him. She recovered his phone from his things piled in the corner and handed it to him.

TAYLOR FELT HER PHONE vibrate in her pocket. She pulled it out and saw it was Sparks. She was expecting to hear Munson, but instead, she got a determined Sparks, and after telling her he was going to be fine, he asked for an update.

"The crews are going through the rubble now," Taylor said. "They just found Leslie's body, the agent I told to grab the documents just before the explosion. I only recognized him by the watch he was wearing. The pouch with the papers survived."

Sparks took a few seconds to take in the news, so much time that Munson put her hand on his shoulder to get him to respond. "We need to work on what links Raven to this attack."

"I've already got a team trying to track the drone," Taylor said. "Initial report says all of Raven's kamikaze drone inventory not already shipped for delivery to the military has been accounted for. But it's obviously too early to track it by metallurgy analysis, or by a serial number if we're lucky."

"Check to make sure all of units shipped were received," Sparks said.

"In the process."

"Have you talked to Mallory yet?"

"Just briefly," Taylor said. "He's mad as hell and quite shaken up as you would expect."

"We have two suspects in this, Bethany," Sparks said. "Raven and the third party that played the two against themselves. I'm going to ask Connelly to be put back on."

"You just had a chuck of metal taken out of your side."

"I should never have let him take me out."

"I know you won't listen to me," Taylor said, "so listen to Brenda."

Sparks looked over at Munson, who was standing with her hands on her hips, those hazel eyes blazing into the back of his skull just like they did on that hot July day in Gettysburg when he realized she was a unique person he had to have in his life. But as it was for the woman he first loved and lost, the job shoved its way into his personal life. He had to see this through.

"She'll understand," he said.

SAM RAVEN WAS AS scared as he had ever been in his life, and that included the time his fraternity buddies had convinced him skydiving was a breeze. Always wary of heights, he couldn't think of anything more terrifying than jumping out of an airplane with only high-quality nylon segmented in small squares keeping him from dying. That was until now.

He had received a text message from an unknown number just seconds before the mansion exploded telling him to get out of the building or die. He staggered to his car with his driver, and they sped off as debris cascaded down on them, looking back to see the structures ablaze, panicked into fleeing instead of staying at the site and giving the authorities his statement. As they headed for the executive airport where his plane waited, Raven's thoughts swirled with possibilities. The warning had to have come from the third party, but it came so late, there was no guarantee he would make it out of the mansion in time. Why would they wait so late to warn him if they intended to keep him as an asset?

So maybe the attack was from someone else and the warning was a last-second attempt to save him. Maybe it was Mallory trying to divert suspicion away from himself, or a terrorist attack, or a competing company from overseas. Raven had downed three scotches by the time they arrived at the airport, and he almost ran to the plane. He was met by two of his security people who hadn't made the trip to the meeting. The young industrialist barked orders to the pair and climbed into plane.

"Get in the air now!" he said.

"Got to file a flight plan," the pilot replied. "Where are we going?"

"Put it in for Boca Raton," Raven said, "but we're going to change it while we're in the air."

"What the hell is going on, Mr. Raven?" one of the two security guys asked as he closed the door.

"I've got to make plans. I've got find out who's been jerking my chain, and I'm going to need to disappear."

The call with Connelly turned out to be as far from difficult as Sparks could have hoped for. It was short, free of consternation from the director on why the agent he had pulled off the case had been at the Mallory estate, and complimentary on Sparks having saved lives. But repercussions were coming down the road, and Connelly made it clear that there would be more discussion. But for now, Sparks found himself sitting uncomfortably in a Secret Service vehicle speeding along the interstate heading to a small airport where an FBI plane was waiting. Taylor was driving and had listened with interest to half of the conversation her partner had just finished up with the Bureau's director. Sparks turned off his phone and put his head back as he tried to adjust himself to ease the pain in his side.

"I suppose it would be superfluous for me to again remind you the doctors threw a fit when you signed yourself out," Taylor said. "This is really pretty stupid."

"Yeah, I'll be careful. I'm not going to be wrestling with any suspects, and once we have Raven in custody, I'll go see the docs. And if they want me admitted back, I'll go quietly."

"I didn't see Brenda. What was her reaction? You still have a girlfriend?"

Sparks opened his eyes and glanced at Taylor. "She understands."

"Hmmmm... okay."

The SUV's audio system signaled an incoming call, and Taylor answered. It was from the FBI team, calling Taylor because they hadn't heard of Sparks being allowed back on the detail. Evidence was still being gathered at the attack site, information was coming in on the drone that had been used. A search warrant for the Raven facilities revealed that all the company's drones under construction or in development were all accounted for, but in the process of checking the military's inventory, a shipment to the Air Force just a week ago was revealed to be short one weapon. It appeared that it went missing somewhere in transport, despite having private security en route. An investigation by the Air Force had already begun.

"Raven wouldn't be stupid enough to use one of his own weapons," Taylor said.

"Certainly not when it was still in his possession," Sparks said.

While still on the line, the FBI team member came in with new information. Samuel Raven's private plane had been en route to Florida, presumably because of the Raven house in Boca Raton, but now had just radioed in that it was changing its flight plan and was headed now to Edmonton, Canada.

"Canada?" Taylor said. "What the hell is in Canada?"

"Check and see if Raven has been to that part of Canada in the last year or so, and we need to see if he or the company holds property in that region," Sparks said to the team member on the phone. The update was over, so Taylor cut off the call and continued focusing on the road but didn't say anything for a few minutes as they drove on.

Finally, Sparks cut in. "Why would he fly to Canada? It's not like we don't have an extradition treaty with them. A jumping-off point for somewhere else where we don't have a way to get at him?"

"Maybe he has property up there? A compound or something?"

"Possible," Sparks said. "But again, for how long could he stay up there? He has a multi-billion-dollar business to run now. Is he really going to give that up? That's why this whole drone attack thing from him seems so... not logical."

"Our next move?" Taylor said.

Sparks moved uncomfortably in his seat and reworked the restraint. "Back to Washington. We need to meet with Connelly and Pearson and wait for the information on Raven's Canada ties. We also need to have the RCMP ready to take him into custody when he arrives."

"It's the middle of the night," Taylor said.

"I'll call Connelly and see if he can get them at the airport up there."

Taylor nodded and continued driving as they made their way back to Washington.

SENATOR BRIGHTON MALLORY SHRUGGED off the nurse who was trying to adjust the IV in his arm and spit a command to his executive assistant, the same one who had blocked the two FBI agents in his office just days ago.

"I need my phone," he said.

"Senator, the doctor said you need take it easy and try and get some sleep," she said. "It's almost three in the morning."

He glared at her, so she acquiesced.

He had Taylor's number from before and was silently thankful he had the habit of retaining all contact numbers. But instead of Taylor answering, it was Sparks.

"Senator, are you doing okay?" Sparks asked.

"Taylor said you were off this case."

"I'm back on it."

"What the hell is going on, Sparks?" Mallory asked, continuing before there was an answer. "Someone tried to kill us all. What the hell is that all about? I receive the original documents and bring them together with your departments and with Raven and someone fucking tries to blow us all up. My home is destroyed! Thank God my family wasn't in there. I'd be dead right now if Agent Taylor hadn't cleared us out. You both were tasked to decipher this mess and protect me. You have failed miserably, and I'm going to have an investigation into this whole affair if I don't get answers that placate me. You understand?"

"You received a warning to get out before the drone struck?" Sparks asked.

"Yes... yes, it came just seconds before the agent told us to clear the room, which came just before the explosion. I made it to an outside corridor and about fifty feet away when the building came down around us."

"Your injuries?"

"Broken ankle, a concussion, and more bruises than you could imagine. Sparks, I want protection, and I want whoever is behind this taken down."

"We've already dispatched two sets of teams to the hospital where you're at, and the first shift should already be in place. You'll be transferred back to Walter Reed in Bethesda as soon as you're able, and security will be even better there."

"Was it Raven? I heard he disappeared right after the explosion."

"We are investigating, Senator. And yes, he disappeared after the attack, and we're trying to ascertain his location as we speak. My advice to you right now is to get some sleep and we'll be in touch with you as soon as we know something solid."

"Sparks, it had to have been Raven. Who else has access to a device like that?"

"That's obvious, Senator," Sparks said. "Perhaps too obvious. We just don't know yet, but as I said, get a good night's sleep and we'll see where we are later today." He ended the call abruptly and dropped his hands to his lap.

"You were very diplomatic," Taylor said.

"Whatever."

"Until you hung up on him."

"Does it really make sense Raven would take out Mallory, us, and the documents when he was in such proximity?" Sparks asked.

"And by using one of his own weapons. A weapon of that type could be traced. It doesn't make sense."

"With what we know, the attack doesn't make sense for anyone, even with a third party that was dealing with Raven and Mallory." Sparks cracked the window and shifted in his seat for about the twentieth time. "Which means there is something else we don't know about this."

DONALD PETTIGREW PEERED THROUGH the light mist and clouds that surrounded the airport and finished off his third cup of coffee, tossing the empty cup into the adjacent trash can. The Royal Canadian Mounted Police officer had been a member of the Force for eighteen years and was considered one of the best examples of the country's finest officers. Dark of hair with bushy eyebrows and a thick jawline, he looked every bit the northern lumberjack stereotype, and he lived a life of an avid outdoorsman. He took everything in his life seriously, especially his job with the Force. He turned to his left and saw the corporate-sized jet clear through the 2500-foot ceiling as it approached the runway at the far end of the airport from Pettigrew's position just past dawn.

"Tell Roberson I want no delay in our approach to the airplane," he said to his deputy beside him. "I want us in position as it rolls to a stop."

The jet touched down and decelerated, taking the first exit available off the runway and taxied to the hangar and customs house near the RCMP's position. Without hesitation, it pulled up to the front of the hangar, and, true to Pettigrew's desire, four units surrounded the plane as it eased to a stop. Pettigrew arrived a few seconds later, stepped out of his vehicle, and walked up to where the steps extended down from the left side of the aircraft. Appearing in the doorway was a disheveled-looking man in a dark suit with his tie tugged loose. He stepped down the five steps to the tarmac.

"My name is Pettigrew with the RCMP," Pettigrew said, holding up his identification. "We have a court order to detain Samuel Raven upon his arrival here in Edmonton."

"Uh, I'm sorry, but Mr. Raven is not on this flight," the man said. "I'm one of Mr. Raven's security personnel, and he is not on board."

Pettigrew's prominent eyebrows furrowed, and he didn't try to hide his annoyance. "The flight plan originally to Boca Raton, Florida, clearly listed Samuel Raven as being on board when the plane left Maryland and it diverted in midair, so tell me how he's not onboard."

"The flight plan was incorrect," the man said. "You'll need to talk to the pilot on that one. Mr. Raven was planning to take the flight to Boca, but he changed his mind at the last minute. We were instructed to fly to Boca, then told to divert here. I don't have an explanation. We do what the boss wants." He held his hands out with the palms up.

"Search the plane, and I want everyone out on the tarmac," Pettigrew said to his deputy. In a few minutes, the officers had two pilots, an attendant, and two Raven security men standing beside the plane in the gray, early light. The plane had been thoroughly searched—cabin and baggage compartments, a visual and infrared scan. With an emailed photo of Samuel Raven on his phone, Pettigrew studied each of the faces standing before him. None matched the American industrialist.

Pettigrew hit the button on his phone for a direct-line call to the American FBI agent he was told was in charge. "This guy Sparks is going to be one pissed-off guy," he said.

When Sparks and Taylor made it back to Washington, Sparks had intended to sleep for a few hours at the Bureau and then get back to work, thinking Raven would be in custody in Canada. When he took Pettigrew's phone call, he shifted into "go" mode despite his fatigue and injuries. A bulletin was put out for Raven's arrest, and the Bureau was working to get court orders allowing for a takeover of the industrialist's properties, both personal and business. Taylor finally convinced Sparks to take a couple of hours off and sleep at about 11 a.m. Always a light sleeper, Sparks's vibrating phone woke him at 12:45 p.m. The number was unknown and carried a signal with the display that it was an encrypted call. Sparks swore to himself and answered, lamenting he should have left the phone with another agent while he was sleeping. He was shocked to hear Raven's voice on the other end.

"Sparks, this is Sam Raven."

"This is an unexpected call," Sparks said. "You need to make yourself available, Raven. Why did you leave the building just as the attack happened, and why did you leave the site? And what is this sending a plane to Canada without you even though you were on the passenger manifest?"

"I'm being framed."

CHAPTER THIRTY-FIVE

March 15-16, 1864

BRISON PRESSED HIMSELF AGAINST the large blocks of stone, water running down its face and onto him as he slipped closer to the open door. It opened inward and was all the way back against the interior wall. The light was coming from probably a single oil lamp that barely carried out into the rain.

If I step into that doorway, he'll put me down with a single shot.

A small barrel stood next to the entrance on his side, away from view inside the monument. Brison had an idea. It wasn't a rip-roaring one, but it was all he could think of at the moment. Keeping the Colt in his hand, he picked up the barrel, which had a small amount of refuge, including water, and brought it up to his shoulder. He knew it was going to hurt his bad shoulder, but he braced himself and hurled the barrel through the door and followed it just a split-second later. A pistol report came, Brison didn't know from where, but he knew the bullet hit somewhere near where the shadow of the barrel crossed the light.

He slipped in and found shelter in, of all things, a dressed side of beef. He was protected from the interior of the monument, and the light gave him a glimpse of what circumstance presented itself. It was a maze of metal scaffolding and sides of beef hanging from hooks on a supported frame. He could see thirty to forty sides of beef, with construction equipment stacked all around with partially obscured stairs on the two far walls.

Brison's heart pounded, the blood surging in his head, but he kept his breathing as steady as he could. He had been in this situation three times before with this man, Hartwick. Brison scanned the interior and saw nothing. Only at the very last fraction of a second did he think to look up as well. He saw Hartwick just as the killer fired a shot that struck the wall behind him and grazed his right coat sleeve. He moved behind the beef and came right back with a shot at the figure in the shadows on the far stairs, missing but only because Hartwick was on the move up.

No rain came down from above other than some coming down the interior sides, so the unfinished monument must have had a tarpaulin or some such covering at the top. The monument was about one hundred and fifty feet high, all that was completed before construction was stopped ten years ago. Brison had never seen the interior before, so looking up, he couldn't see how high the stairs and the scaffolding went. All he could see climbed into darkness above him.

Keeping his focus above, he moved to the left, away from where the table with the lamp was located, moving more into the shadows. The rain still came down hard outside and was hitting something up top, but it was menacingly quiet inside. Brison listened for movement and was greeted with nothing until a minute later as he reached the stairs when another shot rang out and he heard footsteps and the clanging of metal on metal above his head. He pushed aside a final side of beef and started up the stairs, keeping to the outside against the wall, always with his eyes above him.

The scaffolding obstructed the levels above, so Brison was confident that Hartwick couldn't get a clear shot at him until they were relatively close. The sound of more movement came from above, again followed by two more shots, neither of which seemed close to Brison. He estimated Hartwick was about fifty feet up when he came upon a walkway across to the wall opposite from his position. It was not across the middle and therefore in the open, but more along the adjoining wall.

Keeping in the shadows, he stepped with haste across to the opposite wall and once saw Hartwick moving up the stairs for just a moment before he disappeared again. When Brison reached the far wall, he found a section of scaffolding that went up with a rope hanging down from some point above him and, taking a chance, pocketed his Colt and started to climb. His shoulder immediately barked at him, but he ignored the pain and quietly climbed, using the metal structure to guide him and take some pressure off his shoulder.

Twenty feet further up, there was a ledge with box of tools. Brison took a mallet and threw it down toward the side of the monument he had been at just seconds ago. It made a satisfactory crash against either the stairs or the scaffolding and brought forth another shot that, best estimate, was another fifty feet above him. More sounds came from above as he continued his climb, and with the pain pushed aside by his relentless will, Brison reached another level, where he could barely make out the surroundings. It looked like a flat work area.

Pistol in his right hand, Hartwick peered back down the stairs about fifteen feet away. Brison pulled the second piece he had taken from the box a minute ago—a wrench—and flung it back toward the same area as before. When it clanged against metal, Hartwick shifted his attention and raised his pistol. Brison swung himself up and hung just above the wooden platform, knowing that as soon as he touched down, Hartwick would likely feel it and spin around. Using his good shoulder to carry the burden, Brison pulled the Colt from his pocket and, taking a risk, dropped down to the platform with a satisfying thud. Hartwick whipped around, his face obscured in the shadows, and brought the pistol up and pulled the trigger but was met by the hammer finishing with no result.

"I counted," Brison said. "You're out. I could tell by the sound that you carried a Navy Colt and you haven't had time to reload... Hartwick."

"So Raven gave you my name," Hartwick said.

"I need you alive." Brison flicked his Colt toward the stairs leading down. "I need your testimony on Raven and Stanton, and you're going to give it to me."

"You know all of our meetings were just business, Colonel. I was just doing what I was paid to do." Hartwick still hadn't dropped the pistol nor raised his hands. "Perhaps there is an... agreement we can come to that would benefit both of us."

"Drop the pistol and put your hands above your head. And turn yourself around so your back is to me."

Hartwick nodded and followed the instructions, turning his back. "I have much information that would be of help to the president. I can make this easy on you and Mr. Lincoln."

"You can discuss it with the president or his representative," Brison said, already thinking how he could control the killer until he had help form a third party. "For now, start down the stairs slowly." If Hartwick bolted, the only thing Brison could do was shoot him, which he didn't want to do, but he wasn't going to let him get away again, not this time. "When I mean slowly, I mean just that, Hartwick."

Hartwick grunted a reply and took a step toward the stairs and stepped onto a plank that was loose and gave way enough that he seemed to lose his balance. It caught Brison by surprise, as he didn't expect something so quickly, and the distance between the two grew closer. Hartwick spun and stabbed at Brison's gun arm with a knife he had brought from under his coat, the blade hitting home even through the coat. The gun went off as Brison reacted, but the shot went wide and high, and the weapon flew out of his hand and over the makeshift railing on the walkway. In the same motion as the knife thrust, Hartwick threw his body against Brison and sent the two of them sprawling onto the walkway. He tried to strike again at Brison with the knife, but the colonel kneed him in the stomach, which gave him time to disengage, and both scrambled to their feet.

When they were set and looked at each other, Hartwick found himself facing a man with a knife of his own, Brison having pulled his hunting companion from the sheath in his boot. Brison grimaced and felt the warmth spreading inside his right coat sleeve but smiled as he switched the knife from his right hand to his left because, while he fired a rifle and shot a pistol right handed, he could handle a knife with either hand.

The rain continued to fall outside and onto the tarp dozens of feet above their heads, but like before, the stillness inside shrouded the two men. Hartwick flung himself at Brison, slashing with his blade, trying once high and then low as Brison threw his head and shoulders back. The second slash cut into Brison's coat but didn't draw blood. Brison countered with a pair of swipes of his own, but Hartwick easily sidestepped them, and the pair moved slowly while looking for an opening to attack. Then, suddenly, they were at each other, their opposite hands holding fast to their knife arms, each trying to push the other off balance as the platform swayed unsteadily.

"I'm going to finally kill you, you son of a bitch," Hartwick said. "Should have done it way back in Newburgh." He shoved his weight against Brison and pushed them both against the railing, which cracked under the weight but still held, albeit barely. Hartwick pushed to try and send Brison over the side, but a post behind Brison's back gave him stability and a chance to reverse the position.

The colonel took a chance. Shifting his weight all to his left, he threw his right knee up into Hartwick, this time hitting with more force and lower than the stomach blow from a minute ago. Hartwick groaned and staggered back, giving Brison a chance to regain his footing. For a second, Brison remembered hearing about another knife fight back on a dusty road outside of Gettysburg.

Hartwick charged again at Brison, lowering his shoulder to try and send the colonel over the railing, but when he reached near the edge, Brison wasn't there. Dropping to his knee with his knife pointed upward and right arm held up to take the blow from Hartwick, Brison used the killer's momentum and pushed up while rolling onto his back, throwing him up and over as the railing broke away.

Hartwick let out a scream as he realized he was going over, flailing his arms to grab anything. He caught part of the railing as it broke free, but it did nothing to help him, and he disappeared into the gloom with his cry echoing off the stone walls.

Brison fell to the edge and started to go over when he grabbed the vertical post with his right hand to keep himself from going over as well. Hartwick's scream would be a chilling memory for Brison in his later years, one of many. It continued for just a handful of seconds until Brison heard the crash of a body onto metal. He climbed onto his knees and grabbed his arm. The blood was still spilling forth aggressively. He needed medical attention soon.

"Yes, you should have killed me in Newburgh," Brison said, peering down into the monument's shadowed base floor.

TWO MEN FROM LAFAYETTE Baker's staff met Brison at the monument's door and tried to take him into custody, but he showed them his identification and the letter from the president he carried in a waterproof bag that gave him passage anywhere. They had been watching the area because there had been a report of smoked government meat being stolen. Brison ordered the two men to secure the area until Baker and other staff could be notified. They had already tied up the man whom Brison had left in the mud back by the buildings.

Hartwick's body had landed partially on an empty meat hook, leaving a horrible sight for those who would venture into the monument. A rope outside hung down from the top on the north side, which Hartwick might have planned to use when he reached the top while his accomplice shot Brison in the back from below. At least that is what Brison deduced from a first look at the surroundings. After a brief discussion with the two agents, he walked back to the horse he had appropriated and rode it back to the Willard. He rode his own horse to a private doctor's residence, woke the man, and got his arm stitched up. Around four in the morning, he finally made to his bed at the boarding house, falling asleep in his uniform moments after lying down.

AN HOUR SHY OF noon, Brison found himself standing in the president's office, tired and sore with his hands in front of him holding his hat. His uniform was, of course, covered in dirt, as he had no time to get it washed before being summoned before Lincoln. In fact, he had been awoken barely three hours after he had collapsed on his bed. A major had pounded on his door until he had struggled to his feet and answered it. Then came a ride to the Old Capitol Prison and a brief meeting with Baker, where the head of the Secret Service demanded a verbal report on the happening at the monument. Brison held his anger and gave his rendition of what he had gone through, only leaving out the meeting with Raven and Stanton and their ties to the dead assassin. Near the end of their discussion came a revelation that shook Brison to his core.

"The man who shot at you was shot trying to escape within two hours of his capture," Baker had said. "We'll have someone's head for that, I can assure you."

"That man could have given us details on the man who tried to kill me once I was lured to the buildings near the monument," Brison said. "How the hell did he get free, and who decided it was proper to kill the man?"

For once in Brison's brief experience with Baker, the chief was almost contrite over the incident but quickly returned to the offensive. "You should have gotten men to assist you instead of running off like a fool to fall into a confrontation in the monument."

"I would agree."

"This doesn't make sense." Baker stared at his desk before looking up again at Brison. "You're absolutely sure you don't know this man who became a side of beef?" There was no humor in his question.

"No, I don't know him."

"Well, I do."

"I don't understand."

"His name was Hartwick, and he used to be one of my operatives based here in Washington, though he was very adept at tramping around Richmond if the occasion suited us."

Brison, stunned into silence, could only give Baker an open mouth.

"Yes, you killed a former federal agent," Baker said. "One of your own, though I don't think he had the president's ear that you do, Brison. That's why I won't be questioning you beyond this meeting. I've been instructed to shepherd you off to the president's house directly."

"When did Hartwick leave the service?" Brison asked.

"I would have to check our records, but I believe it was just six months ago or so."

Brison decided to head off Baker's next question. "I have no idea why he would want to harm me." He was sure the president wouldn't want Baker to have the whole story yet, at least not until he had reported what had happened.

"And you can't reveal to me what the president has you tasked with?"

"As you know, I was looking into the deliberate damaging of the Union's weapons production."

"So you told me before," Baker said, "but there is more to this intrigue, isn't there?"

"Nothing of consequence to your charge."

Baker swore under his breath. "I can't protect the president and the people of this city if I'm kept without knowledge of this, Colonel."

"I will ask the president if he will allow you to be told."

Again, Baker swore, but again, not directed at Brison.

"Since Hartwick was no longer with this department, the matter is strictly a simple case of either self-defense or murder… and I have no evidence of murder. Your injuries suggest self-defense, but they alone do not prove your innocence."

"I only know the man wanted to kill me," Brison said.

"And the president's intervention means I take his word that Hartwick wanted to do you harm."

As he had been instructed, Baker had an escort take Brison to the president, and now, at eleven in the morning, the colonel stood alone in Lincoln's office, hearing the activity of business outside the closed door. After another few minutes, he sat down in a chair and held his head in his hands. The fatigue he had fought for the past few weeks got the better of him, and he dosed off in the pale light coming through the window. After the third time he awoke, he found the president standing by his desk, a bemused smile on his face.

"Usually, people fall asleep after hearing me talk, not before, Andrew," Lincoln said.

"My apologies, sir." Brison started to rise, but Lincoln shook his head and motioned with a hand to stay seated.

"Tell me what happened last night," Lincoln said. "I received word you had been arrested by Baker."

"I was never arrested, only questioned," Brison said, but he wondered if maybe he had been arrested, knowing how Baker and his people conducted the business of law enforcement. He described the previous night's events. Brison finished by giving a summation of what Baker had asked of him.

When he was done, Lincoln nodded. "It was prudent of you not to inform Baker of this whole business with... Hartwick was his name?"

"Yes, and a former agent. Raven must have hired him to do his bidding on their more illegal efforts."

"And now he is dead and can no longer bring us testimony as to Raven's and Stanton's involvement in the Richmond affair."

"No, but I can, sir," Brison said. "Raven and the secretary both admitted their knowledge of Hartwick, that he worked for them."

"But you said they also stipulated the illegal efforts where not at their behest."

"You know that can't be true, sir."

"Yes."

"Someone sent Hartwick to Richmond to murder Justice Mallory and also Mr. Davis, either as part of the plan or on his own action."

"Yes. Have you seen the papers yesterday and today?"

"No, sir."

"We have a hornet's nest swirling around this Dahlgren affair." Lincoln dropped down into a chair next to Brison. "The Rebels say they have proof Kilpatrick and Dahlgren planned to execute the Confederate cabinet and Davis, and now my generals and the people of the North are crying for retribution of the most severe kind while the South screams their own revenge. I fear we have come to a fork in the road and taken the wrong way. Meade is looking into whether the orders found on young Dahlgren could possibly carry the truth, but he will not learn of the Raven and Stanton involvement unless you and I, Colonel, present him with those suspicions. And Andrew, I'm not inclined to do so."

"Sir, they are, at best, guilty of obstruction of the government's business for some personal gains. At worse, they are guilty of treason, sir. Yes, nothing short of treason. Their actions have moved us into dangerous times. I can't believe you will not let me bring your authorities like Baker into an investigation."

Lincoln sighed, stood up, and reached over to put his hand on Brison's shoulder. "Son, you have done well by me, and I want you to be safe in the knowledge that your country is indebted to you. For now, I must ask you to be patient. The time for justice in this matter is still in the future. Accept a pass from me and travel home to see your family. I will call you back when the need arises."

"I believe I could serve you more effectively by staying in Washington," Brison said. "You might need me quickly."

"I am satisfied with the progress we have made." Lincoln walked around to his small table and continued with his sparse meal. "This business is not finished, but for a time, I want Secretary Stanton where he presently resides... where I see him each day. I'm giving you a two-week furlough, Colonel. Go home to your family and report back to me upon your return. Are we at an understanding?"

Brison stood for a moment and contemplated resisting again but realized the futility. "Yes, sir. I will return in two weeks."

March 17, 1864

SLEEP WAS DIFFICULT, SO in the morning, Brison arose slowly from his bed. He was feeling poorly, the wounds in his side and arm were paining him like the devil. While he'd spent the night before trying to map out a plan to disregard Lincoln's orders and continue the investigation, the new day brought on a melancholy mood, and he was ready to hang up his fiddle on the whole matter. His charge now was to take the train home and see Louise Elizabeth and the children. Perhaps in two weeks' time, he will have healed up some and could re-form his attack on Lincoln's decision. After the events over the past year and a half, Brison felt like he had gone through much for little reward.

He gathered his things, packed them in his traveling trunk, and signed for the month's rent, as it would be billed to others. He still wasn't exactly sure who paid his expenses, just that they always seemed to be taken care of when needed. A 3:00 p.m. train would leave for Philadelphia and then on to New York, followed by another to Springfield and home.

He had settled into a private seat and drafted a letter to Byrne through Stinson that he would mail somewhere along the way. This was one of the matters that he and Lincoln had failed to resolve. Raven was still out there and most assuredly would want Byrne removed from the situation. Some provisions for her safety needed to be crafted.

Coincidences had a way of unnerving Brison and none more than what happened now as a figure slipped onto the bench next to him and stared straight ahead. Brison glanced at the new arrival, and he couldn't help but take in a quick breath and cover up what he had been writing on the paper tablet in his lap. He gathered himself for a moment so that when he spoke, it would be with a measure of authority.

"Raven. What in the Sam Hill are you doing here?" He folded up his letter and tucked it away in his overcoat.

"I wanted to speak to you, Colonel." Raven looked at Brison and then returned his gaze to an extraordinarily garish hat worn by a woman four rows ahead of them. "I heard about your fight with Hartwick at the monument and the outcome. I'll come right out and ask you if he gave you the name of the person or persons who hired him to assassinate President Davis."

"No, he didn't. Obviously, if he had, we would be having this conversation at the Old Capital Prison."

Raven smiled and shuffled the book he held out apart from his satchel. "As I said before, Hartwick was acting on someone else's orders, not mine. Any further investigation on your part won't find evidence to the contrary."

"And an investigation into Secretary Stanton?"

"Politicians and government servants aren't permanent," Raven said. "They often change with the wind. I only wish to retain my contracts."

"Let's put our cards on the table, Raven. I think you're a no-account murderer who tried to have me killed a number of times. You had Hartwick murdered your partner to get out of compensating him for his half of the company. And while I can't count treason among your crimes yet, your deliberate destruction of your competitors' factories could put you in the neighborhood." Brison touched his gun under his overcoat, resting his hand on the handle of his Colt.

"Before you go and bring me in under arrest, you should remember two items." Raven's eyes narrowed. "Your family and Miss Byrne. It is a dangerous world out there, and you never know what could happen during these violent times."

"Raven!" Brison's voice remained hushed but full of anger.

Raven held up his hand. "If you go forth and declare I threatened your family, I will deny it, but I believe you understand the implication. Call them my... insurance. I hear you are headed home on furlough. Congratulations. A well-deserved reward from the president. When you return to Washington, I trust he will have other daring investigations for you to handle."

"I'll not be threatened by you."

"Yes, Colonel, you will. Calm your horses down there. You really had success here. You stopped an assassination that could have made the war more difficult to win. See how just the Dahlgren letter suggesting such an event has caused a stir? Take satisfaction in what you prevented. Now leave me alone, and the fates will be kind to those you care about... at least as far as I can be a party to."

"How can I trust you?"

"I have many faults, but I always keep my word, and you have it on this particular point."

The train whistle sounded, and the cars began to slow.

"This is where I get off." Raven smiled and rose from the bench. "Perhaps I will see you in the dining room of the Willard some time. I would rather enjoy that, I believe. Good day to you, Colonel."

Brison glared as the industrialist disappeared through the car's rear door. Only after he was gone did Brison remove his hand from the Colt.

March 20-21, 1864

A BIT OF SNOW fell on his farm as he rode up the afternoon before. Louise Elizabeth and the children had been suitably happy to see him and had hugged him multiple times until he could not breathe. The evening had been one of the special ones since the war began, filled with stories about what had been going on at school, in town, and at the farm. Despite the flurries outside, there had been some unseasonably warm days this March, and the children had been taking advantage by exploring the area around the farm. Little Patrick had even fallen in a stream just off their land and had been pulled out by his two sisters, who both boasted they had done more to get their brother back on dry earth but less responsible for having allowed him to end up soaked through in the first place.

Brison had laughed his way through a dinner of lamb and potatoes and had read three stories to the children before they were worn down enough to sleep. Louise Elizabeth had played the piano for them and had cleaned up the dishes while he had been preoccupied with the children. She never asked about his sudden appearance or what had transpired since the night many weeks back when a bullet had been left on the table. She had not said anything when they had retired to their marital bed and had spent a good portion of the night satisfying each other, one time in the haste of lustful longing and then later in a more gentle, loving manner, even when she saw the bandage on his side. She had not said anything as they had drifted off to sleep in each other's arms.

She reserved her questions for when they awoke just before dawn.

He calmly gave her as many details as he felt he could without scaring her, though that wasn't the true reason. He worried about being able to deal with her anger if she knew how close to death he had come in the recent weeks or how his future was likely littered with more of the same. And while Hartwick was dead, the strange relationship between Raven and Stanton hung in Brison's mind. He didn't reveal the details of either the strike at Richmond or the fight inside the monument. That time would come after the war when stories would come with the ease of reminiscence.

As he lay in her arms on another chilly morning, he pushed the war away and talked of the warm spring approaching until young children's feet pounded in the hallway floors outside their bedroom door. The spring would be followed by another summer—the fourth of the war—but for a short time, those worries would be left outside the Brison home.

Chapter Thirty-six

ABSOLUTE DARKNESS ENVELOPED THE dirt road. As a test, Sparks turned off his headlights for a moment and marveled at the result. He could have been in a sealed room buried in the ground, the darkness seemed so complete. He admitted to himself it was intimidating. He was somewhere close to the Canadian border in the Northeast Kingdom of Vermont, what the natives called the extreme northeast corner of the state, bordered to the east by New Hampshire and to the north by Canada. Sparks had been here just weeks ago at the home owned by the history professor Arthur Collins. It was where he'd had his hands on the Raven papers for a brief few minutes.

As he was leaving the Hoover Building earlier this day, it was confirmed that the papers had been recovered from the rubble of Mallory's estate in Maryland. They were intact, and their ownership was now headed for litigation, as Mallory had indicated he would have his lawyers file paperwork to make sure the papers stayed either with him or in protective custody as their authenticity was confirmed. All of that because Samuel Raven had disappeared and his own staff didn't know where he was located.

And now, Sparks, on his own with no communication with Connelly or even Taylor, drove on this dirt road to meet Raven in the middle of the night.

The tree canopy encroached on the road he was driving on and the rental car. Sparks had no company car and no cellphone that could be tracked, just a simple four-door sedan. Sparks figured he must be near the border, though this dirt road was not on any map. He didn't dare use the GPS feature on his phone for fear of being tracked, since Connelly was probably busting down the walls because Sparks was off the grid.

Raven had said he was being framed by some organization and begged Sparks to meet him without backup and promise not to take him into custody. Taylor had warned against this very action and even cursed him out for the first time since they had worked together. Sparks had been amused and noted it was the longest anyone had ever worked with him before swearing at him for something.

The headlights swung around a corner and fell on a lone car sitting in a rest area, facing the same direction as Sparks was headed. Sparks pulled to a stop about fifty feet away and killed his main lights so as not to blind the person getting out of the car. It was Raven, and he appeared to be alone. Sparks holstered his gun as he rose from the open car door and walked around, meeting Raven halfway between the two cars. The running lights from the two cars cast a mixture of white and red hue over them.

"Thank you for meeting me under these circumstances," Raven began, his voice tired and strained. "I know you're going out on a limb for me even though I haven't earned your trust."

"You got that much right, so begin building that trust right now."

"I didn't authorize a strike on that meeting, though I'll bet it was one of my drones."

"It was. Preliminary investigation points to your company signing off on a shipment of six drones at your manufacturing plant, but only five were delivered to the Air Force."

"Like I said, a frame." Raven walked over to Sparks's car and sat on the hood. "I'm going to give it to you straight. I was unhappy with my father's roles for me with the business and probably had said too much in public to friends and far-too-casual acquaintances. I was approached by an organization's representative. A woman told me about my father being blackmailed with the documents from the Civil War. They promised me I could get control of the company by providing me with information that would force the board of directors to force my father to retire. In return, I would kick back a portion of our next five major defense contracts to this unnamed entity. I knew I was selling myself to the devil, so to speak, but I did it anyway."

"But they killed him instead," Sparks said.

"Yes." Raven took out a cigarette and lit it. "They never made it clear that murder would be part of their removal plan. I believe my father's attempt to retrieve the papers in Arizona must have spooked them, so instead of a forced transfer of power to me, they took him out. The next time I was contacted, I made it clear I was furious at what they did, and I told them to fuck off. The papers ended up in Mallory's hands, and he called the meeting at his estate."

"And you got a call just before the drone hit?" Sparks asked.

"I did, and I don't know why other than they want to have control over my company in the future. They used one of my drones to frame me. I'm sure you're going to find evidence in your investigation that will somehow tie me into the theft of the drone during delivery. And that I, not my father, was tied to the attack in Arizona and any other illegal goings-on during this affair."

"There have been five other murders."

"Jesus." Raven was genuinely rattled. "I had no idea."

"So why meet with me?"

"I wanted you to have this in your mind when you continue the investigation," Raven said. "Question the information you come across. Double check. Verify."

"Come back with me and help us. Clear your name with us."

"You and I both know there are others in the Bureau and inside the Beltway that will push to have me taken care of. I don't have my father's political connections yet, and I have no illusions as to what would await me. That is, until you discover how it all fits together. Then I can come back and testify. Problem is, the only person I had face-to-face contact with was a woman. I didn't see her after my father's murder, and the male voice in contact with me since was just that, a voice on the phone."

"Was the woman blonde, athletic looking?" Sparks asked.

"Yes."

"She's the one who murdered your father, but she herself was taken out by this organization," Sparks said. "I think the blackmail against your father and then you was about getting money from your contracts, but that was a secondary goal. The primary goal was to blackmail Mallory out of the presidential race this cycle."

"Really? So if he dropped out, he'd get the papers and would have grounds to sue for a large portion of the company."

"That's right," Sparks said. "Would the document stand up under contract law?"

"Not at the full forty-five percent." Raven ground his cigarette into the dirt in front of the car. "I had already resigned myself to the fact that Mallory would get part ownership. I don't have enough capital to buy him out at that percentage, but I'll bet a figure could be arrived at. He struck me as a man more interested in the presidency than in being more wealthy than he already is."

"Is there anyone at the company you can trust?"

"Outside of my security team, I don't know, not with how this has played out. I have funds set aside and in accounts not connected to the company and offshore, so what I plan to do is wait until you can flush out your investigation. I can't help you with this mystery organization. I've only had limited contact, but Mallory might have had more contacts. If I can think of any leads on my end, I'll contact you."

"I'm really putting my career on the line here, Raven," Sparks said. "If you're playing me..."

"I'm not. Look, I met you here completely exposed. You could take me in right now if you decided that was the best course."

"I doubt that. I count at least two men of yours just on the edge of the woods on either side. I caught the movement in my peripheral vision a few minutes ago."

"Trying to hedge my bets, I guess." Raven offered a weak smile. "Still, if you brought the calvary with you, my security guys would be pretty useless."

"You need to give me your location. These people will try to eliminate you if they find you."

"I'll only tell you I'll be in western Canada. No hiding in a country without extradition for me, so that should be a point in my favor. I have your cell, and I have equipment that can bounce a call all over North America, so I'll be hard to trace. Keep me updated." Raven started for his car, and the two security men appeared from the woods.

"I like how you assume the posture that I'm working for you." Sparks' sarcasm was evident. "You're a suspect in a criminal investigation. If you've been playing me, we'll find you... with absolute certainty."

"I have no doubt, but there are bigger fish than even me in this whole mess." Raven continued to the right rear car door. "Why would someone want a source of funds through a defense contractor and, at the same time, remove a strong candidate for the presidency? Think on that for a while."

Raven and the two men pulled away as Sparks got back in his car.

"I've already been pondering those very same thoughts," Sparks said.

June 17

CONNELLY STOOD WITH HIS back to the room, hands behind his back, staring through the Hoover Building window at the activity in downtown Washington, D.C. Sparks and Taylor were sitting in chairs center stage in front of the massive desk the director called home. Pearson sat off to the side, his briefcase opened in his lap, a designer pen shifting in his right hand as he stared at Connelly's figure framed in the window.

Sparks's entire body hurt like nothing he had experienced before. It felt like he had been thrown inside a cement truck and spun around for a time with a few boulders tossed in for good measure. Plus, he was tired beyond tired and mad as hell about the entire hellhole of a case. He and Taylor had been behind from the start and never caught up. His only break had come when Streeter tried to clue him in on what was going on.

And now he and Taylor sat with the directors of the FBI and the Secret Service and didn't know whether they could trust either of them.

"I think, Agent Taylor, your director would agree with me." Connelly turned around slowly. "That this has been one massive clusterfuck from the beginning. Not all of your doing, I'll admit. Sparks here deserves much of the credit." He looked at Sparks. "My predecessor had a very high regard for your abilities, Sparks, and I don't know how we got through the investigations up on the hill last year. Somehow, his reputation survived, and you came out smelling a damn sight better than a dozen roses."

"Yes, sir," Sparks said.

"But this time around, you two were following the bodies around like you worked for the frickin' morgue. The president's chief of staff, the professor, the Vermont state trooper, two of our own in Tucson, the muscle guy for Raven Industries and his girlfriend, Raven himself, the women who worked on the president's staff in the West Wing for Christ's sake. It's an illustrious list. And I haven't even addressed the drone attack at Mallory's place. Five people dead, the papers almost lost, and Raven junior there disappearing. And now you tell me he's telling you that he was being framed?"

"Yes, sir, and I'm leaning on the side of believing him," Sparks said. "The attack on Mallory's place in Arizona was his father's doing, and his father's murder was carried out by an operative who I believe had ties to this third-party group that was playing Raven and the senator against each other."

"We've got to look for leads to this group that had the papers originally," Taylor said. "They're behind everything except the attack in Arizona."

"I took you off this case, Jason, and you forced yourself back on with—of all people—Sam Anderson, and you could have gotten him killed along with the others."

"But he didn't, Director," Taylor interjected. "And he gave me a few seconds that saved some lives."

"Taylor," Pearson said quietly.

"Nevertheless, I'm putting Josh Kinder back on point... after getting a briefing from the two of you," Connelly said. "Director Pearson will decide how much you'll be involved, Taylor, with your part of the investigation. How did a rogue organization operative get past our vetting processes?"

"Yes, sir," Taylor said, the resignation clear in her voice.

Sparks registered no reaction. The fatigue stunted what would have been a vigorous protest against Connelly's decision. The professional side of him was losing out to what extreme exhaustion and prolonged physical pain can do to a person, wear them down until they are no longer effective. All he wanted right now was a couple of days sleep and a chance to see Brenda.

"All I need is a couple night's sleep, and I can get back to it," he said.

"I want you on the sidelines, Jason," Connelly said. "For now. Perhaps down the road here if we remain stymied on Raven. Right now, we're going to tell the press it was a drone that had been stolen in route from Raven to the Air Force—"

"Which is true," Pearson interjected.

"—and those responsible appear to have been a terrorist cell backed by an unknown entity that we are investigating," Connelly continued.

"Which isn't true," Taylor said.

"Whatever." Sparks shook his head. "I expect you'll be needing me back on this pretty quick."

"You're lucky you're not suspended pending a formal hearing." Connelly waved his hand in dismissal. "I want you gone for a couple of weeks."

Sparks rose to his feet and slid away from the chair. "That's your prerogative, sir. Call me when my services are required."

Taylor looked at her own director and followed Sparks out of the room, leaving the two directors alone. She had to quick-step herself to reach Sparks as he reached the elevators.

"Fight to keep on the investigation of Raven's killer," Sparks said when he saw her approach, "and be prepared for backlash, depending on how it goes."

"I will."

"Something is not right here, Bethany, something that rotten doesn't begin to explain. Watch yourself. And let me know what's going on."

"I really don't want to risk my job, Jason," she said.

The doors opened, and he got on, keeping the door from closing with his arm. "You might have to if we want to know the truth here."

June 18

THE THREESOME OF GOLFERS reached the fourteenth tee, which happened to be on the most remote section of the golf course in northern Virginia. It was a brilliant summer day, but the back nine was closed to other groups and eight interested parties were placed well about this select trio. President Douglas, Pearson, and the House speaker climbed out of their carts when a lone man rode up in a golf cart from the opposite direction. Pearson saw who it was and asked the others to give him a minute, taking the man aside and out of earshot. Douglas and the speaker went ahead and hit their tee shots on the par-5 and made it back to their carts. In two minutes, Pearson was finished with the courier, who was obviously bringing information the Secret Service director wanted verbally. Pearson waved Douglas over.

"Mr. President, could I have word with you alone?" he asked.

The speaker waved them off and went over to the restrooms a short way off, leaving the two others alone.

"I asked for a confirmation," Pearson said. "Raven is somewhere in Canada, but our source in his company says his whereabouts are unknown, even by his top vice presidents or the board. The guy has properties in three different provinces, but I'll bet when we check, he won't be at any of them."

"Raymond, now doesn't he have any direct knowledge of whom he was dealing with?" Douglas asked.

"No, sir. We made sure of that."

"But you don't believe in taking chances."

"No, sir, I don't."

"Do what you can, Raymond, but spare me the details of the operation."

"All in all, sir, we did set out and accomplished our main goal, getting Mallory out of the race," Pearson said. "And the funding may still come from Raven Industries. We'll see about the younger Raven."

"You still believe our people on the board will make sure he stays in place once he is cleared of wrongdoing?"

"Yes, sir."

"I still would feel calmer about this once he is back in place." Douglas absentmindedly took Pearson's driver from the director's hand and made a couple of practice swings. "And what about your agent Taylor and Connolly's man Sparks?"

"For the time, they are neutralized. Out of the loop, so to speak." Pearson winced as the president dug into the turf on a third, poorly executed practice swing. "We can always eliminate them in a worst-case scenario. The man I have leading the investigation now is ours and will make sure to steer it in the direction we require."

"Good. Well, let's finish. I believe I'm two up with five to play."

Pearson walked to the tee box, placed his ball on a tee, and prepared to hit his drive. His swing was smooth and without restraint and sent the ball soaring defiantly down the middle of the fairway. The Secret Service director was confident he could make up the two holes on Douglas and maybe even steal the match right at the end.

ABOUT THE AUTHOR

Steven P. Locklin is a semi-retired freelance editor after having worked as a writer and editor for thirty years with seven newspapers in five states – West Virginia, Illinois, Tennessee, Vermont and Florida. He spent most of his youth growing up in New England – where his family history dates back eleven generations – reading every Alistair MacLean, Robert Ludlum, and Clive Cussler novel he could.

The final novel that completes this Brison-Sparks trilogy told in *Beneath Hallowed Ground* and *Strike at Richmond* is in development.

He lives in South Florida with his wife.

MORE FROM STEVEN P. LOCKLIN

Beneath Hallowed Ground

BRONZE MEDAL WINNER - 2013 FLORIDA BOOK AWARDS

After a professor's murder leads FBI Agent Jason Sparks to a $150 million Civil War gold cache, his daughter's kidnapping turns the investigation deadly. As Sparks decodes century-old letters, he unravels Lieutenant Jackson Prescott's 1862 undercover mission for Lincoln to infiltrate Confederate gold smugglers. Both men's destinies collide at Gettysburg, where America's bloodiest battlefield hides secrets worth killing for.

RECOMMENDED READS

If you enjoyed this book, check out these other Grey Gecko Press books that you might like!

Death by Harmony
by Leon Berger

Tense, authentic, compelling – a tumultuous 24 hours in Beijing, as witnessed by those involved.

EACH YEAR, HOWLING WINDS from the Gobi send desert grit swirling into Beijing which then mixes with the existing pollution, causing fluorescent yellow skies and a toxic, throat-burning smog. On one such day in March, youthful activists decide to gather in Tiananmen Square right outside the Great Hall of the People where the National Congress is in session.

Addleton Heights
by George Wright Padgett

New Year's Eve 1901: Six hundred feet above the Atlantic Ocean, the platform city of Addleton Heights balances on massive, soot-covered metal stilts. A grisly double murder interrupts the party in the floating mansion of the city's most powerful man, and for reasons unknown, he coerces detective-for-hire T.H. Kipsey into taking the enigmatic case.

Support Indie Authors & Small Press

IF YOU LIKED THIS book, please take a few moments to leave a review on your favorite website, even if it's only a line or two. Reviews make all the difference to indie authors and are one of the best ways you can help support our work. Reviews help us to earn more readers just like you and keep publishing great indie books!

Plus, you can get any other Grey Gecko ebook FREE with your review!

Visit greygeckopress.com/free-books/
for more information.

GREY GECKO PRESS

9 781944 576058 7